TYPE B

STEVE MITCHELL

TYPE B

iUniverse books may be ordered through booksellers or by contacting:

iUniverse
1663 Liberty Drive
Bloomington, IN 47403
www.iuniverse.com
844-349-9409

Because of the dynamic nature of the Internet, any web addresses or links contained in this book may have changed since publication and may no longer be valid. The views expressed in this work are solely those of the author and do not necessarily reflect the views of the publisher, and the publisher hereby disclaims any responsibility for them.

Any people depicted in stock imagery provided by Getty Images are models, and such images are being used for illustrative purposes only. Certain stock imagery © Getty Images.

ISBN: 978-1-6632-0722-7 (sc)
ISBN: 978-1-6632-0721-0 (e)

Library of Congress Control Number: 2021901449

Print information available on the last page.

iUniverse rev. date: 02/24/2021

CHAPTER 1

It was Wednesday, June 14, 2006, and John Davison was driving in downtown Cincinnati. He sometimes wondered if he should look into getting another job. It wasn't that he minded being a courier; it was just that the traffic lately had become such a pain to deal with, especially with all the construction going on around town. It seemed to be everywhere he looked; all he could see were orange barrels. He knew that traffic in this part of Cincinnati would be bad ever since they announced they would be doing road repairs.

John's company car was old and the air conditioner didn't work, making the drive around town even more unbearable than just the traffic jams. When he wasn't moving, he felt that he was melting. But at least when he was moving, he got some breeze, which helped him endure the drive.

Since John had gotten off at Exit 6 of the I-71 ramp, the traffic seemed to crawl. *I hope things get better once I turn onto Martin Road,* he thought as his patience was wearing thin. *Of course, when you think things will get better is usually when they get worse.* As he turned onto Martin Road, he saw a stalled car in the center lane with a cop car pulling up behind it. *Great,* he thought as he glanced at the time on the dashboard, *this means I'll be late for the pickup.*

With two cars to go before he'd be able to pass the stalled car, what happened? The tow truck showed up. The cop got out of his car and stopped all traffic to allow the tow truck to maneuver into a position to remove the traffic bottleneck. John sat there, waiting impatiently for his turn to drive around the problem. He surveyed the area to find something of interest to pass the time. He started playing with his company badge attached to a retractable clip. He looked at the picture on the badge and thought it was a lousy picture. He read what was printed on the badge: "John Davison, Biological Fluid Courier for Christ Hospital, Cincinnati, Ohio." *Biological fluid courier,* he thought, *What a distinguished title for someone who goes around picking up blood and urine samples to take to the hospital lab for analysis.* He sat there and wondered if a title like that could get him a raise. After all, he was not just a simple courier. *I'm a biological fluid courier,* he thought to himself, chuckling under his breath. "No way," he said.

In the top right corner of the badge was a small pin displaying the number twenty. John had received this pin at the last company picnic for his twenty years of service to Christ Hospital. He had started as a cook in the cafeteria. Later, he'd gone to school and become a phlebotomist. He'd worked in the lab for about ten years after he'd finished additional training to become a lab technician. He'd worked in the back areas of the lab, processing the samples that he now brought to the hospital. However, because of the budget cuts about six months ago, the lab lost several of its lab technician positions. John, being the newest technician in the lab, had lost his position. Since he had such a good work record with Christ Hospital, Tom Mitchell, the lab supervisor and his closest friend, offered John the courier position.

As John was engrossed in inspecting his badge, the cell phone on the center console rang, redirecting his attention to the time displayed on the clock.

"Oh, great," he said in a loud, frustrated tone. "That's got to be Tom. I'll bet a week's pay that he's wondering where the hell I'm at." Tom had called him earlier to tell him he had a rush pickup. John was to go immediately to the Gateway Medical Building to pick up two blood specimens and rush them to the hospital for analysis. It had to be Tom; John couldn't think of anyone else who would call him on this phone. He picked up the cell phone. His suspicions were confirmed once he recognized the number on the caller ID as Tom's office phone.

"Hello," John said congenially, "John here."

Tom's voice on the other end of the line seemed a little upset as he asked, "Where are you? It's getting late. The doctor's office called saying you haven't picked up the specimens yet. You have to get them over to the lab right away."

"I'm stuck in traffic," John said in his own defense, wondering what was so important about a couple of blood samples. "I'm only about a block away, but the road is blocked with a tow truck removing a disabled car."

"How much longer are you going to be?" Tom asked, disturbed with John's delayed progress.

John could tell he was upset with the delay. "It shouldn't be too long," he replied in a hopeful tone. "The car is on the bed of the truck, and the driver is securing it in place. I should be moving soon if this stupid cop ever lets us go by."

"Well, get there as fast as you can. We have two specimens that have to go directly to the hospital lab. Don't worry about the other two pickups. I'll get Mark to swing by and pick them up."

"Okay, I should be there in a couple of minutes. It looks like the cop is about ready to start letting the cars go by."

"Okay, but make it as fast as you can."

"Okay, bye," John said. He placed the cell phone back on the console, where he had a set of flexible hands that held it in place. He sat there waiting to move, wondering why the rush. Having worked in the lab for ten years as a phlebotomist, he couldn't think of any special situation where a blood or urine specimen had to be at the hospital lab within any critical period of time. *I know,* he thought, *some hotshot rich guy probably found out that his daughter's pregnant and wants an accurate test to prove it one way or another.*

Finally, the cop waved the cars past the tow truck. John took the next turn into the parking lot of the Gateway Medical Building. Now he had to find a place to park. Today he was lucky, finding a parking space in the front row, right in front of the main entrance.

John parked the car and rolled up the windows. *I hope I'm not inside long,* he thought as he locked up the car. The dark blue interior would make the car pretty hot if he were to stay in the building too long. Since he had already picked up specimens from two other sites, he had to lock the car. Not that anyone in their right mind would ever want to steal a cooler full of blood and urine samples. *But you never know; this world is full of all sorts of crazy people.*

John entered the medical building and almost died from the shock as the cold air from the air conditioner contacted his sweaty body. The cool air did feel good on his face and neck. John pushed the button for the elevator and waited for the car to arrive as he continued to stand directly under the air-conditioning vent. "Boy, does that cool air feel nice," he said out loud, followed by a sigh.

The doors to the elevator opened, and two elderly women slowly walked out. "Good morning," John cheerfully greeted them as they passed. He held the doors open as the second woman slowly walked out of the elevator. *Tom's in a hurry and I have to wait on these slow old women,* he thought to himself as he waited patiently. John quickly slipped past them and pushed the button to the second floor.

Seconds later, the doors opened on the second floor, and John stepped out into a vacant hallway. He turned down the hallway and proceeded to the third door on the left, which was opened, displaying a sign reading "Laboratory."

"Here I am!" John said with some enthusiasm, trying to keep them from jumping all over his case for being over an hour late.

"It's about time," said Mary, the lead lab assistant at this location. "Here are the specimens that need to go directly to the hospital lab," she said, handing him a Ziploc bag with a biohazard symbol on the side.

"Why the rush?" he asked, taking the bag. "I've never had to rush specimens over to the hospital before, or at least not with the urgency that you are assigning to this run."

"I don't know why," she replied, a little frustrated with his tardiness. "I was told to draw the blood on three people and get the blood to the hospital as fast as possible."

"Who were they?" he asked, wondering what was so important. "Some sort of rich aristocrats?"

"No, actually it was a family," she replied. "A mother, a father, and their fourteen-year-old son."

"Were they sick or something?" he asked, hoping to get some answers to the question of why the urgency.

"No, they seemed just fine," she replied, becoming annoyed with his questions. She knew he was late and that these questions were making him even later.

"I don't get it," he said, shaking his head as if to shake away some of the confusion.

"Well, I don't either, but you had better get going," she said with frustration in her voice. "Tom wanted these there about an hour ago."

"I know he's in a hurry," John said, turning toward the door. "He called me on my cell phone. And you know how he hates calling anyone on the cell phone."

"Well, you'd better get going," she said, sitting down by the computer to enter more information.

"Well, here I go," John said with the flare of a vaudeville actor. With a majestic bow, he turned and raised the plastic bag with the three blood specimens in the air. He stared at it, wondering what the mystery was all about. He had no idea, and he thought no one in the lab did either. Was it a plague that was about to hit the city, or was it a secret test for some high-ranking official they wanted to keep quiet? He didn't have a clue, so he headed for the door.

John stopped suddenly and continued to stare at the bag. Something didn't look right. He turned toward Mary. "There appears to be three specimens," he said, a little puzzled. "Tom said that I was to pick up only two specimens."

"When we first called the hospital for the pickup," Mary said without taking her eyes off the computer screen, "there were only two specimens, but the doctor asked if their son could come in—and he got here before you did. In a way, I suppose it was good that you were late," she said with a slight chuckle. "Otherwise, Tom may have asked you to come back and pick up the third one."

"Well, in every cloud there is a silver lining," John said with a little chuckle. "Of course, I'm not sure Tom would see it that way. See you later," he said, proceeding toward the elevator.

John pushed the button to call the elevator, and the door opened immediately. In the past, it had taken over five minutes for the elevator to stop on this floor. He stepped in and pushed the button for the first floor. He liked to create stories in his mind, so as he waited for the elevator, he wondered if this would be a good story to break to the newspapers. *The secret blood transports to Christ Hospital, or the governor of Ohio and his family all have AIDS, or the mayor of Cincinnati is single and pregnant. That last one wouldn't work,* he thought. *That would require only one specimen.* Before he could envision other far-fetched stories, the elevator doors opened again. As he exited the elevator, he thought, *With my luck, it's probably some test sample to determine if the diagnostic equipment up in the lab is working properly.*

He stepped out of the elevator into a blast of cold air from the air conditioner. "Ah," he said, pausing for a second to absorb as much cool air as possible before going back to the hotbox with four wheels.

He opened the car door and got hit with a blast of hot air. He had become accustomed to this, so he just slid in behind the steering wheel and put the blood specimens in a small cooler that was sitting on the back seat.

He started the car and took a left out of the parking lot onto the main drag in front of the medical center. The traffic was now very heavy as the lunchtime crowds headed out to all the various eating establishments around town. The city streets were crowded, but John found that the traffic was moving pretty steadily, so he made good time back to Christ Hospital. As he entered the hospital, he was again greeted by the cooling effects of air-conditioning. He headed for the employees' elevator and pushed the button to go to the fifth floor, where the lab was located. The doors opened. He got out and approached the lab entrance. He took his badge and put it through the card reader, although it took several attempts to get the card to work. Finally hearing the latch unlock, he opened the door. As he walked through the door, he felt a very strange sensation, as if the rest of his life would be totally different. It was the type of sensation you get when someone dies and you later discover it was your grandmother. John didn't know why he felt this way. Maybe it was the smell of some cleaning chemicals coming from the lab. Maybe it was just the cool air from the air-conditioning that was finally starting to make him feel peculiar. Still, he didn't know why he felt this way, but these strange sensations were making him feel uneasy with the fear you might experience when you walk into the office thinking you will be laid off. Maybe that was it. Tom was upset that it had taken John so long to get back. John was hoping his feelings were wrong.

Just then, he heard Tom's voice from the other side of the room. "John!" he hollered. "Have you got the specimens?"

That was a stupid question to ask, John thought, since that would be the only reason he would be in the lab at this time of the day. John had known Tom for over ten years, and this was the first time he had seen him so serious. So, instead of replying with a sarcastic answer, he raised the small plastic bag with the specimens inside and just said, "Got them right here."

"Good," Tom said. "Take them back to Joyce; she'll start processing them."

"Okay," John replied. He headed toward the back of the office, where the lab equipment was located. As he walked through the lab door, he saw Joyce Wolfe over by the Beckman chemistry analyzer. Next to Joyce were two individuals whom John had never seen before. One was a woman who looked to be in her late twenties, wearing a lab coat over what looked to be a very expensive business suit. She had blonde hair and wore a pair of metal-rimmed glasses. The other was a young man who looked as if he had just graduated from high school. He was also wearing a lab coat over an expensive suit. As John watched them, it was easy for him to see that the woman was in charge as she seemed to be giving instructions to the young man.

Now John would admit that he spent most of his time out on the road, but he was sure he had met everyone who worked in the lab, most of them at last year's Christmas party. But he didn't recognize these two. In fact, they were a little too dressed up to be lab workers. He was wondering if they were hospital administrators. If they were, what were they doing in the lab?

"Joyce," John finally called out, "here are the blood specimens from Dr. Marla's office."

"Thanks, John," she said, taking the plastic bag with the specimens over to a table.

John stood there watching Joyce and the two strangers, who seemed to be interested in this blood. *Boy, this gives me the jitters,* he thought. He stood there for what seemed like forever, watching them from across the room. He was wondering if he should ask what was going on. "Joyce," John said to get her attention after he could wait no longer, "I was wondering, what's so special about those blood specimens?"

Joyce looked up at him and started to say something, but she stopped as if she had been about to say a curse word. She turned and looked at the strangers to her right as if to get some sort of signal. Joyce didn't go in for cloak-and-dagger, but she seemed afraid to voice her opinion. The stranger in the pressed suit shook her head ever so slightly as if to signal to Joyce not to say anything. Joyce looked back at John and struggled with a weak smile, and saying, "Oh, nothing special. Just the normal diagnostic routine." Then she quickly turned back to the bag with the specimens while the two strangers stepped around the table, blocking John's view. John had only worked in the lab for about six months, but he couldn't think of any diagnostic routine that required blood samples with this level of urgency.

John knew that Joyce was hiding something, but he didn't know what. He turned and looked down the hallway, not sure what to do next. He wanted to get more information but was positive he would not get anything from Joyce, especially if the two strangers remained in the back of the lab. He left the lab and headed toward the billing office. If something was going on, they would know because they would be the ones to process the paperwork for it.

John walked into the billing office and over to where Tammy was entering information into the computer. "Hi, Tammy," he said, walking up behind her.

"Oh, hi, John. What can I do for you?" Tammy asked.

"You look tired. Been busy today?" John asked.

"It's been busier today than last week, which was busier than the week before. It seems like everyone in town is getting a blood test."

John turned and looked back toward the doorway, wondering if he should bring up the subject of the two strangers in the lab. Tammy might not know who they were or even that they were there. "Do you know why it's been so busy?" he asked, trying to see if he could get more information as he continued to conceal his real question.

"I have no idea," she replied as she shifted through some papers on her desk. "We just seem to be getting a lot of doctors' offices requesting blood work on their patients." She paused long enough to take a drink of her ice water. "Have you seen much of an increase in pickups on your runs?" she asked John.

"No, not really," he replied. "Most of the time I just grab the bags out of the boxes and bring them in." John paused a second to think about this ritual he performed twice a day. "Most of the time," he continued, thinking out loud, "I have no idea how many tubes are in the bags. Do you know what kind of tests these doctors want to run on all these patients?"

"Most of them are just simple tests to identify their blood type," she said, pausing for a second as if to gather her thoughts. "You know, now that I think about it, there are a lot of tests associated with anemia. I wonder if there are a lot of people not getting enough iron in their diet," she said with a small laugh. "Kind of reminds me of me sometimes when I'm feeling tired. Who knows, maybe I should get a blood test for anemia too," she said with a small chuckle.

"You're not anemic," John said with a small laugh. "You're just not used to working very hard. Or are you?"

Tammy, knowing that John was a bit of a kidder, replied as she played along with his routine. "Well, at least I do some work around here; all you do is just sit around and drive all over town."

"Yeah," John said with a small chuckle as he bent down close to Tammy, "it looks like you do a lot of sitting around also."

With the tension cleared up, John thought, *This would be a good time to bring up the question of the two strangers back in the lab.* "Hey, Tammy," he said in a more serious tone, "do you know who the two strangers are in the lab?" He gave her a possible out by adding to his question, "Do we have some new employees?"

"I don't know who they are," she said, also in a serious tone. "I know they're not new employees. We've had a hiring freeze for the lab for about two months."

"How long have they been here?" he asked, drilling her for more information. He usually stopped by the lab just long enough to drop off a couple of bags of tubes before heading back out on the road. Those people could have been here for weeks and he wouldn't have seen them, especially if they were only here at specific times, when he was out doing his runs.

"They just got here late yesterday afternoon. They didn't even go around and introduce themselves to everyone, which is strange in itself for around here." Tammy was now getting a little curious about John's facial expression and his curiosity about the two strangers in the lab. "Why do you want to know?"

John, in an attempt to recover from his expression, said, "Just curious. I don't get up here very often, and I thought maybe we had some new employees. I mean, would you ever go to work in the lab wearing those types of clothes?" he said, referring to the nice business attire they were wearing.

"I know what you mean," she said. "Even if they are wearing lab coats, I wouldn't want to wear anything that nice in the lab. There is always a chance that something will be spilled—and then there goes a nice set of clothes."

John thought he had better see about making a quick retreat from the billing office before Tammy got suspicious about all his questions. "Well, I'd better get back out on the road. Otherwise, those lab techs won't have a whole lot to do. See you later," he said as he turned and headed for the door.

"See ya," she replied, turning back to her computer to enter more numbers.

John stood in the hallway, wondering what to do next. He could see the two strangers standing in the lab talking to one of the lab techs. He wanted to know more about what was going on. He still had that strange feeling he'd had earlier when he'd entered the lab. *Something is wrong,* he thought, *but what is it, and what can I do about it?*

He turned and took a couple of steps toward the lab, intending just to peep inside to see what was going on. Just then Mark, the other courier, came in with the bags of specimens that John was supposed to pick up.

"I got the specimens you didn't pick up," he said, a little pissed off at John.

"Don't get upset with me," John said, a little upset by Mark's attitude. "I didn't tell you to go get them; Tom did. He gave me orders to rush a blood sample back to the lab, so I did."

"Well, because of your so-called rush order," Mark said in a very sarcastic tone, "I missed lunch, and now I have to go out and start my afternoon run without a lunch break."

"Well, as I said, don't blame me. If you want to get mad at someone, go get mad at Tom."

"Yeah," Mark said, pushing his way past John and heading into the lab. "Here, Denise," he called out toward the lab supervisor in an upset tone. "Here are the specimens," he said, loud enough for John to hear him, "that John didn't pick up and that I had to go out of my way to get."

John just stood there shaking his head. *So he missed lunch,* he thought. *It wasn't my fault; I followed Tom's orders. Mark is acting like I did it on purpose.*

Wait a minute, he thought as an inspirational idea hit him, *Tom is the one who told me to get those samples instead of picking up from my last two stops. Tom has to know what's going on.*

John looked down the hallway toward the lab area but didn't see Tom anywhere. He took a couple of steps back and peeked into his office area. Still no Tom. He walked up to the reception area to see if Tom was up there, but alas, he was nowhere to be found. Wondering where Tom had gone off to, John concluded, *When in doubt, ask someone who knows.* He walked back to the doorway to the office area and leaned over to stick his head in to see who was around. Several other data entry clerks were standing around talking about a problem one of them was having with her kids. "Has anyone seen Tom?" he asked, loud enough for anyone to hear but not directing his question to anyone in particular.

Betty, one of the clerks, heard his question and turned toward John. "He headed down to the cafeteria for lunch."

"When did he go down?" John asked, afraid that if Tom had left awhile ago, John would miss him when he came back up.

"He only left about five minutes ago," she answered. "He said he'd had enough for the morning and wanted to get out of here, even if it was only for a couple of minutes."

"Thanks," John said. He quickly withdrew his head and headed for the elevator outside the lab area. After entering the car, he waited as the elevator descended to the basement, where the cafeteria was located. He tried to determine how he would ask Tom about the blood samples and the strangers in the lab. *Well,* he thought, as the indicator counted down floors, *I can start by asking if I should just do my afternoon run like normal or if I should do a couple of pickups for Mark since he did two pickups this morning for me.* Just then, the doors opened, revealing that John had arrived at the basement level. He stepped out of the elevator and turned right to go down the short hallway to the cafeteria entrance.

Steve Mitchell

John saw Tom over by the cashiers, paying for the indigestible lunch sold by the hospital. He watched and waited to see if Tom would go into the dining area or return to his office. It would be easier to talk to him in the dining area. John never seemed to get a moment of peace in the office. And to ask questions like the ones he wanted to ask would not go over too well, especially up there with everyone trying to eavesdrop on their conversation.

Oh good, John thought, *he's headed for the dining area. Now if he just sits by himself.* That's all he needed was for Tom to sit at a table full of friends and coworkers. Tom would never tell John anything in a crowd.

John followed Tom at a distance as he walked into the dining area. Tom seemed to be heading over to a set of tables by the windows. *Good,* John thought, *he's sitting by himself.* As Tom was getting settled to ingest the indigestible, John walked up and sat down across from him. He didn't even ask Tom if he wanted company or not. He was afraid that he may get a negative answer, so instead, he bypassed that step altogether and sat down.

"Hi, Tom," John said in a friendly manner. "How can you eat that stuff?" he asked, referring to the so-called meat loaf they were serving for lunch that day. This was a good way for him to break the ice and start a conversation. After all, they had made many jokes about the food at the hospital as they compared it to the food their wives would cook.

"Hey," Tom said in a humorous tone. "It beats the stuff my wife cooks."

"I know what you mean," John replied with a chuckle. "Your wife is a terrible cook."

John turned to survey the area to see if there would be any interruptions from other hospital personnel as they migrated through the dining area. To his delight, the closest individuals were about six tables away, and they looked to be were involved in their own discussion. "I understand it's been pretty busy up there the last couple of weeks," he said in a more serious tone. "Is that true?"

Tom conveniently put a forkful of meat loaf into his mouth. With the way things had been going upstairs in the lab, Tom wasn't thinking on his feet too well. He felt that a few seconds gnawing on the piece of tough meat loaf would give him a couple of seconds to think. After all, Tom had his own responsibilities and had to be careful how he answered

John's questions. Tom was pretty sure John wanted to ask questions about the strange actions of that morning. Why had he had John rush a blood sample over to the lab? He wasn't sure if that was where John was going with the questions. However, John was sitting there, watching him chew his food, waiting for an answer.

After some effort to swallow the overbaked dish, Tom responded in a casual tone as if it were the same question asked by everyone in the hospital. "Yeah, we've had an increase in work. You know doctors; they want to run every test under the sun if they can get more money out of the insurance companies."

This caught John off guard. Tom's answer made sense, but was it the truth? Or was he giving him a realistic answer to throw him off track? He didn't know what to do, except that he wanted to know more about the rush delivery and the strangers in the lab. His anxiety was rising, so he changed his strategy to see what other information he could obtain. "Since Mark did two of my pickups this morning," he said, "do you want me to do a couple of pickups for him this afternoon?"

"No," Tom answered as if he were a calm priest, "you and Mark can just do your normal routes. No sense in getting everyone out of their normal routines."

"Well, you know that Mark is complaining that he didn't get to have lunch, and he's blaming me for the change in plans."

"Don't worry about Mark. I talked to him and told him that the change was necessary and that he had to cover for you while you ran the specimens in. I told him to put in for an hour overtime."

John was thinking this could be the lead-in he needed to get Tom to give him some information about why it had been so urgent to get the blood specimens into the lab. "By the way," he started with a touch of anticipation, "why was it so important for me to get those specimens to the lab so quickly? I don't know of any test that needs to be run that quickly after the blood has been drawn."

Tom sat there, looking deep into John's eyes in an attempt to read his soul. He paused for a minute, although it seemed like a lifetime. This made John feel a little uneasy. Tom took a bite of his biscuit to allow himself a couple of seconds more to contemplate his response. "John," he started, again in a calm manner, "that was a test the doctor ordered to have done right away. I'm not a doctor, so I don't know why he was so impatient about getting the specimens analyzed."

John pondered Tom's response. It could be true, although he had never heard of a doctor wanting a test result so quickly. He couldn't tell whether Tom was telling him what he knew or whether he was making up some lie to cover up something more important. His gut feeling was that something was wrong. He wasn't sure he should continue with his questions. For his own satisfaction, he felt he had to know.

"Come on, Tom," John started in a soft whisper as if afraid someone nearby might hear him. "I know you know that no doctor has ever wanted to have a blood specimen analyzed so quickly." He paused for a couple of seconds to see what reaction he would get from Tom.

Tom sat there, not speaking a word in reply to John's statement. Because of Tom's hesitation, John added to the question. "Also, who are those two strangers up in the lab? I know they are not new employees. And it seems everyone up there is doing what these two individuals tell them to do."

Tom still sat there, staring at the wall on the other side of the cafeteria. He almost appeared to be in a trance. John was wondering if he was even alive, sitting there like a corpse with rigor mortis having set in. John sat there looking at Tom. "Tom!" John called out, trying to get Tom to come back to reality. Tom's reactions made John even more uneasy than he had been when he first got the call to bring the blood specimens directly to the lab.

Tom took a deep breath, bringing life to his dead soul, and turned to look at his close friend. "What I'm about to tell you can't go any further than you and me. You can't even tell your wife. This situation has to be kept quiet."

"Tom, you know me," John replied, trying to allay Tom's concerns. "I can keep a secret." He was good at keeping his mouth shut when it came to matters of confidence. And he really wanted to know what Tom had to say.

"This is no ordinary secret," Tom said, pointing a finger at John. "You can't tell anyone," he said in a stern voice that John had never heard from him before. "I mean no one."

"Tom," he started in the same serious tone, "I won't tell a soul."

"Okay," Tom said in defeat. He looked as if he had been beaten up to reveal secrets to an enemy spy. "I need someone to talk to about this situation before I go crazy. But remember," he said in a serious tone, "you can't tell a soul." Life can throw various problems at you, and most times, it's easier to handle these problems when you can turn to your friends for help. In this case, John was Tom's best friend. In the last ten years, together they had survived some of life's hardest ordeals. When John lost his parents in a car accident, Tom was by his side. Tom discovered that his wife was having an affair and confided in John, who never mentioned a word about it to anyone.

"I promise," John said, slowly leaning closer to Tom so that the secret could be whispered softly. Tom's actions were giving John chills of fear. He had never seen him this serious about anything going on at work. Whatever was going on had Tom on edge.

"Well," Tom began in a very soft whisper, "about a month ago, several patients started dying of some sort of anemic condition. No one knows why these people died. I guess it started with the patients complaining about being tired and then they seemed to get weaker and weaker over a short period of time. At first, the doctors thought it was an anemic condition, so they were giving the patients iron shots and other treatments associated with anemia. The problem was, these treatments just didn't appear to be working."

John sat there, staring at Tom in pure disbelief. John had been working in and around hospitals for most of his life, but this was something he had never heard of.

"Those two individuals upstairs in the lab," Tom continued, "are from the CDC" (Centers for Disease Control and Prevention). "They came yesterday when they learned that we've had five deaths due to this anemic problem. I contacted my counterpart at Saint John's Hospital, and he said that there have been four deaths over there. I also talked to several other hospitals. Apparently, this problem has only surfaced in the last two weeks. It seems to be covering a good part of this area. And from what I understand, this problem is occurring all around the United States. I don't know how bad it is because everyone seems to be keeping a lid on this problem."

"What do you think is going on?" John asked, absorbing everything that Tom was telling him.

"I don't know." Tom paused for a second as if to gather his thoughts. "I heard the two CDC people talking on the phone to Washington. They don't even know whether we have a major epidemic or if people are just dying from other causes such as poor eating habits. They just can't seem to figure out what the problem is—or even if there is a problem. All I know is that I'm a little concerned about CDC agents showing up in my lab." Tom had run the lab for over ten years, and the CDC had only stopped by once, to get information on the flu outbreak.

"Well, if they don't think there is a problem, why are you so worried?" John asked.

"Simple," Tom replied. "Those blood samples you brought in."

"Yeah?" John asked, waiting patiently.

"They came from Dr. Marla's office. He had a husband and wife pair come in complaining that they felt really tired and needed to see the doctor. The wife, who was in the examining room with the nurse, died while sitting in the chair getting her blood pressure taken. The husband wasn't doing so well either, so they wanted to get an analysis of their blood as quickly as possible to see if they were anemic. Outside of that, I'm not sure what's going on."

"Wow" was about all John could say. Now he joined Tom as they both stared into the distance with looks of disbelief. John didn't know what to think about the story Tom had just told him in confidence. He was imagining a person dying while having his or her blood pressure taken. It sounded like something out of *The Twilight Zone*. The silence went on for several minutes.

Tom was the first to return to reality. "You'd better get going on your afternoon run," he said, which brought John back around.

"Yeah, I guess I'd better get going," John said. He added with a chuckle, "I don't want Mark to have to pick up any of my stops this afternoon; otherwise, we'll never hear the end of it." John stood up and headed for the cafeteria exit.

Tom watched John walk off, feeling a little better after having revealed the news to someone. But a feeling of concern came over him as he sat there, wondering whether it had been wise to pass this secret onto someone else. Would John keep this secret, or would he accidentally or purposely let the secret out? Tom couldn't even imagine what the population would do if they were to discover a possible epidemic. He didn't even know what he would do if something like that did come true.

CHAPTER 2

John returned to his courier route to take care of the afternoon deliveries and pickups. His first stop was the Blue Ash Medical Center off Montgomery Road. The traffic, as usual, was heavy, but this time it didn't seem to bother him as it usually did. His thoughts were still back in the lab, wondering about the things Tom had said and about the two CDC agents. And what about those blood specimens he had taken in? What about the patients? He again got that feeling that something was wrong. Would the same condition lead to the deaths of the others Tom had referred to? Would they die like the others, or would they be survivors? John just didn't know what to think, especially since he had little information to work with.

A sudden sound from behind caught his attention as an ambulance came up on his rear. This brought John back to reality as he looked around to see where he was. Finally, he realized he had passed the medical center by about a mile. He looked at the clock on the dash and noticed he still had plenty of time to make the pickup, so he pulled into a gas station to turn around.

This time he tried to keep his mind on the traffic as he pulled out to head back down Montgomery Road. As he approached the medical center, he turned in and pulled up in front of the door where the employees entered. He got out of his car and looked around, wondering what was happening around him. He felt as if many eyes were watching him. This made him feel very uneasy. But as he surveyed the surroundings, he could see nothing different from any other day—or at least nothing obvious.

But what was happening behind the closed doors of the doctors' offices in this building and the other buildings where he picked up specimens? And what about the specimens? Would they be the bearer of the bad news Tom was talking about?

John just shook his head as if to shake the strange thoughts and feelings out of his mind. He was trying to concentrate on what was happening now. He walked toward the building, still feeling as if eyes were following him. Could this be because he knew something that no one else knew? He almost wished he knew nothing. He entered the medical center and walked up to the lab door, where one phlebotomist was taking a blood sample from an elderly man. As John watched her draw the blood, he couldn't help but wonder if that sample of blood would bring this old gentleman bad news. As John stood there, Debbie, the receptionist, called his name, but he was still in a daze, staring at the old man's arm and at the blood flowing into the small tube.

"John!" she shouted a little louder, but still there was no response from him. Then Debbie stepped out from behind the counter and walked up to him, "Hey, John," she said, "is there something wrong?"

John finally realized she was standing there. "Oh. No," he replied quickly, trying to return to reality. Looking toward Debbie and then back at the old man, he tried to come up with a believable story. "I just thought I recognized that man over there," he said, pointing to the old man. "He looks a little like my uncle."

"Oh, really?" Debbie exclaimed with a tone of excitement. "That's pretty cool. Did you bring the supplies we asked for?" she asked, having noticed that he wasn't carrying any packages.

John had to stop and think for a second. He shook his head as he replied, "Oh yeah, they're in the car. I forgot who ordered what supplies. I'll run out and get them." He turned and headed for the door before Debbie could ask why he had forgotten them. John felt like a fool for having forgotten the supplies. He had never done that before. He told himself he had to concentrate on what he was doing and stop worrying about Tom's comments and the two CDC agents. Sometimes it is easier to ignore physical pain than it is to ignore what's happing inside your own head.

John quickly returned with the packages of tubes and a box of needles. "Here you go," he said, handing Debbie the boxes. "Do you have the pickups ready?" he asked before she could ask any questions about why he had forgotten the supplies. He knew it was a dumb question since the main reason he was there was to pick up the specimens, but at least it redirected Debbie away from asking about why he had been so forgetful about the supplies.

"They're on the shelf, ready for you to take them away," she said, pointing to a small shelf by the back door where John always picked up the specimens. "Or did you forget where we put them?" she said with a chuckle.

"Thanks," he said with a flat laugh. "I was just kidding around. If they weren't ready yet, I could've enjoyed this nice air-conditioning instead of getting into that hot car." With that, he turned and quickly headed for the door. He picked up the bag of specimens and turned to say goodbye. Noticing the perplexed look on Debbie's face, he knew why she looked that way: because he was perplexed and didn't want to explain why to Debbie or anyone else. He gave her a quick wave and made a hasty retreat out the door.

As the afternoon wore on, John's mind kept wandering back to Tom's comments. He had to force himself to concentrate on what he had to do to finish his other pickups. Once done, he headed back to the lab at the hospital. Most of the day shift at the hospital had just left for home, and only a small night staff was on duty. John walked into the lab and placed the cooler full of specimen bags on the counter, where one tech came over to check them in. "Been a busy day?" John asked, trying to start up a conversation.

"Not too bad," replied the technician.

"I understand you had some visitors today," John said, hoping to get more information.

"Oh," she said, not sure what he was referring to, "do you mean the two agents from the CDC?"

"Oh, is that where they're from?" he asked, playing dumb.

"Yeah," she continued. "They were using our lab equipment to run some tests."

He didn't think that such was the case, but he believed that was the story she probably had been told. "Any idea what tests they're running?" John asked, hoping for more information.

"Well, Sharon," she said, referring to the female from the CDC, "she's a doctor with a PhD in blood sciences, and she wanted to use our equipment to verify the accuracy of some other equipment at another facility. She said she wasn't sure of the results she was getting at her facility, so she and, I think she said his name was Robert, decided to rerun their tests here."

"So was her equipment accurate?" John asked, just trying to keep the technician talking.

"I don't know," she replied, becoming a little disturbed by his questioning. "She and her buddy just did their thing and then left."

"Oh," John said. He thought he had better make a hasty retreat before the technician began wondering why he was awfully curious about what was going on. "See you tomorrow," he said, and turned to leave the lab.

"See ya," the technician replied, glad to see him leave.

John wasn't allowed to drive the company car home, so he had to drive to the hospital every morning to drop off his personal car and pick up the broken-down clunker called the company car. Then he had to return the company car to the hospital before heading home in his own car.

John dropped off his company car and climbed into his own car for the trip home, where he hoped he could put some of this information out of his head. However, thoughts of the two CDC agents and the old man at the doctor's office kept migrating back into his head. He was so preoccupied that he didn't even notice the heavy traffic on the highway.

He pulled into the driveway of his home in Walnut Grove, on the southeast side of Cincinnati. He had a nice three-bedroom house sitting on a small piece of land. One of the doors to the two-car garage was open, and it looked as if his oldest son left had his bike in the driveway again. As John stopped the car, he looked around to see if he could spot the tall skinny fellow who was fourteen going on eighteen. He half expected his son would be playing basketball with his friends, but no one was around. John just parked the car and decided to let the situation with the bike slide for now. As he approached the front door, the storm door almost clobbered him as it came flying open, and the tall skinny fellow he was looking for went flying by. "Peter!" John said with a strong tone of authority. He didn't get to say another word as a sweet little woman he used to think was his daughter came charging by, chasing her brother with a water balloon.

"Beth!" John yelled. This time his children gave some acknowledgment of his presence. Both kids stopped and turned toward their father. John looked the kids over and could see why one was chasing the other. Peter had a shirt on that was a little wet on the right shoulder, and Beth was almost completely soaked. "What started this?" John asked, not expecting to get an honest answer.

"He threw a water balloon at me," Beth said, "so I threw one back at him."

"Well, you look awfully wet from one balloon," John said. "It must have been a huge balloon.

"How did you ever pick it up and throw it at her?" he asked Peter.

Peter, looking a little guilty, knew that Beth had been hit with more than one small water balloon. "After she hit me with a balloon," he started, "I soaked her with the water hose."

John turned and looked into the house, where he saw a path of small wet footprints indicating Beth's path as she tried to intercept her brother. "Well," John said, "since you both seem to enjoy the water, Beth, why don't you go and mop the hallway. And, Peter, since you started it, you can mop the kitchen and dining room floors."

"That's not fair," they both said in unison as each tried to explain that the other had started the whole thing and therefore was responsible for cleaning up the entire mess.

John just turned and looked at the two of them with an expression that indicated he was not in the mood to listen to their complaints. His two offspring clammed up quickly and rushed past their father, who was holding the door open for them to go inside. The guilty kids entered the house to perform the tasks assigned to them.

John walked into the living room and found his wife, Paula, sitting on the couch, working on one of her cross-stitch projects. She would spend many hours after work and after dinner sitting in front of the TV and working on a new creation. "Hi, honey," he said in a monotone voice as he bent down to give her a quick kiss.

Paula looked up from her cross-stitch frame to connect with the exchange of affection. "How was your day?" she asked.

John didn't want to talk about his day at work, so he changed the subject. "Looks like they were at it again," he said, referring to the two kids.

"I tried yelling at them to stop, but that didn't do any good. And I couldn't go after them because I'm in the middle of trying to get this knot out of this thread." Having just pulled out the last knot, she looked up and saw the troubled look on John's face. "What's the matter?" she asked, hoping to get him to open up. John was the type who, if he was in a good mood, would open up to his other half like floodwaters after the floodgates had been opened. When he was troubled, it sometimes would take an act of God to get him to say anything. Paula knew something was wrong, and not only from his facial expression. Usually, he would come home and give her a kiss and then start joking around with her. She expected him at least to say something like "Knot again," using the play on words, but today he didn't even acknowledge the problem she was having with the thread.

"Nothing," he said with little enthusiasm, "just another day fighting the traffic." He turned to go upstairs to change into some old clothes so he could do some small projects around the house. John was the type of individual who loved to keep busy fixing things around the house. Paula just watched him leave, knowing that at this moment, he wasn't going to discuss the problem. She would just have to bide her time and wait him out.

John changed into a pair of old cutoff jeans and went outside to the backyard to test the chemical levels in the swimming pool. This was a routine for him. Even though he spent little time in the pool, he enjoyed taking care of it. This gave him time to think and be by himself, with no one around to bother him. It also gave him a few minutes of peace and quiet. After testing the water and discovering that the chemicals were all balanced, he couldn't figure out what to do next. He kind of wished the pool needed vacuuming, but it still was pretty clean. He just stood by the pool thinking about the two CDC individuals in the lab. What were they doing there, and what was this bit about the blood? John knew he was just driving himself crazy standing around thinking about it, so he went inside to watch some television.

As he entered the house, Paula asked, "Would like a glass of iced tea?" She knew something was wrong. Given that tea was one of his favorite drinks, she hoped the tea would make him feel better. Then maybe he would tell her what was bothering him.

"That would be nice," he said, trying to be a little more pleasant. He had a feeling his wife was picking up on his mood, as she normally would not stop her cross-stitching to get him a glass of iced tea. He sat down in his recliner and turned on the local news. He was primarily interested in the weather because, so far, it has been a rather dry year and he was worried about his garden.

As John was watching the national news, Peter came in and announced that he had finished mopping the floors. "Dad," he said, addressing his father with a tone of reverence, "can I go over to Ken's house? We have some things to finish up for a project we're working on."

Ken Moore had been Peter's best friend ever since first grade. They lived at opposite ends of the short street. They were both on the same summer soccer team and spent a lot of time with the Scouts.

"How long will you be over there?" John asked Peter, knowing that the two boys stayed together until very late on occasion.

"I'll be home by ten o'clock," Peter said. This was not unusual; the boys were usually over at one house or another until after dark. If Peter wasn't over Ken's house, then Ken was over at his.

"Are your chores done?" John asked. Peter usually had several chores to do, especially in the summer months. Most of the chores revolved around working in the yard and keeping his room picked up, which at times seemed like mission impossible. However, the only job he had for today was to go out and pick up trash around the yard.

"I got it all done," Peter replied, knowing that his father was just giving him a hard time.

"Well," John said, slowly, dragging things out, taking a long time to say a simple word.

"Come on, Dad," Peter pleaded, knowing that his father was just giving him a hard time.

"I suppose. But what about dinner?" John asked, knowing that Peter's mother had something in the oven that sure smelled good. John was hoping it was his favorite dish, meat loaf.

"Ken is ordering pizza, so I can eat over there," Peter said. This was also a normal ritual that the two seemed to perform. John sometimes wondered if the two of them were going to turn into pizzas themselves someday.

"I suppose," John said. However, he knew the boys well enough to ask, "Are the girls going to be there?" John was referring to the two girls whom the boys spent a lot of time with. Carla Matthews, who was Peter's girlfriend, had beautiful brown eyes and long brown hair. They were not close, more like good friends who spent a lot of time together doing various activities. They never considered themselves a major couple. Laura Cook, who was Ken's girlfriend, had blue eyes and short blonde hair that appeared to be dyed and colored with streaks for highlights. Ken and Laura were very close. If the two were together, then they were very together. One would be lucky to get a toothpick between them. They were always hugging and kissing each other.

"Well," said Peter, "I'm not sure if they were planning to stop by or not. We plan to spend most of the time trying to get his computer to work properly so we can get this project done." Peter and Ken were both into computers and were good at fixing them.

"I suppose," John said for the third time. He watched Peter turn and bolt out the door. He sometimes wondered how the door remained on the hinges, thinking, *Boys will be boys.*

Paula brought John his iced tea and said with laughter in her tone, "I don't know about that boy, but one of these days …"

John took a sip of his iced tea, looked down the hallway at the front door, and just nodded.

John turned his attention back to the television, but the news was the same old junk. It mentioned more problems with the military in Iraq and Turkey. Another bomb had been set off, killing more civilians.

Just then the lights went out, and John could no longer see the television screen. From behind, he heard a soft voice say, "Guess who?"

John knew immediately whose hands were covering his eyes, but he decided to play the game. "Is it Paula?" he asked, knowing it wasn't her.

"No," said the soft voice.

"I know!" he said as if he'd just had a spark of inspiration. "Carla, what are you doing here? Peter's already left for Ken's house."

"Daddy," the small voice said in a tone of disgust, wondering if she had let her identity slip, "I'm not Carla."

"Well," John said, carefully placing his glass of tea on the end table, "I think you are." Then he reached behind the chair and grabbed the small arm attached to the hand that was blocking his eyesight. Then with great care, he pulled his daughter around the chair and into his lap. "Beth!"

"Oh, Daddy," she said, "you knew the whole time." Beth was now eleven years old. The two of them had been playing this game off and on for many years. John loved the way his daughter played the game, and he always loved the outcome.

Beth was now in his arms, hugging him. "I got something for you," she said with excitement, and jumped up and ran to the counter. She came running back to her father with a pen and an ink picture she had created. "See," she said, pointing to the picture, "I drew a picture of some sort of flowers in the front garden."

"That looks great," John commented, impressed with her ability to create beautiful works of art. Beth had always been interested in drawing and had drawn various pictures since she was able to hold a crayon. She enjoyed doing various types of art, but pen-and-ink drawings were what she most loved to do. She took after her mother in this regard as Paula, too, was very good at drawing. By way of contrast, John couldn't draw a straight line even if he was using a ruler.

Paula was standing at the kitchen doorway, watching her daughter play up to her father. She knew how much she meant to him. He was a proud father when his son was born, but when they had a daughter, he was in seventh heaven.

The newscaster on the TV caught John's attention as he mentioned the death of a woman named Denise Masters. A picture of the woman was displayed in the corner of the screen behind the announcer. "She was transported from the Gateway Medical Center to Christ Hospital," the announcer continued, "where she was pronounced dead on arrival. The strange situation surrounding this woman's illness and death has got doctors at the medical center scrambling to determine the problem. Apparently, her husband of twenty-eight years is experiencing similar symptoms. There were no comments from the doctors at the medical center or the hospital."

John sat there staring at the screen, wondering if that was the woman Tom had been talking about. Was it her blood John had taken back to the hospital to be analyzed? How was the husband doing, he wondered, as his daughter tried to regain his attention by putting the picture she'd drawn right in front of his face. Paula, seeing John's fixation on the story on the news, noticed that it was hard for Beth to get John's attention again. His daughter's actions finally brought him back to the reality of his recliner and his little Beth. "What are you going to do with the picture?" he finally asked her.

"Do you want to hang it in your office at work?" she asked.

"I would love to have it framed and hung at work," he answered. He proudly took the picture from her and carefully laid it on the end table. "I'll pick up a frame on my way home from work."

With her objective to present her latest masterpiece to her father accomplished, Beth jumped off his lap and headed outside to the backyard. As she departed, John grabbed the remote to see if any other news stations might have information on the old woman's death and what had caused her to die. However, by the time he surfed through the channels, the main part of the news was over and they were into the weather.

John would have normally watched the weather with great interest, but this time he just sat there for several minutes, contemplating what was happening. That strange feeling that something was wrong kept haunting him. He couldn't come to any resolution to the mystery. He just leaned back in his recliner and closed his eyes, trying to get the feeling of concern to float out of his mind.

Paula was standing at the kitchen door watching him. She knew something was wrong from the minute he'd walked into the house. But she couldn't figure out what was troubling him. She had a feeling there was something about the news broadcast that was bothering him, but she hadn't paid enough attention to what was being said to get an idea. Feeling there wasn't much she could do to help him at this time, she just took a deep breath and returned to the kitchen to finish getting dinner ready.

CHAPTER 3

The next morning, John heard the alarm clock go off, sounding like a sledgehammer pounding on his head. He quickly reached over to turn it off. He wasn't feeling well and just wanted to stay in bed but knew that he had to get up to go to work. His feelings of fatigue were primarily the result of not getting much sleep. He'd kept tossing and turning all night, dreaming about tubes of blood with flashing lights on them being whisked around town so they could get from a doctor's office to the hospital fast. John took a deep breath and tried to stretch the stiffness out of his aging body. He turned around and noticed that his wife was still asleep.

John's normal routine was to get up and take his shower before waking his wife. Then, as she was taking her shower, John would wake up the kids. Since this was summer and the kids were out of school, they got to sleep in. He was wishing he could sleep in, especially this morning. But tomorrow was Saturday, so then he could sleep late. For now, he had to get up and start his shower.

While in the shower, John's mind kept returning to thoughts of the blood specimens he'd had to rush to the hospital. His mind kept flashing back to the old man getting his blood drawn at the doctor's office. What were the results of that blood sample? Did it bring bad news, or were they just testing his cholesterol? John just didn't know. As much as he tried to think of other topics, his mind kept returning to those mysterious specimens. Suddenly, the door to the bathroom opened and in walked

Paula. "You've been in there a long time," she said to John. "I hope you plan to save me some hot water."

"I'm getting out," he said, not realizing he had taken more time than usual. He quickly rinsed off the remaining soap and turned off the water. "It's all yours," he said, grabbing a towel and stepping out of the shower.

"Thank you," Paula said, giving him a quick good morning kiss. This was her normal routine, except she normally didn't get into the shower until he had gotten out and called to her. "Is everything all right?" she asked.

This caught John by surprise. He tried to think of some answer that would keep her from asking a bunch of other questions. However, he was too tired to think up something clever, so he said, "I just didn't sleep too well, that's all," and stepped out of the way, creating a clear path for Paula to step into the shower. "Why are you up so early?" he asked, hoping this would distract her from asking any more questions.

"The alarm went off again," she informed him. "Apparently, you hit the sleeper button instead of turning it off."

"I'm sorry," he said, starting to wave his arm. "I must have slept on my arm funny last night because it felt like rubber this morning. I guess all the buttons felt the same."

"That's okay," she said, stepping past him. "I wanted to get up early today anyway." She may have been convinced that his actions resulted from not getting enough sleep, but what she wanted to know was why he hadn't gotten enough sleep.

John felt that his performance wasn't very convincing, so he quickly got dressed before Paula could get out of the shower. Then he headed downstairs to start breakfast.

John had the eggs ready by the time Paula had come down to the kitchen. He placed the small plates on the table, went over to the TV, and turned on the morning news. He and Paula always checked the morning news to determine what the weather would be like and to find out if there were areas of heavy traffic or traffic jams they needed to avoid on the way to work. Paula worked a few miles north in Oakley and normally didn't have too much trouble with traffic. However, John had to go to Cliffin to get to the hospital, which was almost all the way downtown. He nearly always had some trouble with traffic. Watching the news helped him figure out which way to go to get to the hospital.

John sat down and ate his breakfast while Paula grabbed the orange juice. He was watching the news, but since they were running a little late, the first section of the news was over and they were already talking about the weather. "Another day in the high eighties to low nineties with lots of humidity and little chance of rain," the announcer said. John wasn't too happy about the forecast as it meant another hot day driving around town.

John was a little disappointed about not seeing more information about the death of the woman with the blood problem, but all he could do was see if there was any news on the radio. He said goodbye to Paula and gave her a quick kiss before going out to the driveway. Then he got into his car and headed toward the hospital. He didn't mind using his own car to go to the hospital; at least the air conditioner worked.

John normally made seven pickups every morning, and today he had to deliver supplies to three sites. When he got to the hospital, he went to the lab to get the supplies instead of going directly to the courier car. This was his normal routine, but today he seemed to have an added expectation. Today he wanted to see what kind of information he might pick up. As he walked into the lab, he surveyed the actions of those throughout the lab area. He looked around, but everything seemed normal. Some of the workers were running around like idiots trying to find the front door in a fire. Those sitting around trying to keep from falling asleep were, in some cases, actually snoring away. John looked around to see if Tom was in yet, but the clock on the far wall indicated that it was only 7:35; he wouldn't be in until 8:00. Sometimes he would come in earlier, but such cases were rare.

John walked over to the door of the lab area and looked around to see if the CDC people were in yet. He didn't even know whether they would be in at all. Maybe they had come in only yesterday and didn't need to come back. As much as John wanted to believe this, deep down he knew they would be back. He didn't know why he felt that way, but he had such a strong feeling that he would have bet money on it.

John saw Tammy come in through the back door to the billing office. He was wondering if she knew any more about the two CDC strangers. She hadn't seemed to know much yesterday, but he wondered if his questions had sparked her curiosity. If they had and she asked some questions of her own, then maybe she discovered something more. However, if his questions had fallen on deaf ears, would she be even more suspicious now? He decided just to say good morning and see what happened.

"Good morning, Tammy," he said in an upbeat tone, which was especially difficult to muster since he was still on the tired side. "Aren't you glad it's Friday?"

"Good morning, John," she said, placing her lunch bag on her desk. "What are you doing here?"

"I have to pick up some supplies to take to one of the medical centers," he replied, afraid to get too involved in asking questions.

John decided he should just pick up his supplies and head out to the various sites on his route. Who knows, maybe by the time he came back with the morning pickups, not only would Tom be in the office, but also he might have more information.

The rest of the morning went as expected, although it seemed to take ten times longer than usual. John would stop and pick up the bags of tubes containing mostly blood specimens the doctors had ordered for their patients. However, this time he took notice of how many tubes were there. This first stop was the Crossroads Health Center. This was a smaller site that had only forty-four tubes. The problem was, he didn't know if this was the norm for this site. He had never paid any attention to how many tubes he picked up. He just picked up the bag of tubes and delivered them to the hospital.

John's second stop was at Hyde Park Internists, where he picked up fifty-one tubes. He paused and again began wondering if this was the normal number of tubes for this site, or had there been an increase as mentioned by Tammy yesterday? He was feeling a little frustrated not knowing what the normal count should be. He decided to keep track for a while to see if there was an increase and, if so, how much were they looking at. He reached for his clipboard that held his run information. He took a pen out of his shirt pocket and, on a blank piece of paper, wrote down the names of the sites where he was going to be picking up specimens.

With the first two stops written down, he started to get into the car. He looked around to see if anyone was watching him. He still had the feeling there were several sets of eyes staring at him. This made him feel a little uneasy. Even though he wasn't doing anything illegal, he felt as if he was. He shook off the feeling, slid in behind the steering wheel, and headed for the next stop.

At the Forest Park Health Center, there were only thirty-three tubes. John entered this information on his sheet. The largest facility was the Tri-Health Medical Center, where he picked up seventy-seven tubes. The next stop was the Gateway Medical Building, which was where he had made his emergency pickup. This site had only thirty-seven tubes. John continued his rounds that morning to the last two sites. Before he headed back to the hospital to drop off the specimens, he tallied the results of the morning run. In total, he had picked up three hundred sixty-four tubes. He had never realized how many tubes he brought in on an average day. The problem was that he couldn't tell if this was an average day's pickup or if it was an increase over the number of tubes he used to bring in. He was also wondering how many tubes Mark was bringing in and whether it was an increase or if it was the normal number he usually brought in.

As John pulled into the courier's parking spot at the hospital, he couldn't shake the desire to know what kind of day this was. He climbed out of the driver's seat and opened the back door of the car. He was already sweating from the humidity. After wiping the sweat from his forehead, he dove into the back seat to retrieve the cooler containing all the tubes. As he walked toward the back door of the hospital, he tried to determine if the cooler felt heavier than normal. Again, he tried to dig deep into his past memories, but he couldn't come up with any reference point against which to compare this load.

He entered the elevator and headed for the fifth floor. His concentration on solving this puzzle put him off his normal routine, and for some reason, his passkey worked the first time. He was standing there swiping his passkey over the electronic reader repeatedly, waiting for the light to turn green, not realizing that it had already done so.

"Having trouble again?" came a voice from behind. John looked down the hall toward the direction of the voice and saw Roberta, a lab technician, approaching the entrance to the lab. John wasn't sure at first what she was referring to, but then he looked down and noticed the light was green.

"No, I got it now," he replied, not knowing when the passkey had worked. "It still acts up from time to time.

"Anything new happening around here this morning?" John asked, trying to make small talk.

"No, not really," Roberta said, leading John back to the lab area. "Another load of specimens for us to process?" she asked, knowing that this was what John was carrying, just wanting to keep the conversation going.

John saw an excellent opportunity to find out if this was a normal delivery or was larger than normal. "Yeah," he said, trying to determine what words to use, "I don't know if I'm getting old or if there seems to be more specimens these days."

"Oh, John," she replied with a slight giggle, "you're not getting old."

This wasn't what he'd wanted to hear. This could mean that today's load was larger than normal, or it could just be her reply to his comment about being old. To get more information on the size of the delivery but not tip his hand and reveal his concerns, he said, "That's good. I was getting worried that I might be too old for this job. It must mean that these deliveries are getting larger."

"You'll never get too old for this job," she countered as she walked into the lab area.

"Well, the number of specimens sure seems to be getting larger," he said, disappointed that he hadn't gotten the information he was hoping for.

Roberta, not realizing that John was looking for a specific answer, just followed his lead. "Well, there has been an increase in the number of tests doctors have requested," she said, looking back at him with a smile, "but I think you can handle it."

This was what he wanted to know. She had confirmed there was indeed an increase in tests requested by the doctors. Now he was wondering how big of an increase. It couldn't be too big; otherwise, wouldn't he have noticed? The other question was, Why all these extra tests? Were people being tested for the same medical condition that had killed the people Tom was referring to yesterday? John didn't know if Roberta knew, but he had to take a shot to find out. The problem was how to ask the question without sounding as if he was interested.

"Roberta, do you think the increase in tests is due to a problem," he asked as he placed the bags on the lab counter, "or do you think these doctors just want to charge more for a bunch of tests?"

"I wouldn't be surprised if the doctors were just trying to get more money from the insurance companies," she offered, sliding the bags of specimens across the counter. "My sister had to go through several tests because of a gallbladder problem. By the time she was done, she discovered that the insurance company wouldn't cover the cost of all the tests. They said the doctor had ordered tests that were not necessary and not related to her medical problems."

John wasn't interested in Roberta's sister or the fact that many doctors ordered more tests than others. He was interested in why there appeared to be an increase in the number of tests right now. He felt he had better leave before generating suspicion with his questioning. "Well, see you later," he said as he turned to leave.

"See ya" was all Roberta said in reply as she dove into the pile of specimens and attacked the paperwork.

John scanned the lab, looking for the two strangers he had seen yesterday. The two CDC agents were nowhere to be found, so he went looking for Tom.

Tom wasn't in his office, which is usually where a lab manager would be expected to spend most of his time. Tom was more of a hands-on manager. He liked to get in with his staff and work with them to understand what they did and what he could do to help them do their jobs better.

John was unable to find Tom anywhere. He decided to ask Kathy at the front desk. If there were any comings or goings, she would know of them. Kathy was sitting at the front counter, banging away on the computer keyboard.

"Hi, Kathy," John said in a cheerful tone as he had done many times in the past.

"Hi, John," she replied, glancing up from the monitor. "What can I do for you today?"

John and Kathy were good friends who had an ongoing tradition of playing games and cracking jokes. "Well, you could check the air-conditioning on that car I drive around all day, and when you finish with that, it could use a good washing and wax job too."

Kathy, in a calm voice, said in response, "Okay, I can get to it in about five minutes, but it will cost you about seventeen thousand dollars."

"That's great. Send the bill to Tom." This gave John the perfect lead-in to asking the original question he had on his mind. "By the way, do you know where he went?"

"He's upstairs in a departmental meeting until two o'clock," she replied. "It's one of those quarterly luncheon meetings that allows you to pig out on food, but you have to sit there without falling asleep and listen to the bigwigs holler and complain as they spill their guts about what's happening around the hospital."

That wasn't what he'd wanted to hear, but there wasn't much he could do about it except go back on the road and complete his afternoon run. "Okay," he said, as he turned and headed into the hallway.

"Okay," Kathy said in a laughing voice. "I'll send you a bill!"

"Go ahead!" John hollered back over his shoulder, also chuckling at their little game. He continued down the hallway to pick up a small box of supplies for one of the afternoon deliveries. With the small box under his arm, he took one last look around the lab for the CDC personnel. Seeing no one who resembled the two new strangers, he headed for the door.

John's afternoon pickups were miserable. The afternoon heat had progressively risen to over ninety degrees. The humidity made it feel more like one hundred ten degrees, especially in the car. John had finished his afternoon route and returned to the hospital just in time to take his new collection of two hundred eighty-five tubes into the building seconds before Mother Nature started a downpour. Some summer thunderstorms provided lots of rain, which helped drop the temperature and the humidity to make the weather a little more comfortable. John just wished that it would rain like that right after lunch so his drive around town would be a little more bearable.

This time when John walked into the lab area, he saw Joyce talking with the female CDC agent, who was named Sharon Frenette, and Robert Caldwell. He recognized her from before. The outfits those two individuals were wearing were definitely not what the normal employee would wear in the lab. He paused as he waited for Joyce to finish talking with them. He stood there quietly listening to Joyce as she explained the results of a test she had just finished.

"The coagulation on this test," Joyce said to Sharon, "for type O blood is much higher than the coagulation for this test on type B blood. I don't know why it's so high, but you can see the results for yourself. Do you have any idea why it's so high?"

John stood there with his eyes fixed on the paperwork he had brought up with the specimens, but his ears were tuned into the conversation between the two women in front of him.

Sharon then asked Robert to review the test data from the report that Joyce was holding. "This is interesting," he ventured, rubbing his head as if to concentrate on the test results. "I've never seen a test result look like this. Have you?" he asked, directing his question to Sharon.

"I've never seen anything like this either," she replied with a tone of disbelief.

Joyce noticed that John was standing there. All three turned and looked at him. Joyce, realizing he was waiting for her, stepped forward. "Hi, John. Are you waiting for me?"

"Sorry," he started. "I didn't want to interrupt your conversation, but here are the afternoon pickups," he said, sliding a large number of blood specimens across the table toward her.

"That's okay," she said. "We were just going over some test results."

John didn't want to leave without trying to get more information about the test Sharon had just run. Was this test associated with the blood problem he had been dealing with, or was it some test to see if the equipment was working correctly? He was sure it wasn't an equipment test, but he had no way to tell if the test was related to the blood problem Tom had referred to yesterday. And what was with the comment about type O and type B? Those were two different blood types. He had to start up some conversation with Joyce without asking a direct question.

"Looks like you're having a busy day today," John said by way of opening the conversation.

"Oh, I suppose it's been a little busy," Joyce said, pointing at the two CDC agents, "especially since they came by to use our equipment. But other than that, it's been just another day." Joyce received a stern look from Sharon as if warning her to watch what she was saying. "Thank you, John," Joyce said, and with that, she turned and went back over to Sharon and Robert to continue the conversation.

John wanted very much to stand there and listen, but he was afraid that they might get defensive and ask him to leave. "See ya later," he said, then turned to leave the lab.

He had an overwhelming desire to get more information, but with Joyce preoccupied with the CDC agents, there wasn't much he could do.

John left the lab in search of Tom. He headed down the hallway and looked into Tom's office. As expected, Tom wasn't there. John continued to look into the offices along the hallway, but with no luck. He walked back down the hallway toward the lab area and took two steps in to look around again. The two CDC agents were now standing alone over in the corner, watching one piece of equipment in the lab. He figured they were watching as a machine ran a test.

The two appeared to be arguing about something, but John couldn't tell what their disagreement was about. The sound was garbled, but their voices occasionally rose in intensity during their discussion. Then they suddenly turned to look at John as if surprised to see him still there. Either they had eyes in the backs of their heads or they had seen his reflection in the large piece of glass on the equipment door. When they turned and saw who was standing at the counter, they turned back toward each other, but now began talking in much softer voices.

John looked around and saw Mike standing in front of a computer terminal at the other end of the lab. There was no sign of Joyce or Tom. "Mike!" John called out in a voice loud enough for him to hear. Mike looked up from his computer screen and saw John standing at the counter.

"Hey, Mike," John said, "have you see Tom?"

"No," Mike answered, walking over to the counter. "I just got here." Mike could see that John was very interested in locating Tom because he continued to survey the lab area. "Do you want me to tell him you're looking for him?" he asked.

"No thanks," John replied, disappointed about not having found Tom. He headed back down the hallway in search of his boss.

John stopped in the middle of the hallway as if he had nowhere to go. Joyce wasn't around, and his hopes of getting any information from her had gone out the window since Sharon appeared to dislike Joyce's comments about what she thought might be going on in the area in the back of the lab.

John continued his search throughout the lab offices, but Tom wasn't anywhere to be found. He reached the front of the office, where the receptionist was sitting. "Have you seen Tom?" he asked Betty, who was reviewing some paperwork in one of the patient's folders.

"As far as I know," she replied, not looking up from the page she was reviewing, "he's back there somewhere." John looked down the hallway where he had just surveyed the offices. Tom didn't appear to be in any of them.

"Thanks," he said, disappointed about not having learned his whereabouts. He turned to retrace his steps, hoping to be luckier the second time through, but his level of disappointment was increasing. He continued down the hallway, checking each office space one at a time. Still no Tom. He was getting a little depressed about not finding him and not getting any more information about the strange problem associated with the blood specimens.

John reached the end of the hallway outside the lab area, still with no luck. This was the place where the employee mailboxes were located, so he got his mail before continuing the search. Standing at his mailbox, he overheard a familiar voice coming from the lab area.

"What have you been able to determine?" asked the familiar voice. John was positive it was Tom's voice, but he wasn't sure whom Tom was talking to.

"It seems to destroy the cysteine amino acid within the erythrocytes," replied a familiar voice. John finally recognized the voice as belonging to Joyce. She was referring to a specific amino acid found within a red blood cell.

"Do you know how it destroys the amino acid?" Tom asked.

"We haven't been able to determine that," replied an unfamiliar female voice. John had a feeling this was the female CDC agent named Sharon.

"Do you know what's causing this?" Tom continued.

"We don't know that either," replied Sharon.

"Do you have any idea where this started?" Tom asked, becoming frustrated with the lack of positive answers from the CDC personnel.

"No," replied another unknown voice. This time John suspected this was the male CDC person, named Robert. "All we know at this time is that this is not an isolated case. In fact, there have been cases reported across the United States and in many other countries around the world."

"Any idea as to how it spreads?" Tom asked, the concern evident in his voice. "I don't want my employees to come down with this, whatever you call it."

"We discovered a new virus that we are calling the Sanguis virus," replied Robert. "This virus is responsible for the disease we are calling B Antigen Resistive Disease, or BARD for short."

"As far as we can tell," Sharon added, "it is not contagious. We haven't been able to determine how these individuals are coming down with the illness. At first, we thought it might be airborne, but tests of contaminated patients have proven this is not true. So the best thing we can come up with is that it has to be spread through some form of ingestion."

"Do you mean it attaches itself to some form of food or liquid and then we eat or drink it without knowing it's there?" Tom asked with much concern in his voice.

"Don't get too concerned," Sharon cautioned. "We don't know all the facts yet."

"That's right," said Robert. "I wish we knew more."

"So do I," said Tom, becoming agitated with the lack of information. "It seems to me you really don't know much at all, do you?"

"Well," Sharon said in an obvious attempt to save face in front of the lab manager, "we're working on it."

"Have you issued any sort of national warning describing the symptoms to watch for?" inquired Tom.

"Not at this time," Sharon replied. "Can you imagine what kind of panic we would have if this were to get out?"

"Well, how in the hell are you determining how big the problem is?" Tom questioned, becoming more and more frustrated with the lack of concrete information.

"We have contacts, like us," Sharon said, referring to Robert and herself, "at various sites around the US, and we all report to Washington. They, in turn, keep the teams notified as to what progress is being made."

"You mean if any," Tom commented with a tone of sarcasm. "I understand the symptoms resemble those of anemia," he added.

"That's the problem, and that's why we didn't make a national announcement," Sharon continued cautiously. "Can you imagine what would happen if we were to release an announcement that there is an anemia-type blood disease killing people? Every individual in the country who is feeling tired and run down would go flying to see their doctors. There are so many people in this country complaining of being tired that

I would bet over 75 percent of the population would go see their doctors, complaining they have the disease. That would cause massive hysteria and would make one major impact on the economy."

"I suppose," Tom responded, reluctantly giving in to her logic, "but it sure seems that it would also make it harder to gather information about this problem."

"Well, in a way it does," Sharon said, glad to see a decrease in Tom's aggressive attitude. "But in a way, it's easier than trying to sift through the millions of blood specimens trying to find those that are infected and those that aren't."

"Okay," Tom said, feeling there wasn't much more they could tell him. "Well, if there is anything else we can do to help, don't hesitate to ask. But I would appreciate it if you kept me informed as to your progress on this problem."

"No problem," said Sharon, obviously relieved that Tom was leaving.

John stood there in front of the mailboxes, acting as if he'd been looking at the paperwork the entire time the conversation was going on. However, now that he could tell that the conversation was winding down, he thought it would be better to avoid being seen standing there. So he took his mail and quickly walked down the hallway to the first door on the right. This led into the small office area where his infrequently used desk was located. He sat down and tried to comprehend the information he had just heard. Some blood disease that resembled a bad case of anemia was affecting people all around the United States and the world. They had no idea of where it started or how it spread, and from the sound of things, they didn't know how to treat it. All John could do was stare out into the distance while sitting at his desk holding a few pieces of mail in his hand.

CHAPTER 4

The rest of the week seemed to go by slowly as John continued his rounds. He continued to keep track of the number of tubes he picked up each day, but there didn't appear to be much of a difference from one day to the next. Wednesday showed a rise in the number of tubes, but then things dropped off a little on Thursday and Friday. Every time he stopped by the lab to drop off the specimens, there seemed to be no one around, or else they were so busy that they barely even noticed he was there. He was thinking this was all in his head. He didn't know what to think. Indeed, the hot days of summer were making it difficult for him to think while fighting the congested streets in town.

As John was heading down Reading Road, he had to stop for a train blocking the street. This happened frequently as there were probably more train tracks in this section of town than in any one area anywhere in the rest of the country. This train was moving relatively slow, which meant he would be there awhile. He put the car in park and turned off the engine. As he sat there, other cars pulled up behind him and waited for the interference to run its course.

John had been waiting for only about three minutes when his cell phone went off. He kind of expected that this call was from Tom. He picked the phone up off the holder and looked at the caller ID. Yep, it was Tom. John, having no idea why Tom would call him while he was out on the road, was a little worried about the reason for the call. Well, there was only one way to find out. "Hello, Tom," John said, worried about what information Tom would present. "What's up?"

"Where are you?" Tom asked with urgency in his voice.

"I'm sitting at the train crossing on Reading Road." He paused, wondering why Tom sounded so concerned. "What's up?"

"How long would it take you to get to Price Hill Medical Group and pick up another stat?" Tom asked with a tone of urgency.

John could sense a touch of concern in Tom's voice. "Isn't that one of Mark's sites?" he asked, wondering why he was being asked to travel to the other side of town. This bothered him a little because he knew Tom was aware that the Price Hill Medical Group was on Mark's route and not his.

"They have another stat specimen and they want it evaluated as soon as possible. I'm asking you to go pick it up because you are already aware of the problem that is going on out there with these blood tests. How long will it take you?" Tom asked, repeating his original question.

"I'm not sure, but if I push it, I could probably be there in about twenty-five minutes and then be back in the lab within an hour," answered John as he tried to figure out the route in his head. "Would that be fast enough?"

"It's going to have to be," Tom replied, wishing John could do it faster. "I want you to get there as fast as possible, but don't get stopped by the police for speeding. It wouldn't look good on your record. Plus, it will take longer for you to get here. Cops can be slower than molasses when you are in a hurry."

"Okay," John said, starting up his car. "I'll do the best I can. Maybe we should see if Scotty can beam me over," he said, using a little humor to relieve some of the stress he was feeling.

"See you when you get here," Tom said.

With that, John put the car into drive and made a quick U-turn to go in the opposite direction from the train crossing. It was a good thing the train was passing at this point because if he had to wait for the traffic to clear before turning around, he would have been there awhile.

John quickly drove to Interstate 275 West, where it took him only sixteen minutes to reach the Price Hill Medical Group. He was lucky there weren't any cops around with a radar unit as he easily approached eighty miles an hour.

He walked into the doctor's office and approached the counter. A short, redheaded receptionist asked what she could do for him. "I'm here from the lab at Christ Hospital to pick up a stat blood sample."

"Wait right here," she said. She picked up the phone and called an extension in the back area of the office. She told the individual on the other end of the line that John was here to pick up the stat blood sample. The person on the other end indicated that he or she would bring it out. The receptionist informed John of this response.

There were two individuals dressed in blue nurse's uniforms standing behind the receptionist. The first nurse turned to the second and began talking about the stat. John stood there looking at a magazine but listening in on their conversation.

"Do you think she has the blood disease," asked the first nurse, "or do you think she is just anemic?"

There's that anemic condition again, John thought.

"I think she's just anemic," replied the second nurse. "According to her chart, she has type B blood. So odds are she doesn't have the disease."

"You said she was about sixty-eight years old, right?"

"Yeah. And she is so skinny, I wouldn't be surprised if she's also suffering from malnutrition."

"Well, the blood test will prove it one way or the other."

Just then, another individual wearing a colorful lab coat came out carrying a small plastic bag and some paperwork. "Here you go," she said, handing the bag to John.

"Thanks," he said, "I'll take it directly to the lab." With the bag in hand, he headed for the door. He made it to the lab in twenty-five minutes, again glad there weren't any cops around. For the entire trip to the hospital, John did nothing but drive and think about the conversation the two nurses had had. What was this about having type B blood? It sounded as if they didn't think the woman had the disease if her blood was type B. Another thing bothering him was that as far as he knew, no one in the lab knew for sure what the two CDC agents were working on. No one was supposed to know anything about this blood problem, and yet here were two nurses talking out loud as if everyone in the office knew all about it. This puzzled John as he continued to drive to the hospital.

He entered the lab and saw Tom waiting for him. "Here you go," John said, handing the bag to Tom. Tom, without saying a word, turned and headed to the lab. John stood in amazement, wondering what was going on. Could this test be so important that even a simple hello would have taken too long? Tom's strange actions increased John's curiosity.

John knew he had better get back out on the road, but he wanted to know more about what was going on. Instead of leaving, he decided that since he had listened in on a conversation in the lab before, while reading his mail, he could do the same thing now. So he, as naturally as he could, walked up to the mailboxes and tried to listen in on any conversations going on in the lab. However, the voices were much lower than before, so he could not make out what they were saying. He did hear "type B" several times, but he wasn't able to determine what it meant.

In an effort to hear more, John stepped closer to the door. However, this move still didn't allow him to hear what was being said with any more clarity. He wanted to get closer but was afraid that he might be seen by someone in the lab. Also, if someone were to come into the hallway, it would look very obvious that John was eavesdropping on the conversation instead of reading his mail.

John continued to strain to hear the conversations, when suddenly he heard footsteps approaching the doorway from inside. He quickly moved back to his spot in front of his mailbox to give the illusion he was reading his mail. As he was standing there, shifting through several envelops and notices, the footsteps came closer until John saw that they belonged to Tom. Tom passed behind John without saying a word. John turned his head to watch him go down the hall and into his office. He didn't know what to do. Tom hadn't told John he needed to go back and finish his route, which is what he normally would have done when he saw John standing there. Why was he acting this way? The sudden request for this blood test and Tom's actions made John wonder what was going on. Was the blood problem that had come up over a week ago getting worse? Was there something Tom knew that he wished John knew? John just stood with more questions than answers. He felt he had to get some answers. So, he aggressively shoved his mail back into his mailbox and headed for Tom's office.

Tom was sitting behind his desk, staring at some papers in front of him. "Tom," John said softly, trying to get Tom's attention. Tom just sat there with no acknowledgment that John was in the room. John stood there wondering if he should interrupt Tom or leave and come back at a later time. He shook his head; no, he had to know more about what was going on. The suspense was getting on his nerves. Plus, Tom was his friend, and he may need someone to talk to.

Ever since the first request to quickly bring in a specimen, John kept hearing little comments on the news about individuals having a blood disease resembling anemia. The reports stated that some of these people died and others didn't. There was also a somewhat clear indication that no one knew what was causing the problem, where it came from, and so on. Was this a disorder or a disease? At least with the AIDS virus, the scientists knew where it came from and how it spread. John was getting more uncomfortable as he stood there watching Tom sitting there and staring as if looking through the papers on his desk. John couldn't just stand there any longer. "Tom!" he said in a much louder tone, which caused Tom to look up from the papers in front of him.

"Oh, hi, John," Tom replied as if he had been drained of all energy.

"Is everything all right?" John asked, walking up to the desk. He sat down in the chair in front of Tom's desk, deciding not to give Tom an opportunity to ask him to leave. If he were to make himself comfortable, then Tom might give him more time to talk.

"Yeah" was all Tom said, but it was clear, even to a blind man, that this wasn't true.

"Come on, Tom," John said, trying to persuade him, "I know you better than that. Something happened in the lab that has you all shook up. What's going on?" He paused for a couple of seconds to see if Tom would open up, but he just sat there staring at the stack of papers. John knew he had to give Tom a push if he was going to get him to open up. "Tom!" John called out in a louder tone to get his attention. "Does it concern the blood disease?" he asked in a much softer tone.

Tom looked up at John and peered deep into his eyes. He sat there as if to analyze the individual sitting on the other side of his desk. Who was this individual? What was his character like? Could he be trusted? John just sat there, waiting, looking back at a set of eyes that seemed to look past him.

"Well," Tom started, taking a deep breath to revitalize his soul, "it looks like this blood disease is going to be worse than originally anticipated."

"What do you mean?" John asked, sitting on the edge of his seat, knowing this was the information he'd been waiting for.

"There have been quite a few deaths attributed to what appears to be anemia. This isn't unusual in itself because it does occur, especially with the elderly and malnourished. However, it has started to occur in healthy individuals as well. I mean individuals of all ages. According to the CDC agents, they've had several die from this disease as young as fifteen. The CDC doesn't know what's causing it or how someone gets it. The worst thing is that they have no idea how to cure it. And"—Tom paused as if to acquire the courage to continue—"it appears the death rate is 100 percent."

John sat there waiting to see if Tom would continue, but Tom looked as if he was lost without knowing where to go next. So John decided to see if he could give Tom something else to think about. "I heard one of the nurses over at the Price Hill Medical Group indicate that she thought this woman whose blood I just brought over was just anemic because her chart showed that she had type B blood. Do you know what that means?"

Tom took another deep breath and looked over at the door to his office as if checking to see if someone was eavesdropping. Afraid that he might be overheard, he got up and walked over to the door. He stood in the doorway as if he'd forgotten why he had walked over there. After a short pause, he looked up and down the hall and closed the door ever so carefully, not making a sound. Then he turned and looked at John. He stood there looking as if he might be analyzing how he would attack the prey sitting in front of him. John started to feel a little uneasy about Tom's actions. However, Tom took a deep breath and returned to his desk.

"It appears," Tom continued in a soft tone, almost inaudibly, "that people who have type B blood are not affected by it. All other blood types seem to be susceptible. That means anyone with a blood type other than type B could die from this disease."

John seemed to imitate Tom's earlier actions as he sat there staring into space. Neither man seemed to know what to say next. Time seemed to stand still. Tom was the first to break the stalemate. "Do you know your blood type?" he asked John with great concern in his voice.

John had to stop and think about it. He hadn't thought about that since he'd given blood a long time ago. "I believe," he said, searching deep in his memory, "I have type B blood." After answering the question, his mind formed a hypothesis as to why Tom had asked it. John wondered if

Tom was concerned about the possibility of John's dying from this disease. Then he looked at Tom and asked, "What's your blood type?"

"I have type O blood," Tom replied. A sinking feeling came upon them both. Was Tom a candidate like the others who didn't have type B blood? This would mean that if he were to catch the Sanguis virus, he could die from the disease.

As John sat there, he thought about the disease. He was type B, so did that mean that if he had the Sanguis virus, he wouldn't be affected by it? And if that were true, could he spread the virus by being around others?

"Tom," John said, "since I'm type B and theoretically not affected by this disease, is there a way to see if I am a carrier? I don't want to spread this to anyone else, including you or my family."

"According to Sharon," Tom said, trying to remember information he had heard earlier from the CDC agent, "there is a test that can be performed, but it's not foolproof at this time. They hope to have a better way of testing for the Sanguis virus soon, but right now we have to assume you're all right."

This didn't reassure John much. He could go home that night and possibly give the disease to his entire family, but what else was there to do? "Tom," he continued, "how long is it between the time someone gets this infection and the time they show symptoms of the disease?"

Tom shrugged his shoulders. "Sharon doesn't know for sure. By the time they find out someone has the disease, the person has died before anyone can get much information from them. Most of the time people just feel tired at first, and then they become very weak very quickly and then die. So until the scientists discover how it's contracted, they can't determine the incubation time or how long a person will last once becoming infected. However, according to Sharon, once someone starts showing signs of being very weak and fatigued"—Tom paused for a second, determining not to say the word *die*—"he or she will generally pass away within a couple of hours. Some may last longer, but that's rare. The big question is how long between the time they are exposed to the Sanguis virus and the time they reach this condition."

John sat with Tom not saying a word, pondering the new information and what impact it might have on their lives, their jobs, and the world around them. "John," Tom said, interrupting the silence, "first, you can't tell anyone what you know, not even your wife. If word of this gets out, there could be a major panic."

"I understand," John replied reluctantly. "But it looks like the newscasters have already gotten some of this information. I hear bits and pieces on the news." John didn't want to say that the nurses at the doctor's office were a lot freer about discussing the situation regardless of who might be within hearing range.

"Well," Tom continued with a tone of deep concern, "at this time, the CDC agents would like to keep this a secret as long as possible, until they can find some of the answers they need in order to solve this problem."

"I understand," John said, not knowing whether he could keep this to himself. After all, some people need to talk just to work out the confusion and fear surrounding a circumstance outside their control. Isn't that what Tom just did with John? And now Tom wanted him to keep it a secret?

"Okay," Tom said after a short pause, "I think you had better get back to your afternoon route. I'll have Cindy call the other sites to tell them that you are running a little behind and not to worry; you will get there."

"Okay," John said as he slowly got up to leave.

"Remember," Tom said sharply, "don't tell anyone."

John stood there for a second shaking his head, knowing that Tom was right but wondering if he could indeed refrain from saying anything to anybody about what he had just learned. It would drive him slowly insane to know what he knew and not tell anyone about it. Plus, he wanted to know what his wife's and kids' blood types were and whether they could die from this disease. How was he going to ask them what their blood types were without arousing suspicion? He slowly turned and headed for the door, then went out to his car to complete his afternoon run.

CHAPTER 5

John finished his afternoon runs then headed home, which seemed to take him forever to reach, partly because of the traffic, which John didn't notice, and partly because his mind was still in Tom's office going over the conversation he'd had with him. Repeatedly in John's mind, he kept thinking about Tom's question about his blood type. Now he was thinking about his family and what blood types they were. Could they be in danger of catching the Sanguis virus and dying from the disease if their blood types were not type B? The idea of them dying was the predominant thought on his mind. His parents had died in a car accident when he was young, but he could still remember the funerals, that dismal day standing in a black suit looking at his father and mother in their caskets. He tried to replace the faces of his parents with the faces of his wife and kids. He suddenly got a shiver from the thought of a casket being lowered into the ground and then covered with dirt. The thought of never seeing his family again was almost more than he could take. A tear came to his eye.

His mind then shifted to thoughts of being a carrier of the Sanguis virus and going around infecting his family without knowing it. He could be condemning them to death without even knowing he was the culprit who had caused their demise. He had visions of everyone pointing fingers at him at the funeral, accusing him of killing the entire family in cold blood, the mourners yelling "Murderer!" at him through surgical masks they wore to prevent him from infecting them. As the moaners walked toward him, they picked up stones and threw them at him. The shower of stones seemed to increase in number and size until he was beaten to his knees.

A sudden blast from a car horn brought John back to reality as the car across the intersection started to advance at the same time John did. John let the car pass, then continued to turn onto his street. He finally pulled into his driveway and stopped the car at the top of the driveway next to Paula's car. He was exhausted from the mental workout he'd been putting himself through. He sat there for several minutes as he tried to dump the thoughts he'd had on the way home so he would have a more pleasant disposition when he entered the house. However, his efforts failed, so he just shook his head and opened the car door.

As he walked through the doorway, he stopped to survey the surroundings in front of him. The hallway was cluttered with some of Beth's junk, as usual. Her stuffed animals and several pairs of shoes were sitting by the little table on the right side of the hallway. Peter had left his card collection scattered all over the table; some of the cards were on the floor. Down the hall toward the back of the house was a basket of clean clothes that someone was supposed to put away several days ago. Able to see part of the kitchen counter, he noticed that it was covered in various kinds of junk from today's mail. Next to that was Paula's and Beth's art supplies. In other words, the house was in its normal state of disarray. Normally, John would have come in and started complaining about the mess, but tonight he just paused and was grateful to have the mess and those who had created it. But for how long? Would the future reveal a cleaner house with fewer individuals around to make the messes? He just couldn't dream of what it would be like.

"I'm home!" John called out in as happy a tone as he could muster, but there wasn't any response; the house remained absent of voices. The only noise he could hear was the TV in the living room. The lack of response was making John feel a little uneasy, especially with the information he had learned about the blood disease. Where was everyone? He feared the worst. *They are all lying on their beds dead,* he thought. However, to get control of his emotions before he could get too carried away, he called out again. "I'm home!" he said in a louder tone, just in case they were out of normal hearing range.

From what seemed to be the deepest depths of the earth, he heard, "I'm down here!" John felt more at ease now that he had gotten a response.

If there had been a major problem, odds are he would have heard from someone before now. "Right," he said to himself, trying to convince himself there was nothing to worry about.

"Where are you?" he called back as he started down the basement steps.

"Over in the corner," came the reply. Knowing it was Paula, he headed over to the corner.

"What are you doing over there?" he asked when he saw Paula rummaging through a box on an old table in a corner of the basement. There were also several other boxes on the floor that indicated that she had just rummaged through those.

"I lost my cross-stitch needle, and I think I have some extras in one of these boxes, but I can't remember which one."

"Wouldn't it be easier to just go out and buy a couple of new ones?"

"Yeah," she replied as she dug into the next box, "but I didn't want to go out. It's too hot, and they are expecting heavy thunderstorms this evening."

"I noticed it was getting a little dark outside," he responded. But in reality, the sun could have been blazing down on the house and he wouldn't have noticed.

"Found them!" she cried out in triumph. She quickly closed the boxes and began heading back upstairs, holding a small pack of needles as if they were a trophy.

John followed her as she climbed the stairs. "Where are the kids?" he asked, wondering why it was so quiet around the house. Normally, the house would have qualified as a noise hazard zone with the kids and all their friends hanging around and likely fighting with each other.

"Beth is over at Hailee's. She asked if she could spend the night. Hailee's parents said it was okay, but I told her to be back by nine o'clock tonight. We have an early day tomorrow. As for Peter, he is over at Ken's and will be back later tonight."

"I wonder if the girls will be at Ken's house as well?" John asked, trying to keep his mind off the disease.

"Well, you know those kids. If they're not, then those boys are going to be awfully bored," Paula replied, sitting down on the couch to continue cross-stitching. "Peter said they were going to watch movies, so that means the girls are probably going to be there too. You know what else that means?" she asked, an excited tone in her voice.

John was standing in the center of the living room watching his wife thread the new needle. She quickly picked up the cross-stitch project she was working on, but before starting the first stitch, she looked up and gave him a questioning look. "Well?" she said.

John just stood there, not sure what she was getting at. "Well what?" he asked, slowly shrugging his shoulders.

"We can have a quiet night at home together," she replied, wondering what was troubling him. He was always looking for a period when the kids would be out of the house. He was usually the first to jump on the occasion. His attitude was a little out of the ordinary for him, which made Paula suspicious.

John, realizing his inability to recognize the advantages of the situation, tried to act overjoyed. He quickly ran over, plopped down on the couch, and grabbed the remote. "This means we can watch anything we want to tonight," he said, trying to imitate his wife's enthusiasm. He grabbed the remote and turned on the cable listings for the night. "What would you like to watch?" he said with a tone of glee in his voice, or at least as much glee as he could muster.

Paula sat there and wondered what was going on. She knew that her husband wasn't acting right. And he was such a lousy actor in his attempt to be happy. She knew he was hiding something, but she also knew he wasn't ready to talk about it yet. "That's not what I meant." She giggled, slapping him on the arm.

"I know," he said, trying to be upbeat.

"Well, for now," she said, realizing he didn't want to talk about whatever was bothering him, "why don't you find us a good movie?"

"Okay," he said, running through the channel guide to see what movies were on that night. He didn't know what to watch and didn't care to pick a film. As he ran through the listings, he read each title, hoping to find something interesting to watch. There were several science fiction movies, a disaster movie, a couple of so-called teen movies, and two musicals. Tom loved to watch sci-fi and disaster movies but wasn't in the mood for them tonight. He knew Paula liked musicals and felt that if he were to find one, it would keep her interested and make it unlikely that she'd do a lot of talking. "How about *Singin' in the Rain?*" he asked as if he were dying to watch it.

This is not what he would normally do, Paula thought to herself after hearing his selection; he would have recommended one of the other movies. She was suspicious when he suggested *Singin' in the Rain.* However, she knew he liked some musicals, and for sure he liked this one, so she decided not to push the issue about what was bothering him. "That's a good movie," she replied.

"Good," he said, happy she had agreed with no persuading. "We have about thirty-five minutes before the movie starts. Do you want me to make something to eat?" It was not unusual for John to make dinner. When it came to certain dishes, he was a good cook.

John went into the kitchen while Paula continued to cross-stitch in the living room. They could still see each other and talk, but he wasn't in the mood to talk. He had offered to cook so that he could be out of conversational range until the movie started.

He made cheeseburgers with all the fixings and french fries. The two were sitting on the couch eating their dinner when the movie started. After they'd finished eating, John took the dishes back into the kitchen and came back to sit on the couch. He sat on one end put his arm on the top of the couch, allowing Paula to reposition herself next to him. She cuddled up to him but allowed enough room to work on her project.

They sat comfortably for about fifteen minutes, watching the movie. The only verbalization was an occasional melody from Paula as she sang along with the film. John sat quietly watching the movie but was preoccupied, thinking about what his wife's blood type might be. Finally, he felt he had stalled enough and he wanted to ask her about her blood type. But how could he ask this question without making her suspicious?

He turned and looked over at Paula, who was counting the number of stitches on the row she had just finished. He concentrated on sounding as if he were holding a casual conversation. "Paula," he said without taking his eyes off the TV, "do you know your blood type?" He tried to act as if he were more interested in the movie than in getting an answer, but somehow he felt he hadn't done a good job of hiding his real intentions.

She stopped counting the stitches and looked up at him. "Why do you want to know my blood type?" she asked, mostly confused by this strange question.

"Oh, the hospital is gathering information for some stupid survey, and that is one of the questions. I knew mine, but I didn't know yours," he continued, struggling to act as if he were still holding a simple conversation. However, deep down he was terrified as to what her answer might be.

"What kind of survey are they doing where they want to know your blood type?" she asked as if not having believed a word he had said.

John became a little more uneasy because he knew his little white lie was about to crumble into a heap of rubble. He was struggling to come up with a story that not only would sound realistic but also would open up other possible avenues to go down if she continued to ask questions. "Well," he continued, as if he were more interested in the movie than in answering her question, "from what I understand, they are just getting an idea of what type of people are in the area so that management can be prepared to handle medical emergencies. You know, like how many smokers are in the area, and what their ages and sexes are. It's just some simple demographics information." John liked the sound of his little story, which wasn't completely untrue as the hospital had done a survey like this about two years earlier.

"I see," she said, still not convinced, although she did admit to herself that it sounded like something a hospital would do if they were engaging in future planning. But the blood type just didn't seem to fit into the survey picture very well. "But why do they want to know our blood types?"

John hadn't been ready for this question. He sat there staring at the TV as if involved in the movie while he tried to devise an answer to her question. "I don't know," he started, which would sound just right to Paula, "they don't tell us everything. Maybe they want to know so that they can determine what they should have in the blood bank." He continued his explanation about not knowing the answer but felt he had given enough. More might make it sound untrue.

"Well," Paula said, accepting John's answer of not knowing what was going on, "I believe I have type A blood."

John got an immediate sinking feeling in the center of his chest. He also began to feel a little sick to his stomach. He struggled to stay composed, not wanting his wife to see his reaction for fear it might cause more curiosity. "Okay," he replied, trying to put on a small smile, "I'll enter the information tomorrow when I get back to the lab."

John sat there trying to envision what the future would be like if something were to happen to Paula. He revisited the visions of a funeral and everyone pointing their fingers at him and saying he had killed her by exposing her to the Sanguis virus.

He now knew what her blood type was, but what about the kids'? John wasn't much of a geneticist and wasn't sure what the possibilities would be for the kids. He did know that if one parent was type B, then the kids could also be type B and therefore would be safe. However, since his wife was type A, there was a possibility that one or both kids had a blood type other than type B and could become infected with the Sanguis virus and die. He knew he would have to ask a second question but wasn't sure he could pull it off without Paula asking a ton of questions he didn't want to answer. But he had to discover, and there was no way to do that without asking. He took a deep breath and continued the conversation in as casual a tone as possible. "You don't by any chance know the kids' blood types," he asked, trying to maintain a small smile, "do you?"

This time Paula was suspicious. Not only did the questions themselves seem unrealistic, but also an awfully long period of time had passed when John just sat there not saying a word. If he wanted to know all the blood types, why didn't he just ask for them all at once? This time she couldn't just supply an answer without knowing more information. "Why would the hospital want to know the kids' blood types?" she asked, putting down her cross-stitch material and turning to look directly at John.

John tightened his right fist in an attempt to maintain composure. Paula was on his left, so she wasn't able to see his reaction. However, he knew he was losing composure, and fear started to grip his soul as a bead of sweat started to slide down his forehead. "Well," he started, pausing to clear his throat as he tried to stall so he could compose his response, "they wanted to know the information about all the family members. I guess they consider kids as important as adults." He was kind of happy about the way his answer had come out.

Paula didn't know what to believe. She had a feeling that something was wrong, but then again, John's answer could be true. It wasn't the questions that bothered her; it was the tone in his voice and his actions. He may have had a small smile on his face, making her think everything was normal, but she noticed that he wouldn't look her in the eye. Not that this was unusual, because a lot of their conversations seemed directed toward each other while they made eye contact with something else. However, this time he was concentrating on the TV more than normal, and this was causing doubt in her mind about the validity of his statement.

"I don't know what their blood types are," she answered. "And I would be surprised if any parent knows the blood types of their kids."

"I suppose you're right," he said, shrugging his shoulders as if he didn't care. This seemed to relieve some of her concerns; she started cross-stitching again. However, how was he going to discover the kids' blood types? Again he turned toward Paula and tried to ask his question as casually as if asking for the time of day. "Do you know how hard it would be to have the kids tested?"

This time Paula stopped the needle in the middle of a stitch and looked up at John. She couldn't believe what she was hearing. She knew this wasn't a simple survey. "Okay, John," she started with a tone of authority, "I don't know what is going on, but I'll tell you right now that I don't like your attitude at all. Now, what the hell is going on?" Paula was not one to swear, so for her to say *hell* was way out of character. John knew he was in trouble.

John sat there staring at Paula, her blazing eyes staring deep into his soul. He knew that his story wouldn't hold water now, and to say anything but the truth would be useless. However, what was he going to do? He wanted to discover how much danger his family was in, but he was afraid to tell his wife about the anemia-type disease for fear this information might be made public and thereby start a panic. And a neighborhood panic that had been started by something John had said was a reality he didn't want to be involved in. After all, he had given his word to Tom not to tell anyone, including his wife. He sat there a little longer, trying to figure out what to do. Paula sat next to him on the couch, staring him down like a vulture waiting for something to die.

John tried to settle himself down by taking a deep breath before telling his wife what was going on. All he could think of was to give her the basic facts and not go too deep into the hazards of the disease. "Well," he started with a nervous tone, "do you remember a couple of news stories on TV about some sort of blood disease that has been showing up in the area?"

Paula looked at him with a puzzled expression. "I don't remember anything specific about it," she replied. "Why, what's going on?"

"Well," he continued, "first, you can't tell anyone about this. The hospital is afraid that it might start a panic if everyone knew about this. Only a handful of people at the hospital know what's going on."

"If only a few people know about it, how did you get to be one of the lucky ones?" she asked, then paused for a second. "Or should I say one of the unlucky ones?"

He just gave her a strange look as if he couldn't figure out why she couldn't see the connection. "I pick up blood all day long," he said as if it were the most obvious thing in the world.

"I know that," she replied snappily. She didn't like his tone, which insinuated that she was ignorant about what he did for a living. "It's just that I didn't think you were in the hospital long enough to hear any information," she said sarcastically. But the more Paula thought about it, the more she realized that he didn't spend much time in the lab, so the chances of his hearing anything that was supposed to be a secret would be pretty slim. However, this time he was lucky to have heard something—or unlucky to have heard it.

"Anyway," he said in a tone of defeat as he decided not to argue the point, "the TV has indicated that there have been several unexplained deaths of people who had symptoms of anemia. The news doesn't know that much, but according to the information from the lab, the Sanguis virus seems to affect people who have a blood type other than type B," John said, emphasizing the word *other*. "So," he said, trying to figure out how to summarize his comments, "I was just wondering what your blood type was because if it was type B too, then we don't have anything to worry about."

John didn't want to say too much for fear of upsetting his wife, but unfortunately, he had said too much. Her face took on an expression of panic. "You mean I could catch this Sanguis virus and die?" she asked, trying to fight back the tears. She had a nice disposition, but at even the slightest hint of crisis, she would get very emotional and sometimes would even cry.

John repositioned himself on the couch so he was looking directly at Paula. "Honey," he said in a soft, loving tone as he reached for her hands to console her, "there hasn't been that many cases, and they have no idea how it spreads, which means it could just be some hereditary problem." As hard as he tried, he couldn't seem to get her to calm down. She just sat there thinking about what would happen if she were to catch the virus.

After a long pause, Paula looked up at her husband. "Do they have a cure for this disease?" she asked with a tone of desperation.

"I don't think so," he replied in a defeated tone. He didn't like how it sounded. Fearing to upset her further, he added a small white lie: "At least not yet. In fact, the CDC is at our hospital right now working on the problem. It shouldn't be too long for them to determine how to cure this thing." He sat there hoping there may be some truth in his statement. At least it seemed to make Paula feel a little better. She took a deep breath as if to inhale more oxygen into her system to lift her spirits.

John sat there thinking about what he had just said. The CDC was indeed at the hospital, and indeed they were working on the problem. However, could they find a cure? As far as he could tell, they didn't even know what was causing the problem, let alone have the knowledge to find a cure for it. Look at the AIDS virus. It didn't take them long to find the cause, but after many years of research, they still didn't have a cure. All he could do was pray this problem had an easy solution.

As John was contemplating the future of this new bug, Paula suddenly sprang to her feet and looked down at him. "John!" she said in a voice that seemed loud enough to break the windows in the house. "What about the kids?" The blood drained completely out of her face as she took on the look of a frightened ghost. "That's why you wanted to know their blood types," she said hopelessly.

He didn't know what to say. He sat there totally dumbfounded, not knowing what to do next. Finally, he just said, "Yes."

The two sat quietly for over five minutes, not wanting to say anything that might bring up more bad news. They were staring at the TV but not watching it, wondering about the kids and what the future might bring. John decided to break the silence. "Do you have any idea how we can get the kids' blood tested?"

Paula was a little slow to respond. She took a deep breath, wiped the remaining tears from her eyes, and looked over at John. "We can call the pediatrician and schedule an office visit."

"But I don't think most doctors will do the blood test without some reason for performing the lab work," he replied, deflating her hope.

Paula hadn't been ready for his negative comment. She just assumed that it would be an easy thing to do to test the kids' blood. She thought about it for a second and was wondering, *When do doctors draw blood?* "We can tell the doctor that the kids have been running a fever and we think they might have an infection," she answered.

"Yeah, but it's not going to be easy for the kids to pretend they have a fever, especially since they use those infrared thermometers these days. One shot in the ear and the doctor will know their temperature." Again, Paula's hopes were dashed.

They both sat there a little longer, trying to figure out how to get the pediatrician to order the blood test. Paula looked up at John. "Honey, do you remember Marsha McFarlene?" she asked, hoping for a glimmer of recognition. However, all she got was a blank stare of confusion from her husband. "You know," she continued, "she's the nurse over at the kids' pediatrician's office. She is also Hailee's mother. She might do it for me if I ask her."

John saw a possible glimmer of hope at the prospect of alleviating this feeling of concern about the kids' possible health problems. "Do you think she will do it without a doctor's request?" John asked, knowing it takes a doctor's request for lab work.

"She might," Paula answered, but John saw a motion of hesitation as if she wanted to say more but was reluctant to do so.

"Okay," he said, "what are you holding back? She might do it, but what?"

She didn't want to tell him what she was thinking, basically because she knew what he would say. "She might want to know why I want to know the kids' blood types," she replied, and then cowered down as if expecting to receive a beating.

"No!" he said in an outraged tone as he jumped up from the couch and walked over to the window. "You can't tell anyone," he said, staring out the window as if to be sure no one was peeking in to see what they were doing. "You know what kind of panic this would cause if this got out?" he said in a loud, panicky voice. He walked back over to the couch and sat down next to Paula. "We can't tell her," he continued in a much softer voice. "We have to think of something else."

"Well, I can always ask her and see what she says," Paula said, having recovered from John's outburst. "Who knows? She might do it."

"She would be taking an awfully big risk to do this without having any idea of why we want it done," he replied. He tried to think of another way to get Marsha to do this for them. The two sat on the couch for what seemed like forever, when Paula started laughing. "What's so funny?" John asked, a little annoyed that Paula wasn't taking this seriously.

"I could tell Marsha that we want to test the kids to see if you're really the father," she said, still giggling some. "I saw it in a movie last week. Can you imagine what she would think of me if I told her I didn't know if you were the father of our kids?"

He didn't think it was funny at all. He just sat there staring at her, wondering why she was thinking such thoughts. Soon it became impossible for him to sit there any longer wondering about her statement, so he had to ask: "Is there any truth to the story?"

She stopped giggling immediately and looked at him in total disbelief. "Oh yeah," she cried out in a sarcastic tone, "I go around all over the place trying to get pregnant by other men just so that you won't be the biological father of my kids."

John didn't like this comment either, and Paula knew it, so she tried to change the tide by being honest. "Of course there's no truth to that statement. I saw it on a Lifetime movie last week; I was only trying to make a small joke out of this chaos. You are the only man I've been with, and you're the father of my children." She paused for a moment and leaned over to give him a small kiss. "And that's the truth."

"I'm sorry," he said as he reached out for her hand. "I just don't know what to do about all of this. I wish I didn't know about any of this. But on the other hand, I'm glad I know so that I can try to do something about it."

"We'll work it out," she said with a level of optimism, "but we still have to determine how to test the kids' blood type." Paula, who spent a lot of time on a computer at work, was familiar with a lot of the possibilities offered by the internet. "I wonder if we can get the testing supplies on the internet and do this ourselves."

"Yeah," he said, trying not to sound too negative, "but that would take awhile, and I would like to know as soon as possible. I think our best course of action is for you to call Marsha and see if she will test the kids' blood without asking a lot of questions."

"Okay," Paula said, reaching over the arm of the couch and picking up the phone. She nervously punched in the numbers and waited.

"Hello," came a familiar voice.

"Hi, Marsha," Paula answered, trying to maintain a cheerful tone to her voice. "How's Beth behaving over there tonight?" she asked, knowing well that Beth was a good kid and never seemed to cause any trouble when she went over to Hailee's house. But Paula didn't want to come right out and ask Marsha to draw the kids' blood.

"Oh, you know those two," Marsha replied. "You couldn't separate them with ten sticks of dynamite."

"Marsha," Paula began. She paused, trying to figure out how to ask the next question.

The delay caused Marsha to wonder what was going on. For Paula to pause like that was not like her. This was causing Marsha some concern. "What's up?" Marsha interrupted, trying to persuade Paula to reveal whatever it was that was bothering her.

"I was wondering if you could do a little favor for me," Paula asked with a shaky voice.

"You know I will if I can," Marsha replied, becoming very concerned about Paula's attitude.

"I was wondering if you could test the kids' blood just to determine their blood types."

With a great sigh of relief, Marsha responded, "No problem. Just drop by the doctor's office. I will be more than glad to do it for you."

"That would be great," Paula said with a sigh of relief.

"Why does the doctor want to know their blood type?" Marsha continued.

There was a long silence on the phone before Paula could answer. "The doctor doesn't want to know; we want to know."

Now the pause was on the other end of the telephone line. "Oh," Marsha finally replied, "I can't perform that test without a doctor's order. Is there something wrong that you don't want the doctor to know about?"

"No, we just wanted to know what their blood types are in case we ever need to donate blood, in case of an emergency." This idea sounded good to Paula. She hoped that Marsha would go for the little white lie. "We just want to be prepared. And most doctors are not proactive, which means they won't order the test just because we want to know."

"It's good to be prepared," Marsha answered, "but I can't help but wonder why you are so concerned."

"Let's just say John had a premonition that something is going to happen and one of the kids will need a blood transfusion. He doesn't know our kids' blood types, so he doesn't know whether he could use his blood to save our child. His premonition seems to have upset him quite a bit. I thought that if we knew the kids' blood types, it would set his mind at ease. But a doctor's not going to order a blood test just because John had a premonition of something bad."

John sat there listening to Paula tell the story about his premonition, which was a complete lie, but she sure made it sound good. Even he was believing her story and was wondering if maybe he was just a little paranoid about the blood disease.

"Well," Marsha said, "I can do it, but it would probably be better if I come over to your house and do the test there, versus your coming into the lab. If you go to the lab, they will be expecting paperwork from the doctor before you can even get past the front desk to see me."

"Marsha," Paula started, happy that her friend was going to help them, "I don't know how to thank you. And if John were here, he would thank you too."

"Well, I'll tell you what," Marsha offered. "I'll stop by tomorrow right after work and we can do the test."

"Thanks so much," Paula replied. "I'll tell John. Hopefully, that will help relieve his concerns about the kids. Thanks again. We'll see you tomorrow." Paula hung up the phone, happy that she had gotten Marsha to agree to perform the blood tests.

"She will be here tomorrow after work," she said, updating John, who just sat there shaking his head.

"You did a nice job," he said to her. "I would have never thought of making you the bad guy, but you sure made me feel like one."

"Oh, don't be so sensitive," she said. "Look at it from another point of view: you are a loving father who is concerned about his kids."

Paula and John sat on the couch waiting for the kids to return home. Beth arrived when expected, just a few minutes before her curfew of nine o'clock. She came in, sat on her father's lap, and began telling her parents about what Hailee and she had done all evening. After about fifteen minutes of bonding with her parents, Beth asked for an ice-cream sandwich. Upon retrieving the snack from the freezer, she headed to her room to play computer games.

It was about eleven thirty when Peter finally came home. He walked into the kitchen and opened the refrigerator door like any growing American boy. And like most American boys, he complained there was never anything in the house to eat, even if the refrigerator was stocked.

"Peter!" John called out. "Can you go up and get Beth? Your mom and I want to talk to you two for a couple of minutes."

"Beth!" Peter hollered from inside the pantry while working on opening a bag of chips.

"Peter!" John hollered back. "I said go up and get her. I could have done that."

"Sorry, Dad," Peter replied. Peter didn't like being the gofer in the house, but he knew he would get a lot of static from his father if he didn't do what he was asked. So he quickly ran up the stairs, taking two steps at a time, and told Beth to come downstairs.

When the two came down and settled in the living room, John motioned for Paula to tell the kids what was going on. However, Paula didn't want to do the honors, so she passed the buck back to John.

"We asked you to come down because Marsha will be coming over tomorrow after work to take some blood to determine your blood type." As expected, the response from the kids was a combination of perplexity and their fear of needles.

"Why do we have to get shots?" Beth asked, not realizing that taking blood was not the same as getting a shot.

"Don't worry," Paula said, trying to comfort her daughter, "they only take a small drop of blood from your finger—and it doesn't hurt."

"Yeah, they take this long knife and slice half your finger off so they can get enough blood to test," Peter said, imitating the actions of someone cutting off his fingers. Then he turned toward his parents and asked, "Why do you want to know our blood type?"

"The hospital is doing a survey to see what they can do to be better prepared for emergencies. Getting an idea of how many people of different blood types are in the area can help them better prepare for those emergencies."

"Sounds like an awfully painful way to gather information for a stupid survey," Peter responded. He settled for the fact that there was no way for him to get out of this.

"So, I need you both to be here tomorrow about six o'clock," John said with a tone of authority, "so that Marsha doesn't have to hang around waiting for you to show up."

Both kids acknowledged their responsibility to be there and were dismissed to pursue whatever they had been doing before the short family meeting. As the kids hurried up the stairs to their rooms, John and Paula sat on the couch staring at the TV, which was on but had been turned down so it wouldn't be a distraction during their meeting. Neither seemed to notice that the TV wasn't turned up for them to hear; so they just sat there in silence.

John was the first to break the spell of silence. He suggested that they call it a night and head upstairs to bed. Paula, slow in getting up, accepted John's hand as he held it out, not only to help her up off of the couch but also to provide his support for what was happening within their home. They went to bed, anticipating that it would be a long and restless night.

The next morning arrived much sooner than either parent would have liked, but the two slowly started their morning ritual. A feeling of helplessness seemed to hang over them all day. As expected, Marsha showed up that evening to draw the kids' blood.

"Okay," Marsha said to the two kids sitting at the kitchen table. "Who wants to go first?"

Neither wanted to volunteer to be first. It was Paula who broke the stalemate. "Peter, why don't you show your sister how brave you are and go first? It's not going to hurt."

"Oh sure, it's not going to hurt," he repeated sarcastically under his breath but still loud enough for his mother to hear.

"Peter!" she scolded him for acting the way he was.

Marsha placed her phlebotomy tray on the counter and pulled out a pair of latex gloves.

"What's she going to do," Peter asked, his voice revealing the presence of fear, "perform major surgery?"

"No," Marsha replied. "This is just standard procedure when we deal with someone's blood." She smiled. "In case you start bleeding all over the place," she continued. "I don't want to get your blood all over my hands, now, do I?" Occasionally she liked to tease Beth when she was over at their house, but she'd never had much of an opportunity to tease Peter. This was a great opportunity to do so.

"Very funny," he said in a sarcastic tone, hearing a snicker of laughter from his sister. "Remember, you're next," he said, hoping to get Beth as nervous as possible so he could get back at her.

Marsha reached into her tray and pulled out a small foil packet with an alcohol pad inside. She tore open the packet and withdrew the small white pad. "Okay, Peter," she said, holding out her hand. "Which hand do you want me to do this on?"

"Neither," Peter said in a defiant tone, placing his hands behind his back.

"You're chicken," Beth said, the smile on her face growing wider.

"You're asking for it," Peter said, threatening Beth. The two got along quite well for brother and sister, but occasionally they teased each other to see who could get the other more upset.

"Peter!" John shouted. "That's enough of that! Now give Marsha your hand. It's not going to hurt."

Peter was reluctant, but his father had spoken. He brought forward his right hand and extended it toward Marsha. She reached out and took hold of the middle finger, wiping the end off with the alcohol pad.

"Why are you doing that?" Beth asked.

"I want to make sure that there are no germs around," Marsha replied, placing the pad on its foil package. "After all, we wouldn't want you to get an infection from a little stick in the finger, now, would we?"

"If the infection would kill him," Beth responded, "then don't use it."

"Beth!" Paula shouted. "That's enough out of you too."

"Yes, Mom," she replied, smiling when she saw Marsha wink at her mother. You could easily tell that the two women were good friends. They had been ever since Beth and Hailee became friends.

Marsha picked up a small gray object called a lancet and twisted off one end, revealing a small silver point. "Okay," Marsha said, straightening Peter's finger, "this isn't going to hurt." With a quick stroke, she pricked the end of his finger. "Now that didn't hurt," she said, laying down the lancet.

Peter looked over at his sister and, knowing she was next, decided to lay in on as heavy as he could. "That's not true," he said, sounding as if he might cry. He was clenching his other fist just to try to overcome the pain as Marsha squeezed three drops of blood onto a small slide.

"Man, that hurts," he said, increasing his acting to such a degree that he could have won an Academy Award. "I thought you were shoving it through my entire hand."

At this time, he looked over at his sister and noticed the fear growing in her eyes. However, a sudden cry of "Peter!" from behind caused him to jerk his head in the opposite direction to address the voice.

"I said, stop that," his mother continued. "Now you know darn well that it didn't hurt. You're just saying that to upset your sister. Now tell her the truth, that it didn't hurt."

Peter turned his attention back to his sister and noticed the fear on her face. "It doesn't hurt," he said, trying to sound sincere. Then, without warning, he continued in a louder, more sarcastic tone, "Much."

"Peter!" his mother again yelled at him, getting a little tired of all his sarcasm.

"Beth," Marsha said to the little girl as she finished with Peter, placing a small Band-Aid on his finger, "it will be all right."

Beth sat there looking at the little needle used to stab her brother and then turned to look at Peter to see his reaction. Occasionally, her brother had tried to make life miserable. She lifted her head and, with a brave tone, said, "I'm ready."

"Okay," Marsha said to Beth, reaching into her tray, "but I have to test this first. If I don't do this right away, I will have to stick your brother again."

"In that case, can you do me now?" Beth asked, giggling.

"Okay," Marsha said to Paula. She pulled out two small glass bottles that displayed some strange words. Paula tried to read the label but only made out the word *antigen*. Marsha took one of the small bottles and added one drop of the antigen to one sample of blood on the slide. She watched intently as if waiting for something to happen. However, nothing happened. The two parents seemed to be in suspended animation, each holding her breath while waiting for the results.

"Okay," Marsha said, taking the second bottle and adding a drop to the second blood sample. This time the blood seemed to react with the contents of the bottle. Finally, she took the third bottle and added a drop of the liquid inside to the third drop of blood. "Okay," she said in conclusion, while John and Paula waited in agony, "it appears that Peter's blood is type B positive." John gave out a deep sigh of relief, which caused Marsha to look up to see what he was doing. Thinking she was doing this because of some premonition, she thought John was relieved to know Peter's blood type.

John just stood there and shrugged his shoulders as if he didn't have a thing on his mind, but in reality, he couldn't bear to just stand there waiting to know whether his kids could die from some strange blood disease.

"Okay," Marsha said to Beth, "your turn."

Marsha repeated the same procedure as before. "How was that?" she asked, applying a small Band-Aid to the latest finger stick.

"I hardly felt a thing," Beth replied, proud of her accomplishment and for being brave. "See," she said, gloating at Peter, "it only hurt for a second."

"Ah, she used a smaller needle on you," Peter said, again in a sarcastic tone. "I had to go through the torture of using the big needle." He exaggerated the size of the needle by spreading his arms as far as he could reach.

"She did not," Beth argued. But before Peter could respond to her denial, Paula stepped in.

"All right," the children's mother said in a louder than normal tone to indicate that she meant business, "that is enough between the two of you."

"I don't care," Beth said in a softer tone. She turned to her mother to ask, "Can I go over to Hailee's house?"

"I don't mind," she replied, "but you'd better ask Marsha to see if you can go over there."

"Mrs. McFarlene," Beth said, "can I go with you to play with Hailee?"

"I don't have a problem with that," she said to Beth. "What time do you want her home?" Marsha asked, directing her question to Paula.

"I can pick her up about nine o'clock, if that's not too late for you."

"Okay then, go get your stuff," Marsha said to Beth, who immediately jumped from the chair and headed to her room to get her shoes.

Marsha took the second blood sample and again added a drop of antigen. She watched carefully. This time there appeared to be a reaction with the antigen. Marsha didn't say a word. She reached for the second bottle and placed another drop of liquid on the other sample of blood. Again the second drop of blood appeared to react with the antigen. Finally, she added liquid from the third bottle. Marsha looked up at the parents and took a deep breath before announcing her findings. "As I said," she started, "Peter is type B positive, but Beth is type AB positive."

John and Paula just stood there looking at each other as if they had been sentenced to an execution. Marsha could see the blood slowly drain from their faces as if they were being transformed into ghosts. "Is something wrong?" she asked, feeling as if she had just stabbed them in the heart.

John slowly looked over at Marsha and said, "No, nothing's wrong," trying to sound casual.

Marsha stood there knowing this was a lie, but not knowing why the couple were hiding whatever they were hiding. All she could do was pack up her supplies and get ready to leave. "I hope everything is all right," she said, walking down the hall toward the front door.

John followed her to the front door, trying to compose himself, trying to make believe everything was all right. However, he didn't think he was doing a very good job of convincing her. "Everything's all right," he repeated in a defeated tone. "Thanks for coming over and doing the test on the kids. We really appreciate it."

"Well," she said, standing in the open doorway, "I hope everything is all right."

"It is" was all he could say.

"Well, give me a call if I can be of any assistance," she said, concerned that they weren't telling her what was going on. She headed toward her car with Beth bouncing at her feet.

John slowly walked back to the living room and went over to where Paula was sitting. He sat down on the couch next to her and put one arm around her shoulders. He then reached out with his free hand and gently held her hand. He sat there, not knowing what to say but wanting to comfort her. He was sure of what she was thinking. Peter had type B blood, so judging from the information they had, the blood disease would not affect him. However, Beth's blood type was a combination of John's and Paula's. Was a person with type AB blood affected by the disease because of the A-type antigen, or would the B-type antigen protect the A side, preventing Beth from catching the disease? John didn't know what to say to his wife, who just sat there, on the verge of tears. He felt helpless to reassure her or himself. The two sat there not saying a word for a good ten minutes.

"She'll be okay, won't she?" Paula asked as she turned to look at John, a tear running down her cheek.

He wasn't sure what to say or do. After what seemed like an eternity, he reached up and wiped away the small tear running down Paula's right cheek. He had never felt so helpless. He swallowed hard, trying to swallow the fear that held onto his heart. He leaned over and gave her a small kiss to help reassure her, then said, "If we are careful of whom she comes in contact with, she should be fine." John didn't know if this was true since they didn't know how the Sanguis virus was transmitted, but it sounded good for now. And it seemed to help Paula relax some.

The two sat on the couch in each other's arms for a little while longer. John, not knowing what he should do next, reached over and turned on the TV. The two sat there for the rest of the evening. They appeared to watch the movie, but in reality, they were both staring through the TV as if trying to see the future, hoping to discover what might happen if the virus were to make its presence known at their house.

CHAPTER 6

John sat in his favorite chair, resting quietly after another hot day on the road. It had been only two days since he discovered Paula's and the kids' blood types, but he still felt the weight of the news as if he was carrying a grand piano on his shoulders. He just didn't know what to do. As usual, he sat there watching the six o'clock news. The local newscaster was talking about more fighting in the Middle East. He continued to dream, when his attention was directed back to the newscaster.

"On the local news," the announcer said, "this station has obtained information from reliable sources that there is a new blood disease caused by a virus that has been causing deaths around the world. This new virus, called Sanguis virus, is responsible for the B Antigen Resistive Disease, or BARD for short. This disease has already taken thirty lives locally, and over twelve hundred deaths have been reported across Ohio."

"Paula, come quick!" John yelled upstairs. He remembered having seen her go upstairs a couple of minutes earlier with a load of laundry.

"What's up?" she hollered, running down the steps in a panic, afraid that someone had gotten hurt.

"From what we have been able to determine," the announcer continued, "the symptoms resemble anemia, where the individual complains of being very tired."

"What is it?" she asked, entering the living room to find John sitting on the edge of his chair.

"Look," he said, pointing to the TV as she sat down on the couch.

"Doctors warn that being tired doesn't mean you have been infected with the Sanguis virus. However, if you suddenly feel extremely weak, it is recommended that you go see your doctor immediately. It has been determined that this virus only affects individuals who are past puberty and have a blood type that is A, AB, or O. Type B individuals don't appear to be affected. Doctors from the CDC are working on the situation but as of yet have not determined how this virus spreads, how long the gestation period is, or how to cure the illness. We will continue to monitor this situation and give you further updates as they come in. And now"—there was a slight pause—"let's go to Mike Johnson for the weather."

John looked up at Paula. Her expression of fear told him she would want to talk about this recent bit of news, so he grabbed the remote and turned down the volume. He didn't know exactly how to start. He just watched her slowly sit back down on the couch. "Well," he finally said as he sat there staring at the wall, not knowing what else to say.

After taking a deep breath to relieve the tension, Paula said, "Well, at least we don't have to be quiet about it anymore."

"That's true," John said as a spark of revelation came to him. "Since they announced it on TV, I might be able to get more information from the hospital."

"Think you might be able to find out what we can do to protect ourselves from this disease?" she asked, a touch of hope in her voice.

"Well, all I can do at this point is to ask around and see what I can learn."

"I hope you can find out something," she said, pausing in the middle of her sentence as if she had wanted to say more but had stopped.

"What's the matter?" John asked, picking up on the sudden termination of her statement.

"Oh, nothing," she said in a defeated tone.

"Come on, I know you better than that," he said, trying to comfort her and persuade her to say what was on her mind.

"It's nothing," she said, trying to convince him.

John knew something was bothering her. He got up from his chair and sat next to her on the couch. He reached over and gently put his arm around her shoulders. "Come on," he said in a loving tone, "what's bothering you?"

Paula took a deep breath and blurted out, "I'm scared. Not only for myself, but also for Beth. What's going to happen to us if we get the disease?"

John had a feeling she was scared, but after she'd said it, he had no idea what to say back to her. He just gripped her more tightly around the shoulders and tried to comfort her as best he could. "I don't know what's going to happen," he finally said. "All I can say is that we have to have faith that God will protect us."

John sat there for a couple of seconds and then lowered his head and closed his eyes. "Dear God," he said in a soft voice, "please protect this house and all of us who live within it. Don't let any harm come to Paula or Beth as we try to endure through the troubling times that are coming. We ask for your protection, but if this is not what is to be, please help us to understand. And if Paula and Beth leave us, help us to know that we will again be reunited when we stand in your presence. Amen."

John could tell that the short prayer had helped Paula relax as she gave out a soft sigh once he had finished speaking.

"Okay," John said, "let's go in and start dinner. I will help you cook tonight." He stood up and held out his hand to help his wife to her feet. Paula quickly fell into John's arms and clung to him as if her life depended upon it. John just continued to hold her until the tension subsided, and then the two went into the kitchen.

The next day, John couldn't wait to get back to the hospital after the morning pickups because he knew Tom would be there by then. As he drove up to the hospital, he noticed that the parking lots appeared to be full. However, he was lucky his courier parking space was still empty. He pulled into the space and grabbed the cooler with the blood specimens he had picked up that morning. He followed his normal path to the lab, like a train following a set of tracks. He walked up to the door of the lab and tried his passkey as usual. However, the passkey didn't work on the first pass. He continued to try, but the card wouldn't unlock the lab door.

After finally giving up on the idea that the badge was going to let him in, John turned around and headed for the reception desk. Betty was in her usual spot at the front counter, punching the keyboard to her computer. "Betty," he called through the closed glass windows, "can you let me in? My passkey doesn't seem to work."

Betty looked up as if surprised to see him. "Hold on," she said. She made a few more computer keystrokes and got up and headed for the door.

"Hi, John," she said as she opened the secured door.

"Looks like my passkey is dead," John said as he entered the lab.

"I don't think the problem is with your passkey," she said. "There is a heightened sense of security around here after last night's little news broadcast, so the hospital went and changed all the passkey codes. You need to go see Tom and get a new one."

"Thanks" was all he said as he passed Betty. He headed down the hallway to the lab. As he walked into the lab, he noticed there was a lot more activity going on than normal. As he surveyed the area, he saw Tom talking with the CDC agents. They appeared to be discussing something related to some papers Sharon was holding. John saw Joyce carrying a stack of forms over to Mike to enter the information into the computer.

"Joyce!" John said, but he hadn't spoken loudly enough to catch her attention. He didn't know whether he was talking softly or whether the noise in the room seemed louder than normal. "Joyce!" he repeated with more volume. This time she turned her head and saw him standing by the counter. She made a few more comments to Mike and then turned and walked over to greet John.

"Hi, John," she said, followed by a long silence. "It's been crazy around here today," she continued in a lower volume as if afraid to give away a secret.

"What's going on?" he asked with great curiosity.

"Well," she started, "after last night's announcement on the news, the phones around here haven't stopped ringing all morning. Besides the normal amount of doctors' follow-up calls, we've had every TV station, radio station, and news reporter calling here to get information on the disease. We finally had to have all calls routed through the downstairs information counter."

"Well, I can only imagine," he said, not knowing for sure what it must be like since he hadn't been there.

"Have you noticed much activity at the doctors' offices this morning?" she asked. Now, this was unusual for someone to ask him what was going on outside the lab. To him, it seemed he was always the one asking the questions.

"Not really. I go in the back door to most of these offices, and I don't normally see what's going on up front. However, several of the doctors' offices seemed to have more cars in the parking lots than normal."

"I wonder what's going to happen in the future with this blood disease scare," she said, shaking her head.

"I don't know, and I'm not sure I want to know," he replied. "Here is the morning pickup," he continued, sliding the bags of blood specimens over to Joyce. John wanted to get more information about the disease but didn't think Joyce would be a lot of help. If anyone knew anything, it would be the CDC agents. Except John felt his chances of getting any information out of them would be worse than the chance of a snowball surviving a hot sunny day in Mexico. His next tactic was to ambush Tom to see if he knew anything. Tom may not know as much, but he knew more than John did. "Do you think Tom is busy?" he finally asked, motioning in the direction of where Tom was still talking to the CDC agents. "I need to talk to him about a new passkey."

John was thankful for the change in the passkey system as it gave him an excuse to talk to Tom. Otherwise, he wasn't sure what kind of excuse he would have had to come up with.

"Oh yeah," Joyce said, "you haven't gotten your new one yet, have you? We all had to go down to security and get new passkeys this morning. It was a madhouse down there." She looked over at Tom, who was still talking to Sharon. "He's been busy with those two all morning. I'm not sure what they are talking about, but that's what he's been doing all morning." Even though Joyce worked in the lab, she knew how to run the equipment and obtain the results. But she didn't know how to interpret the results. "Wait here," she said. "I'll go ask him."

John stood there in anticipation, wondering if he could talk to Tom about the disease, not just about the passkey. He watched as Joyce got Tom's attention, then they all looked over at him. To John's surprise, the two CDC agents followed Tom over to the counter where John was standing. John kind of expected Tom to walk over, but when the two CDC agents came over, he felt a little uneasy. He didn't know why. Maybe they had caught him eavesdropping the other day, or maybe Tom had said something to them and now they wanted to tell him he should be quiet about the whole situation. He wasn't sure why he felt this way, but he wished only Tom was coming over.

"John," Tom said in a friendly voice, "this is Sharon Frenette and Robert Caldwell of the CDC. They are here to help us find a cure for this new blood disease. Sharon, Robert," he continued, redirecting his introductions, "this is John Davison. He is one of our couriers."

"Nice to meet you," John said, not knowing what else to do, especially since he knew more about them than he was supposed to.

"Tom tells me you already know a little bit about this disease," Sharon ventured, catching John off guard. He turned and looked over at Tom, seeking some sign of what he was supposed to say.

John didn't know whether to say he'd gotten the information from Tom because that may get Tom into trouble. However, no signal came from Tom, so after what seemed to be a lifetime of delay, John replied, "I heard some information from several of the doctors' offices."

"I didn't know that," Sharon said, which caught John even more off guard. "Tom told me you had some concerns about the blood specimens you were asked to bring in. He told me he could trust you, so he gave you an update on what we were trying to do."

Tom stepped in to add his two cents to the explanation, probably to help John relax and also to indicate to him he wasn't in any trouble. "Yeah," he started, "I've known John for a long time, and I know he can be trusted. That is why I had him bring in the specimens instead of the other courier."

This made John feel better. And he felt glad that Tom would not be in any trouble for letting some of the information out. "Well," John said, "if there is anything else I can do to help, please let me know." He didn't like the playing ground he was on and wanted to make a hasty retreat. He wanted to talk to Tom alone so he could ask several questions without a crowd. He felt that talking to Tom in front of the CDC agents would cause a problem if they were to discover that he knew more than they thought he should.

"Well," Tom said, knowing John was feeling a little uneasy and trying to give him a sense of comfort, "I was wondering if you wouldn't mind doing some extra runs when needed. Sharon needs to have certain blood specimens brought in from time to time, and I would like you to pick them up and deliver them to her. Don't give them to Joyce. These special specimens are to be processed by Sharon or Robert only."

"No problem," John answered, happy that the request was an easy one. He was out on the road anyway. What's an occasional detour? Plus, since he was to deliver the specimens to Sharon, he might, on occasion, be able to ask some questions.

"That's great," said Sharon, a smile coming across her face. "It will be nice to work with you."

"It will be my pleasure," John said in return. He had reached a trouble spot, namely, what to say or do next. He looked around the lab for a second and then looked at Tom. "Oh, Tom," he blurted out as if he was suddenly surprised. "I need to talk to you about my passkey."

"Oh yeah, they did that this morning. Come to my office," Tom said, exiting the lab.

John turned back toward Sharon for a second to say, "See you later."

John turned to follow Tom but paused for a second more and looked back toward Sharon. "It was a pleasure to meet you," he said, staring into her deep blue eyes. She also looked back as if to peer deep into his soul. He felt a little strange as if he were exposed, as if standing in a crowd in his underwear. He continued to stand there for another second or two, examining all the features of her face.

"It was nice to meet you too," she replied with a small smile, and slowly turned to go back to work.

John stood there watching as she took several steps to get back to the far counter. He felt himself examining every feature of her backside. His eyes traveled the entire length of her body, from her heels up to the dark brown bun of her hair. He paused for yet another moment, realizing that he was analyzing her, and took a quick look around the lab to see if anyone was watching him. Assured that he was clear of any speculation from other lab personnel, he turned and headed out the door.

John caught up with Tom and entered his office to get the forms for a new passkey. Tom sat down at his desk and rummaged through the stack of papers. He looked worried and even a little frightened. "What's up?" John asked Tom.

Tom didn't answer at first; he just kept looking through the stacks of paper on his desk. "Here you go," he said, having located the permission forms. "Take these to security. They will give you a new passkey."

"Thanks," John said, but he wasn't sure Tom had heard him. Was he ignoring him, or was he in some other domain so that John's question was lost in a different universe? "Tom," he said again, this time a little louder, attempting to get his attention. When Tom looked up, his whole face seemed to turn to marble. "What's up? You look like a ghost or something. Are you all right?"

Tom didn't want to answer right away, but he felt he had to talk to someone. "I've been talking with Sharon about this disease, and I don't like what I'm hearing."

"What's happening?" John asked. Tom's statement had piqued his curiosity. Because of Tom's appearance, John wasn't sure he wanted to know more about this disease either. He didn't want to have the same reaction or appearance.

"Sharon said that this disease only affects people who are past adolescence and have a blood type other than type B."

"Yeah, I know," John said, interrupting Tom's explanation. He saw that this little interruption seemed to irritate Tom. "Sorry," he added. "Go ahead."

"Well, they don't know how it spreads, which means it could be in the air, in the water, or in our food. They just don't know. And you know that they have no idea of how it works or how to cure it." Tom paused a second, realizing that he was telling John what he already knew, especially since it was all over the news. "Well, what you don't know is that the number of reported cases is small compared to the real number of infections. The CDC has been reporting the numbers as low so as not to start a panic. In reality, there have been over seventy-five deaths in the local area alone and over three thousand across Ohio." Tom paused as if trying to find the strength to continue. "Sharon said that some of the deaths occurred as a result of accidents, but some of these accidents occurred when the disease suddenly made the patients so weak that they couldn't function. Remember the small plane crash that was on the news last week, the one that crashed when trying to make a landing?"

John just stood there listening and nodding his head when appropriate. He knew about the plane crash from the news. Apparently, a small passenger plane with eight people and the pilot and copilot had crashed just moments before making what would have been a perfect landing. The plane had taken a last-minute nosedive into the runway, causing a huge fireball when the fuel tanks exploded. Several days later, the news indicated that the pilot had had a sudden heart attack and fell forward onto the controls. The copilot didn't have time to react and didn't have the strength to pull the plane back up with the pilot lying on the controls. Unfortunately, all on board were lost.

"They said the plane crashed because the pilot had a heart attack while landing the plane," Tom reported, repeating the same information that had been presented on the news. "However," he said, pausing again to trying to gather his strength, "according to Sharon, who analyzed the pilot's blood samples, he crashed as a result of the disease."

All John could say was "Oh my." He had heard several small stories on the news about people with some sort of blood disease, but he hadn't realized that the disease could be the cause of death for others.

"The man suddenly became so weak," Tom continued, "that he fell forward, unable to move. And with his dead weight on the control stick, he dove the plane right into the runway."

John just sat there listening and shaking his head in disbelief.

"There's more," Tom continued. "About two weeks ago, when all this started around here, there was that fire over in Arlington Heights where all seven members of a family died of smoke inhalation. The fire department said that the father had fallen asleep smoking a cigarette, and the kids were sleeping at the time and didn't get out. Well, according to Sharon, who also worked on that case, the father lost all his strength when he dropped the cigarette, and he didn't even have enough strength to put it out. When the fire started to spread"—Tom paused, trying to keep from crying—"she said he was probably still alive but didn't even have enough strength to call out for help. The kids also had the disease, and they died, not because of the smoke and fire, but because they didn't have enough strength to get out of the house."

As Tom continued with his tale, John slowly sank down into the chair. He was shocked at what was happening. He just couldn't believe what he was hearing.

Tom took a deep breath and leaned over closer to John. "John," he said in a barely audible tone, "I'm scared. Scared for myself and my family. We could all end up with this disease and die from it. And you know what scares me the most?" He sat there watching as John shook his head. "From the time the disease hits you until the time you finally die, you lie there helpless to do anything. I think I would go mad. Can you imagine how that father in the fire must have felt between the time the fire started and the time he died? He must have been in agonizing pain from the flames. He must have gone insane," Tom concluded, shaking his head in terror. "I just don't know what to do."

Tom and John just sat there for several minutes as the new information settled into John's brain. To suddenly lose your strength and not be able to do anything—John just couldn't fathom the situation. The idea of lying there, unable to move out of a dangerous situation and not having enough strength to call out for help, overwhelmed him.

"John," Tom finally said, looking up at his close friend, "did you find out Paula's and the kids' blood types?"

John sat there, realizing the consequence of the question Tom had asked him. "Peter is type B," he started, "so it appears he's in no danger. However, Paula is type A and Beth is type AB, so I assume they are both in danger of catching the disease."

Tom was quick to respond, afraid that John may get the wrong impression of the consequences that could affect his family. "But how old is Beth?" he asked, knowing she wasn't old enough to have reached puberty but not being sure exactly how old she was.

"She's only eleven."

"That's good," Tom said with a sigh. "At least you won't have to worry about her anytime soon. I just pray that these people," he said, waving his arms in the direction of the lab to indicate the CDC personnel, "can find a cure fast so that neither one of us has to worry about our family."

Tom lowered his head for a couple of seconds and then looked up into John's eyes. He seemed to turn even whiter. "John," Tom continued in a soft tone that lacked any emotion, "I'm type O, and so is everyone in my family. I don't know what's going to happen."

This caught John totally by surprise. How do you respond to your friend's comment when he and his whole family might be on the list to die from this disease and you know that you're immune to it? To survive while others around you are dying is almost impossible to accept. What do you say to your friend, "Don't worry. If it happens, it's God's choice"? Now John knew what the soldiers who were the only ones to have survived a major battle, when the rest of their companies were killed, must have felt.

"Oh my," was all John could say again, not knowing if he could take any more bad news. He got up from his seat and stepped over to his friend. "I just don't know what to say," he finally said, putting his hand on Tom's shoulder. "If there is anything I can do to help, please let me know."

"Thanks," Tom said, placing his hand on top of John's hand. After several minutes Tom added, "You'd better get down to security and get your passkey and start your afternoon rounds."

"Okay," said John. He walked out of the room and then exited the lab basically in a daze. He didn't know what to think or feel about the events he had learned about within the last hour. He obtained his new passkey and headed out of the hospital to start his afternoon run. He didn't even notice the scorching hot weather or the normal blast of hot air that came out of his car when he opened the door. He just got in and drove to his next stop.

CHAPTER 7

It was several hours before John returned to the hospital. There seemed to be a lot more specimens than usual from the offices where he made his afternoon rounds. He was in a hurry to get back to the lab, so he didn't take the time to count them. He wanted to tell Tom about some strange happenings at the Tri-County Medical Center. However, when John arrived at the lab, Tom was nowhere to be found.

"Have you seen Tom?" John asked Betty at the reception desk.

"He went home early," she said. "He wasn't feeling very well."

"Did he say what was wrong?" John asked. Fear started to rise within his soul because he knew Tom's blood type.

"Apparently, lunch wasn't settling too well in his stomach," she replied. "He said if he was going to be sick, he might just as well get sick at home, where he could do it in private. I guess he doesn't want anyone to see him barf all over the place," Betty said with a little humor in her tone.

John knew that she was only kidding and wasn't trying to make Tom look bad, so he decided to kind of play along. "Do you know what he had for lunch?"

"All I can tell you is that he ate in the cafeteria," she replied with a chuckle.

"Well, that explains that," John said with a chuckle. "I'd better drop this off in the lab," he said, holding up the cooler full of specimens.

"Okay," she replied, turning back to her computer.

John walked into the lab, which appeared to be empty. But that wasn't right; there should have been someone on the second shift to run the tests for all these specimens. "Hello," he said, but all he got back was the soft whine of some of the equipment just sitting around waiting for some test to be started. "Hello," he called out again, only this time in a much louder tone. This time he got a response. At the back part of the lab, from behind a large Xerox machine, he saw Mike's head pop up.

"Oh, hi," Mike replied from a distance. "I'll be right there." Simultaneously, another head, belonging to Sharon, popped up. Mike bent back down, and John heard a metal door slam shut. Then Mike reappeared and headed over to the counter where John was standing. "Sorry about that," he said as he stopped in front of the counter. "The stupid thing had a paper jam." Mike paused a second as he looked over the large bags of specimens. "You've got quite a collection this afternoon, don't you?"

"Yeah," John replied. "These doctors sure know how to ask for tests."

"Okay," Mike said. "I'll start processing these right away." He grabbed the large bags and carried them over to where the computer was located.

At that time, Sharon was walking by the counter. "Hi, Sharon," John called out, not sure of what he would say.

"Hi, John," she replied, stepping up to the counter. "What's up?"

"I have a question," John started. "I was at the Tri-County Medical Center this afternoon. This is one of those locations where I have to walk in through the waiting room. Most of the time I can enter into the back area through a back door." John paused for a moment, realizing that he was rambling and thinking he should get to his question before he began to look like some sort of idiot. "Anyway, many of the patients in the waiting room were wearing surgical masks. Do masks help?"

"Well," Sharon started, "they would help if this Sanguis virus is transmitted by air. If not, then the masks are a total waste of effort."

"Can you catch this disease by breathing in particles?" John asked, wondering if he should even stand in the room where all this blood was being tested.

"No," Sharon replied, seeing that John was getting a little nervous, "it doesn't appear to be spreading that way. The best guess that we have come up with is that it is ingested by eating something that is contaminated with the virus. The problem is that we don't know how it's getting into the food we eat or the water we drink."

"That can be an awfully scary thought," he said, a little concerned about how the Sanguis virus might be spreading. "You mean we may not be able to eat something because it may be contaminated?"

"Well, there are some things that you can do to protect yourself," she said in a comforting voice, seeing he appeared to be a little afraid after what she'd just told him. Just like many other food contaminants, like germs, the goal here is to make sure you cook food thoroughly and not leave food out. Don't eat food prepared by friends as you don't know amid what circumstances the food was prepared."

"Would I be safe eating a candy bar out of the vending machine?" he asked with a touch of humor in his tone.

Sharon laughed a little at his little joke. "Yeah, I think you would be safe to do that. But be careful," she said in a warning tone. "You can gain a lot of weight from all that sugar. And your cholesterol will go up too."

He looked down and protruded his belly out farther than normal. With a couple of quick slaps to his gut, he looked up and said, "Too late," and started to laugh.

She also started to laugh at his little routine.

John couldn't let this opportunity go by without trying to get some information about what was going on with the research. "How's it going in here?" he asked.

Sharon's glimmer of delight suddenly faded to despair. "Not good," she replied in a defeated tone. "We haven't been able to make any progress on how to cure this disease, and we haven't even been able to determine where it comes from. Every time we start to get close to some conclusions, some discovery seems to throw the whole idea out the window."

"What kind of conclusion?" John asked, hoping she would continue the explanation. There was no one else in the area except Mike, and he was on the other side of the lab. This meant that they were the only two around, so no one could overhear what was being said.

"Well, we know that it attacks the red blood cells, and it appears to cause them to coagulate. Have you ever seen what happens when you do a test to type someone's blood?" she asked, not knowing exactly how much information a blood courier would know.

"As a matter of fact, I have," he replied, remembering when Marsha had come by and tested the kids' blood.

"Well, you use an antigen to test the blood." Sharon continued the explanation in a low tone so as not to be overheard by anyone nearby. "Depending on the results, you can determine the blood type. The Sanguis virus seems to act like a type B antigen. However, if it is type B antigen, it shouldn't have any effect on type O blood. But this has the same effect on type O as on any other type, except type B."

He listened with great intensity, wanting to catch every word she had to say.

"Then we thought that it might have something to do with the hormones that are produced in the body when humans reach puberty since the Sanguis virus doesn't seem to affect young kids. When we did some research on kids with different blood types, we found they were carrying the Sanguis virus but weren't affected by it. So, our efforts to determine the link between this virus and how it is affecting people of different blood types, along with the differences between kids and adults, have been unsuccessful so far."

John stood there nodding his head as he listened to every word she said. Deep down, though, he wasn't sure he had understood everything. He felt very nervous about asking a specific question he had in mind or whether he should even ask it. However, curiosity got the better of him. "Sharon," he started in a low, somber tone, "do you know what your blood type is?"

She just stood there as if turned to stone by Medusa. It took her several seconds to recover and come back to life. "I'm type O," she replied, staring into the counter as if afraid to look John in the eyes.

He just stood there. What should you say to something like this, "Sorry you might die from this disease"? How about "Too bad for you"? He stood there not knowing what to say. It was Sharon who took the initiative to speak.

"That's okay," she said, "I know what that means. What about you?" she asked, wanting to know whether she had company during this crisis.

"I'm type B," he replied. He could see this was not a comforting thought for her. Here she stood with the possibility of dying from this disease, talking to this individual who could end up at her funeral. "My wife is type A, and my daughter is type AB," John continued, hoping that Sharon would know that he had similar concerns about the disease.

"I understand," she replied in a tone of despair.

"If there is anything I can do to help," he said, hoping he could cheer her up some.

"Thank you," she replied. Without another word, she turned and walked over to the equipment in the corner.

John stood there for a couple more seconds and then decided it was time to go home. So he turned and headed out of the lab to fight the evening traffic.

John arrived home after a lighter than normal traffic jam, although he didn't seem to notice it that much. His mind was still on the stories that Tom had told him about victims who had the disease but had died by another form of death. John was especially fixated on the man and his family who had died in the house fire because the disease had made them too weak to get away.

John was a little concerned when he first entered the house. It was morbidly quiet. The TV was off, and the kids weren't yelling or fighting with each other. At first, he was wondering if anyone was home, but a quick glance at the driveway confirmed that Paula's car was there and that someone should be home. "Hello!" he yelled, but the empty house seemed to reverberate his call. "Hello!" he yelled one more time, this time with much more volume. Still no response. He didn't know what to make of it. He walked into the kitchen, only to find the counters clear and clean. The sink was empty of dishes, and the floor was swept and mopped. It was nice to see the place cleaned up, but what was going on? Where was everyone?

John went down into the basement to see if Paula was doing some laundry, but the silence from down below indicated that the machines were not running. He then went upstairs. Who knows? Paula could be taking a nap. It would be a little unusual but not unheard of. She usually fell asleep in the evening, but much later, usually while watching a movie.

No one was upstairs either. John was getting worried. No one seemed to be at home, and there were no signs indicating where they may had gone. All he noticed was a cleaner than normal kitchen and living room.

He went downstairs to the back door to see if anyone was in the backyard, but he found no one. There didn't seem to be a soul anywhere.

What had happened to the neighborhood kids always playing baseball in the field behind the house? They, too, were nowhere to be seen. He stood there staring out the back door as his fear grew.

Suddenly, the front door flew open and in stampeded a herd of animals, commonly known as his kids. They came barreling into the house, followed by their mother. "Where have you been?" John asked, relieved to see them but furious that they hadn't left a note.

"It's all right," Paula said, giving him a quick kiss on the cheek, "we just came back from Elizabeth's house next door. I helped her take some boxes over there."

"Well, that answers the question about where everyone was, but why is the house all cleaned up?" he asked, wondering if they were going to have company that evening.

Paula walked into the kitchen to prepare dinner. John followed. "Well," she said, taking some chicken out of the refrigerator, "several of the mothers in the neighborhood decided to get together to see if we could set up a community support group. Elizabeth wanted to know if she could have everyone get together over here, and I said yes. I didn't want them to come into a dirty disaster zone, so I cleaned up the house a little."

"Well, you did a great job," he said, complimenting her efforts, "especially if you had a lot of people over."

"Thanks," she said, appreciating his compliment. "However, I had help. There were twelve mothers here, and we discussed the situation we're facing with this disease. After the meeting, they all pitched in and helped clean up. So it was quick and easy."

"So how was the meeting?" he asked, trying to get more information on what they had discussed.

"Well," she started, "we discussed the news about this disease and what we should do. Some of the other mothers wanted to stay home and keep their kids out of school to minimize exposure, but most of them are going to wait until just before school opens to make their decision."

"What do you want to do?" John asked, a little concerned about how Paula was feeling about the whole situation.

"I'm not sure," she replied, wondering if she should tell him how she felt.

"It's probably a good idea to wait until the schools are ready to start before you make a final decision," he said, trying to agree with what he thought she was thinking. "After all, it's still more than four weeks before school starts. Although, if you think about it, Peter doesn't appear to have anything to worry about, and Beth is still too young to worry about it. So," he said, having finished formulating his conclusion, "I don't see a problem with them going to school."

"I suppose you're right," she said, not totally agreeing with him but not feeling it was worth an argument.

"I'm more worried about you," he said to her. "You have all those people coming and going at that office of yours, and you never know when someone with the disease will come in and spread it to everyone in the office."

She knew he was right to some extent. However, she mustered the courage to debate the situation. "I'm in the back office, and I don't have that much exposure to the clients who come in to see the lawyers."

"Yeah, but the lawyers have a lot of exposure, which means you could get the disease from one of them and not even know it," he said with a little fear and anxiety in his voice.

"I suppose," she said, "but I would be in the same situation if I went to the grocery store."

"I just don't want you to come down with the disease," he said. His face and his voice showed signs of his fear of the outcome if she were to catch the disease.

"I understand that," she said, trying to reassure him, "but I have to go to work; we need the money."

"We can make do with my salary."

"We wouldn't make it for long," she replied. "We barely make ends meet each month as it is. I can't even imagine what we would do if I were to quit and stay home just so that I could be a little safer from the disease."

"Paula," John said in a louder than normal tone, "this disease is not like the common cold where you have a bowl of soup and then, after a few days, you're all better. With this disease, you get it, and you've had it. Sharon, the CDC agent at the hospital, said that the fatality rate for this disease is 100 percent."

"I'm not going to get the disease working in the back room of the office any more than I would get the disease from you," she responded with an increase in volume, pointing at John. "After all, you pick up all that blood. How do you know that this virus won't get on the outside of one of those blood tubes and get spread around to everyone who comes into contact with the damn thing?" she said, not worrying about the type of words that came out of her mouth.

John stood there for a second, envisioning the chain of events his wife had just described. Was it possible that the Sanguis virus could contaminate the outside of one tube and then spread to all sorts of other surfaces that anyone could touch? The thought that he could pick up the virus and bring it home scared John. "I would never do that," he said, trying to defend himself from the accusation that he might possibly be a carrier of the Sanguis virus without even knowing it.

"You would never do that on purpose," Paula concluded, "but you could do it and not even know it. I could catch it and die, and it would be your fault. You know what's so silly about this whole situation?" she asked, her voice continuing to get louder and becoming a little shaky. As she looked into his eyes, a tear came to one of hers. "You could be the cause of my death and you wouldn't even know it." She cried as she thought about the situation. Her husband, to whom she gave a good night kiss every night and a goodbye kiss every morning before going to work, could be the carrier of the deadly Sanguis virus and the poor sucker wouldn't even know that he was the instrument of her death.

"That would never happen," he said, attempting to relieve her fears. "I could easily find out if I was a carrier by having Sharon at work check my blood from time to time. I'm sure that I'm not a carrier."

"You mean you would have your blood checked every night before you come home to see if you have the virus or not?" Paula asked with a glimmer of hope.

This might be one way to calm her fears, John thought. "If I have to," he replied, not liking the idea of becoming a pincushion for the next period of who knows how long before they could find a way to beat this thing.

"What will you do if you do get the disease?" she asked, not sure of what would happen. "What would you do to protect us from getting it from you?"

"I don't know," he replied, a little frustrated as he tried to work it out in his head. "I could always stay somewhere else until they find a cure for this disease."

"But that could take decades," she said, tears of fear filling her eyes again.

"I don't know what I would do," he said, shaking his head in disbelief. "Let's not worry about it right now." He tried to put his arms around her and help her feel better, only to have her jerk away in fear.

"But we have to worry about it!" she stressed. "You could go to work tomorrow and come home with the disease, and then I could catch it and die." She became more and more agitated as she continued to look at the worst-case scenario.

"I'll tell you," he said, getting a little louder as he tried to overcome her hysteria and get her away from the negative aspects of their situation. However, he never got the opportunity to finish his sentence as Paula looked up at him with enough fear in her eyes to turn his blood cold.

"Oh no!" she said in a high shriek as if she had just spotted a speeding train about to hit her. The tears started. "What about Beth?" she screamed, grabbing John's arm.

He didn't know what to say at first. He was trying to keep from screaming himself as she clutched his arm with a death grip. "She's going to be fine," he finally responded. Paula started to break down and cry again. "She's too young to get the disease."

This statement of reality didn't hit home as strongly as John had hoped. Paula looked up with tears in her eyes and asked between sobs, "Do you think they will find a cure in time?"

"I'm sure they will," he answered, hoping to get his wife to stop crying, but somehow he didn't feel that he was succeeding. "The CDC is working on the problem right now, so I don't think it will be long before they find a cure."

Paula paused and looked deep into his eyes as if to discern if he was telling the truth, but she didn't seem to want to have anything to do with a positive attitude. She took a deep breath and, in a low tone, remarked, "If they don't, you could be the murderer of your own wife and daughter." And with that, she turned and left the kitchen, leaving John standing there feeling as if he had been stabbed in the heart. The thought that he might be the one to bring home the disease scared the hell out of him, but he didn't know what else to do. There were many ways Paula could catch this disease other than getting it from him. What about all the other people she would come in contact with? Even her own son could be the culprit who brings the deadly menace into their once peaceful home. All John could do at this point was to let her be and hope she would settle down later.

Peter had overheard most of the verbal exchange between his parents from his hidden position by the corner in the hallway. He had never seen his parents act this way, and he had never seen his mother display the amount of fear she apparently was feeling in light of the possibility of catching this disease and dying. Peter, too, thought about what would happen if his mother died from this disease. He had heard his mother blame his father for killing her by bringing the disease into the house. But what if his father wasn't the one to bring the disease into the house? What if it was Peter who had brought it in? How would he even know if he had the disease? There was no way to tell. The more he thought about the situation, the more depressed he felt. He had to talk to someone other than his parents. He decided to go talk to Ken and Carla. He normally would have asked one of his parents if he could go, but he felt that his mom was too far gone to discuss it, and his father was too upset. So instead of asking, he wrote a small note indicating he was over at Ken's house and would be back before eleven. He grabbed his baseball cap and quietly slipped out the back door.

CHAPTER 8

John woke up the next morning and reached over to turn off the alarm clock. He shook his head as if trying to deny the fact that it was time to get up. He felt as if he had been wrestling alligators, when in reality he was wrestling more with his conscience. He kept thinking about the idea of bringing the Sanguis virus home from work and Paula dying from it. He turned to see if she was awake, only to discover that she hadn't been to bed, or at least not to this bed. The pillow was still fluffy, indicating that no head had been resting on it. All John could think of was that she was still upset about the conversation the night before and was sleeping somewhere else in the house.

He got up and went downstairs to see if she was on the couch. Sure enough, she was sleeping on the couch with a blanket pulled over her. "Paula," he called out to wake her, "we've got to get ready for work." She slowly opened her tired eyes to see who was calling her. "Good morning," he said in a cheerful tone as he tried to wake her up in a friendly manner. "We've got to get moving or we will be late for work."

"Okay," came a soft response, as if spoken by someone in a dream.

"Time to get up," he said again. "What would you like for breakfast?" he asked.

The question seemed to raise her awareness to the degree that she was able to internalize that the cause of her demise was standing relatively close. "Get away from me," she yelled in a loud tone as she jumped up off the couch and, using the blanket like a filtered mask, ran to the corner of the living room. "Get away from me!" she said again. "I don't want to have anything to do with you or that stupid disease. Get away from me!" With that, John turned toward the kitchen, knowing he would be making breakfast for one.

John's morning rounds seemed to take longer than usual as his mind kept going back to whether he might be a carrier of BARD. He wanted to hurry up and get back to the lab to talk with Sharon to see if there was any news she could tell him about the disease. However, the morning's drop-off revealed that Sharon was not in the lab.

As John was driving to collect the samples for his afternoon run, he noticed several people walking around the shopping centers wearing masks. He even noticed drivers wearing them. Thinking about the things that Sharon had said about catching the disease, specifically that it didn't appear to be transmitted through the air, he figured that all those individuals were wearing masks for nothing. As John waited for the red light to change, he was wondering if Sharon could be wrong. She had said they didn't know for sure how the disease spread. Maybe these people were doing the right thing wearing those masks. John just didn't know.

He was glad to return to the lab to see what information he might learn, but first, he had to unload another large batch of blood samples. As he walked into the lab, he saw Sharon over at the far counter, reading some notes. Joyce, as usual, came over to retrieve the specimens he had brought in. "Hi, Joyce," John said as she took the paperwork out of the bags. "How have things been going here?"

"It's been busy, that's for sure," she replied. "We are falling a little behind on all the paperwork that has come in. You should have seen how many samples Mark brought in today," she said, indicating to John that Mark had beaten him to the lab. "That stack of papers over there on the counter," she said, pointing to a stack of forms that had to be at least four inches high, "that's just the morning run, and now we'll add all these." She held up about three inches worth of forms from John's afternoon pickup. "We are going to be here all night processing all these forms."

"Well, at least you'll make some extra money from working overtime," John said jokingly, but Joyce simply didn't seem to be in the right mood for a simple joke.

"Yeah," she said in a sarcastic tone. "Who wants to process all this blood knowing that any one of these samples could be contaminated with the Sanguis virus and that we could catch it and die."

"Well," he said, not sure of how to respond. After all, what do you say to someone who is working with a potentially deadly organism? "You're all so good back here," he continued, trying to encourage her not to worry. "You don't have a thing to worry about."

"I'll believe that," she said, again in a sarcastic tone, "when I'm still alive after this crisis is over." She turned, with the papers in one hand and one large bag of blood samples carefully cradled in the other arm, and headed for the workstation on the far side of the lab.

John looked over in Sharon's direction and noticed she had been watching him. When Joyce walked away, Sharon came over to see him. "Hi," she said with a small smile on her face. Not sure of what else to say, she had wanted to start up a conversation. After what seemed a rather long uncomfortable pause, she continued, "How's it going?"

"Fine," John replied, also feeling a little awkward and unsure of how to get the conversation going. "That was going to be my question to you," he continued. "Any luck with the mysteries of this disease?"

"Nothing spectacular," she replied. "I wish I had something better to tell you." She stood there for several seconds in agony, wanting to say something but not sure of what to say or how to say what was on her mind. In the back of her mind was some disturbing information she desperately wanted to share with someone. However, she didn't know if she should tell anyone. But bad news can sometimes be hard to contain within the soul, causing a person to feel the need to tell someone else. Sharon shifted her posture several more times, transferring her weight from one foot to another as if waiting for a Mr. Wonderful to give her a first kiss. Finally, she stopped fidgeting around as she looked directly at John and asked, "Have you heard how many died from this disease this morning in this hospital alone?"

John was not privy to this information. Since he didn't spend much time at the hospital, he had little time to hear any gossip. "No," he replied, a little concerned by the way she had asked the question, as he could see she was greatly distressed by the information. He feared that she would announce to him that hundreds had died of the disease in the last twenty-four hours.

"Today, there have been ten deaths from this disease in this hospital alone, and my contacts at Saint Joseph's Hospital say they've had twelve. I'm afraid that this is only the beginning."

John didn't know what to say. Was this number of deaths a big deal? He didn't think it was. After all, people die every day. Some die of natural causes; others die in accidents; and still others die at the hands of other people. This was a big hospital; it couldn't be that big of a deal to have that many die from the disease. After all, how many died every day from cancer or heart attack? John had no frame of reference to judge the numbers, but Sharon's reaction made him think twice about the numbers and what they may mean in the future.

"How bad is it?" he asked.

"According to the limited information that we have gathered from across the United States and from some overseas locations, at this rate, most of the adults who have a blood type other than type B could catch this disease and die within six months to a year. That gives us very little time to find a cure," she said with a slight quiver in her lower lip as if about to cry. She took a deep breath before saying, "Before we won't need the cure."

Her last statement about not needing a cure didn't connect in John's brain at first. *Why wouldn't they need the cure in the future?* he wondered. But then he realized that they wouldn't need it if all the possible victims of the disease had died. The only ones left would be those who had type B blood.

"Only six months," John repeated, envisioning the calendar. *Six months doesn't seem that far away,* he thought. *That would put it around the end of the year.* "Boy, what a lousy way to start the New Year. Do you think you'll have enough time to find the cure?" he asked, thinking about how long his wife would be around before she caught the disease and died.

"I don't know," Sharon said, shrugging her shoulders in doubt. "We are working on it, but we have made very little progress. There are a lot of people working on this problem, but as I said, there hasn't been much success."

"Well, I have confidence in you. You'll be the one to find the cure," he said, trying to raise her spirits.

"That's very doubtful," she said in a defeated tone as a tear came to her eye.

John saw the tear and the change in her mood. He was concerned about why she seemed so defeated. "What's wrong?" he asked.

Sharon didn't look up; she just continued to stare at the floor. John stood there, waiting for her to answer his question but not wanting to rush her into responding. So he just stood there waiting for a response. Sharon, on the other hand, was standing there wishing he had never asked the question. She desperately wanted to answer the question, but she also didn't want to say anything else. She stood there waiting for him to leave, but it was soon obvious that he wasn't going anywhere.

Why is he just standing there? she thought. Was he just nosy, or did he truly care about her and what was going on? All she knew was that she wasn't going to get out of answering his question. So with a deep breath as if she were going to shout the answer at the top of her lungs, she whispered, "I have the disease."

This little whisper of news hit John like a Mack truck running through a stop sign. He almost fell backward from the news. He caught himself and regained his stance before she could look up. He was afraid that his lack of control might make it appear that he was retreating from her because she had the disease. He stood there looking at this young woman, thinking that if she were to die, it would be such a loss. He had to ask, "Is there anything anyone can do to help?"

She finally looked up at him and gazed deep into his eyes as if seeking reassurance that he was sincere about his question and that he was not just trying to discover if he might be in any danger from her if she was contagious. She felt a sudden calming that told her he was indeed concerned about her welfare.

"Well, we are trying one test," Sharon said at last.

She paused for a second to wonder if she should divulge the information about this test. She didn't want to get anyone's hopes up about a possible cure. After taking a deep breath, she continued, saying, "I had a blood transfusion this morning of uninfected blood. We don't know what the results will be, but for now, all I can do is wait. According to some other sites, giving a patient a blood transfusion of noncontaminated blood seems to slow down the effects of the Sanguis virus. It depends on the individual, but they have had some success with this treatment. In each case, the patient has lived for about a week before the symptoms started to reoccur. The problem has been catching the disease early so that a blood transfusion can be administered before the virus destroys too many of the red blood cells. They are also trying red blood cell injections in place of a normal blood transfusion."

"So," John said with encouragement, "this means you have a chance then, right?"

She paused for a second before answering. "I suppose," she said, still displaying a defeated expression, "but I don't know how much of a chance it will be." And in reality, she had no idea. After all, no one had survived the disease as of yet, and most attempts to control the disease, at this hospital and at other locations, had resulted in fatalities. "Only time will tell," she finally concluded.

"Well, if there is anything I can do," he said, "please let me know." He sincerely wanted to provide her with whatever help she might need, but he was also afraid that he could catch the disease from her and infect his wife and daughter.

"Thank you for caring," she said, trying to bring forth a smile. "Please don't tell anyone. No one here knows. Only the CDC knows."

"No problem," he said, trying to reassure her. "I won't tell a soul." He stood there, not knowing what to do or say. How do you talk to someone who knows she will die if a cure isn't found for the disease? He felt he needed to talk to someone else, but if no one else knew, then how could he possibly find someone to talk to? The only one he theoretically could talk to was Sharon. "How about taking a break and going down to the cafeteria for some coffee?" he asked, hoping it would cheer her up. This would allow her to talk, which might help her feel better.

Sharon just stood there for a second, not sure of how to answer the question. She sure could have used a friend just then, but she wasn't sure how much she could trust John or herself for revealing information. She stood there, caught between what she felt she wanted to do, which was go for coffee and talk, and staying in the lab and being quiet about the whole thing. However, she had just told him something that she really shouldn't have revealed to anyone outside the CDC. Her thoughts were interrupted; she looked up at him. "What?" she asked, acting as if she hadn't heard what he said.

"Come on," he said in a friendly, persuasive voice. In a humorous tone, he started singing the familiar McDonald's theme song: "You deserve a break today."

This brought a smile to Sharon's face as she realized that he didn't have the greatest singing voice. He was quite tinny and way off-key. *Maybe he just sang it that way to get a laugh,* she thought to herself. With a little reluctance, she said, "Okay, but just a quick one. I still have a lot of work to do."

John and Sharon sat in the cafeteria, each with a cup of coffee and a small piece of cherry pie that John so gallantly had offered to buy for Sharon as a way of treating her. They sat at the table not saying much at first, other than commenting that the coffee was a little bitter and the pie was a little stale.

John sat at the table wanting to talk about the disease, but he wasn't sure how to get started. He felt that talking about it would also help Sharon feel better, but he just sat there, continuing with the small talk. Knowing she would have to go back up soon, he had the sense he was wasting time. He had to start something.

On the other side of the table sat Sharon, not saying much unless John said something first. She sensed that he wanted to talk about the disease but seemed to be avoiding the subject. In a way, this made her feel a little relieved, but on the other hand, she wanted desperately to talk to someone about her situation. She just sat there nibbling on her piece of pie.

John, unlike Sharon, took large bites of his pie, partially because he was hungry and loved cherry pie, and partially because he didn't want to waste too much time eating, when all he wanted to do was talk. He took the last bite of his pie and quickly tried to wash it down with the bitter coffee. He looked up and noticed that Sharon hadn't finished the pie. She was poking her piece with her fork while she was daydreaming. He knew he had to start the conversation soon, or else she would have to return to the lab. So he drew in a deep breath and kind of blurted out the question: "If the transfusion doesn't work, how long do you have before the disease wins out?"

The increase in the volume of John's voice startled Sharon but brought her back to the reality of being in the cafeteria. She wasn't sure exactly what he had asked, but she knew it had to do with something related to the disease and her. To make sure she had understood his question, she asked, "What did you say?"

He felt a little at ease because she hadn't caught the question and, more likely, hadn't caught the way he blurted it out. Now he could repeat the question and put a little more feeling into it. "Oh," he started in a more casual tone as if discussing the weather, "I was just wondering if you knew how long you have if the transfusion doesn't help?"

Sharon understood this question, and although it was difficult for her to talk about the fact that she could drop dead at any time, she felt that talking about it would make her feel better. "It's not certain," she started. "According to some experts in the CDC, they have found that a transfusion can add enough good red blood cells to keep the individual going for a week or more. Unfortunately, the Sanguis virus soon kills off the new blood cells, and then the patient has to have a new transfusion."

"Well, that sounds promising," he said, hoping to raise her spirits.

"Yeah," she said, and then took a deep sigh. "But we don't know how many transfusions you can give someone. I mean, we don't know if giving transfusions will help the individual keep ahead of the Sanguis virus, or if the virus will eventually take control and kill the patient." She didn't realize that she was answering his question in such a way that it sounded as if she was talking about another patient and not herself. To John, she seemed to avoid the concept that she had the virus.

"Well, at least there is some sort of a plan to address the survival possibilities with this disease," he said, not sure where he was going with the conversation. Because her comments were not related to her situation, he was a little afraid of continuing. He didn't want to accidentally force her to realize that it was she in this situation, not some unknown patient. An awkward silence fell between the two with neither wanting to continue the conversation. Sharon didn't know what to say, and John didn't know what to say that wouldn't upset her. Finally, he broke the silence. "Do you know how you caught the disease?" he asked, hoping a slight change in subject would get her talking again.

"I'm not sure," she replied. "We know that you can become infected if you ingest something contaminated with the Sanguis virus. We have also determined that the virus can be transferred by the exchange of body fluids from an infected person to a noninfected person. However, I don't think I have ever come in direct contact with anyone's blood or any other body fluids."

As John sat there thinking about it, he realized that the human body has a lot of different fluids other than blood that can transfer germs and viruses between individuals. Simple kissing can transfer the common cold, while more intimate actions can transfer other viruses such as HIV.

"What about touch?" John asked, wanting to see if the scenario Paula had described might be a possible way of transmission.

"What do you mean?" Sharon asked.

"What I mean is, if someone who is contagious touches a surface, can they leave the Sanguis virus? And then when someone else comes along and touches that same surface, will they catch the Sanguis virus?" He didn't like his question and also felt he hadn't asked it well. "You know," he continued, "like the Lysol commercials on TV about spreading cold germs on surfaces. If the Sanguis virus ended up on someone's hands, could they spread the virus to other surfaces where someone else, like me," he said, not really wanting to throw himself into the picture, but having his reasons for doing so, "could come along and touch that same surface and catch the Sanguis virus?"

Sharon kind of laughed at his question. "That is a good thought," she said. "Maybe you should work in the lab." The two had a brief laugh at the idea. John didn't tell her that he used to work in the lab before the cutbacks. "However," she continued, "we have determined that the Sanguis virus is not passed by direct contact between the infected person and anyone they come in contact with."

"That's good," he said, not wanting to say what he was thinking. However, she caught the gesture he was making and knew what he was referring to.

"Don't worry," she said. "You will not get infected by me touching you." She paused for a second and stared out the window. "But we really don't know all the possible ways it spreads," she finally said.

John was afraid that his comment might have the effect of alienating him from future conversations. He didn't want Sharon to think that he was afraid she might contaminate him. "I wasn't thinking about that," he said, trying to ease her concerns about the way he was acting. "I was thinking of my wife and all the paperwork she handles. There would be no way to tell if someone handling the papers has left the Sanguis virus on the paper. And then my wife might pick up the papers and catch the virus."

His statement seemed to help relieve some of Sharon's fears. "I'm sorry," she said in an apologetic tone. "I meant nothing by it."

"No problem," he said, trying to raise her spirits.

Since there seems to be so many ways to transmit the Sanguis virus, he thought to himself, *is it possible that I could have given the virus to Sharon? Could I be the culprit who may end her career and her life?* This made him a little nervous to ask Sharon about this possibility, since if true, it could make all that Paula feared about the disease materialize. However, he just had to ask. "Is there any way that I could be carrying the Sanguis virus and you caught it from me?"

Now, this was something that Sharon hadn't thought of. She already knew that someone with type B blood could be a carrier and could contaminate others. However, she hadn't even thought of the idea that the carrier who had given her the Sanguis virus could be the same person sitting across the table from her. As she reviewed the situation in her head, she wondered. She had had the disease for at least several days with symptoms and had had a transfusion. She had only just met John a couple of days ago, so odds were that he couldn't have given her the virus. Also, the virus was said to be transmitted by a transfer of body fluids, and there was no way any of his body fluids could have come into contact with Sharon. So she concluded that she had been infected by someone else or by some other means they hadn't determined yet.

"We know that it's not transmitted through the air, so you couldn't have breathed it on me. It can be spread by certain body fluids, but unless you bled on me or we have been participating in more intimate actions," she said as she winked at John, "then I doubt that I caught this virus from you."

John caught the wink. "So is it possible for me to spread the Sanguis virus?" he asked.

"Well, if you have been exposed, you can spread the Sanguis virus without knowing," she replied. She noticed his repelling action as he shifted his weight backward, as if to distance himself from her. She assumed his actions resulted from an unconscious fear that he might contaminate someone if he were infected.

"How hard is it to determine if I'm carrying the virus?" he asked, his fears of being a carrier having increased.

"It's easy," she answered. "We use a simple blood test up in the lab to test patients to see if they are infected." She stood up from the table.

John and Sharon dropped their paper dishes into the trash can and headed back up to the lab. Sharon escorted John over to a chair by a small table. Walking over to a glass cabinet, she unlocked the glass door and reached into the back of the cabinet for what looked like a small vial. She returned to where John was sitting after a quick stop at a drawer, where she had pulled out a small needle and a small glass slide. "Okay," she said, "stick out your finger."

He wasn't too sure he liked the idea of being stuck in the finger, even if it would be only a small poke. However, the idea of the needle entering the skin and making the small puncture wound gave him chills as he thought of the pain. He tried to cover up the fact that he didn't want to be stuck for fear Sharon might think he was chicken.

"Oh, this isn't going to hurt," she said in response to his hesitation. "Give me your finger." John complied but was still slightly hesitant as she wiped off the end of his finger with a small alcohol wipe. Then, she took the small lancet and, holding his finger, placed it against his finger. She could see the fear in his eyes as he stood there like a statue. It was evident that he didn't like needles, which to her seemed kind of strange since he saw needles every day on his runs. "John," she said, trying to get his attention, "I can't stick you when you're so scared of this little needle."

John looked up and sighed with relief as he started to relax his tense muscles. He started to say thank you, but before he could get the first word out, a sudden feeling of pain shot through his finger as Sharon had released the little clip and the small needle penetrated his skin. "Hey!" he shouted as if he had been stabbed with a fourteen-inch Bowie knife. "That hurts."

"Oh," she said, applying a small drop of his blood onto the glass slide, "you'll live. Here," she said, handing him a small Spider-Man Band-Aid.

"You mean if I want to be tested for this virus, I have to get stuck each time?"

"That's how it works," she replied as a smile formed on her face. She started the test by adding a drop of dye to the drop of blood.

John, a little embarrassed holding a Spider-Man Band-Aid, applied it to his finger and tried to rub away the small pain that was present. The pain may have been small, but to him, it felt like he'd had major surgery. "What does that do?" he asked, continuing to massage his little wound.

"Boy, you're a wimp," Sharon said with a chuckle as she watched him continue to rub his finger. "Anyway, this dye makes the Sanguis virus turn blue. I wish it would kill the virus, but all it does is make a protein chain associated with it turn blue so that I can see it under a microscope."

"So," John said, deducing from her explanation, "if it doesn't turn blue, then I'm not carrying the virus?"

"That's correct," she answered, focusing the microscope so she could see the small blood cells on the glass plate. "Well," she said as if talking to the microscope, "let's see what we have. Hmm." She was speaking in a loud enough tone that John could hear her. Time seemed to drag on. "Now that's interesting," she said, making him feel uneasy as he stood there waiting for her conclusion.

"What?" he asked as he stood in suspense. He was getting a little uptight about the results or, rather, the lack thereof. Was he or wasn't he infected with the Sanguis virus? The results could make a major impact on his life. The waiting was becoming unbearable, especially since Sharon kept making simple little statements that didn't give a clue one way or the other.

Sharon stood up from the microscope and turned to face John. "Do you feel a little tired from time to time?" she asked, continuing to drag him along in her little joke.

"Not really," he said, knowing that fatigue was a symptom of the disease. He had type B blood, so the disease shouldn't affect him. So why was she asking if he was tired?

She could see he was getting uptight about her little joke, so she told him what was going on, instead of driving him crazy. "It's all right," she started. "It just looks like you're a little anemic. You might want to try taking some iron supplements for a while. As for the Sanguis virus, you're clean. No sign of it."

John felt so relieved that he almost collapsed where he was standing. Then he realized what she had done. "Okay," he said in a seditious tone, "two can play that game." He noticed a smile come across her face. "Just remember," he continued, using a tone that would scare Vincent Price, "I don't get even; I get revenge." And then the two of them laughed. The tension they'd felt from discussing the Sanguis virus and from the fact that Sharon was infected seemed to melt away. "Well," he said, the giggles decreasing, "I'd better get home."

"Okay," she said. "Have a good evening."

"You too," he replied. As he started to turn and walk out of the lab, he added, "Don't work too hard."

"Okay," she said, turning to head over to a counter where Robert was standing.

After John walked out of the lab, he stopped by the mailboxes to see what mail he might have. As he was reading a notice about the hospital's quarterly blood drive, he was interrupted by someone down the hall calling his name. He looked up to see Tom standing by his office door.

"Can I see you for a minute?" Tom called down to John.

"Coming," John replied, crumpling up the blood drive notice. "What's up?" he asked, walking over to Tom's desk.

"I was wondering how the runs are going?" Tom asked, concern in his voice.

"They're going fine," John replied. "Why?" he asked, wondering what Tom might be hiding. He didn't know how to take his question. In the past, Tom had never asked how things were going unless there was some sort of a problem. But John couldn't remember anyone complaining about anything recently.

"Nothing much," Tom responded. "It's just that Mark has been complaining about the larger number of specimens he has been picking up. He's concerned that he may not be able to handle all the tubes that have to come in. Also, Joyce has commented that they are starting to fall behind with processing the specimens because of the large numbers that are coming in."

"Well," John said, sitting down in the chair across from Tom. He thought about the list he had been keeping. He didn't want Tom to know that he'd begun counting the number of specimens he was bringing in each day. "Now that you mention it," he continued, "I have noticed that there are more orders than what we used to get. In fact, I've had to get a second cooler to bring in all the samples."

"That's kind of what I expected," Tom continued. "With the budget cuts, I can't hire anyone. With all these orders coming in, it's going to be hard to keep up unless either we get some help from somewhere or the hospital authorizes overtime."

"I thought you could authorize overtime," John said as if to remind Tom of something he already knew.

"I can, but only for short periods. I have a suspicion that this disease is not going to be a short-term problem," Tom said a bit sarcastically. "And now I have to have the lab techs supporting the CDC agents. There just isn't enough time to get everything done."

"Can you get some help just for the CDC agents?" John asked.

"No," Tom said in a defeated tone, "they won't pay for that either."

"Can Sharon authorize any help?" John asked, not realizing that he had referred to her by her first name.

"Apparently not," Tom answered, and then paused as he took a long look at John. "I didn't know you knew her first name." Tom was surprised that John would refer to someone he didn't know by her first name, especially since was always forgetting names.

John felt a little uneasy at first. He didn't want Tom to get the wrong idea. He took a deep breath as if trying to exhale some of the anxiety. "You introduced me to her, remember?"

"Oh yeah," Tom replied, "but I'm surprised you remembered her name."

"Well, I was just talking to her a minute ago," John said in his own defense, "so I was able to read her name tag."

"Oh," Tom said, satisfied with his explanation.

John thought this would be a good time to bring up some of the things that Sharon had told him. "I understand that one possible way to treat this disease is to give the infected patient a blood transfusion?"

"Yeah," Tom replied, "I read about that in yesterday's report that they submitted to Washington. It apparently works for a short time, but it's not a permanent solution to the problem."

"I found the information interesting since Paula is a possible candidate to catch the disease."

"Well, don't count too much on transfusions as a solution," Tom said as if announcing a warning.

"Why?" John asked, concerned about Tom's reaction. "Sharon said that it seems to be working."

"It does," Tom replied a little less aggressively. "However, the blood banks are empty. I noticed you were looking at your mail."

"Yeah," John said, a little puzzled. "So what?"

"Did you see the notice for the blood drive?"

"Yeah," he answered, not sure of where Tom was going with this.

"That notice says that it is the quarterly blood drive, but we had a blood drive about eight weeks ago. This isn't the quarterly blood drive; it's a necessary blood drive. The Hoxforth blood bank has tripled their drives to try to bring in more blood."

This news made John a little uneasy. "You're telling me that if Paula does catch this disease, she may not be able to get a blood transfusion?" he asked with great concern.

"You'd better pray that she doesn't catch the disease, because her chance of getting clean blood is almost nil. Not only is there not enough blood, but also they're finding that about 50 percent of the blood they do get is infected and can't be used. They don't even want to separate the blood into its components for fear the Sanguis virus is still present. They won't even keep type B blood around if it's contaminated. So, if it tests positive for the virus, they just have to dispose of it."

John sat there evaluating the news Tom had just presented. What was he going to do if Paula were to catch the disease? According to the news and Sharon, if you catch the Sanguis virus and do not have type B blood, you are considered terminal and will die. John had been feeling really good earlier when he discovered he wasn't a carrier, but now he discovered there may be no way to save his wife if the worst should present itself. "Is there nothing they can do either to get more blood or to clean up the blood they do get?" he asked Tom with a tone of despair.

"According to the CDC report," Tom continued, "they can obtain some blood from normal donors, but it will not be enough to provide for the needs of the hospital and to provide transfusions for everyone who comes down with the disease. They say that the only noncontaminated blood source is from preteen children who have not yet reached puberty. Apparently, once they reach the point where the adrenal glands start to produce puberty-related hormones, they can become infected. But before that, their blood can be used for whatever needs present themselves. The problem is that most kids who haven't reached the puberty stage are too small to give blood."

"How old do they have to be to donate blood?" John asked.

"Well," Tom said, trying to remember all the requirements for qualifying as a donor, "I believe the big one is that they have to be eighteen years of age. But I think that is more for legal reasons than medical. The only other requirement is that they have to be at least a hundred pounds and in good health. Any smaller than that and taking a pint of blood from them could cause them to faint. If they are really small, taking a pint of blood could put them into a coma and they could die."

"Wow," John said in a low tone.

"John," Tom said, looking up at the clock on the wall, "you probably should get home. Paula is going to want to know what's taking you so long."

"Yeah," John responded, as if he had been defeated by a sumo wrestler, "you're probably right." He got up and headed for the door. "See you tomorrow," he said, although he wasn't too sure he ever wanted to come back to this frightening place of chaos.

CHAPTER 9

John headed home, glad of the fact that he wasn't carrying the Sanguis virus, but concerned about how he would help Paula if she were to contract it. The downtown streets were not as congested with pedestrians as usual, but many of the people who were out were wearing surgical masks. John, lost in his own thoughts, paid little attention to the pedestrians. Under other circumstances, he would have thought it strange to see all those people walking along the streets wearing masks. But today he just drove home through the heavy traffic and was glad to pull into his driveway.

"I'm home," he called out as he entered the front door. Paula's car was in the driveway, letting him know that she was home, but he had no idea if the kids were around. He was hoping that they weren't around so he could spend some time with his wife to let her know he wasn't currently a carrier.

"Up here," came her familiar voice from the bedroom.

As he entered the bedroom, he saw Paula changing out of her business attire and into some housework clothes. She had just removed her skirt when John entered and was standing in front of the dresser in her bra and panties. John, hoping to regain some ground after she'd gotten upset yesterday, decided to whistle a catcall at her. "Sexy," he said in a seductive tone as he, too, started to change into some work clothes.

"Oh, shut up," she said, a little embarrassed at being considered a sex symbol but knowing he was only teasing her. However, Paula did have a good figure and did look good in lingerie. To her husband, she was pretty sexy. He occasionally told her so, but somehow she just didn't believe it. "How was your day?" she asked, pulling a pink T-shirt over her head.

"About as normal as can be with the chaos that has been going on around the hospital," he answered as he also pulled on a T-shirt. He walked over to her. She was brushing out the mess in her hair from having pulled on her T-shirt. "I've got a small boo-boo," he said, mimicking a toddler's voice, showing her the small Spider-Man Band-Aid on his finger.

"I guess," she said, seeing how small the Band-Aid was. "What did you do, get a little paper cut?" she asked in a sarcastic tone.

"No," he replied in a gallant voice, standing tall to show her how brave he was. "I had my finger stuck with one of those stupid needles—and you know how I hate needles."

"Oh no!" she screamed in fear, which caught him completely off guard. "You were stuck with a needle! There's no telling what kind of diseases you picked up from that needle." The panic of what could happen overwhelmed her. She backed away from John.

John didn't know what to say or do as Paula jumped over the bed and headed for the master bathroom. "It's okay," he called after her, but the only response he got was the door slamming shut. Her fear of the disease was intense. He had never seen her act that way. She would climb up on the roof to hang Christmas lights and never had the slightest fear of falling off the roof and onto her head. This reaction of hers was something he had never seen before.

John walked over to the locked door and lightly knocked. "It's okay," he said in a soft tone, trying to get Paula to calm down. "I didn't accidentally get stuck with a needle. It was one of those sterile needles that they use to stick your finger to test your blood. You know, the same type of needle Marsha used to test the kids' blood. Those things are thrown away immediately after they are used. You know me; there's no way I would ever get near a needle, let alone get stuck by one of them, unless it was being done on purpose like to test my blood to see if I have the Sanguis virus," he continued, trying to emphasize the idea that he had been tested for the virus and hadn't just gotten stuck with a needle by accident.

This explanation eased Paula's fears, but she still worried about what could happen if he were to contract the Sanguis virus and bring it home.

"Sorry," she apologized, opening the bathroom door. "I didn't mean to jump to conclusions like that."

"It's okay," he said in reply. "Everything is fine." He stepped toward her to see if she would continue to back away. But for now, she seemed content to trust him, at least partway.

"Guess what?" John said in an attempt to ease the tension by making a small game out of the situation.

"I'm not in the mood for any games," Paula answered, wondering what kind of information he would pass on to her. She was still not ready to accept that everything was okay, and she didn't want to be convinced.

"Well, I had my blood tested," John said, taking another step toward her, "and I'm fine. I am not carrying the Sanguis virus, so you are safe."

She wasn't totally relieved, but he could see the tension drop away from her as she slowly sat down on the bed. She didn't know what to do or say as she felt kind of like a fool for having jumped to conclusions.

"Honey," John said. He walked over, sat next to her on the bed, and placed his arm around her shoulders. "It's all right," he continued as he tried to comfort her. "We'll get through this together." He leaned in and gave her a small kiss on the cheek.

Paula, not ready to handle the sudden rush of emotions, turned and cried on John's shoulder. He just sat there holding her and letting her cry her emotions away. After about five minutes, her sobs had decreased to small sniffles. "Are you all right?" he asked. She started to wipe her eyes with the hem of her T-shirt.

"Yeah," she said, taking small gulps of air to recover from the sudden flow of tears. "I will be," she replied.

"Why don't you lie down for a couple of minutes and rest?" he said, helping her adjust the pillows since she was too far down on the bed to reach them. "Later you can finish getting dressed. Then I'll meet you downstairs."

"Thank you," she said, closing her eyes to let Mother Nature help her to relax.

John finished getting changed and then headed downstairs. He was interested in finding Peter as he wanted to discuss a problem with him. As he walked into the living room, he could see that Peter was out on the back porch playing a game on his Game Boy unit. John sometimes wished that Peter would lose that game unit and do something else, but right now he wanted to use his son's computer skills.

"Peter," he said, trying to interrupt the game the boy was playing.

"Just a minute, Dad," Peter replied, his fingers flying across the controller.

John had always hated that line, even though he had used it himself. But when Peter used this line, it seemed more like hours than a minute. However, John knew how much his son enjoyed playing the game, so he waited for what seemed to be a minute. Still, when one is waiting, a minute seems awfully long. "I need to talk to you," John said, again trying to interrupt the game.

"Come on, Dad, just a second," Peter responded with a touch of frustration. "I'm almost there."

John was getting impatient, but he tried to control his desire to tell his son to get off the game. He stood there waiting and watching, wondering how many more seconds it would take before he could get his son's attention. His level of patience was dropping fast as he stood there waiting. Just as he was about to interrupt with a much firmer tone, Peter suddenly yelled out, "Made it!"

"Sorry, Dad," Peter said, turning off the game and putting it to one side. He knew that when his father wanted his total attention, he had better put the game away and listen. He didn't like it because this usually meant that his dad wanted him to do something he didn't want to do—and that usually meant no more game time. "What's up?" he asked.

"I want to talk to you about your mother." John had started in a soft tone, hoping no one else would hear him. "You know about the blood disease that has been going around, right?" he asked, which was, in reality, a dumb question since it had been on everyone's minds for the last week or so.

"Yeah, Dad," Peter replied. "Why?"

"Do you know your mom has type A blood and could catch the Sanguis virus and die?" This statement was a little on the heavy side and was one that Peter wasn't ready to hear.

"I talked to someone at work today," John continued in a serious tone of voice, "who said that if someone catches the Sanguis virus, they can get a blood transfusion to help them stay alive."

"That's cool, Dad," Peter said, not having known this tidbit of information.

"Yeah," John continued, "but the problem is that the hospitals are basically out of noncontaminated blood. The only blood that can be considered safe is blood from a young person who has not reached puberty. I say someone who is ten to twelve years old."

"Are the hospitals trying to get kids to donate blood?" Peter asked, still unsure of where his father was going with this conversation.

"No," John replied in a sad tone. "I wish they would. Instead, I was thinking of going out and trying to find a kid who would be willing to donate blood for your mom. Then we could make arrangements for the kid to stay here with us."

"What about the parents?" Peter asked.

"Well," John said, a little hesitant, "according to the news, there are some kids who are on the streets because their parents have died. I thought we could ask one of them if they would like to stay here in return for some blood for your mom."

"Well," Peter said, "do you think these kids will donate their blood?"

"I don't know," John replied, afraid the answer might be no. "I guess we would have to go out and ask some kids. The first thing we have to figure out is how to do a blood transfusion. It won't do any good if, once we can get a kid, we can't get the blood out of them."

"You mean we have to perform the blood transfusion?" Peter asked, stressing the word *we*. He was terrified by the idea. "Why don't we just take the kid to the hospital with Mom and have them do it?" he asked. It sounded like a reasonable question.

"Because, according to the hospital, and from what I understand," John replied in a discouraged tone, "they will only take blood from a donor if the donor is at least eighteen years old. At that age, a kid is too old to be immune and could be infected. Another problem is that the kid may not be the right blood type."

"I don't think I can do it," Peter confessed.

"Don't worry," John said to reassure him, "I can draw the blood. I just don't know how to put it into another patient."

"What do you want me to do?" Peter asked, trying to resolve the idea that they may have no other way to deal with the situation.

"Well," John answered, "you're good at finding information on that computer of yours. I was wondering what you might be able to find out about blood transfusions. We also need to know how to get the supplies for the transfusion, as well as the testing supplies to test the donors for their blood types."

"No problem," Peter said, confident that he could find information on anything. "I'll go see what I can find. Maybe I can get lucky."

John was always impressed by Peter's ability to locate information on the internet. Peter had been surfing the internet for many years to find information for school and other projects, so this should be easy for him to do. "Okay," John said, "but don't tell your mom." He knew that if she were to discover what he was contemplating, she would scream. "She's upset enough, so let's not add fuel to the fire."

"Okay," Peter said. He headed to the computer in his room.

John made a simple dinner consisting of soup and grilled cheese sandwiches. After dinner, he decided to kill some time relaxing in his recliner and watching the news. Paula had slept for about an hour and was now in the kitchen helping Beth do her hair. Peter was upstairs on the computer searching the internet. John used the cable remote to change to the news station. He sat there half watching the news and half daydreaming about what the future would bring. He was only half listening when the news broadcaster said something that caught his attention.

"A small number of kids are now without parental supervision because their parents have died from the disease. These kids have started to cause trouble in various communities. Small gangs have started forming, consisting of children as young as ten to as old as sixteen. These gangs are responsible for a rash of vandalism and looting. One gang of seven young boys was caught and arrested for breaking into the Great Woods Hunting Shop in an attempt to obtain several rifles and handguns. Luckily, none of the boys got away with any merchandise, and no one was hurt. The boys had several guns in their possession but didn't know how to remove the store safety locks. The seven boys will be arraigned in Hamilton County District Court tomorrow at ten o'clock.

"A late afternoon fire at a house in Colerain is being blamed on three boys ages twelve and thirteen. They broke into an abandoned house and set the carpets on fire in several rooms. Officer Davenport caught the boys in the woods behind the house, watching the firemen put out the blaze."

John was listening to the newscaster when Peter came into the living room with several pieces of paper he had printed off the computer. "Dad," he said, carrying his small stack of papers, "here is some information you might be interested in."

"What have you got here?" John asked, not knowing what his son was referring to. To hand him a small stack of papers didn't give him much of a clue as to what Peter was asking him to look at.

"It's some of the information you wanted me to find out about. You know, like how to do a blood transfusion," Peter said, passing the papers to his father.

"Oh," John said, not realizing that Peter had located all this information in less than three hours. John sifted through the papers, wondering where to start. "How about giving me the simplified version?" he asked, giving the stack of papers back to Peter.

"Well, Dad," Peter started, "I did find out that you are right about the age limit. You have to be at least eighteen years of age to give blood. This is basically a legal condition. According to one site, all you need to be is over one hundred pounds, and you should have enough blood to donate. According to another internet site, young donors can actually recover faster than older donors. So, as far as I can tell, if we can find young kids who are at least one hundred pounds, then they can donate blood. The problem is that you're not going to find too many kids over one hundred pounds who have not started puberty."

"That could be a big problem," John said, a little disappointed in the news. "What else did you find out?"

"I found out that once someone donates a pint of blood," Peter continued, shuffling through the papers in his hand, "they have to wait fifty-six days before they can donate again. If they don't wait, they could become anemic themselves. Remember your idea of having some kids stay here in return for their blood?"

"Yeah," John said, a little disappointed as he saw where Peter was headed.

"Well, if we need new blood once a week, and if each donor has to wait fifty-six days before donating again," Peter continued, not wanting to reveal more bad news, "that means we need to have eight kids who are each over one hundred pounds, who have not yet reached puberty, and who have type A blood. Do you know how hard it's going to be to find that many who fit these criteria?"

John didn't know what to say. He'd had an idea of how he could help his wife, but the odds that they would find kids who fit into these categories would be almost impossible. "I never thought it would be that complex," he said. Noticing that Peter had many pages in his hand, he continued, asking, "What else do you have there?"

"First of all," Peter answered, continuing to shuffle through papers, "I did some research on how to do a transfusion. There are several ways we can do it, but I think the best way is to collect the blood from the donor in a sterile bag and then give the blood to Mom."

"Well," John interrupted, "I can find the vein, but I've never tried putting blood into anyone, only taking it out."

"One problem we have is getting the supplies to do this. We need to get some special needles, and they have to be sterile or else Mom could end up with an infection that could kill her just like the disease itself. The nice thing is that I found a company on the internet that sells the supplies. It's about fifteen dollars for each collection. The hard part will be finding the veins in Mom's arm. If we miss, we could end up pumping a lot of blood under the skin on Mom's arm and not into her veins."

"This sounds almost impossible," John said as he shook his head. He had a lot of experience drawing small samples of blood from someone's arm, but he had never tried to insert a needle that had to be in the exact position or else something terrible could result.

"Don't give up yet," Peter said, searching through the stack again. "First, I've found a website that teaches you how to find the different veins. I just need to try a couple of times for practice. I think I can do it." Not that he wanted to. He hated needles, but if it was a choice between sticking his mom with a needle and watching her die, he would find it easy to make the choice.

This news was making John feel a little more optimistic. He had made a request of his son to find answers to the problem, and it looked as if Peter had done a good job so far in working out the details.

"This same supply house also sells a kit to test for blood type," Peter continued. "We have to make sure we have the right blood type, or we could kill Mom ourselves."

"That's great," John said with enthusiasm, but his enthusiasm didn't last long. "What about the donors?" he asked. "Didn't you say it would be almost impossible to find enough donors?"

"Yeah," Peter answered, a little depressed because he hadn't figured out how to solve that problem. "I'm still working on that aspect. I was wondering if I can go over to Ken's house and talk to him about some other ideas I have?"

"Well," John said, a little disappointed, "don't you think it's getting a little late to go over to Ken's? Why don't you go over tomorrow and talk to him then? Who knows, you may get some other ideas if you sleep on it."

"All right," Peter said, a little disappointed. He had wanted to work on this situation while his thoughts were still fresh in his mind. But he knew his father was right—and it was getting late. It was already ten thirty. Peter was sure that if he went over to Ken's, he would be up for many hours discussing this situation.

"Peter!" John called out as his son headed back upstairs.

"Yeah?" Peter replied.

"Don't tell Ken too much about why you're talking about this. I don't want too many people to know that we may be taking in homeless kids for their blood. I don't mind if they think we're being nice to take in the kids, but I don't want them to know why we want them to stay here." John could only imagine what the people in the neighborhood would say if they were to discover that he wanted to take in kids who were homeless, not for unselfish reasons, but because he wanted to extract their blood so he could save his wife's life if she should come down with the disease.

"No problem," Peter said, and headed back upstairs.

Peter had plans to meet with Ken the next day about seven in the evening at Peter's house.

*   *   *

"Hi, Ken!" Peter called out as he saw his friend jump over the backyard fence. Ken's house was at the other end of the street. Cutting through the backyards was the quickest way to Peter's house.

"Hi," Ken said as he approached the porch. "Sorry to be so late, but you know what my dad's like when he gets to working in the yard." Ken sat down in a lawn chair across from Peter.

114

"Yeah, I know," Peter replied. "My dad's the same way when it comes to taking care of the pool. He can spend hours at it. And I'm not even sure what he does."

"Well, what do you wanna do tonight?" Ken asked.

"I want to talk to you about something," Peter started, his voice shifting to a more serious tone. However, he wasn't sure how to direct the conversation toward the disease and the possibility that his mother could die if they couldn't find donors to give blood. He had rehearsed his conversation repeatedly, but now that Ken was here, he couldn't figure out whether his rehearsed speech would work or if something better would do.

Ken, having noticed Peter's hesitation, asked, "What's up? Something bothering you?"

Peter, continuing to meditate for a couple of seconds more, looked up at Ken and asked, "Do you know your blood type?"

"Sure," he replied. "Remember last year in biology when we were doing that exercise on genetics? Mr. Caldwell tested our blood to see what our blood types were."

"Oh yeah," Peter answered. "I remember the exercise, but I forgot what the results were. So, what's your blood type?"

Ken had begun to question Peter's actions. He thought that his friend sure was acting strange. Finally, he answered, "I'm type B—like you, if my memory serves me correctly."

"Yeah," Peter replied. "I found out that I'm type B also."

There was a long silence as neither boy knew what to say next. Peter didn't know how to continue the conversation, and Ken didn't know where Peter was coming from with his question. Suddenly, Ken said in a loud tone, "Don't tell me that you're worried about that dumb blood disease I've been hearing about on the news. You have type B blood, and the news said that we're immune and can't catch the stupid bug."

"I know," Peter said in a soft tone, trying to get Ken to talk in a lower tone. He was afraid that someone in the house might hear them. "Come on," Peter said as he got up off the lawn chair and headed over to the deck by the pool. Ken, not sure of what was going on, followed, mostly because Peter was his best friend, but partly out of sheer curiosity as to what Peter was up to.

When they were settled on the deck, Peter turned to Ken. "Listen," he said, looking around to see if anyone was within hearing distance. His primary concern was that either Beth or his mom might overhear them. He didn't want to have to explain what he was talking about with Ken. "I know I can't catch the disease," he started. He paused as he looked deep into Ken's eyes. "But my mom and Beth can."

Ken just sat there looking at Peter, not knowing what to say, which for Ken was a bit unusual. He had heard the news about the disease but didn't know anyone who had died from the disease. It's strange how you hear about bad news affecting people you don't know, and you don't think much about it until the bad news affects someone whom you are close to. Finally, after several seconds of silence, all Ken could say was "Wow."

"My dad and I have been talking," Peter continued in a soft tone, "about my mom and what to do if she catches the virus. He said that some people at work said if someone catches the Sanguis virus, they could survive if they get regular blood transfusions of good blood."

"That's great," said Ken, not understanding why Peter was acting so dismal.

"That's what you think," Peter said, causing Ken's eyes to open wider. "According to my dad, all the blood banks are empty of noncontaminated blood. There aren't enough donors. Either they don't want to give, or their blood is already contaminated, so the blood banks won't take it."

"Man, that's bad news," replied Ken. He stared into the distance as if looking for a glimmer of hope.

"There isn't much hope from what I can tell. I did some research on the internet and found out how to transfer blood from one person to another. I also found out how to test for blood type."

Ken listened intently as Peter continued to explain the details he had found online. When Peter appeared to have finished his summary, Ken was more confused than ever. "What are you going to do?" he asked with great curiosity. And then with a touch of sarcasm, he added, "Open your own blood bank so that you can get blood for your mom?"

Peter again paused and looked around to verify that no one was within hearing distance. "No," he replied, disgusted because of Ken's sarcastic remark, "the only donors who would work are kids who have not reached puberty. They are the only ones who would not be affected yet.

The problem is, where do we find these kids, and how do we get them to donate their blood?" He paused to let this question settle into Ken's brain. "My dad thought we could take in some homeless kids in exchange for their blood, but that would require us to take in at least eight kids. And there is no way we can get that many kids in our house. I don't think we could afford it either. That's a lot of mouths to feed."

Ken and Peter sat on the edge of the deck with their feet dangling in the pool, trying to determine a way to get the blood they needed.

Ken cocked his head as an idea came to his mind. His idea wasn't exactly legal, but what Peter and his father were thinking about doing wasn't exactly legal either. He didn't know what Peter would think of the idea, so he decided just to present it.

"I know what you can do," Ken said proudly.

"What?" Peter asked, hoping that Ken had a good idea. Ken was a nice guy who was friendly and was fun to be with, but usually, he didn't have the greatest ideas.

"Well," Ken said, continuing to formulate the idea, "why don't you find some kids, put them to sleep, and take their blood? If they are asleep, they won't know the difference."

"I don't know," Peter said reluctantly as he thought of stealing blood from kids. "It sounds wrong." He basically would have to kidnap some kid, put the kid to sleep, somehow stick a needle in his or her arm, and take his or her blood. It not only seemed wrong but also sounded impossible to do without getting into a lot of trouble.

"It would be easy," Ken continued his explanation. "We just wander around some section of town, and when we see a kid who is alone, we can quietly walk up behind him and use that liquid stuff they use on TV to put him to sleep."

"You mean chloroform," Peter interrupted, having an idea that this was what Ken was referring to. "But that only happens in the movies."

"That's what?" Ken questioned. He hadn't been listening to Peter as he was concentrating on how to set up the plan to get blood from kids.

"That liquid used to put people to sleep is called chloroform," Peter explained.

"Well, what do you think I am," Ken kind of snapped, "some sort of pharmacist?"

"No," Peter snapped back, "but if you're going to dream up a plan, you'd better know what you need to pull it off."

"Well, can you get chloroform?" Ken asked.

"I can look," Peter replied in frustration, not sure he wanted to waste time looking for a substance to use for doing something that only happened in the movies. He had spent a lot of time on the internet and had concluded that one could get almost anything over the internet. But chloroform? He was sure this chemical had some sort of government control and would be almost impossible to get.

"Anyway," Ken said in a long, drawn-out way. He was a little frustrated about having his plan interrupted and wanted to get back to his idea. "We can put them to sleep." Ken paused to continue building on his concept. "Can you get the stuff we would need to determine their blood types?"

"Yes," Peter replied, not sure he wanted Ken to elaborate.

"We test a kid's blood," Ken continued with his idea, "and if it's a match, we carry the kid back to your house and give your mom a blood transfusion. When we're finished, we take the kid back to where we got him from and let him sleep the rest of the night away."

Peter sat there for a short time thinking about the plan he had just heard. It sounded simple, but there would be some small problems they would have to work out. But it might work. "We would need to have some sort of a wagon to take the kid back to my house," Peter responded, trying to follow Ken's line of thinking. "I don't want to carry some hundred-pound kid all the way home and then take him back again."

"That's a good idea," Ken said, continuing to run through the plan in his head. "And if any of the kids are not a match, we just leave them in a comfortable position and let them sleep it off. We'll have to be careful with the chloroform because we don't want to put ourselves to sleep." He laughed a bit as he thought of a movie. "Yeah." Ken chuckled, thinking about three kids lying on the ground somewhere, all asleep because he and Peter had been careless with the chemical. "We would have to make sure we always carried some extra chloroform with us in case the kids started to wake up before we got them back to wherever we had picked them up from."

"Yeah, that would be a problem," Peter said, thinking about a kid coming to and asking where the hell he was and how he had gotten there. "It sounds like it might work," Peter concluded, hoping that Ken was right. "But I'm still not sure it's the right thing to do," he continued, his conscience creeping into his thoughts. After all, they would be stealing blood from kids. And what would Peter's mother say about getting a blood transfusion from some kid without the child's consent or knowledge? She would probably have a fit. But if the alternative was dying from the disease, what would she do? Peter also wondered that, were he and Ken to get caught, if they could be charged with kidnapping.

"Do you want your mom to die?" Ken asked in a damning tone as if Peter didn't know what the right thing to do was. "And from what you've said," Ken said in a louder tone, "there's nowhere else to get the blood except from kids. And it's pretty obvious to me that they won't just give it to you. So the only way I can see to keep your mom alive is to steal the blood. It should be okay as long as we don't take all the blood from any one particular kid," Ken said, laughing a bit as he dramatized being a small kid shriveling up as all the blood was drained from his body.

"That's not funny," Peter snapped, thinking of what would happen if they did draw too much blood from some kid. "The kid could die." Or what would happen if they tried to get blood from some kid who wouldn't stop bleeding once they'd taken out the needle? Again, all Peter could think about was that some kid could just die. The thoughts of these scenarios were bothering him, but the mental image of his mom in a casket was something he didn't want to manifest in reality.

"Well, I guess we could at least try it and see what happens," Peter said, finally giving in to the idea that there may not be another way to get blood for his mom. "But remember," he emphasized, "we don't need to do anything until my mom gets the disease, if she ever does."

"Yeah," Ken said. "I hope it doesn't happen, but if it does, you can count on me."

"Also," Peter said in a soft tone, remembering what his father had said about telling Ken too much, "we can't tell a soul. Otherwise, we could end up in a lot of trouble."

"No problem," Ken answered, understanding the seriousness of the situation. If they were to be caught, not only would they be thrown into jail, but also Paula would most likely die from the disease.

The two sat on the deck for a couple of minutes more and then went to get on the computer to see if they could find some chloroform.

CHAPTER 10

It took over two weeks for the chloroform and the blood-typing supplies to come in. So far, the Davisons had been lucky in that Peter's mother had shown no signs of having the disease. In the interim, the news channels seemed to be devoting more and more time to stories associated with the disease and the ramifications it was having on society. The news indicated that there had been more deaths and that more individuals had been diagnosed with having the Sanguis virus. The latest count showed that over seventy-five hundred had contracted the virus in Ohio alone, with over twenty thousand victims in the United States. The progression indicated that if the epidemic were to continue to spread at the same rate it had for the last four weeks, then more than 50 percent of the adults in the United States would contract the virus and die before Christmas. Communications from the medical field indicated there was a strong chance that the predictions would come true. This would result in a decrease of the world's population by over ten million by year's end—all adults. At this rate, the number of unsupervised children between the ages of under one year old to about twelve years old would increase to over a million. With no supervision, a large number of street gangs could spring up, making them uncontrollable, and could cause all sorts of trouble for the authorities. The number of reports of gang violence had increased over 200 percent. These gangs were responsible for an increase in robbery, assault, and arson, especially in or of people's homes. There also had been an increase in gang fights that resulted in the deaths of young people.

The outlook for the future, as impressed by the media, was very dismal, to the point where some were implying that this was the beginning of Armageddon.

As everyone within hearing distance of media listened to the latest news on the disease, Ken and Peter continued to make plans.

"Are you ready?" Ken asked Peter, watching his friend slip a small backpack onto his shoulders.

"Yeah," Peter replied as he tried to straighten out one of the straps that had twisted, "I think I've got everything."

"Okay," Ken said with a touch of enthusiasm, "let's go."

The two boys slipped out the back door on their first dry run to see if their plan for getting blood donors would work. It was after nine o'clock when they headed out. They were dressed in dark clothes and dark shoes to minimize their ability to be seen in the dark. In Peter's backpack was a small bottle of chloroform, the blood test kit, Band-Aids, and smelling salts, just in case. He also had some alcohol wipes to clean the end of the kid's finger. Since he and Ken would be out late, they had brought some snacks and drinks in the backpack, which added to the weight.

Their original plan was to go over to the Lakota Cliff apartment complex since the kids there were usually running around late at night. As they headed out, their goal was to see how many kids were running around and how hard it would be to put one to sleep to test his or her blood. With type A blood being fairly rare, the odds were that they would find one possible donor out of every ten kids they tested. So tonight, again, was a dry run to see what kind of problems they might encounter. They had been working on the details for over a week, trying to visualize any possible problems that could crop up. They also had discussed what they needed to take with them. No matter how hard they had worked on planning this excursion, they felt they were still missing something.

"I'm scared," said Peter in a soft whisper. It was hard for him to speak as his lower lip was quivering in fear.

"I know." Ken acknowledged having the same feelings, but he would never admit it to anyone other than himself. "But this is going to be interesting. I mean, it's kind of like being an undercover spy or something, and we're out to save the world, or at least a small part of it if your mother ever catches the disease."

"I hope she doesn't," Peter replied with a tone of helplessness, "but according to the TV, it's not a question of if she'll catch the disease; it's more like when will she catch it."

They continued through some of the backyards of their neighborhood over to the apartment complex. They figured it would take about fifteen minutes to walk there in the dark. This dry run didn't include the dragging of the noisy wagon that they would use to transport the donors back to the house. For now, they wanted to see how well they could travel in the dark without the wagon.

As they approached the street, they both crouched down behind some bushes to see if anyone was outside before they attempted to cross the street. "It looks clear," Ken whispered after one last look around. "I don't like that streetlight over there. It makes it too bright. We should either find another way or bust the light."

"What do you have in mind?" Peter asked in a sarcastic tone. "Shoot out the light?"

"Hey!" Ken exclaimed as if he'd just had a great idea. "That's not a bad idea. I have that small .22-caliber rifle. I could shoot that light out from here." Ken didn't believe in shooting animals, but he had learned to shoot as a Boy Scout and had discovered that he was a good shot.

"Yeah, and have every one of the neighbors hear the shot and the breaking glass," Peter said, attacking his friend's idea. "I'm sorry," he announced in a low tone of authority, "we're not going to go around and shoot out streetlights to make it easier for us to get around. It's just too dangerous, and we don't want to get caught. It wouldn't take the police long to figure out what we're up to with the stuff that's in this backpack."

"I guess," Ken said in a defeated tone. "You're right."

"Well, then let's go to the end of the block and cut across to that field down there," Ken directed as he was pointing in a southerly direction. "I don't see any lights down there."

"Okay," Peter said. He backed up and retraced his steps toward the backyard, with Ken close behind.

As they crossed the street and entered the tall grass that covered the field at the back of the apartment complex, they could hear kids running around outside. The complex had plenty of lights for the parking areas, but there was little or no lighting facing the back areas. However, when it got dark, the kids migrated to the front of the apartments and played where there were more lights.

"We can get real close without having to worry about being seen if we stay in this tall grass," Ken said.

"Yeah," Peter responded, "but watch your step. You have no idea of what might be in this tall grass. All we need to do now is to step in a hole and break a leg."

"That would really suck on our first patrol," Ken said. He liked to visualize himself as a marine out in the woods hunting for the enemy, only they were looking for the prize that would save Peter's mother.

As the two boys approached the edge of the grassy area, they could see several kids playing Frisbee at the end of the apartment building in the center. They continued to creep slowly through the tall grass to the far end of the apartment building on their right. "Look over there," Peter said in a low whisper, pointing to a young boy sitting on the side of a sandbox. "He looks to be about ten years old. And there is no one else around. You think we should try him?"

"Well," Ken said, a touch of excitement in his voice, "we've got to do it to someone, so it might as well be him."

"Okay," Peter uttered in a soft whisper, slipping off the backpack. He opened it up and took out some of the supplies they had brought. First, he pulled out a Ziploc bag with a soft white washcloth inside. "Here," he said, handing the washcloth to Ken. "You'll need this and this," he said, handing Ken the small bottle of chloroform. He then pulled out a pair of thin gloves, which he handed to Ken. They didn't know what kind of problems they may encounter, but they wanted to be safe by not leaving any fingerprints. The last thing Peter pulled out was a baseball glove and a ball.

"Okay," Ken said, preparing to give a summary of the instructions, "you take the baseball glove and ball and walk in front of him. When you get his attention, I'll come up from behind him and apply the chloroform to his face."

"Right," Peter agreed, looking over the area in front of the kid.

"And once he's out," Ken continued, "you come and help carry him back over here, where you will test his blood."

"Okay," Peter said again. "Remember, don't apply the chloroform to the cloth until we are in position, and then don't hold it too close to

123

your face." With a small chuckle, he added, "We want him to go to sleep, not you."

"I know, I know," Ken came back, giving his friend a dirty look. What did Peter think, that Ken was stupid or something?

Ken made his way through the tall grass to a point right behind the young boy. His heart, which was racing very fast, sounded so loud in his ears that he was afraid that the boy might hear him. He had to walk carefully so as not to step on something that would make a lot of noise. He kept an eye on the boy to see if the boy had spotted, but so far, so good. As he approached his intended position, he paused and took a deep breath. With his stomach a little on the queasy side, he was trying not to get sick. This wasn't a good spot to throw up the hamburger he'd eaten earlier that evening.

He reached his point of attack and knelt down on the ground to get ready. He was about fifteen feet from where the boy was sitting on the edge of a homemade sandbox and playing quietly in the sand, building a castle that looked like something out of a fairy tale. Ken could see only a small part of it as the boy was in the way, but from what he could see, this boy had a talent for working with sand.

Ken took the washcloth out of the plastic bag and slipped the bag back into his pocket. With the cloth in one hand and the bottle of chloroform in the other, he quickly applied the chloroform to the washcloth. Now ready to go, he raised his hand to signal Peter that he was ready.

In the meantime, Peter was waiting in the tall grass for Ken's signal. His stomach was giving him problems, and he hoped the discomfort would go away, but he doubted it would. His left hand was sweating profusely in the baseball glove. He wished this was over. But he knew he had to do something to help his mom if she ever caught the disease. If a blood transfusion would help, then that was what he was prepared to do.

Peter saw the signal from Ken indicating that he was ready. He wondered if anyone in the complex could see the white washcloth flying back and forth over by the tall grass like a flag of surrender. Peter took one more quick look to see if anyone was around. The coast looked clear. He stood up and walked the two steps out of the tall grass. He tossed the ball into the air, catching each volley. He just hoped that he wouldn't drop the ball. That would be a disaster if he were to go chasing after the ball with Ken standing there, waiting for him to help to move the boy.

Ken saw Peter step out of the tall grass onto the asphalt of the parking lot. The boy didn't look up, which caused Ken concern. All Ken could do was to keep waiting for the boy to look up. However, he had to make a move soon or else Peter would be on the other side of the parking lot and out of the scene. The young boy still didn't look up. Ken knew he had to do something fast; otherwise, this whole event would be a waste of time. *Okay,* he thought to himself, *here goes.*

Ever so lightly, Ken stepped out of the cover of the tall grass and crept toward the young boy. The boy still didn't see Peter. But then the boy didn't seem to know that Ken was there either, which was good as far as he was concerned. He paused for a second as he heard some kids over on the other side of the parking lot yelling, "You're it." He was concerned that he and Peter might soon have some uninvited company. However, everything appeared to be safe.

Ken continued his advance. He was now only three feet away. He looked up and saw Peter crossing about twenty feet away. Taking one more step, he was now only two feet away. His heart was racing so fast that he thought it would explode through his chest. One more step. It was now or never. He quickly reached around the boy and placed the washcloth over his face. At the same time, Ken dropped to one knee and put his other arm around the boy to limit his struggling.

It seemed to take hours for the chloroform to do its thing. But in reality, it was only about two seconds before the boy relaxed in Ken's arms, indicating that he was now asleep. With a great sigh of relief, Ken slowly removed the washcloth from the boy's face. He had to be careful not to leave it there too long for fear the chloroform might put the boy to sleep permanently.

Peter arrived at about the same time the boy went under. "Quick!" he commanded. "Let's get him over to the tall grass." Ken stuffed the washcloth into his pants pocket and put his hands under the boy's arms. Peter put the baseball into his pocket, placed the glove on the boy's stomach, and grabbed his legs. As they lifted him, the pole-bearers quickly carried the boy to the tall grass.

Once in the grass, the two quickly looked behind them to see if they had been spotted. The sound of the kids at the other end of the parking lot hadn't changed. There were no parents outside yelling for their kids to come in. "It looks like we did it," Peter whispered with a big smile on his face.

"Yeah," Ken replied, a little out of breath. He felt as if he had held his breath from the time he left the tall grass until the boy went to sleep.

"Okay," Ken said. "You know what to do, so test his blood."

Peter quickly grabbed the backpack and removed a white plastic kit about the size of a small first aid kit. Inside were three small bottles containing the antigens needed to test for blood type, along with several sterile glass slides. Finished with that, he handed the backpack to Ken, who reached in and pulled out a Band-Aid and some small packets of alcohol wipes. "All right," Peter said, still with a slight tone of fear as he started the blood-typing process, "grab a finger, and clean it off with one of the alcohol wipes."

"Wait," Ken said with a chuckle, pulling the white washcloth from his pocket. "I had better put this back into the bag before we put ourselves to sleep."

"Good thinking." Peter laughed softly. "It wouldn't be a good idea to go to sleep now with all this stuff here."

"Well," Ken said, opening the alcohol wipe, "which finger do you want to use?"

"I don't care," Peter replied, a little annoyed since they had discussed each step of this operation in great detail before this night's excursion. They had agreed that Ken would just pick a finger and wipe it off with the alcohol.

"Okay." Reaching for the boy's right hand, Ken cleaned the middle finger with the alcohol wipe. "Look, he's flicking you off," Ken said sarcastically.

Frustrated and nervous, Peter reprimanded Ken for his lack of seriousness. However, Ken's humor was helping him to relax a little.

"Sorry," Ken apologized. He held out the boy's hand, allowing Peter to start the extraction process.

Peter carefully twisted the end off the gray-colored lancet that was to be used to pierce the skin. He placed the lancet against the tip of the boy's finger and pushed on the small release button. A soft click could be heard that, to Ken and Peter, seemed to echo throughout the complex. The sharp point extended from the end with enough force to penetrate the boy's skin. Peter quickly removed the lancet, at which point a small drop of blood formed on the end of the boy's finger. Peter carefully took the glass slide and lightly touched the small dome of blood to make three small spots of blood on the glass slide.

"Okay," he said to Ken, "go ahead and put on a Band-Aid while I test his blood." The lack of light was making it hard to see. But since they had been in the dark, their eyes had become accustomed to the small amount of light that was coming from one of the lights in the parking lot. Peter applied a drop of A antigen on the first drop of blood and waited to see if there was a reaction. But no reaction occurred. Next, he applied a drop of the B antigen to the second drop of blood. Again, there was no reaction. This indicated that the boy's blood was type O. Peter didn't even try the third test to determine if the boy's blood was positive or negative. "Well," he said, a little disappointed with the results, wanting to swear but refraining from doing so, he is type O.

"So," Ken summarized, "I guess he's not going to work."

"No, I don't think so," Peter replied. He started putting the various supplies back into the backpack.

"Shit!" Ken said, realizing for the first time that not every kid they put to sleep would have the blood type they sought and that they may have to do this many times to find a donor.

"Okay," Peter said, slipping on the backpack, "let's get this kid back over to the edge of the sandbox before he's missed or he starts to wake up."

Just as Peter lifted the boy's legs, Ken cried out in a loud, panicky whisper, "Get down! Someone's coming."

They both dropped to the ground and peeked through the tall grass at an adult male who had come out of the door at the end of the apartment complex. The boys didn't move a muscle for fear they may be spotted. The man walked over to a small blue two-door car parked under one of the lights in the parking lot. Although Peter and Ken didn't recognize him, they gauged that the gentleman was in his midtwenties. He opened the car door and climbed in, apparently unaware that he was being watched by two shadows in the grass. Peter and Ken heard him start up the car, and then suddenly two bright headlights came on, shining intensely right at the two boys in the grass.

"Duck," Ken ordered in a soft tone. He buried his head in the grass close to the ground, as did Peter. Their biggest fear was the potential visibility of the white T-shirt the boy was wearing. All they could do was hope that the driver of the car didn't get suspicious of some white object in the grass.

It was only about twenty seconds, but it seemed more like twenty minutes, before the driver started to back the car out of his parking spot and the bright lights moved away from their position. "Damn, that was close," Ken proclaimed, rising from his prone position.

"Yeah," Peter said in a soft whisper, shaking from the ordeal. "I guess next time we had better get a little farther away so no one can see us. But right now we need to get this kid back over to the sandbox and get the hell out of here."

"Agreed." Ken did an extensive search of the area for anyone who might be around.

Peter also looked around and carefully checked each window in the apartment building to make sure no one was looking out. "It looks like the coast is clear," he said, grabbing the boy's legs.

"Looks good to me, too," Ken said, lifting the boy from under his shoulders. The two quickly walked back over to the sandbox and laid the boy down in a comfortable position to let him sleep off the chloroform. Then they quickly headed back to the tall grass. Ken thought the boy looked as if he might be dreaming of a life in his fairy-tale sandcastle.

Once in the grass, the two stopped to look around again to see if they had been spotted, but all was quiet. "Okay," Peter said, still having the feeling of being watched, "let's get the hell out of here."

"I'm right behind you." They cut across the field.

"Man, that was scary," Peter said, using his normal voice for the first time since they had set out on their excursion. "I wonder if it will get any easier after we do this several times."

"I don't know," Ken responded. "It was scary at times, but I think it was cool that we were able to just go up and grab this kid, put him out, and test his blood without anyone knowing about it."

"Well, I hope no one ever learns about it," Peter said, concerned that they may be discovered someday. The fear of what the law would do to them made him feel very uneasy about the whole ordeal.

"Like I want to get caught," Ken said in a sarcastic tone. He paused a couple of seconds before continuing. "Which is why we should do it again."

"What?" Peter asked in a surprised tone, "Are you crazy? Wasn't that scary enough?"

"No," Ken said, replying to Peter's first question, "and yes, it was scary. However, sooner or later we may have to do this for real, so we need to have attempted this exercise several times to see if we need to make any changes. Like tonight, we should have retreated deeper into the tall grass. We may even want to bring a dark blanket just in case our donor is wearing something white, like that kid."

Peter paused for several seconds as he massaged Ken's comment in his brain. "Okay," he said in defeat, realizing that Ken was right. He didn't like the idea, but soon they may have to do this for real, and the more practice they got, the better they would be at finding donors without getting caught. "Well then, where do you want to go?"

"I don't know," Ken replied, "but I do know that we shouldn't go in a circle around our houses. The cops might think the ones kidnapping these kids are in the middle of that circle, so let's not give them the right place to look."

The thought of the cops looking for them gave Peter a cold feeling. He knew it was just fear and was afraid to let Ken know, especially since his friend seemed to be a little more relaxed about the whole situation. Peter just didn't like the idea of looking over his shoulder to see who could be following them.

"Let's go over to Carmel Street," Ken said. An idea came to his mind. "We can travel through the woods behind those houses and see if anyone is hanging around outside." Ken thought this area would be easier to travel since most houses didn't have backyard lights on. And if they did, and if the boys were in the woods, odds were that the light wouldn't be bright enough for them to be seen. Also, they would be less likely to have a car light shine on them in the woods.

"Okay," Peter said, not knowing what other options to explore. He followed Ken down the street the short distance to Carmel Street. The first problem they had to overcome was where to go from the street up into the woods behind the houses without being seen. There was no reason for someone to be cutting through the yards to get to the woods unless it was someone who was going hunting. Otherwise, it would be someone looking to cause problems. Since it wasn't hunting season, that left few other options to use as an excuse if they were to get caught.

"Ken," Peter said, "what should we say if someone catches us back in the woods?"

"We'll tell them my dog got loose and we saw him run into the woods," Ken replied after he had thought about it for several seconds. "Everyone around here has dogs, so it shouldn't be a big thing to see one running loose."

"What kind of dog are we looking for?" Peter asked, trying to think of what someone might ask them if they got caught.

"I have that little white dog," Ken said, referring to the little white ball of a dog at Ken's house that always loved to get attention.

"What kind of mutt is he?" Peter asked, not remembering.

"He's a bichon," Ken said.

Peter paused for several seconds as he tried to walk through a scenario in his head. "Okay, I guess that will work, but I hope we don't have to use it."

"Hey," Ken said, pointing up the street, "those two houses on the curve are dark, and from the street, it will be hard for the other houses to see us." Ken was referring to two houses one of which had some large bushes lining part of the driveway. That would provide them excellent cover.

Ken and Peter walked very slow as they approached the driveway of the first dark house. They were looking around for anyone who might see them. It wasn't uncommon to see joggers or someone walking a dog at this time of night, especially in this small housing community. "Let's go," Ken said. The two darted up the driveway and crouched down at the side of the garage.

"Whoa!" Ken said suddenly as he approached the back corner of the garage. It would probably have been a good idea to check out the area first, because in the backyard was a large German shepherd, which started barking in their direction. "Come on," Ken said in a loud whisper, motioning for Peter to follow him. They dashed for the woods with the dog barking as if it would bite their heads off if it hadn't been chained up to the tree in the backyard.

The two reached the woods and ran several yards past the edge just to get out of sight of anyone who might come and investigate the dog's barking. "Okay, now what?" Peter asked, confused as to what they should do next, and panting hard from the run and from the fear that now had put a lump in his throat. He was all for giving up and going back home, but he felt that Ken was enjoying the adventure.

"Come on," Ken said in an enthusiastic tone, "let's go down toward the other end of the street and see if there is anyone outside." They walked in the direction Ken had indicated, but it was difficult to see where they were going. The darkness of the night and the darkness of the woods made it easy to stumble over downed sticks or large roots. Their biggest fear was stepping into some raccoon burrow and breaking an ankle. What would happen if one of them had to help the other out of the woods? Everyone would be asking questions as to why they had been there in the first place, and the boys didn't want to answer any of those questions.

Ken, seeming more sure of his step, walked through the woods a little faster than Peter. Ken stopped, knelt by a large maple tree, and peered into the distance. Peter took a couple of seconds to catch up and join him. "What's up?" he whispered, looking past the tree in the direction Ken was looking.

"Look," Ken whispered, pointing to a girl sitting on the steps of her porch. "I put her at about ten to eleven years old." She appeared to be writing in a small book.

Peter's adrenaline started pumping again as he saw another possible donor. "Okay, but how do I get her attention so that you can get up behind her?" Peter asked, concerned because this situation was very different from that of their first run. "Also, what about the possibility of the parents coming out of the house? You'll have to get awfully close to the house to get her."

"Piece of cake," Ken said with confidence. "I'll tell you what I want you to do. Go down to the other side of that shed, and then pretend to fall and get hurt. Then, call that girl for help. But don't call out too loud; we don't want her parents to come out."

"Yeah, but what happens if she runs into the house and calls her parents?" Peter questioned Ken's plan. "I don't want to explain why I'm lying in their yard pretending to be hurt."

Ken just shook his head as if he didn't believe Peter could be so stupid. "If she goes into the house, you get up and run down the edge of the woods toward the other end of the street. And I'll go this way," Ken said, indicating the opposite direction from where he would have Peter exit the scene.

"Easy for you to say," Peter said, not sure he wanted to attempt this.

"But," Ken continued, "if she does come toward you, then I will slip around the other side of the shed and put her to sleep. Then we can simply carry her to the area behind the shed and test her blood."

It sounded feasible to Peter if the girl indeed did come over to see him, but he still didn't like the idea of what might happen if she went into the house and they had to beat feet to get out of there. "All right," he finally agreed as he put on the rubber gloves. Ken did the same and took out the white washcloth, which still smelled a bit like the chloroform. "I guess I'm as ready as I ever will be," Peter said, getting up and heading to the far side of the shed.

Peter took a deep breath and then stepped past the shed so the girl on the porch steps could see him. Then, with dramatic execution, he took a massive fall, groaned softly, and held his ankle in pain.

Peter looked up and noticed that his groan was enough to catch the attention of the girl on the steps. "Can you help me?" he asked in a soft whisper, loud enough for the girl to hear him. He hoped with all his heart that no one else would hear him. To his surprise, the girl quickly got up and ran over to where he was sitting on the ground. She looked to be about eleven. She had long blonde hair and was dressed in a short skirt and a T-shirt. She wasn't very tall. Peter was wondering if she might be over a hundred pounds. But before he could do anything else, a hand came around the girl's face. She quickly fell asleep after a minor struggle.

"Quick!" Ken said, fearing that they may be spotted. "Grab her feet!" The two carried the girl to the area behind the shed. "Okay," Ken said, "start the test." Peter sat down by the girl's head while Ken sat down by her side. They prepared to test her blood.

Peter again took out the glass slides and the antigens to test her blood. Ken did his part by wiping off the end of her finger and holding it out for Peter to puncture. After the blood was withdrawn, Ken applied a small Band-Aid as he'd done with the boy earlier that night. Peter quickly tested the blood and discovered that the girl was also type O and, therefore, would be of no value to them.

"Well," Peter said, putting the supplies back into the backpack, "let's carry her back to the porch."

"Okay," Ken said, but he was intrigued by the young girl's long legs. "Hey," he said, "watch this." He slid his hand up to the edge of her skirt and pulled it up, revealing a pair of Barbie panties. "I didn't know girls this age still wore this kind of underwear," he said with a chuckle.

"Stop that," Peter said in a stern tone. "We are not doing this for your enjoyment."

"I know," Ken agreed, "but don't you think it's kind of neat that we could do just about anything we wanted to her and she'd never know?"

"Yeah," Peter replied in an authoritative tone. "Well, we are not going to be doing anything to her."

Ken never had a sister and never really knew much about younger girls. Unlike Peter, who had a younger sister, Ken's exposure to the female sex was basically with Laura, who had helped him learn plenty.

Peter didn't like what Ken was doing or saying, and he didn't understand why Ken didn't feel the same way he did. To Ken, here lay a young girl who was asleep and would never know if they did anything or not. "Haven't you ever wondered what it would be like to have an opportunity like this?" Ken asked, lightly sliding his finger up and down over the girl's crotch area.

"Stop that!" Peter said, almost loud enough to be heard at the house. "And no," he said with emphasis, "I have a sister, and that's like playing with her. And that's just not right."

"I know," Ken said, continuing to caress the girl's genital area. "But she's not your sister, and she'll never know that I'm doing this."

"Yeah," Peter said in a stern tone, "but I know, and I said stop it."

To Ken, this seemed like an opportunity to explore a situation that normally would get him into a lot of trouble. But in this situation, he could do almost whatever he wanted with no consequences, as long as Peter told no one and as long as Ken himself did nothing that would indicate that the girl had been touched. Ken sensed a type of power he had never experienced before—and here was an opportunity to experience it. This new power was hard for him to ignore.

"Ah," Ken said in a devilish tone. "Wouldn't you like to take a peek?" he asked, grabbing the Barbie waistband and pulling the girl's panties down enough to see some light-colored pubic hairs.

"That's it," Peter said, disgusted, "I'm leaving."

Power without authority can lead to losing control of one's actions. In this case, Peter's moral conscience was the authority that helped limit Ken's immoral actions. But without this authority, how far would Ken have gone to continue feeling this kind of power over someone?

Ken could see Peter wasn't interested in exploring this power over others that was available for them to explore. "Okay, okay," Ken said, letting the waistband snap back into position, "you're a party pooper." He didn't want to give in and abandon this power he was experiencing, but deep down he knew Peter was right.

"I'll take her legs," Peter said. He got up and walked around Ken to get the girl's feet. He didn't want Ken to grab her feet and look up her skirt, and he wanted no more comments about it either.

"Okay, okay," Ken said. He stood up and reached down to grab the girl beneath her shoulders.

After a quick check of the area, they quickly walked over to the patio and placed the girl on the steps as if she had fallen asleep. The book she'd been writing in was lying next to her feet. They placed the pencil next to the girl's hand as if it had simply fallen out.

"Okay, let's go," Ken whispered. The two headed back into the woods to head home.

They took awhile to return to the place where they had entered the woods. They were quiet so as not to draw any attention from the dog they had passed earlier. They took one last look around to see if anyone was nearby and then made a reverse dash back to the street.

"Hey, Peter," Ken said as they were walking down the side street close to Peter's house. "I'm sorry about what I did to that girl back there," Ken apologized. "It felt strange that I could do that and, for all practical purposes, get away with it."

"Yeah, not only was that wrong," Peter said, scowling him, "but it's not what we are out here to do."

"I know," Ken said, holding his head down, a little ashamed that he actually had done it. "I suppose the situation got the better of me." He kind of enjoyed the power that stemmed from the knowledge that he could do just about anything he wanted to her. But on the other hand, he had this stone in his stomach, knowing that what he'd done was wrong.

"Well, I don't want it to happen again," Peter ordered, accepting Ken's attempt at an apology for his actions.

"It won't," Ken said with conviction. "I'll help you to get blood donors and that's all. No more fantasies."

"Okay," Peter said, relieved that Ken would behave himself. "Let's go to my house and watch a late movie."

CHAPTER 11

Peter was sitting on the couch, reading more information about transfusions that he had found on the internet, when his mother called everyone to dinner. Peter put the stack of papers on the couch and went to the table. Beth came bouncing down the stairs, still wearing her bathing suit from having gone swimming earlier that day with some friends. John was half asleep in the recliner, but he roused and came to the supper table once Paula announced dinner. The TV was on, but apparently no one was watching the Lifetime movie except Paula, who would take quick glances as she prepared dinner. John looked up at the kitchen clock and noticed that the evening news was coming on, so he took the remote and changed it to Channel Twelve to catch the local news.

"John," Paula called out in disappointment, "I was watching that."

"I'm sorry," John apologized in a soft tone, "I didn't know you were watching it." John looked back at the television but didn't change the channel back to the Lifetime movie. "It's time for the evening news," he continued in a whining tone, trying to justify his actions. "You know I watch the news every night."

"All right," Paula said, giving in to John's plaintive comment. Indeed, John usually did watch the evening news. Besides, Paula felt that if she tried to argue her way back into watching the movie, it would upset John and eventually the rest of the family.

As the family settled down at the dinner table, Paula continued to bring the dishes out and set them down. She finally sat down herself, and the family enjoyed the dinner.

John wasn't paying a lot of attention to the newscaster as she was talking about some accident that had happened on Martin Road. "Some young kids were driving too fast and lost control." John had started to take another bite of his baked chicken when the announcer said, "The latest on the BARD epidemic. The epidemic continues to grow here in the tristate area, as well as across the US. There have been over nine hundred deaths in the local area alone, and the national numbers have reached over fifty thousand and are climbing. It's almost impossible to get an accurate count since the number continues to increase at a rate of more than one death an hour. Scientists are still puzzled as to how to treat this disease."

John just sat there thinking of the thousands of people who had died and especially of those who had died in the local area. He was wondering about all the blood samples he had delivered to the hospital for testing. How many were positive for the Sanguis virus with the people now dead or dying? What about those who had just discovered they had the Sanguis virus and would die soon? He looked over at Paula, who was talking to Beth about coupons they could use when they went shopping. He wondered how long it would be before they too would have their names on the list of the dead. He lost his appetite as he continued to think about losing his family.

The newscaster brought John's mind back to the room he was in when she said something about the police and stray kids. "The number of children who have lost their parents but who have not contracted the Sanguis virus themselves has risen. These kids are free to do whatever mischief they want. There are too many for the local police to handle. They have been blamed for many break-ins, many fires, destruction of many properties, and numerous attacks against each other. The problem has risen to the point that the governor has called out the National Guard to help police patrol the streets and keep order. There is now a curfew, and no one, especially young kids, is allowed out on the streets after eight o'clock. If any kids are out after curfew, the police have orders to round them up and take them to various local schools, where supervision has been set up to watch these kids and provide some form of order. There, they will be provided food, clothes if needed, and a place to sleep until more permanent arrangements can be made."

John couldn't think of what kind of arrangements could be made when thousands of people were dying of the disease and leaving their young children behind. There weren't going to be enough adults left to take care of the large number of orphaned kids.

"The police have also registered an increase in kidnappings of younger children," the newscaster continued. This immediately caught John's attention. He gave Peter a quick kick under the table. Peter looked at his father with a questioning expression, wondering what the hell he was doing kicking him. He hadn't been doing anything wrong. John nodded his head ever so slightly toward the TV, enough for Peter to get the message, but not so dramatic as to catch Paula's attention. Peter turned around and looked at the TV as the announcer continued the story.

"Police have indicated that the number of kidnappings has increased over the last two weeks," continued the newscaster. "There have been so many that the police haven't been able to keep up with the reports. Detectives working on the cases have indicated that most of these abductions are related to the desire to obtain noncontaminated blood. Many of the kidnapped kids have been located close to their homes, and many were wearing a Band-Aid on one of their arms. Police think there are gangs kidnapping kids, stealing their blood, and then letting their victims loose afterward. This blood has been found to sell for as much as five thousand dollars a pint. Unfortunately, these gangs may be responsible for the deaths of twelve kids so far due to the removal of too much blood. Jamie Bottoms of Anderson Township was found dead last night, lying on the back steps of the library. An autopsy indicated that she had had more than three pints of blood removed from her body. Police believe she had three different individuals take blood from her, not knowing that she had been a donor earlier. The police ask that everyone keep their children within sight at all times, especially at night."

There were others out there at night looking for blood donors. That meant not only that he and Ken would have competition for donors, but also that parents would be watching a lot closer to make sure their kids didn't become a target for these blood collectors. Unfortunately, that meant Peter too.

As Peter played with his broccoli, his mind drifted to the night he and Ken had gone on the prowl for blood donors. They hadn't been successful in finding a donor that matched Peter's mother's blood type, just two kids, one in a sandbox and one sitting on the porch steps. Would the girl's parents now require her to stay inside, where she couldn't be abducted? And what about the boy in the sandbox? Would his parents also require him to stay inside? Peter didn't know whether he and Ken could find donors or not. He just wasn't sure what to do. Finally, he gulped down the broccoli, disliking its taste, and got up from the table to head to his room to think more about the situation.

John was still sitting at the table watching the news. "The price of gas has jumped again as the supply continues to diminish," continued the newscaster. "Many refineries have stopped production or have drastically decreased operations due to the decrease in manpower. Many workers have refused to go to work for fear of catching the disease. Some small businesses have had to shut down because of the number of deaths within their business. This is having a ripple effect on the rest of the economy as prices across the board have started to climb because of a decrease in manpower. On the other hand, several small businesses have started to prosper. Doctors' offices are reporting a major increase in patients, along with an increase in drug sales. Unfortunately, there is also an increase in business for mortuaries and businesses that manufacture coffins and headstones."

This bothered John. How was this going to affect his job? With this epidemic going on, there were lots of blood tests being requested, which meant there were lots of samples that had to be picked up and delivered to the hospital for testing. But with the increase in the cost of gas, would they cut their costs by eliminating one driver? He just didn't know, but the whole situation made him feel uneasy. He looked over at Paula and waited for her to finish talking to Beth.

"Honey?" John said, trying to get his wife's attention.

"Yes?" Paula said.

"I was wondering," he started, but he paused as he tried to compile his thoughts, which seemed more difficult with all the problems being presented on the news. "Have the prices for groceries been going up over the last couple of weeks?"

"Are you kidding?" she said in a mocking tone. "The price of milk is almost four dollars a gallon, and the cheap ordinary hamburger is as expensive as the steak I bought at the beginning of summer. It's absolutely ridiculous," she cried out. "If the prices keep going up as they have been, I'll have to make my own bread and butter—and that's all we're going to have to live on. Either that or we're both going to have to get second jobs just to pay for food. I mean, it's absolutely ridiculous what they're charging nowadays. That's why I'm looking at coupons, to try to make our food money go further."

"Okay," John said, trying to get her to calm down, "I was only asking."

"Yeah," Paula continued as she got up to clear the table, "and have you seen the price of gas?"

This was a silly question since John spent most of his time driving a car, which meant he had to stop and buy gas regularly. He bought gas almost every other day, so his knowledge of gas prices was a lot more up to date than Paula's. "I know," he finally replied. "The gas over at the Speedway station was at three dollars and eighty-seven cents this afternoon."

"That's what I mean," she said. She stopped picking up the plates and leveled a long stare at John. "That is absolutely ridiculous," she said, the third time in less than two minutes.

John kind of laughed under his breath at the way Paula was acting about prices. It was funny listening to her repeat herself. But the prices were going up to the point of being ridiculous. How was John ever going to keep food in the house and pay the bills with the cost of everything going up? He wasn't exactly the most skilled person in the world, so trying to make extra money on the side would be almost impossible. But he felt he might have to start looking for something if things didn't improve soon. With this disease around, it didn't look as if things would improve anytime soon.

"Well," John started up again after Paula had returned to the table, "all I can say at this point is that we're going to have to start tightening our belts a little."

"What do you think I've been doing these last couple of weeks?" she snapped back, feeling she was being accused of wasting money. "I mean, I have a budget to run this house on, and I can't stretch it any further. Look at what we had for dinner," she said, pointing at the rest of the dishes on the table. "Hot dogs and broccoli with instant potatoes. That's not what I would call a great dinner, but we don't have the supplies to make something better, at least not until payday."

"The dinner was fine," John said in an attempt to change the subject. "I was just saying we need to tighten our belts."

"Well, I have," she concluded as she picked up more dishes. "What else would you have me do?" Paula asked with a slightly defensive tone.

"I'm just saying we need to watch our spending," John stated flatly, afraid she was getting defensive.

"Don't you think I am?" Paula asked, but this time the tone of her voice was serious.

"I'm sure you are," John said. "I'm just saying that we shouldn't spend money on things we don't need."

"Like what?" Paula asked, wondering what John was accusing her of doing with the money in her budget. It wasn't as much as it normally would be, but then again, the price of everything seemed to have risen out of control. This had put a big dent in the amount she normally would have had at this time in the budget cycle. So what was he trying to say, she wondered? Did he think she was just throwing money away?

"I don't know," John said, trying to figure out how to say that he thought she was spending money on things they didn't need. However, he couldn't just come right out and say that. She would go out to the store and come back with things they didn't need, such as a new purse. What was wrong with the old one? She had had that one only a couple of months. Had she bought a new one because she needed one or because she just wanted one? But how could he ask those questions without causing an argument? "Well," he finally said, knowing that he wasn't going to get out of this without saying something, "like that catalog you and Beth were looking at. What are you going to get out of there that we need right now, another new purse?"

This infuriated Paula as she felt that she was being accused of spending money without thinking of the consequences. "For your information," she said in an almost threatening tone, "we were looking at coupons to see if we can find the items we need at a cheaper cost. We have no plans to buy anything until we need it. Is it some sort of crime to search for possible sales?"

"No, of course not," John said, getting a little defensive since he felt as if he had wrongly accused her of planning to spend money on stuff they didn't need. "But you do tend to buy stuff we don't need." As soon as he finished his statement, he wished he could have retracted it.

"I do, do I?" she snapped back. "And you don't?"

"I don't spend money on stuff we don't need."

"You don't?" she said with the tone of a defense attorney. She walked over to the entertainment center and picked up three science fiction DVD movies. "And what were you planning on doing with these that makes them such a necessity, line the bottom of your shoes?" John liked sci-fi movies, but Paula didn't care to watch them. She rarely complained about the number of science fiction movies he purchased.

"Okay," John replied, on the defensive, "so I bought a couple of movies a couple of weeks ago. I didn't know then that prices were going to go up this high and that we were going to be so tight on money. Otherwise, I wouldn't have bought them."

"Well," Paula continued, her voice growing more aggressive, "then what about the purse you so eloquently indicated that I didn't need? I bought that purse before you bought those stupid movies."

"Okay," John said, walking over to the beginning of the hallway, "all I'm saying is that we are going to have to watch how much we spend."

"Yes, Your Majesty," Paula said, bowing down like a slave would bow to her master. This did nothing but make John even madder. He turned and went upstairs to the office, leaving Paula upset and a little angry for having been accused of wasting money. She'd had control over the household money almost since the day they were married, and now wasn't a good time to complain that she wasn't doing a good job.

Paula stood there for several seconds, her level of anger growing as she continued to contemplate what John had said. All she could think of was that he was making an accusation about how she was handling the money. After several seconds, she turned and picked up a book that was on the chair and threw it across the room into the kitchen. You could hear the book crash into the kitchen trash can, and then what sounded like a glass jar and several metal cans went rolling across the floor. She then turned and headed out onto the back patio to cool off.

John sat at his desk, wondering what he had said that had made his wife so upset. He didn't think he had accused her of doing anything wrong, or at least not at first. He was just concerned with the money situation. Maybe that was enough; he didn't know. Maybe the stress of trying to make ends meet with a limited amount of funds was getting to his wife. All he could think of to do was just to stay out of her way for a while.

Beth and Peter had seen the beginning of the argument. As the discussion between their parents escalated, Peter had motioned to Beth that they should leave the room, so the two went upstairs to their rooms. Beth went into her room to continue on a paint-by-numbers picture she had been working on. Peter, having decided it was time to leave, called Ken to see if he was free.

Peter walked up to Ken's house and saw him sitting on the steps, whittling a small piece of wood. Ken almost always carried the small knife he'd gotten from his father two Christmases ago. He liked to whittle. He was never very good at it; he just liked to make wood shavings. "Hiya, Pete," Ken said as he saw him cutting through the backyard.

"Hi. What are you doing?" Peter asked as he noticed Ken creating another pile of wood shavings. "Trying to create a supply of kindling for the fireplace this winter?" he continued with a chuckle.

"Ha-ha," Ken said as he folded the knife with one hand and slipped it into his pocket. "Well, friend of mine," Ken continued as he got up to his feet, "are we going to try another dry run tonight?"

They had discussed the results of their first attempt and had made several changes to their approach. The primary changes were that they would watch out for lights and also get their victim further out of sight. They also had gotten a small red flashlight so they could have some light to see the results of the blood test. It was difficult to see using just any ambient light that might be around, and the beam from a regular flashlight would be too easy to see. They also had made plans to transport their victims from where they found them to Peter's house to see how long it would take to move them. This meant that they would use the wagon this time after they had carefully lubricated the axles and tightened all the bolts so the wagon would make as little noise as possible.

"That's the plan," Peter said, "but my parents were arguing about the high prices of groceries and stuff, so I decided just to get out of there. Plus, you could use the company, right?" he said, trying to shake the depressing thoughts of his parents' argument.

"Okay," Ken said, "we have about an hour and a half before it starts to get dark enough for us to go out, so let's go watch a movie."

There didn't appear to be anything of interest to watch, so the two boys passed the time by playing games on Ken's Xbox. "I win," Ken said once he had beat Peter in another car race.

"I let you win," Peter said jokingly, knowing that Ken almost always won at these games, primarily because he played them all the time.

"Oh, sure," Ken said sarcastically, "that's very nice of you."

Peter didn't want to get beat in another game, so he placed his controller on the coffee table and looked up at the clock. "It's almost nine o'clock," he said with a slight indication of fear as they were about to go out on another excursion.

"Well," Ken said, also putting his controller on the coffee table, "I guess we should get going."

Ken slipped into a black long-sleeved shirt and led the way to the back door. Outside, Peter pulled his black shirt from his backpack and donned the cover for night hunting. Then he grabbed the backpack and slipped the straps onto his shoulders. Ken walked over to the side of the garage, where they had the small wagon sitting. He grabbed the handle. The two stood in the backyard, surveying the neighborhood.

"Where do we want to go first?" Peter asked, not sure of where would be the best place to go to find kids running around.

"Let's try over by the Deer Run housing complex." That complex was filled with mostly inexpensive homes for new homeowners, which generally meant that most of the owners were younger parents and would hopefully have kids playing outside.

"That's okay with me," Peter replied. The two headed east across the neighbors' backyards. Ken was leading the way, pulling the wagon, which wasn't as quiet as they would have liked it to be, but it was all they had.

As they approached the Deer Run complex, they could hear kids playing in some of the backyards. However, when they got closer, they could see that the kids were only about six years old, and they were playing with their parents.

Peter and Ken continued to walk down the main street, surveying the various houses to see if any candidates might satisfy their requirements for a donor. They were also looking for ways to get in and get out without being seen. As they approached the end of East Path Road, they could hear several kids playing behind a house. They continued walking down the street until they could see around the house. There were about six boys playing football. This wasn't going to work; they needed a kid all by himself or herself.

"You know," Ken said as if hit with a glimmer of logic, "if we can hear the kids, we can't use them. We need to look for silence and see if there are any kids around. We know this complex has kids, and if they are making a lot of noise, we'll never get one of them for a donor."

"That makes sense," Peter agreed. "But it's sure going to be hard to find a kid who is quiet when we can't hear him," Peter continued, emphasizing the catch-22 situation. "Any ideas?" Peter asked, knowing he had no idea of how they would find a kid who wasn't making noise.

"What we need to do," Ken concluded, "is to go along the backyards so that we can see who is outside. More than likely if the kids are outside, they're not going to be in the front yard."

"That makes sense, too," Peter said after he'd analyzed Ken's evaluation.

"Let's sneak into the backyards and see who's outside," Ken said, pointing to a side street where they could enter the backyards without being seen.

They had gone through seven backyards with no sign of anyone playing outside. "Look," Ken said quietly as they approached the eighth backyard. Over by the corner of the house was a young boy of about eleven. From where they were standing, they weren't sure what he was doing. "Want to try him?" Ken asked.

Peter looked out over the large backyard. There was a shed on the right side that could provide them some cover as they approached the boy. It was still a long way to cross before they could grab him and put him to sleep. "I don't know," he said, the anxiety growing. "It's a long way over to the house."

"Yeah" was all Ken said as he tried to figure out a way to capture this potential donor. The more he thought about it, the more he was convinced this one wouldn't work. The child was just too close to the house with way too much open space. "I'm afraid that we will have to let this one go."

"I agree," Peter said, a little relieved but also a little disappointed. This was the first possible target they had seen in this housing area, and it was one they would have to pass on.

"You know," Ken said as he surveyed the remaining backyards, "all of these yards are awfully big. If we do find a possible target, it's going to be very difficult to get close enough to catch the kid without being seen by him or by a neighbor three or four yards down the street."

Peter also surveyed the yards and could see what Ken was referring to. The success rate in this area would be low, and anyway the prospect was very risky. "Think we should go somewhere else?" he asked.

"We had a lot more luck with an apartment complex," Ken concluded. "I think we should go over to Spring River Apartments." These apartments were about a mile up the street. A lot of young families lived in the complex, so they figured there should be kids around. However, they had no idea if these kids would be outside. There was no way to determine if a change in plans would provide them with more opportunities or if another possible donor was just two houses down. There was just no way to know.

"Okay with me," Peter answered. He stepped back as if to distance himself from all the people who might be up by the house.

Ken also took a step back when the boy by the corner of the house started chasing another boy who had come around the corner of the garage. The two boys were playing a game. The one by the corner attacked the boy running from the front of the house; they were pretending to commence in battle. "Boy, I'm glad we didn't try to catch that kid. We would have been right in the middle of the yard when that other kid came around the corner."

"Well, let's get out of here before something does happen," Peter pleaded. The two continued on their way to the end of the woods and onto a small side road.

They immediately headed over to the Spring River Apartments, hoping to find a possible donor. The side street had lots of trees and only a couple of streetlights, making it easy for them to hide if they were to encounter someone walking down the street. The last thing they wanted to do was be spotted by someone wondering if they were out to cause trouble.

It didn't take long for them to find their first victim, a small boy of about ten years old playing with what looked like a Game Boy unit. He was sitting on the step to the side entrance.

"Now he looks like a possible candidate," Ken said, pointing to the boy.

"Yeah," Peter agreed, but he was getting that uneasy feeling again.

"Okay," Ken said, a plan forming in his head. "If I go in the front door, I can come down the steps and wait by that door," he said, pointing to the door behind the boy. "Then when you walk across the sidewalk over by those cars," he said, pointing to several cars parked about twenty feet from the doorway, "you can drop something to catch the boy's attention, and then I'll step out and put him to sleep."

Peter surveyed the area and tried to visualize his role in attracting the boy's attention. "That may work," Peter finally agreed. But something bothered him. "Where do we take him to test his blood?" he asked with a tone of concern. There was at least twenty feet of open space in all directions, and it would not be easy to carry the boy to an area of seclusion without being noticed. Also, the light over the doorway entrance would not be helpful.

Ken continued to survey the area as he tried to review the sequence of events in his mind. "Well," Ken started, and then paused. "We could first carry him behind the building," he said, pointing to the darkness behind the building. "There don't appear to be any lights back there." About fifty feet down from the rear of the apartment building was an electrical transformer cover, probably used to supply the apartments with power. "We could carry him down behind that metal box over there," Ken offered, pointing to the transformer unit.

Peter could see the transformer unit, but he didn't like the distance between the spot where they would have to pick up the boy and the hiding place. But at least it was in the dark. "Okay," Peter finally agreed, feeling that there wasn't much else they could do. He didn't like it, but they had to try something.

"All right," Ken said. "I'll go the long way around to the front door. When I get over to that doorway where he's sitting, I will wave to you. In the meantime, if he seems like a good donor, we will need the wagon to carry him home, so you go the long way around," he said, pointing toward the wooded area and the tall grass behind the apartment complex. "Leave the wagon behind that metal unit. Then," he continued, trying to visualize the rest of the exercise, "come back around to that end of the parking lot. When I give you the signal that I'm ready, start walking toward those cars."

Peter, after walking through the exercise in his head, finally responded, "Okay." Then he took off his backpack and removed the Ziploc bag with the white cloth soaked in chloroform that Ken had used the last time. He handed Ken the bag, along with the small bottle of chloroform. "Okay," Peter said, slipping the backpack onto his back, "I guess I'm as ready as I'll ever be." And with that, he grabbed the handle of the wagon and headed into the wooded area.

Ken headed in the opposite direction to make his way to the front of the building.

Peter was in position and ready to start across the open area toward where the boy was sitting. His stomach was jumping as his fear increased. He didn't want to try this, but based on the information presented by the news, his mom would get this disease sooner or later. If he was going to keep her from dying, he had to get good at finding blood donors. He crouched down behind the last car in the parking lot, waiting for Ken's signal. Finally, he saw a face in the small window mounted high in the door. The problem was, he wasn't sure it was Ken. The light over the entranceway didn't illuminate the interior behind the window. Again a face popped up. Was that Ken? Peter couldn't tell. Suddenly, a red light could be seen in the window. "That's Ken's flashlight," Peter said, almost loud enough for someone nearby to hear him. Peter stood up from his hiding place and walked toward the apartment complex. He was relieved that the face belonged to Ken because it meant that it wasn't someone looking outside to see if something was going on. However, it did mean that Peter had to do his part. As his fear increased, so did his adrenaline. This was causing the butterflies in his stomach to feel less like a fluttering nuisance and more like a bombing raid.

Holding his backpack in his hands, Peter approached the cars that Ken had pointed to earlier. He was ready to drop the backpack, hoping to attract the boy's attention. He kept one eye on the boy and continued to look around to see if someone might be watching. However, instead of his dropping the pack, the loose strap on the pack got caught on the trailer hitch on a pickup truck that was backed into its parking space. Peter was concentrating so hard on the boy that he didn't notice he had caught the hitch until suddenly he was restrained from continuing his forward motion. The action of catching the hitch caused Peter to shout out, which caught the boy's attention. As Peter quickly untangled the strap, he looked over to see the boy slumped over in Ken's arms. Peter's job had been to attract the boy's attention by dropping something, but this unexpected event had done the job just as well. Peter's fear that something may go wrong had come true, but in this case, it resulted in a positive outcome for them.

Peter, running over to where Ken was standing, grabbed the boy's feet. The two boys carried their victim around the corner of the building and into the darkness. After a quick look around, they felt it was safe to head over to the transformer.

Ken laid the boy down on the ground and looked up at Peter. "That was great, man," Ken said, trying not to laugh at Peter's mishap with the tow hitch. If it weren't for Ken's fear of being heard, he probably would have laughed as soon as he'd seen it happen. Instead, he'd held in the laughter and completed his part of the job.

"Shut up," Peter commanded, opening his backpack. "It worked, didn't it?"

"Yeah," Ken said. "We're going to have to use that routine again."

"Shut up," Peter repeated, a little embarrassed by and disgusted with Ken's attitude. "Let's get to work."

They were getting into a standard routine for testing for blood type. Peter handed Ken the alcohol wipes and a Band-Aid, and then he pulled out the slides and the antigen bottles. Ken did his part of wiping off the boy's finger and holding it out while Peter released the lancet. The puncture produced the desired effects, and Peter put three drops of blood onto the slide. Peter applied the antigens to the samples while Ken applied the Band-Aid to the boy's finger. "He's type O," Peter said, announcing the bad news. "He's not going to work."

"Well, at least we're getting the practice," Ken said.

"I know," Peter said, a little disappointed, "but I wonder if we'll be able to find enough donors to save my mom's life."

"We're just going to have to try again," Ken said, trying to give Peter some encouragement, even though he too was a little disappointed with the blood results.

"Well," Peter said, stuffing everything into the backpack, "I suppose we should take him back over to the steps."

"You know," Ken said, "we should use him as a test case to see how hard it's going to be to get our donor back to your house. We have the wagon, so let's take him a little way toward your house. Then we can bring him back."

"That sounds like a good idea," Peter said, a little more enthusiastic that this run wasn't going to turn out to be a total waste of their time. "He's already out, so a short ride won't hurt him," he agreed, slipping on the backpack.

The two boys picked up their donor and carried him the short distance to the other side of a row of trees where Peter had left the wagon. They carefully placed him in the wagon, but since the boy was asleep, he was dead weight. They tried to sit him up in the wagon, only to have him fall sideways out of it. Then they tried to lay him on his back, but his legs were hanging out the back of the wagon.

"That's the best we can do," Ken said, a little tired from repositioning the boy. "Let's see how hard it's going to be to move him in the wagon."

"I'll start pulling," Peter said, reaching down for the wagon handle. The plan was that the two boys would take turns pulling the wagon. While one of them pulled, the other would walk beside the wagon to make sure their passenger didn't fall out.

"Go for it," Ken said.

The two boys started their journey toward Peter's house. The first part of their journey was through some tall grass and across a small field. Even in the dark, it wasn't too hard to see what was in front of them. They had traveled about a block, when their journey became a lot harder than expected. Since they had to travel out of sight of the general population, they walked through the woods and fields. The fields weren't too bad, but the woods were something else.

"Hold it," Ken said. Their passenger had shifted to the right and had almost fallen out of the wagon again. Crossing the fields wasn't too bad for their passenger as he stayed in place. However, as soon as they entered the woods, their load of dead weight shifted from side to side as they tried to traverse the rough ground. The boy fell out of the wagon twice before they had gone fifty feet into the woods. That's not counting the number of times he had shifted and almost fell out, which he probably would have done if Ken hadn't been fast enough to catch him.

"Okay," Ken said. He repositioned the boy. Peter began pulling again.

They hadn't gone ten feet when Ken cried out, "Damn!" He had stepped into another hole. "If I didn't know any better, I would swear someone deliberately put each of these holes in the way just so that I would step into them." If it wasn't a hole that he'd stepped into, it was a tree root the two of them would trip over. Any way they looked at it, pulling a wagon through the woods was much more difficult than they had thought it would be.

"Yeah," Peter said as he wiped the sweat from his forehead. Since he was doing most of the work pulling the wagon, he was perspiring from the exertion. "We're stuck again," he said, trying to pull the wagon over another tree root.

"I'm coming," Ken said. He stepped up to the right side of the wagon and lifted the front wheels so the wagon would clear the root as Peter resumed pulling it forward. However, they hadn't gone ten feet before the wagon got stuck again.

"This is ridiculous," Ken said in disgust as he caught the boy falling out of the wagon again. "I'm not lifting this stupid wagon over another root."

"Well," Peter said, also frustrated as he threw the handle of the wagon toward the ground, "what do you want to do, leave the kid here in the middle of the woods?"

"No, of course not. But I'm not going to move that damn wagon another inch," Ken replied, disgusted. He threw up his arms and walked over to lean against a large tree. He was not one to put out a lot of extra effort, even when it would be to his own benefit. So, all this energy he was expending to transport this kid was more than he was willing to burn.

Peter walked over to another tree, near the one Ken was leaning against. "What do you want to do?" he asked as Ken started to calm down. "We can't leave him here."

"Of course we can't leave him here," Ken said in disgust, reinforcing his earlier statement. He didn't care for the idea that Peter was making a statement that made him feel as if he were stupid or something.

"Got any ideas on how to take him back?" Peter continued, hoping to spark some ideas from Ken. Ken was good at dreaming up ideas for how to get things accomplished.

"I know," Ken said, giving Peter the evil eye as various thoughts of ways to get out of this situation started to pass through his mind. However, in the dark, it was hard for Peter to see the expression on his friend's face.

"What?" Peter asked, waiting to hear Ken's idea. However, since Peter couldn't see Ken's expression, he didn't know if Ken was being sarcastic and actually did not have a constructive idea.

"Let me think a minute," Ken said as his frustration drained off.

"Do you want to try to just drag the wagon back, or do you want to try something else?" Peter asked, trying to give Ken an alternative. He didn't want to drag the kid back in the wagon, but at least it was an option.

It was several minutes before Ken replied: "Well, I'm definitely not going to try to take this kid to your house, or at least not by using this method. That means we're going to have to take him back." Ken stood there thinking about the problems they had. "All right, let's take him back," he said as he stood up, away from the tree. "Let's switch jobs. I'll pull, and you control the kid."

Ken hoped that Peter's job was easier than his. Pulling the wagon had to be easier than trying to keep the boy in the wagon. Plus, Ken was larger than Peter, and he felt he could pull the wagon faster than Peter could.

"Okay," Peter said. He also stood up, moving away from the tree. He'd had to work awfully hard to move that wagon along, so he didn't mind changing jobs. Handling the boy had to be easier.

Ken walked over and could barely see the wagon's black handle lying on the ground. He lifted the handle and, with Peter at the boy's side, turned the wagon around and headed back toward the apartment complex.

As they reached the edge of the woods, Ken realized how hard it had been for Peter to pull the wagon, and Peter realized how hard it was to keep the boy in it. The trip back through the woods was hard, but it became much easier once they reached the field. However, this part of the journey wasn't without its problems. They constantly had to look around to make sure no one was watching them. It would look awfully strange to see two kids pulling a wagon with an unconscious kid in it. Indeed, from a distance, it might look as if they were transporting a dead body.

As they approached the edge of the tall grass, all appeared to be quiet at the apartment complex. As they approached their hiding place behind the transformer, the boy started to stir.

"Ken!" Peter called out with a tone of excitement, probably louder than he should have spoken. "I think the boy's starting to wake up."

Ken stopped and looked down at the boy as he moved about. None of their other victims had shown any signs of movement when they were put to sleep. The problem was that Peter and Ken never had hung around long enough to see what happened when the chloroformed kids woke up. Was this boy waking up, or was he just unconsciously moving?

"Well, we had better get this kid back over to the steps," Ken said. He dropped the handle of the wagon and slid his hands under the boy's armpits. In the meantime, Peter started to reach for the boy's feet. "Ready?" Ken asked.

"Yeah," Peter replied.

The two lifted the boy out of the wagon. They quickly headed for the back of the apartment complex, taking no time to see if anyone was watching. As they approached the back wall of the building, the boy stirred. He didn't realize he was being carried—or at least not yet. As they moved down toward the corner of the building, Ken looked around to see if anyone who might be able to see them was nearby.

"Oh shit," Ken said in an almost inaudible tone.

"What's the matter?" whispered Peter, huffing and puffing from carrying the dead weight.

"There are two guys over by the cars," Ken said with a touch of fear in his voice. "We can't go around the corner without them seeing us."

"Now what are we going to do?" Peter asked. His fear of getting caught increased, especially since the boy was waking up.

"I don't know," Ken said, feeling the same fear as Peter. Before they could plan their next move, the boy opened his eyes. He appeared a little dazed at first, as if not sure of where he was, but neither Ken nor Peter knew what was happening. Suddenly, the boy lunged, pulling himself free from Ken's support, and he went crashing headfirst onto the ground. But Peter still had the boy's feet in the air, so the boy was now almost upside down. This sudden drop in altitude and the sudden stop at ground level resulted in a loud verbal response that caught both Peter and Ken by surprise.

"Ken!" Peter shouted, not realizing that they wouldn't be able to get the boy back to the steps. "Let's get out of here!"

Peter, still holding the boy's feet, dropped them. The two headed for the tall grass. Neither stopped to see if anyone was following them or what the status was of the poor boy who had been dropped on his head. Instead, they ran into the tall grass with Peter pausing only a second to grab the handle of the wagon. Then they ran as fast as they could with the wagon clanging behind them. They didn't slow down until they were deep into the woods on the other side of the field.

The two boys dropped to their knees and turned to survey the area behind them. "It doesn't look like anyone is following us," Ken said, panting harder than he had ever panted before.

Peter didn't even have enough energy or breath to respond. He just knelt there panting as if he were in a vacuum, unable to catch any air.

Ken and Peter repositioned themselves against a large tree as they continued to watch the field at the edge of the woods. "That was close," Ken finally said.

"That was too close," Peter finally said, his system slowly recovering from their exhausting exit.

"Well, now we know how long the chloroform lasts before they start to wake up," Ken said with a slight chuckle.

"Yeah," Peter replied, "but I don't want to find out like that again."

The two boys sat there for about ten minutes, watching the field and the distant apartment complex. There were no signs of anyone chasing them or any signs of the police arriving at the apartment complex. At least they hadn't heard any sirens. Since all appeared to be peaceful, they decided it was safe to head home. The fifteen-minute walk home was quiet except for the slight clanging from the wagon they were pulling behind them.

As they approached the edge of the woods, they could hear loud voices nearby. "Quiet," Ken said in a whisper as he crouched down behind a large bush. Peter followed his lead, also kneeling down behind the bush.

Ken separated the branches ever so slowly so as not to attract any attention. They were about forty feet from the edge of the street, where they would have normally crossed to enter the backyards of their neighborhood. In the middle of the street were five boys. Two of the kids looked to be about eight to ten years of age, while the other three were much taller and appeared to be in their midteens.

From Ken and Peter's observation post, the streetlight did a good job of illuminating the entire scene. The three older boys were dressed in jeans and old T-shirts with the sleeves cut off or rolled up. The shortest of the three older boys had several chains and other accessories attached to his clothes. Ken and Peter, able to see the faces of two of the boys, noticed that they appeared to be into body piercings. One boy must have had five or six earrings in each ear and a dozen other piercings on his face alone. Ken and Peter couldn't see the face of the third boy all that well, but they could see his arms. This individual had many tattoos on both arms.

From where these hoodlums were standing, it appeared they were blocking the path of the two younger kids. Those two boys were dressed in shorts, T-shirts, and sneakers. They appeared to be normal kids out having some fun in the evening. One boy was carrying a skateboard, and the other appeared to be carrying Rollerblades.

"Where do you think you're going?" asked the shortest hoodlum. It appeared to Ken and Peter that he was probably the leader of this trio.

"We're going to my house," said the boy wearing blue shorts. There was a quiver in his voice, indicating that he was experiencing some fear related to this encounter.

"Well," the leader said as he walked behind the boys, "you need to pay a toll to pass."

"What do you mean?" asked the boy wearing the brown shorts. "We live right there," he said, pointing to a brick house two houses down from where they were standing.

"You still have to pay a toll," the leader repeated. "How much money do you have?"

The two boys looked at each other. The brave boy in the brown shorts replied, "We don't have any money. And if we did, we wouldn't give it to you."

The leader didn't appear to like the younger boy's comment or his attitude. He wanted to have control over the boys, which meant he had to instill fear into them. "You wouldn't," he said in a soft, kind tone. Then he turned, looked into the eyes of the brave boy, and grabbed him by his shirt. "That's not the answer I want to hear." And with that, he shoved the boy halfway across the street.

The brave boy stumbled backward and then fell, landing on his back, scraping his elbows, and hitting the back of his head on the road. Ken and Peter looked on in shock, as they had never seen anyone act that way, at least not in real life.

"Should we go help them?" Peter asked in a soft tone, concerned for the two boys' safety.

"I don't know," Ken said, also concerned for the boys' safety but also worried that his and Peter's intervention could cause more problems. "Let's wait a couple of seconds and see what happens."

The other two hoodlums walked over, picked up the brave boy, and roughly dragged him back to the leader. "Did you like that?" the leader asked the now frightened boy.

"No," he said, on the verge of tears.

"Now," the leader said, talking in a soft voice, "do you have any money?"

"No," the frightened boy replied.

The leader now turned to the other boy, who was also frightened. "Do you have any money?"

The sudden transfer of the leader's attention to the boy in the blue shorts made the latter shake with fear. "No," he replied, his lower lip quivering.

The leader turned to his friends and said in a sarcastic tone, "They don't have any money to pay the toll." Shaking his head from side to side, he continued, "What should we do with them?"

"Let's just beat them to a pulp," said the boy with all the facial piercings, "and leave them in the street like dead animals that have been run over by a truck."

"What do you think?" the leader asked, addressing the two boys. This made the boy in the blue shorts cry as his fear of being beaten up by these thugs continued to increase.

"No," responded the braver boy, "you would get into a lot of trouble."

"No, we wouldn't," the leader replied. "Not if you're dead." He proceeded to poke his finger into the brave boy's chest, hard enough to cause him to cry out and almost lose his footing again.

"Let's just take their toys," the second hoodlum suggested.

"Now that's not a bad idea," the leader said, looking at the skateboard and the Rollerblades. "They won't be needing them while they're recovering from the injuries I'm going to give them."

The fear within the two boys grew as the power of their assailant grew in proportion. "But these are ours," exclaimed the braver boy, holding his skateboard close to his chest.

Peter and Ken watched from their secluded position, wanting to help but afraid of the consequences. "Let's go over to that house," Ken said, pointing to the house the boy had pointed to earlier. "We can tell their parents, and maybe they can call the cops."

"Okay," Peter replied, "but let's leave all this stuff here. If they do call the cops, I don't want to be carrying all this on my back." They put their stuff into the wagon and took several steps back into the woods so as not to be seen by the gang in the street, then quickly traveled through the woods to the house.

Ken paused a second at the edge of the woods to see who might be watching them. He didn't want to explain why he and Peter were coming out of the woods. He stepped out of the woods, followed by Peter, and the two quickly ran to the front door. They knocked and rang the bell repeatedly to get whoever might be home to respond quickly. A middle-aged man opened the door, holding the daily paper. He must have been relaxing and reading the paper when the two boys made all the racket at the front door.

"What the hell do you boys think you're doing?" he asked in an angry tone.

"There's a gang over there beating up on two little kids," Ken said, pointing down the street where the confrontation was occurring. The man inside the house couldn't see what was going on, so he opened the door and stepped out onto the sidewalk. He had to go about five steps down the sidewalk before he could see the group of kids Ken was referring to. The man watched for a second, wondering what was going on, as the group didn't seem to be doing much to attract any attention.

"What do you mean?" the man asked, convinced that nothing was going on. But before Ken could respond, the man yelled at the top of his lungs, "Stop that!" Ken and the man watched as the three older boys picked up the boy in the brown shorts and threw him across the street. The boy landed halfway on the edge of the grass and halfway in the street. The other small boy ran down the street, but one thug ran after him and gave him a hard shove. The little boy went flying down the street, landing on his stomach.

The man dropped his newspaper and pulled a cell phone out of his pocket. He quickly dialed 911 and told the police what was happening as he ran to help the two younger boys. The thugs, seeing the man come running down the street, started calling him names and flicking him the finger. This lack of respect infuriated the man, who increased his efforts to reach the scene quickly. As the man got closer, the thugs threw the skateboard and the Rollerblades at him before turning to leave. You would think that they would have been a little concerned about getting caught. But instead of running away, they just walked away, laughing about the whole situation. In the meantime, the man started to help the two boys who were now in need of medical attention.

Ken and Peter didn't know whether to follow the man to see if they could help or to disappear. "Come on," Ken said, "let's get the hell out of here and let the police take care of this. I don't want to have anything to do with the cops."

"But we might be able to help those boys," Peter said, not sure of the right thing to do. He wanted to help the boys, but at the same time, he didn't want to get involved with the cops either.

"No," Ken said with conviction as he turned to head for home. "I don't want to hang around here for someone to ask why we were at this location at this time. I would just like to disappear."

Peter felt a little guilty about leaving the boys behind, but he was somewhat consoled by the fact that the man was helping them. He and Ken could hear sirens, indicating the cops were coming, so there would be more than enough help to take care of the boys. "Okay," Peter said. "What about the wagon?"

"We'll come back later tonight and pick it up," Ken replied, not thinking about it. "Let's just get out of here." The two boys quickly crossed the street and headed into the backyards of their neighborhood to head for home. For the rest of the night, they could think of nothing other than the events they had just witnessed and/or been party to.

CHAPTER 12

John, pulling into the parking garage at the hospital after his afternoon run, grabbed the collection of specimens and headed into the hospital. As he walked into the lab, he saw Joyce standing by the counter. "Been waiting for me?" John asked. She normally didn't wait at the counter.

"Of course not," Joyce replied with a smile. "I wouldn't be waiting for you, because when you show up, it means I have work to do."

"Well," John started as he placed the bags of specimens on the counter, "you'd better get to work then."

"Oh, thanks a lot," she replied in a sarcastic tone. She grabbed the bags and carried them over to the computer to enter all the information.

John saw Sharon over in the corner working on the equipment. She seemed preoccupied with running a test. John wanted to talk to her to see how things were going, but she seemed to be paying a lot of attention to the equipment and he didn't want to interrupt. So he decided just to leave and try another day.

"Hey, John," came a familiar call from behind as he was almost out the door. He turned around and saw Sharon walking over to the counter. "Well," she said in a weak voice, "I guess you don't say hi anymore."

"It looked like you were involved in something important. I didn't want to interrupt," John said, retracing his steps to return to the counter.

"Come on over," she said, motioning John to come around the counter and follow her over to the machine.

As John followed her, he could see she didn't seem to have the energy she had when he had first met her. Her walk was slower, and she took shorter steps. It was almost as if she were an old woman.

"I want to show you something," she said, pointing to the machine. "We've discovered how the Sanguis virus is spreading," she said weakly but with excitement.

"You discovered how it spreads?" John asked excitedly, not realizing he just had asked a question that Sharon had already answered.

"I just said that," Sharon said, starting to giggle.

"Oh yeah," John said as if he were in a spelling bee and had misspelled a simple word. "So how does it spread?"

"Well, the first thing we noticed is that there are more fatalities in the suburbs than in cities. So we tried to determine the big difference between being out in the suburbs," she said, holding out her left hand, "and being in the city." She held out her right hand and then continued holding out both hands as if to make a distance comparison between two known bits of information. However, John didn't seem to catch the relationship. "Trees," she announced. "There are more trees and plants in the suburbs. It appears that the Sanguis virus lives on the chlorophyll in plants."

John had to stop and think about this for a minute as he tried to remember his high school biology class, where he remembered hearing the word *chlorophyll*. As if a light bulb of recognition had gone off, he responded, "You mean this disease is the result of some dumb plants?"

"It appears so," Sharon continued. "We're not sure where it came from or how it came about, but we do know that it can be found in any plant that is contaminated. It doesn't appear to affect the plants, but it is definitely there."

"What plants are contaminated with it?" John asked, hoping to avoid whatever plants may be spreading the disease.

"That's the bad part," Sharon continued, her tone changing from one of excitement to one of defeat. "It appears to be in almost every plant we tested."

"You mean, like, every flower that's out there probably has this disease in it?"

"Just about," Sharon said. "But we have found some that, so far, don't appear to be contaminated. However," she said, pausing for a second as if not wanting to share the next bit of news, "it can be found in flowers, grass, and trees and in almost every type of organic product we consume."

John had to think about this for a minute. The thought of the Sanguis virus being carried by organic products people consumed didn't seem like a big problem at first. "Do you mean like vegetables?" he asked as the concept started to become clearer.

"Yes," Sharon said, realizing that John didn't quite understand what she was saying. "It can be in every type of food we eat. It could be in any fruit, any vegetable, or any of the many types of grains. Anything that can grow in the ground could be contaminated."

The two stood there for several seconds as John began to grasp the seriousness of what Sharon had just told him. "That means if I go to the store and buy some grapes, there is no way of knowing if I'm eating contaminated food. That means I could catch the virus just by eating lunch."

"I'm afraid so," Sharon responded.

"What about meat?" John asked, wondering if there was anything safe to eat.

"Apparently, animals that eat contaminated food may be carrying the Sanguis virus, but they don't appear to be affected by it."

John's spirit became defeated at the thought that if one wished not to catch the disease, then one shouldn't eat. The vision of people dying of starvation versus dying of the disease—boy, what a choice. The thought of skinny people walking around because they wouldn't eat gave him a crazy idea. "I know," he announced with a sudden rise in enthusiasm, "let's advertise this disease as a weight loss program." He sucked in his stomach, mimicking starvation. "Save your life and lose weight." He paused. "At the same time."

Sharon could see that John was making a joke about the situation because her news was very distressing. "However," she said, to catch John's attention, "you can eat any food, even if it is contaminated, as long as you cook it at a heat of three hundred seventy-five degrees. This seems to be a high enough temperature to kill the Sanguis virus."

John's eyes opened wider as some hope came back into the picture. "That's good," he said, slapping his oversized belly. "I wouldn't want to lose my figure because of a stupid disease.

"Have you determined how the Sanguis virus spreads?" John asked, hoping for more good news.

"As a matter of fact," Sharon said, "it appears to travel from plant to plant by way of water. If a contaminated plant gets watered, the Sanguis virus appears to come out of the roots of the plant and into the water. It then travels to another plant, going up through the roots to contaminate other parts of the plant. As long as the virus is in the water, it appears that it is not dangerous to humans. However, once in the plant, it seems to combine with the chlorophyll in the plant and to change just slightly enough to be fatal to us."

John just stood there listening to Sharon's explanation of the actions of the Sanguis virus. He couldn't imagine anything like it. When Sharon had finished her explanation, he had one question he simply had to ask, although he dreaded the answer. "Have you found a cure?"

Sharon looked back at John, the expression on her face becoming a cold, blank stare. The only response that she provided was "No."

The two stood there for several minutes as if frozen in time. Neither knew what to say next. What do you say when you're standing there knowing one of you will die from this disease and the other one will never become infected? What words of encouragement do you offer when there is nothing to be encouraged about? "Well," John said finally, "if there is anything I can do to help, please give me a call."

Sharon looked up at him and smiled. "I know," she said in a weak tone, reaching out with her hand. John held out his hand, and Sharon pulled herself toward him, wrapping her arms around him. Instinctively, he put his arms around her. The pressure of her hug caught John off guard. He didn't know what to think at first. Was this an act of friendly support, or was there a romantic element involved? He didn't know what she was thinking and also didn't know what he was feeling. He felt he had better be careful, especially in the lab. One never knew what kind of rumors could be started if someone were to wrongly interpret their actions.

John wanted to do more but didn't know what to do. He wanted to know more but didn't know what questions to ask. *How are the blood transfusions going?* he wondered. He wanted to know but felt he had better relent until another day. "Well, I'd better get going," he said as he released his arms from around her. Sharon was a little more reluctant in releasing her hold, but she soon lowered her arms and stepped back away from him.

"Have a good evening," she said, turning to return to the equipment she had been working on. She took two steps and then paused. She wasn't sure why she had stopped, but she felt she couldn't go any farther. She turned toward the doorway of the lab to see John just walking out of sight. "John!" she called as loud as she could, but with all the background noise in the lab and given her weakened condition, she was just barely audible.

As John walked out the door, he felt that something was wrong. Thinking he had heard his name being called, he looked back into the lab to see if someone was calling him. He looked around, but no one appeared to look in his direction. He turned and peered more closely into the lab to see if Sharon was over by the equipment she'd been working on. No Sharon.

Now John was feeling very uneasy. He had that feeling of doom as he continued to survey the lab, waiting for Sharon to reappear from behind some piece of equipment. This feeling kept him from moving. He didn't know whether to leave or go back into the lab. Shaking his head as if to shake loose this feeling of dread, he walked back into the lab and around the counter. As he stepped past the counter, his eyes opened as wide as they could open. Over on the floor in front of the machine, he saw Sharon lying on the floor. He quickly ran over to her and lifted her head. "Joyce!" he called at the top of his lungs.

Joyce, hearing John, came quickly out of the back room where the blood specimens were prepared for testing. She had no idea why John would be calling her in such a loud voice. She turned the corner and saw John kneeling next to Sharon. "Oh my God," she said, holding her hands in front of her mouth.

"What do we do?" he called back to her. John may have been around hospitals for several years, but he'd never needed to use any of his training on basic first aid.

Joyce ran over to the phone and dialed a couple of numbers. Within seconds, a coded announcement came over the hospital's public address system indicating to those who knew the code that there was an emergency in the lab.

It couldn't have been more than two minutes before several doctors and nurses came storming into the lab. Several nurses were rolling a gurney; others were bringing other equipment; and one was carrying a mobile drug case. A doctor and a nurse were the first to reach Sharon's side. They asked John to leave, telling him they would take good care of her. Tom also came in, along with the rest of the equipment and personnel entering the lab area.

"John," Tom said, pulling him out of the way, "let's go to my office and wait to see what happens."

"I'd rather stay here," John said with a tone of concern.

"I know," Tom replied, giving John a slight push toward the doorway. "It'll be better for you to wait in my office." Just then, several hospital security personnel came in and tried to direct people away from the scene so the doctors could get the equipment in and get the patient out if she had to be moved to another location. They also liked to minimize the number of people in the area who could get the wrong information and spread rumors all over the hospital.

"Come, sirs," one of the security officers said to Tom and John. "Please leave this area." At the same time, the other security officer was asking Joyce to return to her duties in the back room.

Tom continued to walk John down to his office, but neither said a word. As they walked into the office, John sat down on a chair facing Tom's desk. However, he didn't want to see Tom's face. He wanted to see the medical personnel take Sharon out of the lab. He wanted to know how she was doing before they took her too far.

It was only about fifteen minutes, but to John, it was an eternity, when he saw the gurney slowly rolling past Tom's office door. "Wait!" John said as he jumped up from the chair and ran to the door. "How is she?"

He got his answer when he reached the doorway. On top of the gurney was a white sheet covering a body. But instead of seeing a smiling face looking up at him from one end of the gurney, he saw that the white sheet went from one end to the other. *She didn't make it,* John thought, feeling as if a Mack truck had hit his heart.

The gurney never stopped; it just kept rolling past Tom's office and past John's now tear-filled eyes. "I'm sorry," said the doctor, as he could see how Sharon's death was affecting John. "If there is anything I can do," he continued, "please come and see me." The doctor then followed the others out of the lab.

John just stood there, not knowing what to do. He hadn't known Sharon all that well, but her loss felt the same to him as when he'd lost his sister several years earlier. Was her last hug an indication that she knew what was about to happen? Was this last action her way of saying goodbye?

"John," Tom said, placing his hand on his shoulder, "I know she was a good friend, and I know you're going to miss her." Tom had said what he thought he was supposed to say in a situation like this, but he didn't know what else to add. "Why don't you go home and take tomorrow off?"

"Yeah," John said in a soft tone. He stepped out of Tom's office and headed for the lab door. He didn't even register what Tom had said, other than that he was being directed to leave.

John left the hospital, almost oblivious to what was happening around him. He almost climbed back into the courier car without realizing he was supposed to go home using his car. He tried to shake off the thought of Sharon dying. She might have died in his arms if he had continued to hold her for another minute. He tried to concentrate on what he was doing as he climbed into his car and pulled out into traffic. His thoughts continued to go from Sharon's death to what would happen if Paula were to come down with the disease.

Occasionally, his mind would shift to Sharon's comments on how the Sanguis virus spreads. Through plants! He never had heard of such a thing. There were all sorts of plants at his house: house plants, a garden, several trees, grass, weeds. Could they all be a threat to his family? He didn't know, and he didn't know what to do. His avenue of information had just passed away. Now he didn't know whom to go to, to get information. Tom was there, but his information also had come from Sharon. He didn't know Robert that well but thought maybe he could be an avenue for information.

As John was running through this information, the small SUV driving in front of him suddenly hit the brakes, causing John to respond the same way. The chain reaction between all the cars on Clifton Street caused a three-car collision involving the three cars in front of him. Luckily, John was a driver who always tried to leave plenty of room in front of him just in case the driver in front had lead weights on his shoes and liked to stop quickly. The first two cars were locked together as the third car rammed the second car, going under the first one. The third car was now sitting sideways, blocking the right lane, and the other two cars were blocking the left lane. With the heavy oncoming traffic, there was no way to get around this mess, at least not until the police showed up to direct traffic while a road crew cleared away the obstructions.

John decided to turn off his engine to save gas, especially since gas was so expensive, figuring he wasn't going anywhere soon. He watched as the driver of the third car got out of his car and walked over to the driver of the second car. This driver seemed as if she might be hurt as she made little effort to move or get out of the car. The driver of the first car also got out of his car, wiping a little blood from his forehead. John figured the collision must have caused him to hit his head on the steering wheel. He didn't seem hurt, but if looks could kill, his expression would have brought death upon anyone nearby.

The third driver turned to ask if the first driver was all right, when the latter started yelling at the former. John couldn't hear any of the comments since his windows were closed because there was a light rain coming down. However, the actions of the first driver seemed neurotic, which gave him an idea of what the man was saying. John reached for a small umbrella he had in the side pocket of the door and stepped out into the rain. As expected, when John stepped out of the car, the rain intensified. Despite the heavy rain, a small crowd started to form around the accident site as they watched the first driver's actions.

The first driver was accusing the third driver of causing the accident, which might have been partially true, but some of the blame had to go to the second driver. The third driver tried to calm the first driver by offering him a handkerchief for the small cut on his forehead. However, this action seemed to infuriate the first driver. He started ranting louder, saying that the third guy was trying to infect him with the disease so he would die. The third driver said he had no such intentions; he was only trying to help him with the cut on his forehead.

The first driver took a swing at the third driver, causing the latter to stumble back several steps. He then retaliated with a swing of his own, knocking his opponent down onto the ground. At this time, several other bystanders came running over to break up the fight. This caused the first driver to go nuts as he swung at anyone who came near him, screaming that they were all out to contaminate him with the disease. As he continued to swing wildly, he made his way back to his car. Most bystanders were backing away from him or checking on the condition of the third driver.

The first driver opened the back door of his car and withdrew a small automatic rifle. "No one's going to contaminate me and get away with it!" he yelled at the top of his lungs. And before anyone could react, he fired several shots into the small group standing around the third driver. The driver and two bystanders were hit as their flesh and innards exploded at the exit wound sites. Blood from the victims' wounds went splattering all over the third car, converting the light blue car into an expressionist artwork. However, the rain transformed the red splotches on the car's surface into artistic red streaks.

The three victims immediately collapsed to the ground, creating a pool of blood that started to mix with the puddles of rainwater now forming from the downpour. The first driver didn't seem satisfied that he had shot the third driver; he seemed to be afraid of anyone who got near him. He continued screaming that no one would contaminate him without paying for it, and he continued to shower bullets in every direction possible.

John stood there, basically frozen in horror in response to what was happening. To see a body explode from the impact of a bullet at close range was more terrifying than John had ever imagined. The rest of the crowd that had gathered ran in every direction, screaming in fear. He had seen things like this in movies, but to stand less than fifty feet from someone being shot was nothing like on TV. Suddenly, a bullet hit the top of the windshield of his car, cracking the glass but ricocheting off it instead of going through. This brought John back to the reality of the situation and the danger he was in. As the idea of being shot became more real, John quickly joined the rest of the panicking crowd and started to run toward the back of his car. As he turned to duck behind the car, he heard another shot go flying by his left ear. This shot would have hit him in the head if he had been a split second slower. Although this shot missed his head, it did go through his right hand, ending up in the chest of a man who had stepped out of the fifth car behind his. The impact caused the elderly man to fall backward, revealing a woman standing about four feet behind him. She screamed as she stared down at the blood, now all over the front of her dress. John, seeing the elderly man lying on the ground not moving, also saw the blood on the woman's dress and realized that it could have been his.

Excruciating pain redirected his attention from the chaos on the street to a hole in his right hand. He was astonished to see the amount of blood, and the pain caused him to grit his teeth. As he flipped his hand over, he noticed that another hole had been created as the bullet went through his hand before making contact with the elderly man. This hole was also providing a stream of blood that dripped onto the ground just like the blood from the other victims. John, suddenly concerned about the blood coming from his wound, quickly removed his shirt to wrap it around his hand. The effort to remove the shirt added to the pain he was experiencing in his right hand. After removing his shirt, he carefully wrapped it around his hand, trying to ignore the pain, in an attempt to stop the bleeding. John, having never experienced this level of pain before, prayed to God that he would never have to feel such pain again. He could only imagine the pain the other victims must have been experiencing. The fact that he'd been shot in the hand made him realize how lucky he was not to have been shot in a more life-threatening manner.

The shooter continued firing as everyone ran for cover. At this time there must have been more than ten individuals who had been hit. John didn't know what to do. He had never been in this type of situation before. He had never been this scared before either. Suddenly, the firing stopped. As curiosity started to outweigh his earlier feelings of fear, John peeked past the edge of his car to see what was going on. He could see the shooter reaching into the back seat of his car. John hoped this was the end, but the shooter came out of the car, inserted another clip, and started shooting again. The shooter seemed possessed with the idea that these people were out to contaminate him with the disease. He was obviously afraid that he would die.

John could hear the sounds of the police sirens and could see their lights reflected in the store windows. The shooter continued to spray bullets throughout the area as John continued to move slowly toward a safe location around the corner of the building. Detective Mitchell came over and, seeing that John's hand was covered with a blood-soaked shirt, immediately called a paramedic to come over to address his injury.

The paramedic escorted John over to a waiting ambulance and helped him climb up. After making him comfortable, he carefully removed the shirt to examine the damage done by the bullet. Regardless of the care exhibited by the paramedic, the pain John was experiencing could be easily seen in his face. After a quick examination, the paramedic indicated that the bullet had damaged the bones in his hand; he would have to go to the hospital to have the damage repaired. John decided to call his wife while the first responders and the crowd waited for the cops to clear a path so the ambulance could leave.

"Hi, honey," he said calmly, even though he was in a lot of pain. "It looks like I will be a little late tonight. There's been an accident on Clifton Street."

"Are you okay?" she asked in a panicky tone, fearful that he might have been hurt.

"The accident was with three cars in front of me," he said, not wanting to tell her about the lunatic with the rifle or about being shot.

"Oh, good," she said with a sigh of relief.

John knew he would have to tell her what had happened. It would be too hard to hide a large bandage on his right hand, and once she saw it, she would ask questions.

"Well," John started, but he was unsure of how to continue. "The driver of the first car got all upset and was screaming that everyone was trying to contaminate him with the disease. He pulled out a rifle and started shooting."

There was a moment of silence on the line as Paula stood there, frozen, thinking about someone standing on the street shooting people. As a feeling of fear came over her, she asked, "Are you okay?"

"I'm fine," John said.

"As long as you're okay," Paula said with a sigh of relief.

"Well," John continued, fighting the urge to say that everything was all right, "there is a small problem."

"What happened?" she asked, fear creeping back into her voice.

"Nothing much," John said, trying to minimize the situation and hoping his voice didn't betray the fact that he was in a lot of pain. "I had a stray bullet go through my hand.

"But it's nothing major," he quickly added, before she could think up some dark, gruesome thought. "The paramedic here told me I have to go to Christ Hospital to have it taken care of. So I was wondering if you could meet me there."

"Are you sure you're all right?" Paula asked, believing that he wasn't telling her the whole truth.

"I'll be fine once the doctor puts in a couple of stitches," he replied, not knowing how much damage the bullet had done to the bones in his hand.

"Are you sure?" she asked, still not believing he was telling her the whole truth.

"I'm fine," he repeated his previous comment.

"Okay," she said, accepting his word for now. "I'm leaving now."

"See you there," John concluded, glad he had kept the severity from upsetting Paula any more than necessary. He finished his call as the ambulance departed the scene, on its way to the hospital.

It was early the next morning before John could return home after having been in surgery for over an hour to have the bones in his hand repaired. His hand was immobilized with a brace so the bones could heal. He'd been given a sling to support his arm. The injury didn't cause too much discomfort as the pain medication helped. John's biggest concern was whether or not he'd be able to drive so he could do his job. However, given that the last twenty-four hours had confronted him with a little more stress than he was ready to accept, once he was home, he decided he wanted nothing more than to go to bed. He'd worry about driving later.

CHAPTER 13

Several days had passed since Peter and Ken had made their last trip out to find a donor. They decided to get together and talk about the problems they'd had with transporting the donor, and the scary situation they'd found themselves in when those thugs beat up those two kids.

"That kid was just too heavy and too awkward to move in the wagon," Ken said from the porch railing, where he had made himself comfortable. "We need to figure out an easier way to get the donors back to your house."

Peter looked up from his position on the porch steps; he was trying to figure out a good solution to the problem. "We could try to stay closer to the house," Peter said, responding with the first idea that popped into his head. "It would at least limit the distance we have to travel."

Ken was the analytical type who could quickly review a situation in his mind and determine the pros and cons. "That would make the transporting time shorter, but it would greatly limit the number of possible donors we could find."

"True," Peter agreed, knowing it wasn't much of an idea.

"Plus," Ken continued, "if we want the area where our donors are being found to be in a certain direction from our houses, then our odds of finding a donor will be really difficult."

"What?" Peter asked, not understanding what Ken was talking about. He knew what he was saying, but he didn't fully grasp all the details since sometimes Ken had a hard time getting his point across.

"Remember?" Ken asked. "We decided to go looking in one direction from our house so that if the cops were working to find out who was stealing blood from these kids, our houses would be on the circumference instead of in the middle of the circle. This way the cops will assume the culprit is somewhere in the middle and will not come looking for us."

"Oh, now I remember," Peter acknowledged, understanding the situation, but still not having an answer to the original question of how to transport these kids.

"Let's look at it in a different way," Ken said. "How would someone transport a person who is unconscious today?"

Peter wasn't sure how to answer the question or where Ken was heading.

"Let's say that I was knocked unconscious," Ken started, thinking out loud. "What would you do?"

"I would call 911, and they would probably send an ambulance," Peter replied.

"Okay." Ken paused, continuing to visualize the scene as Peter replied to his promptings.

"They have arrived. How do they move me?"

"They have a stretcher on wheels that they would put you on. Then they roll you out to the ambulance, where they transport you to the hospital." Peter wasn't sure where Ken was heading with this line of thinking, but he didn't like the idea of using a gurney to roll through the woods. "You're not thinking of making a stretcher to carry the kids on, are you?"

Ken looked down at Peter and smiled from ear to ear. "Why not?"

Peter stood up and climbed the two steps to the porch to address Ken face-to-face. "It was hard enough trying to drag that wagon through the woods," Peter replied in frustration as the memory of their past experiences came to mind. "And you want to use a gurney! Those things have smaller wheels than the wagon does, which means that, if we use one, it will fall into every little hole along the way. Plus, it would be top-heavy with the kid on it, making it more difficult to handle. We would do better carrying a stretcher with the kid on it."

Ken looked at Peter and grinned even wider. "That's right," he said with a chuckle. "Instead of a gurney, let's use a stretcher and just carry the kids."

Peter looked at Ken and thought about what he'd said for a second. "That sounds good, except trying to carry a kid through the woods isn't going to be easy. Plus, we're going to get awfully tired carrying him to the house if it's a long way away."

Ken looked up this time as if trying to find the answers in the few clouds in the sky. "The weight of one kid divided between us would put about fifty to sixty pounds on each of us. Right?"

"Yeah," Peter agreed, again not sure of where Ken was heading with this train of thought.

"Well," Ken continued, looking at Peter as if he had just won the award for being the smartest person in the world, "then we need to get two more guys to help us carry the stretcher."

Peter didn't like the idea of getting anyone else involved in their attempts to bring blood donors to his house. "I don't know," he said, not sure of what to say. He liked the idea of lightening the load by distributing it between two more carriers, but he didn't like letting others in on what they were doing. "Do you have anyone in mind who you can trust to keep their mouths closed?"

"Let's ask Cory and Justin to help us," Ken replied almost immediately as if he had already had them in mind.

These two boys were a little on the rough side and had had some trouble in both school and the neighborhood, mostly just pranks and mischief. They never did anything that would be considered a felony. They never broke in and robbed a house or stole a car. But they weren't above trying to see if they could get away with something. Peter was friends with these two, but not what one would call close friends. Occasionally, the four would go swimming or skateboarding, but they didn't spend a lot of time together, or not as much as Peter and Ken spent together.

Ken, seeing Peter's hesitation, was concerned that his friend didn't want to use those two boys. "Look at it this way," Ken said. "We need someone who would be willing to help but can keep their mouths shut. Cory and Justin would love to get involved just for the fun of it. I don't think they would go and tell anyone."

Peter sat there for a couple of seconds, unable to think of any alternative friends who might work with them on this project. "Okay," Peter finally agreed, "let's see if they're interested."

Ken got on the phone and had Cory and Justin come over to his house to discuss a possible project that he said he needed their help with. Each agreed to meet over at Ken's house later that afternoon.

"Great," Ken said, excited that they were interested, "see you around four."

Later that afternoon, Cory was the first to show up at Ken's house. He was a tall, skinny kid who didn't look over twelve years old. Occasionally, his blue eyes and baby face gave him lots of trouble in school as the kids sometimes teased him. However, lately, the girls had started to find his features very attractive. Although a skinny kid with skinny arms, he wasn't without muscles. They didn't stand out, but he was as strong as Ken and stronger than Peter.

Justin was the type of kid who always seemed to be ten minutes late. Today was no exception. He knocked on the door exactly ten minutes later than he was expected. Justin was a handsome boy with broad shoulders and a thick shock of dark hair, usually requiring combing. He was built like a linebacker and was hoping to play that position in the coming school year. His voice, unlike Cory's, was deep and raspy, the result of an accident he'd had as a kid that affected his vocal cords.

The four boys made themselves comfortable on the back porch with Ken in his normal position on the railing. Peter stood next to him, while Justin and Cory sat on the porch, leaning against the house. Ken explained the situation and what they were trying to do. Cory knew how Peter must be feeling since his cousin had just recently died from the disease. Peter stepped in and explained the procedures and precautions they had to take in catching a kid, putting him or her to sleep, and testing his or her blood type. Ken continued by explaining the problem with transporting the kids back to Peter's house for the blood transfusion, saying that they wanted Cory and Justin to help as stretcher-bearers. Cory and Justin both agreed to help them in their efforts to carry donors back to Peter's house. They all decided to go the next day on a trial run to see if this plan would work.

Early the next afternoon, the four boys worked on constructing a stretcher to use for carrying their donors back to Peter's house. They started with two long poles that came out of a closet. They took an old dark blue sleeping bag and zipped it up. One end of the sleeping bag was open.

They cut two small holes in the closed end to slide the poles through. To test the stretcher, Ken and Peter held one end, while the other end rested on the picnic table. Justin pushed down on the poles on the table end to prevent them from moving. Cory, being the lightest and the closest in size to the donors they would be carrying, climbed onto the stretcher to see how strong it was. Their efforts paid off; the makeshift stretcher held Cory's weight with no problem. The other nice thing about their stretcher was that the two poles could compress next to each other, making the contraption easy to carry. If stopped and questioned, they could pull out the poles and roll up the sleeping bag. Then they'd be just some boys going to a friend's house for a campout, with two of the boys having brought their walking sticks.

"Okay," Ken said. The sun had started to set. "Let's go." Peter and Ken led the way with Cory and Justin following behind. All four wore dark clothes. Justin had the job of carrying the stretcher.

"Where are we going tonight?" Cory asked, excited to be part of this expedition.

"We're going over to the Lakota Cliff Apartments," Ken answered. "We've had some good luck there."

"Is it wise to go to the same apartment complex you've already been to?" Cory asked, a note of concern in his voice.

"Don't worry," Ken said. "We've been there before, but we only put one kid to sleep. We didn't carry anyone away or take any blood."

This still didn't make Cory feel any safer about going to someplace they had been before. But he was consoled by the thought that at least they knew the area.

They arrived at the apartment complex, only to find the place deserted. "Now what do we do?" Justin asked, hoping he hadn't come all this way carrying the stretcher for nothing.

"Well, there don't appear to be any kids outside," Ken reported. "Peter, do you think we should go over to the Spring River apartment complex?"

"We also had some luck over there," Peter answered.

"You mean if you don't find someone in one complex, you go to another one?" Justin asked, a touch of frustration in his tone.

"We have to go where the kids are," Ken replied. "So if there are no kids here, we have to go somewhere else."

"All right," Justin said, even though he didn't like the idea of walking to another apartment complex carrying the stretcher. But there was no use hanging around this one all night if there were no kids around.

"Okay then," Ken said, retracing his footsteps into the tall grass. "Let's go."

The four walked the two miles to the other complex, where they hoped to have more success.

"I hear some kids," Justin announced, a little louder than he should have.

"Quiet!" Ken scolded him in a stern voice. "We don't want the complex to know we're here."

"Sorry," Justin apologized. Cory slapped him on the arm as punishment for being so stupid.

"Also, we have found that if we hear kids' voices," Ken continued, "odds are there's more than one kid playing. And it's almost impossible to take out two kids, let alone a bunch. So we try to find a single kid by himself."

With that, the four headed off into the woods behind the complex to see who was outside.

They didn't have to travel far. On the patio of the third apartment building was a girl about eleven years of age playing a Game Boy cube. Peter looked at Ken. By this visual exchange of information, it was clear that they had agreed to try to put this girl to sleep.

"You two wait back here in the woods while Ken and I try to put her to sleep," Peter said, giving instructions for the first time all night. Until this point, Peter had let Ken play the role of leader—until they were ready to put the kid to sleep. The two newcomers didn't like being told what to do, especially since Ken had given all the orders up to that point. They felt Peter was their equal and not someone else who should be giving them orders. However, they did comply with the instructions, taking several steps into the woods.

When the two new pole-bearers were deeper into the woods, Peter removed his backpack. He and Ken prepared to capture this girl. "I don't like the idea of those two with us," Peter whispered to Ken.

"They'll be all right," Ken replied. "They can do this with their eyes closed."

"Well, I hope you're right," Peter said, closing his backpack and slipping the straps back onto his shoulders. "Are you ready?"

"Yep," Ken said. He went to the right to get into position on the far side of the porch. Peter crossed the yard behind the porch. He would pretend to trip in the girl's yard, hoping she would come out and check on his condition. Ken would then sneak up behind her and put her to sleep.

The two had been getting a lot of practice, so this one came off without a hitch. Ken and Peter quickly picked up the girl and carried her into the woods. As they laid her down on the ground, Cory and Justin came to the edge of the woods to see what they were doing.

"That's weird," Justin said, watching Peter test the girl's blood. Visibility was limited as darkness had settled over the area, but there was enough light from the red flashlight to allow them to see what Peter was doing. The two newcomers watched Peter add a drop of antigen to each drop of blood. "She's type O," Peter said, a little disappointed that they hadn't found a blood donor.

"Well," Ken said, trying to cheer Peter up, "we may not be able to use her blood, but let's try carrying her on the stretcher."

"You want to try it?" Peter asked, directing his question to Cory and Justin.

"Sure," Justin answered, eager to do something. He was getting bored sitting around in the dark doing nothing.

"Okay," Peter said, "go get the stretcher. Let's see if this works." As Justin went to get the stretcher, which was lying a few feet deeper into the woods, Peter finished putting everything away then slid his arms through the straps of his backpack.

"All right," Justin said, laying the homemade stretcher down next to their new passenger.

Peter lifted the girl by her feet as Ken lifted her from under her shoulders. The two lightly placed her in the center of the stretcher. Peter moved up to the front end by Ken, and Cory and Justin moved over to the other end of the stretcher. Each boy stood beside the stretcher, ready to lift the girl off the ground.

"Okay," Ken said. All four boys stooped down, each grabbing his end of the two poles. "One, two, three, lift," Ken softly instructed them so that no one but the four of them could hear him. The four boys lifted the girl up. The girl may have been around a hundred pounds, but because the weight was divided four ways, she didn't feel that heavy.

"Now," Ken said, heading into the woods, "watch your step." The going was slow in the woods, but the four made good time. They carried the girl through the woods and then across the field. To prevent one arm from doing all the work, they made several stops to switch sides. However, Ken and Peter always took the lead since they had more experience walking in the woods in the dark. They knew what kind of obstacles to look for. When they ran into a hitch, they would notify the pole-bearers at the other end of the stretcher.

"Okay," Ken said as they reached the far side of the empty field, "let's put her down here and take a break." They laid the stretcher down behind a line of bushes along the edge of the field. In this position, they were well hidden but could see the entire field and the road at the end of it. "Let's rest here for about five minutes, and then we'll take her back."

"I thought you wanted to take her to your house?" Justin asked, addressing Peter.

"Well," Peter started, "as we said yesterday, my mom doesn't have the disease, so there's no sense going all the way to my house if she doesn't need this girl's blood. This is more like a dry run."

"Well," Justin said, "it sure seems like a waste of time to come all this way and not take her to your house."

Peter wasn't sure whether he should get into a discussion about it or just drop it. "Are we ready to go?" Ken asked, ending any possibility of a discussion.

The four boys resumed their positions and lifted the girl into the air to transport her back to her apartment building.

When they reached the edge of the woods behind the apartment complex, Ken whispered, "Hold it." Something didn't look right. The four boys stopped and quickly ducked down into the high grass. "I don't like it," Ken said cautiously.

"What's up?" Peter asked, not sure what Ken was seeing or feeling.

"I don't know," Ken replied, confused at what he was feeling.

Peter could sense that Ken was greatly concerned about the situation in front of them. Peter didn't feel the same way as, as far as he could tell, everything was dark and quiet.

"When we were here earlier," Ken whispered with a tone of concern, "almost every apartment had its lights on. Now look," he said, pointing to the building in front of them. "There are only three lights on in the entire building. And look over there," Ken said, pointing to the building to their right. "Those apartments have lots of light on."

Peter wasn't sure what Ken was feeling, but he could see what Ken was referring to, and the nearly dark apartment building made him feel a little uneasy also. "You think they know this girl is missing?" Peter asked as the fear of getting caught rose up in his soul.

"I don't know," Ken said, continuing to survey the apartment windows. "It would be very easy to stand up there and watch for someone to come up in the dark. In fact, it is a lot darker than normal, as if they're trying to make us feel that it's safe because we won't be able to be seen."

Justin and Cory were listening to Ken and Peter's conversation, although they could not get it all because the two boys were talking very softly. "I think we should get out of here," Cory said, sounding concerned.

"You may be right," Ken agreed, and motioned for the four of them to retreat deeper into the woods. "Okay," Ken started, "let's get the girl off the stretcher, and you two head back to my house. We'll give you a ten-minute start before we try to put her back on the porch. That way you will have time to get away with that stretcher. We wouldn't want them to catch us with it and then have to explain why we have it."

"That's not a bad idea. And take this too," Peter said, taking off his backpack. "Do you still have the bag in your pocket with the rag?" Peter asked Ken, referring to the chloroform-soaked rag.

Ken reached into his pants pocket, pulled out the Ziploc bag, and gave it to Peter, who quickly returned it to the backpack.

"Here," Peter said, giving the backpack to Cory. "Drop this off too."

"Okay," Ken said, "get going. I'll give you ten minutes."

As Cory and Justin reversed direction and headed through the woods, Ken and Peter waited and watched.

"You wait here with her," Ken said, pointing to the sleeping girl now lying on the ground. "I'm going to go around to the other end of the building to see if I can see anything suspicious."

"All right," Peter whispered back, "but be careful."

Ken made his way through the woods. They were much deeper than they normally would have been, just in case there was someone nearby who might see him. When he reached the end of the apartment complex, he slowly made his way back to the edge of the woods. He still saw nothing out of the ordinary, except that most of the lights were out. There didn't appear to be anything wrong, but he still felt awfully uneasy about the whole situation. Unable to see anything that would support his suspicions, he retraced his steps back into the woods.

More than ten minutes had passed before he could rejoin Peter and the girl. As Ken approached Peter's position, he again felt something was wrong. He didn't see Peter. Where had he gone? Ken slowly advanced toward where Peter was supposed to have been waiting. Still no sign of Peter. Ken wanted to call out, but that might bring unwanted attention. He continued his advance one slow step at a time, looking around not only for Peter but also for anything that might be abnormal. Ken was sure this was the spot where he'd left Peter, but there was no Peter. Starting to feel desperate, Ken didn't know what to do.

After taking several more steps, he looked closely at the apartment building to see if someone was watching. Had someone seen Peter and come to get him? If that had happened, Ken figured he would have heard something since the night seemed deathly quiet. He didn't know.

Ken took one more step and almost tripped over a small hill in front of him. He didn't remember a hill here. As he knelt down to feel the hillside, he noticed it was made out of some material other than dirt. Suddenly, a corner of the hill moved and a familiar face popped out. "Careful, you klutz," Peter whispered.

"I was wondering where you'd gone," Ken said, getting down next to Peter.

"I didn't know if anyone could see us," Peter whispered, "so I pulled some of the tall grass and covered the girl and then used some to cover myself. Good camouflage, isn't it?"

"Good thinking," Ken replied, a little envious that he hadn't thought of it. "I didn't see anything, but I tell you, something is going on."

"What do you want to do?" Peter asked.

"What I would like to do," Ken answered with a tone of desperation, "is leave this girl by the edge of the woods and get the hell out of here."

"Well," Peter replied, concerned about the girl's safety, "we should put her back so someone can find her." He didn't want to leave her at the edge of the woods. It could be dangerous if she didn't wake up; something could happen to her. He would feel much better if they put her back on the patio.

"Yeah," Ken agreed in a defeated tone, knowing Peter was right. "Okay," he said with a tone of determination. "Let's pick her up and quickly lay her on the patio, then run like hell."

"Okay," Peter said. The two removed the grass covering the girl and lifted her off the ground. To make it easier to travel, this time Peter picked up the girl by her feet, with the front of his body facing away from her. This way both be and Ken would be facing forward. This would allow them to travel faster.

"All right," Ken whispered, taking a deep breath, "let's go." The two walked slowly at first, until they reached the edge of the woods. They again surveyed the area for signs of watchful eyes. However, they saw nothing that would indicate a problem.

"Go!" Ken ordered. The two of them, carrying the girl, quickly crossed the thirty feet of open ground to the patio. *Nothing yet,* Ken thought as they took the two steps up onto the patio. They carefully laid the girl down on the lounge chair and then turned to head back toward the woods. Still, all was quiet.

As they were leaving the porch, Ken thought he heard a noise from the end of the apartment complex. It sounded as if a door had opened and closed. Instead of running for the woods, the two boys froze in their tracks, not knowing what was happening or what to do next. The noise at the end of the building was now joined with the sound of whistling. Whoever it was wasn't very good at it either.

"Let's go," Ken whispered almost inaudibly. He and Peter quickly and quietly returned to the woods. Nothing happened. The apartment complex may have been darker than they had expected it to be, but all appeared to be normal.

As the two boys headed back through the woods on their way home, they didn't say a word. They refrained from speaking until they exited the other side and started across the field. "Man, that was scary," Peter said, first to break the silence.

"I'm sorry," Ken said, feeling that he had caused all the fear.

"Sorry for what?" Peter asked, not knowing why Ken was taking the blame for something that hadn't happened.

"I guess I'm just paranoid," he replied.

"Well," Peter said, trying to reassure Ken, "I would rather you be a little paranoid and be safe than be reckless and get us caught."

The two boys continued the walk home, where they met up with Cory and Justin to tell them that nothing had happened.

CHAPTER 14

John came home after a rather quiet day running around town. He followed his normal evening routine by changing into some cooler clothes and sitting down in his chair to watch the news. Peter sat on the end of the couch, playing his Game Boy. John was a little concerned that Paula was late in getting home. He didn't know what was keeping her. She usually got home before the news started, but she must have been held up by traffic. The only one missing was Beth, and since John had seen her bike in the driveway, he assumed she was somewhere around the house.

John usually liked to watch the weather after work. But today he just wanted to sit in his chair and exist. However, all the silence in the house caused him to think about all the negative problems he had experienced. So he grabbed the remote and turned on the news.

John turned up the volume so he could better hear the newscaster. As he listened, he heard some basic news about the problems in the Middle East. *Will these issues in the Middle East ever be settled?* he wondered.

"Now for the local news," the newscaster continued. "The police have issued a warning that kids should not be outside after dark unless accompanied by a parent or guardian. The number of reports of abducted children has risen 30 percent over the last month. For more information on this story, we go to reporter Mark Martin at the Colerain Police Department."

"Thank you, Dave," Mark replied to the newscaster. "Police have noticed an increase in calls from parents reporting a missing child. I talked to

Detective Chun, whose feeling is that a lot of these abductions are attributed to kidnappers who are after young kids to sell their blood. Ever since the CDC indicated that the BARD disease does not affect young children, the number of missing kids has increased. An extensive search for these children has resulted in some arrests. Unfortunately, several bodies of young children have been found in various parts of the city. The coroner's report for several of these kids indicates that they died of insufficient fluids in the body."

"So what you're saying," said Dave, as the vision of Mark shrank to a small window on a display behind Dave, "is that these kids died because someone withdrew too much blood?"

"That's right," Mark continued. "And the police are requesting that you keep a close eye on your kids, especially those between the ages of eight and twelve. This is Mark Martin reporting for the Colerain Police Department. Now back to you, Dave."

"Thanks, Mark," Dave said as the image of Mark disappeared from the screen. "The number of abductions, in reality, may be lower than indicated," he continued, "as there are reports of missing kids who were later found sleeping close to where they live. An interesting fact about these abductions is that some of these kids were put to sleep with sleeping pills or chloroform. Many of these kids were found with a Band-Aid on one of their arms covering a puncture wound. Police have indicated that someone put these kids to sleep, withdrew some blood, and took the kids close to where they'd been picked up. Police have promised to step up patrols in areas where there are a large number of kids."

The statements made on the TV caught Peter's attention even though he was involved with the Game Boy. Peter looked up at his father. The two exchanged a glance of concern, although neither said a word.

John continued to listen to the newscaster, who used the report on child abductions as a lead-in to news about the disease. "The latest news on BARD indicates that the disease is continuing to spread at an alarming rate. In Ohio alone, there have been over forty-five thousand deaths, and over eight hundred thousand across the United States. The total number of deaths across the world can only be estimated at over one-point-two million."

John sat there and thought about the numbers and how Sharon was now a statistic represented by those numbers. *How many more will there be?* he thought. *And will Paula be one of them?*

"With a large number of deaths," the newscaster continued, "employers are having trouble maintaining a substantial workforce to keep businesses going. Also, many employers are requiring a blood test to determine blood type and are only hiring type B workers. There is a concern in political circles as to whether this may be a form of discrimination.

"Another economic concern is rising prices. Prices of all kinds are on the rise. Gas companies have complained that they've had to shut down two refineries because they didn't have enough qualified workers to run them. Some of the employees who worked at these two sites were transferred to other refineries to help offset some of the manpower problems at those facilities. The future doesn't look good for the consumer as prices are expected to continue their upward momentum for now."

Peter had had enough of hearing about the dismal future the news seemed to be projecting these days. He got up and went upstairs to his room to listen to music and play his Game Boy in peace. This would cheer him up, especially if he beat the game. John, also having had enough of the dismal news, turned off the TV and headed for the kitchen.

John looked up at the clock hanging on the kitchen wall and noticed that it was almost six thirty. Paula was usually home by now. Becoming a little concerned, he called her cell phone. Normally he tried not to call her when he knew she was driving, but he was starting to worry about her, wondering why she was so late. He dialed her cell phone number, but all it did was ring five times and go to her voice mail. Because it had rung as many times as it had, he knew that her cell phone was on and she wasn't talking to anyone. Otherwise, his call would have gone straight to her voicemail. Either she didn't have the phone close enough to hear it or, for some reason, she was out of range. He wasn't sure about anything, so all he could do was wait.

John continued to look at the clock, wondering what was taking his wife so long to get home. He prayed she hadn't had an accident. He reasoned with himself that she was at the store getting groceries and that the cell phone wasn't getting good enough reception. He continued to wait by the window in the front room, while the large grandfather clock behind him chimed seven times. He was really starting to get worried. Finally, at about a quarter after seven, he saw the car pull into the driveway. He watched from the window to see if Paula had a lot of bags to bring in as he assumed she had gone shopping. However, she didn't get out of the car.

John opened the front door and stood out on the porch to get a closer look at what Paula was doing. Examining the person behind the wheel, he wasn't sure it was Paula. Whoever was driving had his or her head down. This made John wonder not only who it was but also what was wrong.

John walked up to the car and opened the door. There, in the front seat, was Paula hunched over the steering wheel. "What's wrong?" John asked, stricken at the sight of her. He had never seen her do this. Was she sick? He knelt down by her and tried to look into her eyes. "Are you all right?" he asked, still with no reply from her.

John leaned into the car and pulled Paula back so she was in a normal sitting position. She finally opened her eyes, but they were glazed as if she was there physically but not mentally. "What's wrong?" John inquired.

"I feel really tired," Paula replied in a soft, almost inaudible voice.

"Come on," John said, putting his arms around her to help her climb out of the car. "Let me help you into the house." John opened the door with one hand as he tried to support Paula with the other. "Peter!" John yelled with a sense of great urgency in his voice. He hoped that Peter would hear him over the music playing in his room.

Peter heard his father's call and was concerned by the tone his father had used. It wasn't the normal call, such as when his dad wanted him to do something. There was more of a sense of desperation in his tone. "What's up?" Peter questioned. He had jumped down the stairs from the second floor in two big leaps.

"Your mother isn't feeling very well," John answered. "Help me get her to the couch." The two supported Paula as they walked down the short hallway to the living room. Then Peter quickly ran around, grabbing several pillows to make her feel comfortable.

"How's that?" John asked as he placed a pillow under Paula's knees. She liked to lie on the couch and place a pillow under her knees. She always said it helped her hips.

"That's fine," she replied in a very weak voice.

"Would you like me to make you a cup of tea or get you something to eat?" John asked, not knowing what to do next. However, Paula just closed her eyes and shook her head no.

John walked away quietly, careful not to make a sound, and motioned for Peter to follow him into the kitchen.

"What's wrong with Mom?" Peter asked, concerned that she might be really sick.

"I don't know exactly," John replied with a touch of fear in his voice, "but I think she has come down with BARD."

"That means she's going to die," Peter responded in fear.

John stood there, not wanting to lose his wife of eighteen years, but not knowing what else he could do.

"Dad," Peter said in a soft voice as if preparing to tell a secret. His father looked up at him, his eyes moist with tears. "I think we can get her a blood donor."

John's eyes widened at the news. "How are you going to get a donor?" he asked, surprised by his son's statement. John and Peter had talked about getting blood donors but were concerned about the risks associated with carrying out the idea, especially since they'd heard the news report this evening. Peter never had told his father that he had been going out at night to capture kids to take some of their blood.

"Well," Peter continued, "Ken and I have gone out a dozen times to see if we can find kids to be blood donors. We've been pretty lucky in finding a couple, not that we've taken any blood from them other than to test it."

"How do you get the kids to let you test their blood?" John asked, a little confused.

"We don't ask," Peter replied. He paused as a puzzled look came across his father's face. "We put them to sleep with chloroform and then test them."

"You mean like they said on the news tonight?" John asked, beginning to realize that the news might have been referring to Peter's actions. "Have you ever gotten caught doing that?" John asked, concerned that Peter's future address may be that of the penitentiary.

"We have been very careful and have worked out all the details. We have tried many times and have made changes to our procedures as we learn from each trip."

John stood there totally amazed that his son had gone this far with the plan. He didn't know what else to do. "Can you get a donor for your mother tonight?" John asked, concerned that Paula may not survive long without one.

"I don't see why not," Peter answered with a certain degree of pride for having pulled this off without his father's knowing anything about it. Although deep down he wasn't sure he would succeed based on their past record, especially since the news had made a big point about parents not letting their kids run loose with no supervision.

"Is there anything I can do to help?" John asked.

"Well," Peter said, thinking about the process that he and Ken had gone through in finding donors, "the biggest problem we have is transportation. When we find a kid whose blood will work, we can carry him or her away from the area, but to carry someone all the way here and then back again is awfully tiring. If we can find a donor," Peter continued, running through some alternatives in his head, "can you come by and pick us up so that we can get here easier and faster? We're still not sure how long the chloroform lasts."

"Sure," John said, willing to help but still surprised that they had worked out the process so well. "Whatever I can do to help keep your mom alive."

"Okay. I'll have Ken's cell phone. You stand by the phone here. We will work out some sort of plan so that you can pick us up."

And with that, Peter went to call Ken and the others to get ready for the actual event: finding a donor and performing a blood transfusion.

The boys had gone out on many dry runs to see if they could find blood donors. During these trips, their biggest fear had always been that they would get caught. Tonight would be a whole new experience. They were going out to find someone with the correct blood type and take him or her back home to transfer healthy blood from their involuntary donor to Peter's mother.

"Where do you think we should go to tonight?" Peter asked Ken, who had played the role of the leader almost since the time Peter initially talked to him. The four boys were busy gathering up the supplies they needed. Justin was carrying the stretcher, and Peter was slipping on the backpack with the other supplies.

"Let's try that housing complex over on Maple Road," Ken answered, not sure of the name of the complex.

"That's Cherry Hills," said Cory. "I have a friend who lives in that complex."

"Great," Ken said, "then you might know some easy ways to get in and out without being noticed."

"Sure," Cory replied, proud to be more than a simple follower. "Let's go." He started off with Justin at his side.

Ken and Peter followed, but Ken felt very uneasy about having Cory leading the way. Cory was a little reckless, and Ken didn't want him to do something that would get them caught. "Let's stay close," Ken whispered to Peter. "I want to head off any trouble before Cory stumbles into it."

The four hiked through several backyards, through a short patch of woods, over a small creek, and through a small field on the edge of the housing complex. "Stop!" Ken ordered in a loud whisper. Something caught his attention, but he wasn't sure what it was. The four boys were kneeling down, trying to minimize their silhouettes in the field.

"What is it?" Peter asked, his voice almost inaudible.

"I don't know," Ken replied in the same low tone. "I heard something, but I don't know where it came from."

The four remained motionless for another two minutes, and then Ken blurted out with a soft giggle, "I'll be damned. It's an owl."

As the boys continued to listen, they also heard the sound that Ken had finally identified. Off to their right came the sound of an owl hooting away and then being quiet for thirty-second intervals.

"That owl's been there for I don't know how many years," Cory mentioned.

"Okay," Ken acknowledged with a sigh of relief. "Let's go." He stood upright again. The four continued toward the back property lines of the houses in the complex. They were on the edge of the field, but the grass in this area was still pretty high. It was high enough that if they had to, they could drop down and conceal themselves from observing eyes.

As the four made their way along the property line, each backyard appeared to be quiet and dark. "I don't think anyone is home," Cory said in a slightly louder tone than Ken would have liked.

"Whisper," Ken scolded in a stern but hushed tone.

"Sorry," Cory apologized in a soft whisper, following Ken's orders.

They were about to give up, when Peter spotted a boy sitting on the porch. The other three didn't see him. Peter almost missed him. He would have if it weren't for the fact that a reflection in that direction caught his eye.

"Okay," Ken said, looking the area over. "We can bring the boy back to that shed over there," he added, pointing to a shed about fifty feet from the house. "We will test his blood there. You two had better wait here," he said to Cory and Justin, "in case there is trouble. If he's a match, we will bring him here, where you will be ready with the stretcher."

With everyone ready, Ken and Peter set out to capture the first candidate of the night. Ken worked his way through a yard two houses down from where the boy was sitting, and Peter worked his way over to the shed next to a stack of firewood. Once in position, Peter reached over and pushed the stack of firewood over, catching the boy's attention.

The boy looked up from his game, stood, walked down the porch's four steps, and headed toward the shed. The boy had gone maybe ten feet when, before he even knew what had happened, Ken put the chloroform-soaked rag over his face and he drifted off to sleep. Peter arrived within seconds, and the two of them carried the boy behind the shed. With high hopes, they tested the boy's blood as they had practiced doing many times before. The test proved he was type B. "Looks like he'll have a future," Peter replied disappointedly. Then, he and Ken quickly carried the boy back to the porch, placed the Game Boy on his lap, and headed back to join Cory and Justin.

When the four were reunited, Ken voiced his frustration at not finding a compatible donor. "I was really hoping," he said with a tone of disappointment.

"Don't worry," Peter said, trying to give him some encouragement. "We'll just keep looking."

The four continued around the far corner of the complex and began traveling on the south side. At first, their travels resulted in empty backyards. At least there appeared to be people home as some houses had lights on. They had passed about ten houses, which was quite a distance since these houses had wide yards, when they saw something moving in the shadows. "Duck!" Ken whispered, warning the group to drop to the ground and out of sight. Up ahead about two hundred feet, an adult was putting something into a shed. All the boys crouched down as they waited for the adult to go back inside.

After they passed this house, they passed several more houses just to be on the safe side—in case that adult were to come back out again. It wasn't a hindering decision as there were no kids outside anyway. They continued looking for possible donors who might fit their requirements. They passed a house with teenagers in the backyard trying to play volleyball in the dark. One house had someone barbecuing on the porch for a late supper, and another house had several adults sitting in a screened-in sunroom, talking about politics.

As they were passing another house, the light by the back door came on, scaring the hell out of the four hunters. "Duck!" Ken again ordered. The four dropped to the ground and slowly crawled deeper into the tall grass. "This way," Ken directed, trying to get as far from the light as possible. As they were crawling along, Ken came to what appeared to be a small path running from the housing complex and across the field. "This looks like a good way to get the hell out of here," he whispered. A minute later, the four of them were heading down the path.

They had traveled only about forty feet when Ken came to a stop to look and see what was happening. They could still see the house, but not as clearly as before because of several large tree branches partially blocking their view. However, they could hear voices from the house. "See ya later," some girl said. The voice sounded like that of a younger girl, but the boys couldn't determine her age.

"I'll see you tomorrow," replied another girl's voice. This girl sounded older, maybe an older sister. "Careful walking across the field."

"You're a big worrywart," replied the first girl.

Ken looked at Peter and could almost imagine what he was thinking. Could this be the path she would walk down?

Ken turned to Cory and Justin. "You two crawl farther into the grass in that direction," he said, pointing away from the path. "Let's get ready." Peter immediately slid off the backpack and pulled out the plastic bag with the white cloth and the bottle of chloroform. The four waited, listening to the gate to a chain-link fence open and close. It was dead quiet as Ken and Peter strained their ears to listen for the approaching target.

As footsteps approached, they could hear the girl singing softly to herself. The small sliver of the moon cast a slight radiance across the grass and off the girl coming toward Ken. Ken could see she was about eleven or twelve years old, which was requirement number one. She was slender but tall, which he hoped put her at about a hundred pounds. She was no more than five feet away now. Several more steps and she would walk right past him, never knowing he was there. In less than two seconds, Ken had the chloroform-soaked rag on her face; she went out without even knowing what had happened. Peter was there a second later to help carry her away from the path to a safe area to test her blood.

Again the two boys went through the ritual of testing the blood of their captive. Peter put the antigen drops onto the drops of blood and then looked up at Ken. "She's type A," Peter said with a big smile on his face. He then applied the third antigen, and his smile went from ear to ear. "She's A positive," he announced. "She's a match!"

"Okay," Ken said in a whisper as they packed up their supplies. "Let's carry her to Cory and Justin, and then we'll call your father for a ride." After the two lifted the girl, they carried her twenty feet or so, to the spot where the stretcher-bearers were waiting patiently. "We've got one," Ken proudly whispered. The two quickly opened the homemade stretcher, and Ken and Peter carefully laid the girl down.

"Okay," Ken said, still whispering. "Let's go. We still need to be careful and quiet and keep a lookout for anything." Ken and Peter lifted one end of the stretcher, and Cory and Justin lifted the other end. Ken and Peter led the way through the field and back to the road where they hoped they could catch their ride.

As they approached the road, they stopped to hide in a nearby ravine. Peter used Ken's cell phone and called his father to tell him where they wanted to be picked up. John was supposed to flash his headlights as he came down Maple Road so they would know it was him.

It seemed like hours waiting in the field—waiting and watching for a car to flash its lights. Every time a car came down the street and didn't flash its lights, Peter had to duck down so that the headlights wouldn't shine on him and reveal his position. Minutes seemed like hours, but Peter finally saw a car flash its headlights. He quickly called his father on the cell phone. "I hope you just flashed your lights," he said to his father over the phone.

"That's me," John replied.

"Hey," Peter said softly to the others, "it's my dad."

"Okay, let's go," Ken said to Cory and Justin. Justin took one end of the stretcher, and Ken and Cory took the other end, while Peter gave his father directions as to where they were hiding.

"You've got about a hundred feet to go," Peter said into the cell phone. The approaching vehicle slowed down, anticipating a stop. "Another thirty feet," Peter directed as he stepped out of the grass. Peter looked quickly in the opposite direction; no cars were coming. John pulled up, pulling partway off the road and into the grass. Peter could see Ken and the two others carrying the girl up the small embankment to the road.

"Quickly!" Ken said. Peter went to the back of the van and opened the liftgate. The boys quickly slid the stretcher into the van, and then Ken and Cory climbed in next to the girl. As Peter was closing the back of the van, Justin quickly climbed into the back seat. Finally, Peter jumped into the front seat next to John.

"Nice job," John said to the four of them. The boys were swelling with pride in their accomplishment, especially since none of them had thought they could do it.

"Thanks, Dad," Peter said, "but this is only the first stage. We still have a lot to do before we can consider this night over."

When John arrived home, he backed the van up the driveway and opened the garage door. Then he continued up the driveway until the back of the van was inside the garage. This made it hard for anyone passing by to see what was going on in the garage.

Peter climbed out of the van and went to the back to again open the liftgate. The boys jumped out, then Ken and Justin pulled the stretcher out. John opened the door to the house so the boys could carry their donor into the house.

"Grab four chairs," John said to the boys not carrying the stretcher, "and place them by the couch." Peter and Cory each grabbed two chairs and carried them over to the couch. John took a chair from Peter. "Position the chairs like this," he said, positioning the first chair so its back was toward the couch. Then Peter positioned the second chair so it was about two feet away, facing the first chair. Cory followed John's instructions and positioned the other two chairs in the same manner. "Good," John said to Cory. "Now position the stretcher between them."

Ken and Justin walked over to the chairs and positioned the stretcher so the poles were resting on the chairs, making a nice cot. Their captured donor was about three feet from the couch, where Paula lay unconscious.

John's past job experience as a phlebotomist had given him the knowledge and ability to draw the blood out of a donor's arm, although he had never tried to put the blood back into anyone's arm. But anyway, because his right hand was all bandaged up, he was unable to perform this procedure. This meant that Peter would have to perform the procedure with his father's guidance.

"Okay, Peter," John said, "it's all up to you now."

Peter had never felt so scared in his life. He had read a lot about how to perform a blood transfusion, but reading about doing it and actually doing it are two different things. However, he had his father to help guide him through the process. Peter put on some sterile gloves and pulled out the sterilized needle and the sterilized hose, the latter of which was connected to the collection bag he had purchased on the internet.

"Ken," John called out, "since you helped with the blood tests, can you get an alcohol wipe and clean this part of her arm?" He was pointing at the inside part of the donor's elbow. Ken quickly pulled out some sterile gloves and an alcohol wipe and cleaned the area John had designated.

Peter positioned a tourniquet around the donor's arm just above the elbow and tightened it to make the arteries and veins hyperextend.

"Okay," John instructed, "press on the skin until you feel a spongy section. That should indicate that there's a vein there."

"Okay," Peter said, taking a deep breath to relax himself. He probed the girl's arm in an attempt to find the vein into which he would try to insert the needle. It seemed to take forever to figure out what was a vein and what was an artery or a muscle. "I think this is it," he said, after identifying a long protrusion along the top of the skin.

"Good," John said. "Now position the needle in line with the vein and slide the needle through the skin. You will feel a small amount of resistance when you first penetrate the vein. Then just slide it in a little more so that the needle is fully inside the vein."

Easier said than done, Peter thought to himself. He picked up the needle and looked over at his father. If he couldn't get the needle into the girl's vein, it meant that his mother could die from the disease before they could find another donor to try.

"Man, I'm scared," Peter said as he looked down at the needle and the girl's arm.

"You can do it," John replied with a tone of encouragement.

"Here goes." Peter positioned the needle on a steep angle in line with what he hoped was the vein. As if in slow motion, he slid the needle into the skin. The girl didn't even flinch from the puncture. He continued to push the needle deeper into her arm. Suddenly part of the plastic tube near the insertion point turned red, indicating that he had found the vein.

"You did it!" everyone said, almost in unison. They had all been staring intently, and they were all relieved when Peter found the vein.

"Yeah, but that's only half the process," Peter replied, not as enthusiastic as the others. He reached up and released the tourniquet. Then, he reached over to the other end of the tube and released the clamp that was preventing the blood from flowing into the collection bag. Suddenly, the tube turned dark red as blood started to flow into the collection bag.

The collection bag would hold a full pint of blood. However, given the size of their donor, John suggested that they not take an entire pint. They agreed to fill the bag between 80 percent and 90 percent full. It took about twelve minutes to fill the bag to the desired volume.

"Okay, that should do it," Peter announced. He closed the clamp on the tube. Then he took the small gauze he had ready and positioned it over the puncture wound on the donor's arm. As he pulled out the needle, he quickly placed the gauze on the puncture wound to prevent additional bleeding. "Can you give me a Band-Aid?" Peter asked, holding the gauze in place. Ken quickly took the Band-Aid out of the wrapping and gave it to Peter, who applied it over the gauze.

"That's the first part," Peter said, glad this part was over. "Now I need to put this into Mom's arm," he said as he hung the bag of collected blood on a hook on the curtain rod above the couch. He started by applying a tourniquet to his mother's left arm. Then he had Ken repeat the process of cleaning her skin with the alcohol pad. Peter took her arm and examined the inside elbow to see if he could find the vein. This time he found the vein quickly. "Here goes," Peter said, still scared that he could kill his mother if something were to go wrong. Positioning the needle on an angle as he had done with the needle used on the donor, he slowly pushed the needle into her arm. The problem here was that he had to make sure he was in the vein and not going through it. If he were to go through the vein, he would just pump blood under the skin and not into her circulatory system. He slowly pushed the needle in farther trying to judge the depth of the vein vis-à-vis the length of the needle. "I think that will do it," he said, silently praying that he had done it right. "Okay," he said, grabbing the clamp on the tube, "here goes." He released the clamp and removed the tourniquet. There was no easy way to tell if the blood was flowing through or not. Peter quickly checked his mom's arm to see if the area around the puncture was swelling up with blood. All looked good so far.

Five minutes seemed to take forever as no one was sure anything was happening. "Well," John said, "it looks like the bag is getting flatter, which means the blood must be going into her vein."

"Okay," Peter replied with a sigh of relief. The bag was basically empty when Peter reclamped the tube to stop the blood from flowing. He again took a small gauze pad and positioned it over the puncture wound in his mother's arm. As he pulled out the needle, he quickly placed the gauze on the puncture wound to prevent additional bleeding. "Give me another Band-Aid," he said, holding the gauze in place. Ken quickly took the Band-Aid out of the wrapping and gave it to Peter, who applied it over the gauze. When he was done, he took the transfusion hose, the bag, and all the trash and put it into a plastic bag. John took the bag and disposed of it in the trash can.

"You did a great job," John said to Peter, who took a deep sigh of relief, glad that the process was over.

"I hope they find a cure soon," Peter said. "I don't want to have to do that again." Deep down he had a feeling that a cure wasn't coming soon and that he would get very good at blood transfusions.

"Okay," Peter said, "I guess we had better get the girl back before she wakes up."

"Right," Ken said as he got up out of John's favorite chair. Ken and Justin took positions at each end of the stretcher. "Ready," Ken said, "lift." With their blood donor off the chairs, Cory, John, and Peter replaced the chairs around the dining room table while Ken and Justin headed toward the back door. John opened the garage door, and Ken and Justin carried the stretcher out of the house and into the garage. Peter and Cory assisted the other two in sliding the donor into the back end of the van. Everyone jumped into the back except Peter, who closed the liftgate and climbed into the front seat. John also climbed in, then started up the van.

The trip back was quiet until they came close to the drop-off point. "Okay, guys!" John yelled to the three in the back. "Get ready." John surveyed the road in front of him and behind him for any approaching traffic. All looked clear. He pulled the van over to the side of the road and stopped. Peter jumped out. But before he could get to the back of the van to open the liftgate, a set of headlights came over the top of the hill in front of them.

"Hold it!" John yelled, pulling the hood release on the van. Pulling out the flashlight he had stored under the front seat for emergencies, he climbed out of the van. He went to the front of the vehicle, where he opened the hood and, using the flashlight, looked around the engine compartment. To anyone passing by, it would appear that he was checking something out, even though in reality, John was stalling, hoping the car would just drive by.

Peter, on the other hand, was on the passenger side of the van, ready to go either to the front of the van to be with his father or to the back of the van to let the group out.

The approaching car slowed down and finally stopped beside the van. "Anything wrong?" the driver of the small SUV asked.

"No," John replied. "I thought I smelled something burning, so I thought I'd better check it out, but I can't find anything wrong. I hate it when cars do that," John said to the Good Samaritan in a humorous tone. "It makes you feel the darn thing has a mind of its own sometimes."

"I know what you mean," said the driver, who accelerated as he continued on his way down the road.

John took another look up and down the street, but the only thing in sight was the disappearing taillights of the Good Samaritan. "Okay, Peter," he called out. Peter headed toward the back of the van to release the passengers.

"Quickly, before someone else comes by," Peter said to the gang inside. They quickly pulled the stretcher out and headed down the ravine where they had hidden themselves earlier. Peter closed the back of the van one second before a set of headlights came into view from behind him.

"Stay there," Ken called back up to Peter, afraid that whoever the driver was in the oncoming car might see him duck into the grass.

Peter quickly walked around to the front of the van, where his father still had the hood open. This time the car was in a hurry; it didn't even slow down to go past them. Once the car was no farther than fifty feet ahead of them, John closed the hood of the van and climbed into the front seat. Peter followed his father's lead, walking around to the other side of the van. However, instead of climbing in, he turned and leaped out of sight into the ravine. Seconds later, the van pulled back out onto the road, and the four boys, along with their donor, were alone in the dark.

"Okay, guys," Ken said, "let's take this girl home." The four took their places, one on each end of the pole, and started carrying her back to the path where they had picked her up. As they approached the path, the four of them crouched down and listened. All appeared to be quiet. "Okay," Ken said, "let's drop off our passenger." The four stopped on the path and laid the girl on the ground. "Let's go," Ken said. Everyone except Peter returned to the tall grass to get out of sight of anyone who might be watching.

Peter first pulled the Band-Aid off the girl's arm to see if she had stopped bleeding. The wound looked good. He didn't want to leave the Band-Aid on unless it was necessary, because then it would have been an immediate sign that something had happened. Since her arm had stopped bleeding, all that was visible now was a tiny spot indicating the needle entrance hole he hoped she would never see. Satisfied that she would not bleed to death, Peter pulled a small capsule out of his pocket. He took the capsule in both hands and bent it back and forth until he heard a small break. The internal chemicals became active as the strong odor of smelling salts filled the air. Peter passed the capsule in front of the girl's nose to help her wake up. He hoped to see some small reaction from her, but she showed no signs of reacting to the smelling salts. If she didn't react, there was a possibility that something was wrong. The girl could be in trouble. They would have to take her to a doctor to revive her. Peter tried again, passing the capsule in front of the girl's nose, hoping to get a response. What he got instead caught him totally by surprise. She came up swinging and swearing as if she were in a fight. Peter was surprised to hear such language from such a young girl, but his thoughts of her diction quickly left his mind as her right fist came flying in his direction. Peter was quick enough to duck and evade the swing. He headed off into the grass, not to hide, but to escape possible injury should she connect with any of the flying punches.

"She's awake," Peter announced to the others when he caught up with them. His announcement wasn't needed as the others easily had been able to hear the girl's voice and thereby determine her attitude.

"What happened?" Ken asked, wondering why the girl was so upset.

"I suggest we get out of here fast, before she realizes what happened to her," Peter said in desperation. He didn't want to hang around for explanations at this time. And with that, the four made a hasty retreat away from the housing complex.

The trip home was quiet for a while as they didn't want to attract any attention. But as they got closer to Ken's house, they began talking about the success of their evening's endeavors.

"I can't believe we pulled it off," Ken said to Peter as they walked up the driveway to Ken's house.

"We only pulled it off," Peter replied, a touch of sarcasm in his tone, "if the blood transfusion helps my mom."

"Don't worry," Ken said, trying to boost Peter's confidence, "you did a great job."

"Well, I'm going to run home and see," Peter said. With that, he turned and headed around the house to cut through the backyards as he had done so many times in the past.

"We're going to head home too," Justin said to Ken, referring to Cory and himself.

"Okay," Ken replied. "I'll give you a call later and let you know how it all turns out."

"Okay," Justin said. The two boys headed back down the driveway toward home.

As Peter entered his house, he was surprised to see his father sitting on the recliner. He thought he would be sitting with his mother. As he walked further into the living room, he noticed that his mother wasn't on the couch. "Where's Mom?" Peter asked, concerned that they may have killed her.

"Oh," John said, looking up from the TV, "she's upstairs taking a shower. She was sitting up watching TV when I came back. The transfusion appears to be working. She appears to be back to normal." With that, Peter sat down on the couch and watched TV with his father as he waited for his mother to come back downstairs.

Several minutes later, Paula came downstairs wearing her bathrobe and a towel around her head. "Hi, Mom," Peter called out, excited to see his mother up walking around again. "How do you feel?" Although glad to see her walking around, he was still concerned about her health.

"I feel fine," she replied. She took the towel off her head and rubbed her hair with it. "I guess I only needed a nap."

"That's great," Peter said, hoping the reason she was feeling better was because of the blood transfusion that she didn't even know she had gotten. He also hoped that she was feeling better because of the nap. That would mean she didn't have the disease, but somehow he didn't think that was the case. Peter looked over at his father and received a smile, indicating that his father was proud of the efforts he had made on his mother's behalf.

"I do have one question," Paula said, addressing the two of them. "Did I get stabbed by something here in my arm?" she asked, pointing to the Band-Aid on her inner elbow.

"I don't know," Peter replied, acting dumb.

"I don't know either," replied John, following his son's lead. "I believe you had that Band-Aid on your arm when you came home. I was going to ask you about it, but you looked tired. I didn't want to interfere with your nap."

Since Paula didn't know where the Band-Aid had come from, she had to accept their answers. She was just going to have to check at the office tomorrow. "I'm going to go upstairs and get dressed," she said, and headed back down the hallway.

"She doesn't remember," Peter said to his father. "That's great."

"Yeah," John replied. The two settled back, proud of their accomplishment that night, as they returned to watching the TV.

Their feelings were quickly shot down as they listened to the news. The newscaster was again reporting the latest news about the disease and the breakdown in society. "The number of victims of the disease in Ohio is now over six thousand, and the number of infected adults is estimated to be over ten thousand. Because of the number of dead or dying adults, the number of homeless kids roaming the streets without any parental supervision is estimated to be over seventy-five hundred. This is making it difficult for police and the military to maintain order. It is believed that many of these homeless kids have organized into gangs and that some of the members are not survivors of the disease but runaways who have joined a gang to get away from their parents. A sunset curfew was put into place to keep kids off the streets, but after three days, the effect of the curfew seems to have had little or no effect on minimizing the numbers of crimes that have been committed on the streets. The looting, vandalism, and arson have all risen to levels that are almost impossible for authorities to cope with. Some communities are on their own as resources have dried up or have been pulled to help in areas where the trouble is much greater."

Peter and John were feeling good about having helped Paula recover from the disease, but the news quickly converted their feelings of accomplishment into feelings of futility.

CHAPTER 15

A week can go by quickly if you're busy. The reverse of this is that a week can go by slowly if you have little to do. In Peter's case, the week seemed to fly by as summer was coming to an end. Ken and Peter had talked about the upcoming school year and the times they would have at football games, dances, and parties with their girlfriends. However, the future plans of the school rapidly had been put on hold.

Peter came home from Ken's house to find his father in the living room with his mother. She was lying on the couch. His father had a desperate look of fear in his eyes.

"What's wrong?" Peter asked, a tone of concern in his voice.

"It looks like the Sanguis virus has used up the blood from the last transfusion," John answered as he looked up from Paula. "It appears that you're going to have to go out and find another donor."

This wasn't the news Peter had wanted to hear. Having been very scared the last time, he wasn't looking forward to going on another excursion. What he feared ran the gamut from getting caught to accidentally killing his mother or the donor. He didn't want to go out again. Since that night, not one of the four boys had said anything about their excursion or about going out again.

Peter went over to Ken's house to discuss going out that night. "Ken," he said after they had gotten comfortable on the back porch.

"What's up?" Ken asked after taking a big gulp of his soda.

"My mom's starting to get weak again," Peter explained, "and I think she's going to need another transfusion soon." He didn't like saying it, but neither he nor his father had any other solution to keep his mother alive.

"Oh no!" Ken cried out, knowing that this meant another trip out to find a donor. He was a little reluctant about going back out. Although their last expedition had been successful, there were many things that could go wrong. He was wondering if they might be pushing their luck. Luck is a finite commodity; one doesn't want to waste it. But someone's life was at stake, and Ken just couldn't say no to trying to help keep his friend's mother alive. "I guess we had better call Cory and Justin," he finally replied, pulling his cell phone out of his pocket.

Later that night the four boys met to prepare for another trip out to find a blood donor who could help Peter's mother. "Where should we go tonight?" Cory asked as he picked up the homemade stretcher.

"I don't want to go to the place we went to the last time," Justin said. "I'm afraid they may be keeping too sharp an eye open for us."

"You're probably right," Ken agreed. "Let's go to the apartment complex over on Chestnut Road."

The apartment complex Ken was referring to was about three miles away and would take a little time to get there. This would be the farthest they had traveled since they started their evening expeditions. They traveled through backyards and down dark side streets to minimize being seen, especially by the cops.

"Because of that stupid curfew," Ken cautioned, "we will have to be very careful not to be seen." Earlier that week the police had set up a curfew to minimize the trouble that was mounting in various areas. The curfew required all citizens to be off the streets at sunset, except in times of an emergency. Even though the boys' efforts were in response to an emergency, they didn't think the explanation that they were kidnapping a kid and stealing his or her blood to save Peter's mom's life would be all that well accepted by the cops.

"We may not need to be as cautious as you think," Justin started. "Cory and I were in that area last night, and there were people everywhere. I don't think many people over there are observing the curfew. And I haven't seen a cop in that area for weeks."

Ken didn't say anything back, partially because he didn't know whether to believe Justin or not. To have a bunch of people ignore the curfew with no fear of getting dragged off by the cops just didn't sound right. On the other hand, not having these kids obey curfew requirements meant that there might be some kids to capture for a blood transfusion.

It took some time, but they finally made their way to the edge of the complex. Their only contact with the authorities had happened about a mile from Ken's house, when the boys had to hide in some tall grass until an army jeep drove by.

"Ken," Justin called softly so as not to attract attention from others who might be around. "Let's hide the stretcher somewhere out here. I don't want to have anyone see us carrying it and wonder what's it for."

"That sounds like a good idea," Cory concurred, liking the idea himself, especially since they had decided that it was his turn to carry the stretcher.

"Okay," Ken replied, "but if we end up on the other side of the complex, you will have to come back, fetch it, and take it around so that it will be close by when we're ready for it." With that, Cory stuffed the homemade stretcher behind a storage shed by the back corner of the first lot they came to.

With the stretcher securely tucked away, the boys continued their hunt for a compatible donor. They spotted a boy sitting on the porch of the third building, playing with what appeared to be another Game Boy. Peter and Ken got into position with Ken by the corner of the porch and Peter behind another small shed. This time Peter pushed over a small trash can that was sitting beside the shed. The racket was a little louder than he expected as the barrel was full of broken glass. When he pushed the barrel over, it not only fell over; it also fell off an upside-down milk crate. The boy who was their target got up from the lounge chair he was sitting in and walked over to the top step of the porch to see what the noise was. Ken quietly climbed over the porch railing to move in for the attack. He was about two feet away, but before he could put the chloroform rag over the boy's face, the sliding glass door of the apartment opened. A tall heavyset man stood in the opening.

"What are you doing?" came a frightening growl from behind Ken.

Ken was taken by surprise by the unfriendly voice from behind him. He turned to see who belonged to the threatening voice and became paralyzed. However, this condition didn't last long as the man stepped onto the porch and came after him. When the boy turned and saw Ken looking behind him, he took advantage of the situation by taking a swing at him. He caught Ken in the stomach, which didn't hurt too bad—but it did bring him back to life.

Suddenly, from out in the yard, Ken heard a familiar voice yell, "Run!"

Ken jumped the porch railing only inches ahead of the man's grasp. He quickly caught up with Peter. The two dashed into a clump of trees, hoping to hide their identities and the direction of their escape. The man jumped down from the porch, and a footrace began. The man was older and a lot heavier, so he wasn't as fast as the boys. However, he also looked as if he could break them in two if he were to get his hands on them. "Come back here!" he yelled at the top of his lungs, adding a few swearwords for good measure.

No way, Ken thought to himself as he and Peter dashed for an escape, afraid of what would happen if the man were to catch them. They weren't as worried about what the law would do as they were worried about what that monster would do if he managed to get a hold of them.

The two boys never looked back as they continued their retreat, running through the fields on the other side of the woods. They passed Cory and Justin without even knowing that they were waiting in the tall grass. However, the hasty retreat of the first two quickly caused the other two to follow suit.

"That was close," Ken reported, gasping for air after the two boys had run about half a mile behind the apartment complex.

"That was too close," Peter agreed, also panting hard.

"Why did you leave us back there?" Justin questioned Ken, upset that he'd been left behind.

"We didn't leave you!" Ken said, starting to regain his composure. "That monster didn't know you were even there." He paused for a second to inhale and fill his lungs completely with air to cleanse them. "You should have stayed put until it was clear to move and then gone in the opposite direction so that he wouldn't see you if he suddenly turned back to go home."

"Well, you should have said something," Justin said, disgusted about having been left behind. "It looked like you were leaving us behind to get caught while you escaped."

"Now you know that's not true," Ken argued. "It would be pretty stupid to leave you behind to get caught, when all you would have to do is say we were the ones who talked you into going. We would get picked up within minutes of you spilling your guts to the cops."

"I wouldn't do that," Justin said in self-defense.

"Well, maybe not at first, but the cops have a way of threatening people into giving them want they want," Ken replied, which infuriated Justin more.

The argument didn't seem as if it would be concluding anytime soon. Peter could see the tension rising between Ken and Justin. "Stop it!" he interrupted in an angry tone. "Can we get the hell out of here?"

"You're right," Ken replied, "this is getting us nowhere. I suggest we go to another location since that guy has probably called all his neighbors by now."

"Let's go over to those houses," Cory said, pointing to some houses built very close to each other.

"I suggest we go farther away from here," Justin interrupted, "as the cops are bound to be driving around looking for anyone who might be trying to cause trouble." He paused a second and then announced, "Like us."

"Okay," Ken agreed. "Any ideas?"

"Let's head back toward Lakota Cliffs," Peter suggested, "and see what we can find between here and there."

"Okay, let's go," Ken said. He turned and took the lead.

They didn't have to go far before they saw their first target. A boy was sitting on his bike just rolling back and forth. It was strange to watch the kid; it was as if he was stuck in a routine and couldn't get out of it. The size of the yard was much smaller than many of the other yards the boys had had to go through to put their targets to sleep. The house next door, also, was very close, and there weren't a whole lot of areas to hide behind.

Ken surveyed the area carefully and suggested that Peter go wait behind a large maple tree at the corner of the lot. He would work his way over to the street, come up between the houses, and wait by the corner of the house.

"Let's go," Ken directed, an uneasy feeling starting to come over him. He didn't know what it was exactly. Maybe it was just the memory of the chase he had experienced earlier. He didn't know, but he knew he had to go on. Otherwise, Peter's mother might die if they didn't find a donor.

Peter quickly moved into position by the tree and watched to see when Ken was ready. It took awhile for Ken to get into position, but he finally saw the silhouette of his friend coming up the side of the house.

Peter was trying to determine a good way to attract the attention of the boy on the bike. It still seemed strange to him that the boy was just rocking his bicycle back and forth as he sat on the seat. Peter reached up and grabbed a one-inch branch and pulled with one great downward yank. The resulting snap caught him by surprise as the audio level was about ten times louder than he had expected. However, the resulting noise did nothing to attract the attention of their target.

Peter then bent down and picked up a large rock, about the size of a large grapefruit. Then, with as much force as he could muster, he sent it sailing at a boulder only about ten feet away. The smaller rock crashed into the boulder with a loud crack, splitting it into halves. The noise it made was so loud that Peter was afraid he would catch the attention of every house within two blocks. Regardless of how much noise he made, the boy made no signs of hearing him. He could see that the boy wasn't looking around; he was concentrating on the bike. So, Peter stepped partway out from behind the tree and waved to Ken to go ahead and put the kid to sleep.

Ken, seeing Peter's signal, carefully crept up behind the boy. Within a second the boy was asleep. Since the yard was small, it didn't take Peter any time to get to Ken. The hard part was picking the boy off the bike while trying to keep the bike from falling to the ground and making a lot of noise.

Ken and Peter carried the boy through the backyard into a small patch of trees. There wasn't a lot of cover, but the trees did provide some camouflage as the two of them tested the boy's blood. They quickly went through the procedure of testing the blood, only to find out the boy was type O. Disappointed with the findings, they quickly packed up their supplies and carried the boy back to the patio where he'd been riding the bike.

Still, with a keen sense of disappointment, Ken and Peter rejoined Cory and Justin, who'd been watching from a dark shaded area across a small field. There were several small trees and some bushes that provided a small bit of cover for them as they hid behind them.

"No good," Ken whispered to Cory and Justin when they arrived at their hiding spot. "I guess it's back to the happy hunting grounds," he added with a sarcastic tone.

The boys continued to travel through the dark shadows of the neighborhood, looking for another possible donor. It was about twenty houses later when they saw another kid outside. From a distance, it was hard to tell if this kid was a girl or boy. It was also hard to tell how old he or she was.

"Okay," Ken said to Cory and Justin, "you two stay here while we get closer to see if he might be a good target." As Ken and Peter slowly moved closer, they could tell this individual was a girl. She couldn't have been any older than seven or eight as she was playing with several Barbie dolls. Ken waved at Peter, indicating that they should go back and skip this one.

"No good," Ken announced. They returned to where Justin and Cory were hiding.

"No," Peter added. "She was too young."

"What is the difference?" Justin asked, a little frustrated. "A kid is a kid. Let's put her under and see if she's the right blood type."

"If we try to take a pint of blood out of a little kid like her, we could kill her. Do you want to do that?" Ken asked, a little frustrated at the lack of progress they were making that night.

"No," Justin answered in a solemn tone, "of course not."

"Okay then," Ken continued, "let's keep looking."

They continued to walk around the neighborhood, hoping to find another possible donor. It had been over half an hour since their last encounter with the little girl who was too young, when they spotted another girl. She was sitting on a lounge chair, writing in a book. "Must be an author," Ken guessed, speaking in a kind of comical tone. The girl was in a brightly lit area illuminated by a porch light, which meant that it would be difficult putting her to sleep without the possibility of their being seen. They wanted to figure out a way to get her to come toward the back of the yard, but there weren't a whole lot of places to hide.

"Ken, look!" Peter whispered, pointing toward the girl. "It looks like she's wearing some sort of headphones."

Ken, looking carefully at the shadows being produced around the girl's head, could see what appeared to be the outline of something covering her ears. "I think you're right," Ken replied.

"If she's listening to music," Peter continued, "you could sneak up behind her and put her to sleep without me trying to attract her attention."

"Okay," Ken said, getting out the chloroform and the rag, "I'll try it." He made his way over to another yard so the girl wouldn't see him. The neighbor's small pool gave him cover as he came within about twenty feet of her. Once in position, he took a quick look around. Satisfied that no one was watching, he quietly crept up behind her and put her to sleep.

Again, Peter was there within seconds of the target's having been put to sleep. They usually carried their donors into the woods to test their blood, but since the neighbor had a nice pool to hide behind, they picked up the girl and carried her behind the pool. Using their bodies to block the red light from their flashlight, they quickly tested the girl's blood. Their hopes were quickly dashed when they discovered the girl was type AB. This was the first kid they had tested with type AB blood.

"Damn," Ken said when Peter told him her blood type. "I guess we had better put her back." The two boys again packed away their supplies and returned the girl to the lounge chair, placing the book she'd been writing in back onto her lap.

The two boys again joined Cory and Justin and gave them the bad news. "It's starting to get late," Justin said, disappointed that they had spent most of the night hiding in the dark and not getting anything accomplished. Not that he was the only one feeling that way.

"I know," Ken acknowledged in a disappointed tone as he looked at his watch. It was almost eleven o'clock. "And the later it gets, the less chance we have of finding anyone outside. Maybe we should call it a night," Ken said to Peter.

"I don't like the idea of not finding a donor for my mom," Peter replied, also disappointed with the night's efforts, "but I guess you're right." He wasn't as concerned about not finding a donor as he was about how long his mom would survive without one.

The four boys headed home. Instead of traveling through the woods behind the properties, they decided to travel more toward some of the back alleys. There the traveling was easier, and there weren't too many people around wondering what they were doing in the dark after curfew. The only concern they had was watching out for the cops since the curfew was in effect.

The boys were walking down some unknown alley when eight boys jumped out from behind some trees and bushes. "And what do we have here?" asked the one who appeared to be the leader of the group.

Ken was about to answer the leader's question, when Justin stepped forward and cut Ken off. Justin didn't want Ken telling the boys they were on their way home. He recognized this type of group. It was a gang of homeless and runaway kids. It would not have been smart to tell them they were going home.

"We're just roaming around to see what we can find," Justin answered, hoping they would fall for the deception.

"What have you got there?" the leader asked Justin, pointing to the homemade stretcher that Cory was carrying.

"We made a stretcher to carry whatever we find," Justin answered. "It works pretty good."

"What did you carry in it?" the leader asked, trying to figure out how much use this contraption might be.

"Well," Justin said, trying to dream up answers as quickly as the leader was asking the questions, "the other night we found several boxes of food and two cases of beer." He tried to think of items that might be desirable to the gang. He felt the more he could make his group of four look like a gang, the better their chance of survival might be.

"That's pretty cool," the leader replied. "Where did you get the beer?" he asked, wondering if he could tap the same supply.

Ken, able to see what Justin was doing, played along. "We found it in an empty house about two blocks that way," he said, pointing in the direction the gang had come from.

The leader liked what the boys were saying and was interested in learning more about them. "Where are you guys staying?" the leader asked.

Justin felt he had to be careful with this answer because he didn't know where these boys were from. He didn't want to pick an area they may be familiar with.

"We stay wherever we can find a place that's empty," Justin answered. "That's how we found the house with the beer."

"Then why are you out here?" the leader asked, getting a little suspicious about how they had ended up in this area of town.

"Apparently one of the damned neighbors called the cops," Justin replied, trying to sound as frustrated as he could, "so we had to abandon the place. And now we're looking for another one."

The leader of the gang seemed to accept Justin's comments but was still a little cautious. "Where are you all from originally?" he asked.

Justin looked over at his friends and tried to compile a picture of where they might be from. "Peter and Cory," he said pointing to the two, "lost their parents to the disease, and Ken and I are runaways."

This seemed to be a satisfactory answer for the gang leader, but he still wasn't satisfied that he knew who he was talking to. "Where are you guys from?"

Justin turned and looked at his friends while he attempted to create a story that would satisfy the gang leader. He had to pick a location that wasn't too far away but also one that the gang members would be familiar with. "We came from the Blue Ash area," Justin said, "and we're trying to get as far south as possible. We don't want to be up here for the winter months."

Peter was fascinated with Justin's ability to create such convincing stories right off the top of his head.

This explanation seemed to satisfy the gang leader as he smiled and, in a much friendlier tone, asked, "So, what have you been doing?"

Justin didn't want to elaborate too much in case the gang leader wanted specifics. "We've just been trying to survive," Justin replied. "We look for empty houses and see what food and clothing we can find. Occasionally we get lucky and find some money, but generally it's not very much. After all," Justin said with a smile, "it takes money to go south."

"Is that all?" the gang leader asked, disappointed in Justin's remarks.

Justin didn't know what else to say, so instead of adding more, he decided to direct the conversation back to the leader. "What have you been doing?" he asked.

"We have been having all sorts of fun," the gang leader bragged. "Last week we broke into some old people's house and stole all their money with them standing there shaking in fear." The leader paused for a second as he tried to recall other events. "We also broke into another house, but we didn't find anything of value, so we torched the place. It was fun watching the firemen put out the blaze."

"Then we threw rocks through business windows to set off the alarms," said one of the gang members behind the leader, "and when the cops showed up, we set off the alarms at another business. It's fun to watch the cops go running around in circles trying to take care of all the alarms."

"We also sell pot and drugs to other kids roaming the streets," added the gang leader. "You'd be surprised how much money you can make selling drugs. In fact, would you guys be interested in a good deal?"

"Aren't you afraid of getting caught?" Justin asked, trying to redirect the conversation away from the topic of drugs. First, because they had no money, and second, because none of the boys had ever tried drugs. A beer occasionally, but nothing stronger.

"Nah," said the leader in a confident tone, "there are so many problems out here that the cops have no idea who's doing what, so basically we can do what we want."

"Tell them what we did with that one girl last week," another gang member called out.

"Well," the leader started, proud of what they had done, "we found this fourteen-year-old girl over by the park, and we dragged her behind a garage and made her take off all her clothes. She didn't want to at first, but we persuaded her to cooperate."

"Yeah," said one of the other guys with a chuckle as he pulled out his switchblade. "A knife to the throat makes for a nice persuader."

The thought of these guys using a knife to force a girl to strip made Peter feel a little sick to his stomach. He didn't want to hear any more.

"Then we grabbed her and bent her over a garbage can and fucked the hell out of her," the gang leader said, laughing as he described the gang's activities. "Then we opened the garbage can and poured a half gallon of sour milk over her head."

Peter started to feel sicker and sicker at the description the gang leader was giving as he continued with his story. The gang seemed to enjoy the gross actions they had subjected the poor girl to.

"Then," the leader summarized, "we tied her hands behind her, put a paper bag over her head, and made her walk down the center of the street. I'd like to see some gang beat that," he said, proud of their accomplishment.

Peter couldn't fathom such actions as he thought about his sister and the possibility that she could have been a target for such a gang.

"Hey," the leader said, having gotten an inspirational idea. "Why don't you guys join us?"

"No thank you," Peter said, disgusted that this pervert would even think that they could do such awful things.

"What?" the gang leader asked in a low tone of disgust.

Justin turned toward Peter, surprised that he had responded so quickly. This caused some concern as Justin knew more about what was at stake. "It's not that we aren't interested," Justin replied quickly, before the leader could react further. "It's just that we were planning on going south. However," he said, looking at Peter, "we do need money to go south, so maybe we should join them for a while."

Peter looked at Ken and then looked back at Justin. "No thanks," Peter answered. He and Ken turned and walked away.

"What the hell do you think you two are doing?" the leader hollered out.

"Let me talk to them," Justin said, stepping in front of the gang leader before he could act on the situation. Justin then turned and ran to catch up with Ken and Peter.

"What are you doing?" he asked as he caught up with them. "Do you know what this guy can do? He could have us all killed if we're not careful."

"I don't want to have anything to do with that gang," Peter said.

"But if you're not careful, they may end up killing us all," Justin said, hoping to change their minds.

"We're going home," Ken said, reinforcing Peter's decision.

"Wait," Justin said, as he turned and saw Cory standing only two feet from the gang leader. He tried to think about what might happen if the three of them just started running. There was no way to know if the gang would let Cory go or what they would do to him.

"Okay, wait here," Justin said. "I'll tell them that you want to think about it." Justin, turning to walk back to the gang leader, paused. "Please don't leave until you see us leaving," he pleaded in a serious tone, "for the lives you may be saving are mine and Cory's."

Justin walked back toward the gang leader, not knowing whether Ken and Peter were still standing there. He didn't want to look back to confirm their presence for fear that the leader might suspect something was wrong. "They said they wanted to think about it," Justin said, hoping this would be acceptable to the leader of the gang. "They still want to go south. I told them that if we went with you guys for a while, we could get the money we need. Who knows, you may all want to come with us to the beautiful sands of the Florida shores," Justin said, trying to paint a lovely picture of being in the south.

"What if we don't want to go south?" the leader said, leaning into Justin's face.

"Well then, we can go on our own," Justin replied, fear tightening his stomach.

"What if we don't want you to leave?" the leader asked, leaning closer to his face.

Justin didn't know what to do. He could just bow down to his wishes, or he could play the comedian and see if he could lighten the seriousness. "Well," Justin said, trying to bring forth a smile, "maybe you won't want us to hang around anymore."

"Funny," the leader said in a sarcastic tone as a small smile formed on his face. Justin thought this might be working, when he saw the leader look toward Ken and Peter. "They haven't started back," the leader said, frustrated that he wasn't getting his way. Then he gave Justin a push right into a light pole.

"Hey, stop that!" Cory said as he stepped up and put himself between Justin and the gang leader.

"And who asked you to butt in?" the leader said, grabbing Cory and shoving him into a mailbox.

Justin quickly went over to Cory to help him back onto his feet. Justin, knowing this guy meant business, needed to figure a way out of this situation. As he helped Cory back onto his feet, he whispered, "Get ready to run."

Justin looked at the gang leader and asked, "Is this how new members are treated?"

"Yeah, why?" the leader asked, not sure where he was heading with that question.

"Well, if you treat all new members that way, I guess we're your new members. See," Justin said, pointing toward Ken and Peter.

The gang leader turned to look down the street, expecting the other two to be walking toward them, but they were still standing in the same spot. Without any notice, the gang leader went flying to the ground as Justin delivered a right cross and decked him.

"Run!" Justin yelled at Cory. The two ran down the street, away from the gang. Their avenue of flight was in a different direction from where Ken and Peter were standing. Justin took a second to notice that they, too, were off at a full gallop.

Since the leader had been knocked to the ground, it took several seconds before he could respond to what was happening. "Get them!" he hollered as he tried to get back to his feet. However, the rest of the gang had been sitting comfortably on a stone wall along the sidewalk, watching the leader interact with the prospective new members, and were not in a position to start a pursuit. Also, since the boys were running away in two different directions, it took the gang even longer to figure out who was to run after whom. This delay gave Cory and Justin the extra seconds they needed to escape.

Later that evening, Cory and Justin finally made it back to Ken's house, where Ken and Peter were waiting. "Thanks for getting us out of there," Peter said. "I didn't mean to cause trouble."

"That's okay," Justin replied, "I'm just glad you waited. If you hadn't, we would have been dead."

The four friends continued to discuss their experiences that evening. Also, realizing that they had not found a donor for Peter's mother, they decided they had better go out the next night since they didn't know how long she could last without another blood transfusion.

Late the next afternoon, after Ken and Peter had finished their chores, they played video games to kill some time. They were waiting for Ken's father to finish making dinner early because he had errands he needed to get done. His father was no gourmet chef, but he had become a pretty good cook after his wife died. The two boys enjoyed some baked pork chops with mashed potatoes and a salad.

"You want to go over to Laura's house and see what the girls are doing?" Ken asked as he finished his glass of milk.

"Sure," Peter said. The two of them got up from the table, took care of their dishes, and headed for the back door.

"We're going over to Laura's house!" Ken yelled back into the house at his father, who was in the kitchen putting leftovers away. The two cut through the backyard, which was a shortcut to Laura's house.

When the two boys walked up to the front door of Laura's house, they could hear the voices of Laura's parents, who appeared to be shouting directions to each other. The door wasn't completely closed, but it was closed far enough that the boys couldn't see what was going on. "Wonder if we should ring the bell?" Ken asked as he turned to look at Peter. He was a little afraid that they might be interrupting an argument.

Peter just shrugged his shoulders and tried to peek around the edge of the door. However, there wasn't enough of an opening for him to see anything other than the corner by the stairs. Ken tried standing on his tippy-toes to see if he could look in through the glass at the top of the door. Ken was tall, but he wasn't tall enough to see into the house. He could only see as far as the light fixture hanging in the entrance hallway.

"Well," Peter said, "maybe they could use some help."

"Okay," Ken said, liking the idea of seeing Laura. He pressed the doorbell.

"Oh no," came a cry from somewhere in the house. "Laura!" the voice hollered, as if she wasn't even in the same house. "Get the front door."

Within seconds, Laura swung the door open enough for the two boys to look down the hallway. However, their vision was blocked not only by Laura but also by Carla. "Hi, guys," Laura said, pleased to see them. "Come in."

"What's going on?" Ken asked as he opened the storm door.

"Oh, my dad's moving the entertainment center to try to hook in a new surround sound system he just bought. He's having some trouble moving the monstrous thing."

The boys had been over to Laura's house often and knew how large the entertainment center was. "Can we help?" Peter asked, trying to be polite. In reality, he didn't want to help; he would rather spend time with Carla. Also, Laura's father was sometimes hard to work with. He seemed to appreciate the help but would redo anything anyone else did because it hadn't been done as well as he could do it.

"No!" Laura replied. "He's almost done anyway. And if that stupid surround sound system doesn't work, I don't want to be around when he explodes." This brought a laugh to the four of them. They decided to go sit out on the back porch.

As the kids sat on the porch talking about the things teenage kids talk about, there was a tremendous explosion of yelling and swearing from inside the house. "Well," Laura said with a small chuckle, "I guess it didn't work. I say we get out of here before he brings the house down on all of us." Laura's father was loud and quick-tempered but was not the type who would resort to major violence. He just did a lot of loud cussing when he got really upset.

"That sounds like a good idea," Ken said, jumping up from the lawn chair he was sitting in. "How about a movie? Let me call my dad and see if he can give us a ride," he said, flipping open his cell phone. The theater wasn't that far away, only about three miles, but they needed to get there soon if they were going to see the next movie. "Great," Ken said, replying to someone on the other end of the cell phone, "see you out front."

"That must mean we have a ride," Peter said, as he too got up out of his chair.

"Yeah. Boy, what good timing," Ken said, closing his cell phone. "My dad was just getting ready to leave and to go to the store over near the theater, so he's not going out of his way or anything."

"That's good," said Laura. "Dad!" she called into the house from the back door. "Can I go to the movies with Carla?" Although in reality, she was going to the movies with Ken, it just sounded better to ask if she could go to the movies with a girlfriend instead of with a boyfriend.

"I suppose," came a reply from the front room. This response was followed quickly by several other swearwords as her father continued his efforts to get the surround sound system to work.

"Here, Peter," Ken said, handing the phone to him, "you'd better call and ask your parents. I don't want them to be mad at me because you went to the movies without permission."

Peter, using Ken's phone, got permission from his father to go to the movies. Not that it would have been difficult to do since the four of them did this regularly. Carla also used Ken's phone and got permission from her mother to go.

So with all the permissions obtained, Ken slipped his arm around Laura and said, "Okay, girls and boys, let's go to the front and wait for my dad." The happy couple led the way as Peter and Carla, hand in hand, followed close behind.

It was only minutes before they saw the blue SUV come around the corner. "Let's go," said Ken's father. "I want to get to the store before it closes." And with that, the four teenagers climbed into the car, Ken and Laura in the back seat and Peter and Carla in the front.

They saw a comedy called *Accepted*. After the movie, the four departed the theater through a back exit and walked out into a beautiful evening with the sun just setting. The sky had a nice orange glow. The two couples decided that since it was a nice evening, they would walk home. It was only about three miles, and the walk would help them work off all the popcorn and sodas they had consumed during the movie. Their conversations ranged from comments about the good parts and some of the dumb parts of the movie to remarks about what a beautiful evening it was. As they entered the community where Laura lived, the conversation shifted over to school. The news had reported that the number of teachers available to teach had dropped drastically because of the BARD disease. This was causing some concerns as to whether the school would open on time for the new school year.

"I don't know," Carla said, clinging to Peter's arm, "it would be nice not to start school right away."

"Yeah," Laura added. "It would be nice to have a longer summer."

"However," Peter interrupted, "if we don't start school soon, we will be going to school in the middle of summer next year to get the hours we need to move to the next grade."

"You mean assuming school starts at all," Ken said with a negative attitude.

"It better start," Peter replied. "I want to go to college on time so I can get a good job while I'm still young."

"You think you're smarter than us?" Ken asked, poking fun at Peter.

"Yeah," Peter said in a joking way, attempting to rile Ken.

However, before Ken could come back with another comment, Laura interrupted. "Can we sit down a minute?" she asked in a very weak voice. "I feel awfully tired." This was not normal for her. She was the captain of the field hockey team and did a lot of swimming. It was unusual for her to be tired after walking only a couple of miles.

"Sure," Ken said. He sat down on the curb next to her and was quickly joined by Peter and Carla. Carla put her arm around her friend's shoulders, concerned about her pale countenance.

After several minutes, Ken got up and helped Laura back onto her feet. "Ready now?" he asked, expecting her normal surge of energy. Instead, she barely had enough energy to stand up again. He helped her up and provided support as they continued toward her house. They hadn't walked a block before she began complaining about being tired again. This time she lay down on the grass in the front yard of the house they were passing in front of. He was getting very worried about what might be wrong with her.

"Peter!" Ken called as he stepped out of hearing range of Laura. "She seems awfully tired," he said, a touch of fear in his voice. "Do you think she has the disease?"

"I don't know," Peter replied, unsure of how to tell one way or the other. "I have an idea," he said, stepping past Ken and walking over to where Laura was lying on the grass. "Laura," he started in a soft voice, "do you know what your blood type is?" He didn't want to bring up anything about the disease for fear it might make her panic.

"I think I have type A blood," she replied in a weak voice.

Peter stood up and walked back to where Ken was standing. "I'm no doctor, but if I had to guess," he started, a little afraid to go on, "I think she has the disease. She said she thinks she has type A blood. She is also exhibiting the same symptoms that my mom had before we gave her the blood transfusion."

"Think you could give her a blood transfusion like you did with your mom?" Ken asked, fearing for Laura's life.

"We could try," Peter said, "but we don't have any of the supplies with us."

"Okay," Ken said, now with a tone of hope in his voice, "help me get her home, and then we can go to my house and get the supplies."

Peter agreed. With Peter on one side of Laura and Ken on the other, the two lifted the weak body of the stricken girl and carried her home. By the time they got to Laura's house, they were carrying her completely as she had no strength left even to stand up.

When they reached the front door of Laura's house, Carla ran inside and called out, "Mrs. Rilmen! Come quick. Laura is really sick!"

Laura's parents came running to the front door to see what the problem was.

"We think she has the BARD disease," Ken said to Mrs. Rilmen.

"Do you know your blood type?" Peter asked, knowing that if neither of them had type A blood, then Laura couldn't have BARD."

"We're both type B," Mr. Rilmen replied, looking at Mrs. Rilmen, "aren't we?"

"Yeah," Mrs. Rilmen responded. "I have that information in our records. We had our blood typed about two weeks ago because of this disease problem. We are both definitely type B."

"That's good," Peter said. Addressing Laura's parents, he said, "She must just be sick with something. She didn't know for sure." He and Ken laid Laura down on the couch. "She thought she might have type A blood."

"Well," Mrs. Rilmen said, pausing as if afraid to say something that would reveal a secret, "her blood type might be type A."

Peter looked up, a little confused, thinking that her parents must not know much about genetics. "If you're both type B," Peter explained to the parents, "then Laura has to be type B also."

"Well," Mr. Rilmen said, acting the same as his wife, "not necessarily."

Now, this really started to confuse Peter. The laws of science can't be changed; she had to have type B blood.

The Rilmens, able to see the confusion in Peter's face, knew that he didn't understand the situation. "Peter," Mrs. Rilmen said, getting him to look directly at her, "she's adopted."

This hit the three teenagers like a bomb. They had never heard Laura ever mention this fact. Mrs. Rilmen could see they were stunned with the information, so she told them the whole story in a brief summary. "When I was nineteen, we had our first baby. She died at childbirth, and I was unable to have any more kids, so we adopted Laura. She doesn't know she's adopted."

Mr. Rilmen quickly changed the subject "We had better get her to the hospital as soon as possible." He quickly called 911, and within minutes an ambulance appeared in front of the house. The paramedics inserted an IV, placed Laura on the stretcher, and loaded her into the ambulance. They took off, heading for Saint Joseph's Hospital.

Mrs. Rilmen ran around the house gathering up her purse, her keys, and other essential items to go to the hospital to be with her daughter.

"You kids can wait here," Mr. Rilmen said to the three remaining teenagers, "and we'll call you when we have some news." The kids agreed to wait for a report. Laura's parents headed for the hospital.

"I hope she's all right," Carla said to Ken, trying to provide some comfort. Ken didn't seem to want to talk much as his thoughts were at the hospital with the girl he loved.

It seemed to take hours. Waiting for news was unbearable at times. They didn't turn on the TV, they didn't play games, and they didn't even read a magazine to help pass the time. They just waited.

Finally, about one o'clock, they got the call they'd been waiting for. "Hello?" Ken said into the receiver, as he had been the first to reach the phone, being no farther than two inches away from it. The first ring hadn't even finished. "How is she?" he continued, hoping for the best. His face went white as if he had seen a ghost. The phone receiver slowly slipped out of his hand and onto the floor. He just stared into space, not saying a word. He didn't even tell the others how she was doing.

"Hello?" Peter said, having picked up the phone. "How is she?" Mrs. Rilmen repeated the outcome. Peter, too, felt like dropping the phone, but he maintained some control. "Thank you," he replied to Mrs. Rilmen. He slowly replaced the phone receiver onto the cradle and looked up at Carla. "She died about ten minutes ago. She had the BARD disease."

"No!" Carla screamed, running into Peter's arms and crying. Peter didn't know what to do. The only experience he'd had with death was the death of a distant uncle he didn't even know. But to lose a close friend—what do you do? He just stood there holding Carla in his arms and letting her cry.

After about ten minutes of Carla's crying, Peter suggested he take her home to get some rest, saying that then he would go with Ken to his house. Carla cuddled close to Peter all the way to her house, while Ken followed behind. "I'll see you tomorrow," Peter told her at her doorway. "I want you to get a good night's sleep. I'll call you tomorrow." He watched as she ran into the house to continue crying in her mother's arms. He slowly closed the front door as he heard Carla sobbing as she tried to explain that her best friend had died.

The walk home with Ken was quiet. Peter, being his best friend, wondered, *What do you say when your best friend loses his girlfriend?* He just didn't know. As they approached Ken's house, Peter saw it was dark. An idea came into his head. "Ken," he called out to get his attention, "why don't you spend the night at my house? We can kill some time watching movies." He knew that Ken would not be in the mood to do much of anything, but he felt he had to keep him preoccupied somehow.

"Okay," Ken said with little or no enthusiasm.

"Come on," Peter said. "Let's get some clothes and go to my house."

As they climbed the steps to the porch of Ken's house, they could hear the TV going in the background, but all the lights were off. The door wasn't locked. Ken and Peter just walked right into the house. Ken walked past the doorway to the living room. As he passed the living room, he noticed that his dad was asleep on the couch. Ken went up the stairs while Peter waited in the hallway.

Playing on the TV in the living room was some movie that Peter recognized, but he couldn't remember what it was about. Quietly tiptoeing into the living room so as not to wake Ken's father, he looked at the TV. He began watching the movie on the TV, but something in the room was bothering him. He quickly looked around to see what was out of place. It took him several minutes to recognize the obvious. Mr. Moore, Ken's father, never went to bed on the couch, and he would never have left the TV on. He was even bossy about leaving lights on that weren't being used.

"Mr. Moore," Peter called out in a soft whisper. There was no change in Mr. Moore's position. "Mr. Moore," he repeated his call in a slightly louder tone, but still no movement from Ken's father. He carefully stepped closer to get a better look, until he was standing over him. Something didn't look right with the way he was sleeping. His hands were still dirty from working on something involving grease. If he was going to take a nap, one would have expected him at least to have washed his hands. Peter knelt down next to the couch and looked closely at Mr. Moore's face. There was no movement to be seen, including any breathing.

"This is not good," Peter said out loud, but not loud enough for anyone to hear, except possibly Mr. Moore—and he didn't appear to be listening. Peter put his ear next to Mr. Moore's nose to listen for any air coming out. Nothing. He then put his hand on the veins on the neck, hoping to find a pulse. Again, nothing. Even the feeling of Mr. Moore's skin was strange. It was cool and a little clammy.

"Ken!" Peter hollered at the top of his voice.

Ken sensed the desperation in Peter's tone and came running downstairs as fast as he could. He found Peter standing by the living room doorway. "What's up?" he asked softly, trying not to wake his father, although Peter's call would have awakened anyone in the house.

"You don't have to whisper," Peter said in a serious tone. "I think your dad is dead."

Ken looked into Peter's eyes to see if he was playing a joke. Peter's sense of humor could sometimes be of bad taste, and Ken was sure this was one of those times. However, fear was in Peter's watery eyes. Ken looked over at his father lying on the couch.

He walked over and knelt down next to the still body of his father. He looked at his face and saw that there was no form of expression. It was as if he had died in peace. Ken remained next to his father for at least fifteen minutes, when Peter finally decided he had better call the authorities.

Peter placed a call to 911 and requested someone to come out and verify that Mr. Moore had passed away. The ambulance had made it to Laura's house, sirens wailing, within minutes of her father's calling 911. This time it took over twenty minutes for the ambulance to pull up. This ambulance didn't use the sirens and had the lights off, and the paramedics actually knocked on the door. It seems that if you're dying, they come running, but if you're dead, they get there when they get the time.

"Come on, Ken," Peter said as he placed his hands on his shoulders. "Let's go to my house so these paramedics can take care of your dad." Ken slowly got up and, walking backward, left the living room and moved into the hallway. Two policemen were just coming in, wanting to get some information on the dead man in the other room.

"His name is Mark Moore," Peter said to the officer, "and this is his son, Ken. He's going to stay at my house for now." Peter gave the officer some contact information, and then one of the other officers drove them to Peter's house.

John was surprised to see a police car pull up into the driveway so late at night. It was almost three o'clock in the morning. Peter wasn't home yet, and John feared that his son was in a lot of trouble. And then to have the cops pull up! He knew that the boys had been planning to go out looking for blood donors for Paula, but he'd never gotten a call indicating that they'd found a donor, so he was getting worried. Now, this.

Suddenly he saw Ken and Peter climb out of the back of the patrol car, looking as if all was well. The officer was walking the boys up to the front door as John opened it. "What's wrong?" John asked the officer.

"This boy just lost his father, and your son said he could stay here for a while."

John was glad to hear that the boys weren't in trouble and was surprised to hear that Ken's father had died. "Oh, that's not a problem," John replied to the officer as he opened the door to let the boys in. "Ken's welcome anytime."

"That's nice of you," replied the officer, who then returned to his car.

John walked the boys to Peter's room and made sure Ken was comfortable. John wanted to know more about what had happened but felt it was late and that they should get some sleep.

CHAPTER 16

The next morning Peter got up early, but he was very quiet to allow Ken to sleep as long as he needed. Ken woke up about one o'clock, still feeling as if he had been up all night. He went downstairs to the kitchen to get something to drink.

"Want some breakfast or lunch?" Peter asked, seeing him walk into the kitchen.

"No," he replied in a soft, depressed voice. Ken was still thinking of the events of the night before. Almost his entire life had been taken in just a couple of hours—first his girlfriend and then his father. The only true friend he had left was Peter.

"You should eat something," Peter said, not knowing what to do to help Ken feel better. He could remember when his grandfather died and how he'd felt afterward. He hadn't wanted anyone to help him then, just as Ken wanted no help now. Peter was feeling helpless and wanted very much to make his friend feel better. "You should eat something," he repeated a little louder, thinking that Ken hadn't heard him the first time. "You might feel better if you put something in your stomach."

"I said I don't want anything," Ken snapped back, not interested in eating or in any conversation.

Peter just sat at the table and watched his friend pour himself a glass of orange juice and stare out the window. He didn't know what to say, so he just sat there waiting for Ken to say something first.

Without a word, Ken turned away from the window and walked out of the kitchen. Peter didn't know where he was going and was a little concerned that he might go outside. He thought he had better get up and follow him, at least at a distance, so that if he tried to do something stupid, he would be close by.

Ken walked into the living room, probably to watch some TV or something. Ken and Peter had spent many hours in front of the TV. Suddenly Ken stopped, as if frozen in an instant. He didn't move; he just stood there staring at Peter's mother, who was lying on the couch.

"Peter," Ken said with a sudden surge of excitement, "we need to go out and get your mom some fresh blood."

For some reason, the excitement made his statement sound funny as if he were Dracula and needed fresh blood. However, Peter knew what Ken meant.

"We were going to go last night before everything went wrong," Peter said, "remember?"

Ken paused for a second and remembered that they were supposed to go out after dropping the girls off at home. "Yeah," Ken said, still acting as if he were in a daze. "We'd better go out tonight. I don't want to see anyone else die from this damn disease."

Ken's actions created a slight amount of fear in Peter. It was as if he was possessed with finding a blood donor. Losing two people you're very close to can make you a little uptight, but Ken's attitude was more than just uptight.

"We have to go out tonight," Ken repeated in an eerie tone. His mind drifted off as he calculated all the things they needed to do before going out. Then, he started talking to himself about finding fresh blood. This, above all, made Peter feel very uneasy about the whole ordeal.

"Okay," Peter said. "I'll go make sure we have what we need in the backpack. Why don't you try to reach Justin and Cory to see if they are available?" Peter felt that having Ken make the calls would give him something to do to take his mind off of Laura and his dad.

Arrangements were made that all four boys would meet at Ken's house around nine o'clock. It would be just getting dark by then, and they would have several hours to find a new donor.

Usually, Ken acted as the leader during their expeditions, but tonight his mind appeared to be somewhere else. It was Ken who usually decided on which way to go, but tonight he just acted as if he didn't know a thing, so Peter suggested that they go over to Lake View Apartments. It wasn't that far away. A lot of middle-aged families with kids around the ages of ten to fourteen lived there. The boys set off on their mission. Now all they had to do was find someone with the correct blood type.

The first several buildings appeared to be empty. As they reached the end of the first apartment building, they saw a small boy. "Do you think he's old enough?" Peter asked as he peered through the bushes along the back alleyway.

"He can't be more than about eight years old," Cory said.

Peter looked over at Ken to see if he would give his opinion, but he didn't say a word. He just stared at the small boy like a vulture waiting to attack its next meal.

"Let's go," Peter said, grabbing Ken's arm as he directed his attention away from the boy. Ken's attitude appeared to have gotten worse. He seemed obsessed, and Peter didn't know why. But hoped that if they kept looking, Ken would snap out of it.

"Hey, Peter! Ken!" Cory called out in a loud whisper. "Look over there," he continued, pointing to another boy sitting on the hood of a car.

Peter paused and looked in the direction Cory had indicated. There was a boy about the right age sitting on the hood of a car. From a distance, it was hard to tell what the boy was doing. However, every once in a while they saw a small reddish glow.

"He's smoking a joint," Justin said in a loud whisper, louder than he should have spoken. He got a quick jab in the ribs from Peter as he tried to get him to keep it down.

"How do you know it's a joint?" Cory asked, confused at how someone from this distance could tell the boy was smoking pot instead of a cigarette.

"I can smell the aroma," Justin said. "Hey, Peter," he said grabbing his arm, "if he is smoking, then it should be easy to sneak up on him and put him out."

"Yeah," Peter said, "but do I want to put his blood into my mom if he's high on pot?"

"I don't think it will hurt her," Justin replied in a sarcastic tone. "After all, it's only a small amount of blood. And by the time we get him to the house, most of the effects will have worn off."

"Okay," Peter said, tapping Ken on the shoulder, "let's go see if he's the right blood type."

Ken knew his job and was ready to perform, but Peter was still worried about the way he was acting. For now, Peter had to trust that Ken would do what he was supposed to do.

About six minutes later, Ken and Peter were carrying the half-stoned boy, now asleep from the chloroform, behind a line of bushes. The two immediately tested the boy's blood. As Ken finished putting the Band-Aid on the boy's finger, Peter announced that the boy's blood was type O. Since he wasn't the right type, they quickly carried the boy back to the car and laid him on the hood.

"No one's even going to know that you put him to sleep," Justin said with a small chuckle. "Whoever finds him will think that he's stoned out of his head." Three of the boys laughed quietly at the little joke, but Ken seemed quite withdrawn from the others. Peter indicated to the others that they needed to continue looking.

Their efforts continued to result in one test after another coming up as the wrong blood type. They found a girl who was type B and a boy who was type O.

Ken was normally an easygoing boy who rarely got upset. However, tonight it was easy to see he was getting frustrated with their failure. The loss of his father and his girlfriend had hit him hard, and now the possible loss of Peter's mother was making him act even stranger. He seemed preoccupied with one thought: *Get some blood.* His actions made Peter wonder if they should return home. The problem was that if they didn't find a donor soon, his mom could die. This could cause a major emotional disaster for Ken. He was liable to go crazy if anyone else he knew died from this disease.

"Well, let's continue looking for another possible donor," Peter said, trying to keep Ken's hopes up. To find someone with type A blood wasn't easy, but they had been successful in the past. The odds were that they would be successful again. At least that was what Peter was hoping for.

The four were walking across the back parking lot where the lights had been shot out. "Look," Justin said, pointing toward a small alcove between two apartment buildings where a large dumpster was located. Sitting on an old wooden box was a young girl who appeared to be concentrating on something in her hands.

"Let's move up," Peter said to Ken. From where they were hiding, the girl looked a little older than what they were looking for, but they couldn't be sure. A small light over one of the back doors to the apartment building was casting shadows, making it hard to analyze her from this distance. Peter and Ken moved closer, hiding behind several cars as they crept closer.

"She's going to be awfully hard to put to sleep," Peter said, seeing that the girl had her back against the wall, which meant that the only way to approach her was from the front.

"I think I can put her to sleep," Ken said in a tone that made it sound as if he were possessed.

This was the first positive statement Ken had made all evening. But it wasn't what he said that caused Peter concern; it was the tone of his voice when he'd said it. "Are you sure?" Peter asked, concerned about what would happen if he weren't successful. She was sitting about six feet from the side corner of the apartment building. That meant that he would have to travel the distance from the corner of the building to where the girl was sitting quickly enough to put her out before she could react. If she saw him, she might scream, and then every inhabitant in the entire apartment complex would come running. Or she might fight, which could make it next to impossible to get the chloroform rag over her face.

"It's a piece of cake," Ken said, sure of himself. "I can go along the building to the corner there and then jump around the corner and put her to sleep."

"Okay," Peter said reluctantly. "I'll follow you up to the corner, and once you put her under, we can carry her to the woods." The woods were about one hundred feet away, but since most of the exterior lights were out, they figured they should be able to cross this distance without being seen.

Ken and Peter quietly made their way to the side of the apartment building. As they approached the corner, they could see the glow from the small light over the doorway. However, from this angle, there was no way to tell if the girl was still sitting on the box. Ken continued his advance, coming within a foot of the corner, and pulled the chloroform-soaked rag from the bag. Then he looked back at Peter and nodded his head, indicating he was ready to make his move.

Ken approached the corner. As he stepped around the corner, he could see the girl sitting on the box communicating with someone using text messaging. Ken no sooner appeared around the corner than the girl looked up and saw him standing there. He rushed toward her and tried to get the rag over her face. She threw the cell phone at him and fought back.

Peter peeked around the corner, expecting to see Ken putting the girl to sleep. Instead, he saw Ken struggling to get the chloroform rag over her face. The girl screamed for help. Peter, realizing that Ken wasn't going to be successful this time, rushed over to the girl and said, "Relax! We're not going to hurt you." Somehow, this didn't convince her. She continued her efforts to break away. Peter was concerned that the girl's screaming would attract someone to investigate the disturbance.

Cory and Justin, who had been observing all the commotion, rushed over to see if they could help subdue their prospective donor. As they arrived, the girl showed no signs of giving in as Ken tried to pin her down on the crate she was sitting on.

"You'd better stop," said Cory. He stepped up next to the girl as she continued to struggle with Ken. Suddenly, she stopped struggling as the light reflected off the shiny part of a knife that Cory had removed from a sheath he had under his pants leg.

Ken stood up, allowing the girl to come up to a sitting position. She surveyed the boys standing in front of her and the knife Cory was holding.

"That's better," said Cory in a seditious tone as he moved the knife closer to the girl's neck. "We want to talk to you," he said, indicating to Ken that he now had the floor. Cory positioned himself on the girl's right side as he continued to flash the light off the blade of the knife and into the girl's eyes. In the meantime, Justin moved up to the girl's left side, while Ken stood in front of her, making it impossible for her to escape. Peter stood to Ken's left, watching the nightmare unfold.

"What do you want?" the girl asked with a quiver of fear in her voice. She sat there, petrified with fear at the sight of the knife, at the presence of the four boys she didn't know, and by the fact that she didn't know what they wanted.

"We were just wondering," Ken asked, "do you know your blood type?" The entire evening, Ken had seemed much more passive than he'd been when out on the other excursions they had been on. But tonight he seemed to let Peter take charge. Now that they had this girl trapped, Ken was acting as if he was in control again. His attitude and actions were scaring Peter.

"I don't know," she replied, a little relieved that all they were interested in was her blood type. She had thought she might be killed or raped by this gang of boys.

"I don't believe you," Ken said, disgusted with her answer. Ken believed that with the situation involving the blood disease, everyone should know their blood type. "I say you know, and I want you to tell us," he demanded in an authoritative tone.

"I'm telling you, I don't know what my blood type is," she repeated, the feeling of fear continuing to grow.

Ken was getting very frustrated, not only because this girl wasn't cooperating, but also because they hadn't been able to find another donor for Peter's mother. He was afraid that Paula might die if they failed to find a donor. Ken looked deep into the girl's eyes and demanded, "Tell me your blood type."

Now the girl, already on the verge of tears, was more upset. "I don't know what it is!" she hollered.

"Ken," Peter said nervously, grabbing Ken's arm and trying to redirect his attention, "we'd better get out of here before someone comes to see why she was screaming."

"No one's going to come," Ken said with a tone of confidence. However, Peter wasn't so sure. She had been screaming pretty loudly. Someone must have heard her and was planning to come to see what the problem was, or at least called someone.

Seeing that the fear of someone coming didn't seem to influence Ken's decision to stay or leave, Peter thought he should try something else. "She's not going to work," Peter said. "I think she is probably type B."

Ken turned and looked at Peter in confusion. "How in the hell can you tell that by looking at her?" he asked angrily.

"She looks too old not to be infected, and she doesn't show any signs of having the disease. So she has to be type B," Peter explained, hoping that he could convince Ken to give up.

"I don't believe you!" Ken said, getting more and more frustrated as if everyone was against him. "I think she knows, and I'm going to make her tell me!" Ken exclaimed. He turned to Cory. "Give me that knife."

Cory, handing the knife to Ken, was wondering what he would do with it. Peter was also wondering—and getting very nervous about Ken's attitude.

"Okay, girly," Ken said in a frightening tone, "stand up." Ken pulled back the knife, allowing the girl to slide off the box she was sitting on.

"Now," Ken said in a soft tone, "what is your blood type?"

Again the girl said she didn't know. She was shaking from fear as Ken positioned the point of the knife by her throat.

"Okay, if you won't tell us …" Ken said. He looked down at the girl's pink shirt and noticed the first button was undone. "Take this off." He slowly positioned the point of the knife at the second button on the front of the girl's shirt.

Through her tears, she said, "I think my blood type is B."

"I don't believe you," Ken said, looking into the girl's eyes. "I think you're saying that because he said it first," he added, referring to Peter. "Now, I said take off your shirt, or I'll cut it off."

Peter stood there, not knowing what to do. He had never seen Ken act this way. To take a knife and threaten someone was something he couldn't imagine Ken ever doing. Picking up a knife was something Ken never did except to do some whittling.

"Ken!" Peter roared louder than he normally would have done, but his fear of Ken's actions outweighed the consequences if they were to be overheard by someone else nearby. "If you think she's lying and not type B, then she's too old and is no good to us. We need to find someone else."

"Shut up!" Ken snapped back. "I'm going to get her to tell the truth, or else."

It was the *or else* that scared Peter, but he didn't know what to do to stop the way the events were unfolding.

Cory and Justin stood by, also not knowing what to do. But unlike Peter, they were liking the way the scene was unfolding. Ken was standing there telling some girl to take off her shirt. That was something that neither boy ever had thought he'd see at this age.

Ken didn't like the girl's hesitation. He looked deep into her eyes and said, "Take off your shirt, or I'll take this knife and cut it off." His threatening tone scared Peter and the girl. He then gave out a small chuckle. "And I'm not very good with a knife, so I might accidentally cut you instead of the shirt."

The girl was now crying loudly as she slowly lifted her arms to unbutton her shirt. As she unbuttoned each button, all the boys except for Peter became more and more entranced by the show. After she had unbuttoned the last button, she lowered her hands to her sides, hoping she could stop there.

"Don't stop now," Ken said with a chuckle. "I didn't say unbutton your shirt; I said take it off."

The tears were running like a river from her eyes as she slowly opened her shirt, revealing a light blue bra. She slid the shirt off her shoulders and stood there holding it in her right hand.

"Take the shirt," Ken said to Cory, who was standing the closest to the girl's right side. "Very good," Ken said to the girl as he leaned forward to look into her eyes again. As he leaned back, he slowly slid the knife from her throat down and over one of her breasts. Ken again looked up into her eyes and could see the fear growing within. This made him feel that he had total power over this girl. "Now," he said, continuing to slide the knife down the girl's stomach to the waistband of her shorts, "it's time to take off the shorts."

"Please," the girl pleaded, "don't do this!"

"I think you had better do what you're told," Ken said, feeling more and more powerful, "otherwise, you might get hurt."

"Ken!" Peter pleaded as he again grabbed his arm to direct his attention away from the girl. "We're not here for this. We're supposed to find a donor for my mom."

"Shut up," Ken said, pushing Peter away. "This is more fun. Plus, we can use her blood later." He turned his attention back to the girl. "I said, take off those shorts," Ken said in a loud, demanding tone as he again threatened the girl with the knife.

Tears were flowing freely now as the girl undid the buckle. Ken followed the girl's hand with the knife as she unzipped the zipper. A matching pair of light blue panties could be seen as she started to pull her shorts down over her hips.

"Very nice," Ken said, watching her slide the shorts to her ankles. However, she didn't stand up again. She remained in a stooped position to hide her private parts from the boys. "Stand up and step out of the shorts," Ken demanded.

The girl, shaking and scared, complied, standing up in full view of the four boys.

All the boys except Peter were eyeing the girl's figure, amazed at what most fourteen-year-old boys would never get to see at that age, at least not in real life. Peter, who could also see the girl in full detail, was concerned about the events that were occurring and feared what the consequences could be. They could end up in a lot of trouble. In the meantime, his mother could be dying and they were doing nothing to help.

"Very good," Ken said to the girl in a polite tone. "You follow directions very well. What do you think?" Ken asked Justin, who was looking over the girl's figure.

"Very nice," Justin replied as he reached over and grabbed a handful of the girl's butt.

The girl jumped forward, surprised by Justin's actions, and almost ran into the knife that Ken was holding. This caused her to scream out in fear as she hadn't seen Justin make his move. She had been focused on Ken and the knife and what he might do with it. The girl's sudden scream caused Peter to wonder why no one was responding to the commotion. He couldn't believe that no one had heard the girl's screams. Was she a runaway, or was there no one in this building? That latter idea didn't seem to make any sense since there were lights on in the windows. The only thing Peter could think of was that no one was around to hear her screams, or else she'd been heard and no one wanted to get involved.

"Well," Ken said with a small chuckle, "if you like what you see now, do you think you would like it more if she took off the rest of her clothes?"

The thought of a young teenage girl standing in front of them with no clothes on caused the boys to soar with desire. "Most definitely," Justin replied with excitement in his tone as he grabbed the waistband of the girl's panties and started to pull them down.

"Stop that!" Ken scolded Justin for his actions. "Don't do that." Ken looked over at the girl and seemed entranced with her. "Okay, Laura, let's see you take off your bra."

The girl looked up at Ken in confusion as he called her by the name of Laura. She didn't know who this individual was, and this caused her even more fear. "No, please don't do this," she pleaded.

The other boys also caught Ken's slipup. Both girls had blue eyes and blonde hair. Peter was wondering if Ken was hallucinating that this girl was Laura and was reenacting some game he used to play with her. Ken mentioned that Laura and he had had many sexual encounters and that they liked to play silly games. Could Ken be envisioning this girl to be Laura? Could he be trying to relieve his feelings about Laura's death by using this girl as a substitute?

"Ken," Peter pleaded, trying to get his friend to give up the game he was playing, "this isn't Laura."

"Leave me alone!" Ken said in a loud, frustrated tone, again pushing Peter away. "This is my game, and I'm going to win."

Peter now knew that Ken wasn't all there, but he didn't know what to do about it. He could try to fight Ken, but Ken was standing there with a knife. The other two boys seemed to be on Ken's side. Peter would have to fight all three of them, and he was not much of a fighter.

"Okay," Ken said to the girl, getting her attention again, "I would like you to take off this bra, or I can cut it off." Ken slowly positioned the point of the knife on the thin section of material between the two cups of the bra.

"Please don't!" the girl sobbed. She slowly reached up behind her and unhooked the hooks. She stood there, not letting the bra fall away from her, attempting to remain covered as long as possible.

"I said, take it off!" Ken said in a loud, stern tone that made the girl jump. She sobbed even more. However, she did what she'd been told and let the bra fall to the ground, revealing two soft breasts.

"Watch this," Justin said with a tone of excitement as he reached up and grabbed the girl's left breast. He stood there, aggressively massaging the breast, while she continued to break down.

"That's enough," Ken again scolded Justin, basically telling him to mind his own business. He was in command; Justin wasn't to interfere.

"I'm sorry," Ken said to the girl in an apologetic tone. "I didn't mean for him to do that. Now," he said as he slowly moved the knife down to the waistband of the girl's panties, "all you have to do is to take off those pretty blue panties."

By this time the girl was beyond fear, so she complied with whatever Ken said. She slowly lowered her panties but again tried to stay in a stooped position, trying to hide herself from the boys' hungry eyes.

"Very good," Ken said in a soft tone. "Now stand up and step out of those panties." The girl seemed exhausted as she slowly rose to a standing position, revealing all her feminine features. Cory and Justin's eyes opened as wide as they were able to open to allow as much of this never-before-seen view to enter into their memories.

"Okay," Peter said in desperation, "you've seen her with no clothes on. Now let's get out of here and go back to finding a blood donor for my mom."

"Leave me alone!" Ken hollered back at him, loud enough for anyone nearby to hear. "Okay, Justin," Ken said, turning his attention back to the girl. "You wanted to see what she feels like; which side do you want?"

Justin looked at Ken, not realizing what he had just said. A minute ago he'd gotten upset and had told him to keep his hands off her, but now he was letting him touch her. Justin reached out and again grabbed the girl's left breast, massaging it. Ken held the knife close to the girl's throat with one hand and reached down to her crotch with the other. Cory looked over at Ken and then reached up and grabbed the girl's other breast.

Peter stood in horror, watching the three boys abuse the young girl. "Ken!" Peter screamed at the top of his lungs as he tried to turn his friend away from the girl. "This isn't right. Leave her alone! Let's get out of here."

Ken looked at Peter with fury in his eyes. "I said, shut up," he growled at Peter and then swung the at him.

Peter quickly tried to duck away from the flying steel, but the sharp blade caught the side of his right arm, creating about a six-inch gash. With the knife away from her throat, the girl tried to make a break for it. However, Justin quickly grabbed her and pulled out a second knife, telling her not to move again.

Peter backed off as he grabbed his bleeding arm. He watched Ken and the others continue to abuse the girl. She stood there like a mannequin being manipulated by a group of window dressers, allowing them to touch her without voicing the slightest opposition.

"Lay her on the boxes," Ken said to the other two as he undid his pants.

Peter watched as the two grabbed the girl's arms and pulled her down onto the boxes. The girl revitalized her efforts to get away as she realized what the boys had in mind. She screamed for help as loud as she could, but no one came. Cory and Justin, who didn't seem worried about the girl's screaming, reached down and grabbed her legs to lift her up onto the wooden crate. Then they pulled her legs apart, giving access easy for whoever wanted to violate her.

Peter, blinded with fear of what was about to happen, ran up to Ken and pulled him around. "This isn't right!" he cried. But before he could say another word, an excruciating pain in his left leg caused him to let go of Ken and drop to the ground. As he looked up, he saw Justin's knife red with his blood. Peter's leg was gushing blood from the puncture wound. He slowly limped off, knowing there was nothing he could do to keep the boys from raping the young girl.

Peter slowly headed home with his left hand over the wound on his right arm and his right hand over the bleeding hole in his left leg. He paused at the far side of the parking lot to look back at the boys who used to be his friends as they were actively raping their victim. He stood there looking around, wondering why no one was coming to the girl's aid. She had been screaming in desperation, but no one seemed to hear her or care. This made Peter wonder how safe it was to be out at night. He finally turned away from the horror his friends were executing and headed home.

It took Peter about two hours to return home. He limped into the house, exhausted and weak from the large amount of blood he had lost.

John, seeing Peter limp into the living room, jumped up from his recliner and ran to help his son to a kitchen chair. "What happened?" John asked as he quickly looked at the hole in Peter's leg.

"Ken and Justin attacked me," Peter said in a very weak voice.

"Why in hell would they do that?" John asked, bewildered as to why they would even have a knife, let alone stab someone.

"We were trying to put some girl to sleep to test her blood, and she put up a fight. Ken kept asking her what her blood type was, and she refused to answer." Peter paused for a second as if giving a short explanation was as exhausting as running a marathon. "When she wouldn't answer, Cory pulled a knife. Then Ken took the knife and had the girl take her clothes off. I tried to stop them, but Ken cut my arm. Then they were going to rape the girl, and I tried again to stop them. That's when Justin pulled a second knife and stabbed me in the leg. And then I came home."

"Beth!" John yelled upstairs.

Beth came downstairs in her pajamas, ready for bed.

"What happened?" she asked in a fearful tone as she saw all the blood on Peter's shirt and pants.

"Never mind," John replied as he helped Peter up. "I want you to keep an eye on your mother while I run Peter to the hospital.

"We'll tell the police when we get to the hospital," John said as he and his son were driving down the street.

"Dad," Peter said in a weak voice, "please don't tell the police it was Ken."

"Well, you know the hospital is going to ask questions," John argued.

"I'll tell them I was on my way home and I was jumped by a gang looking for money," Peter said, remembering the gang they had come across about a week ago.

"Well, I suppose," John said. "But I don't agree with you. If Ken stabbed you, then he should pay the consequences."

"But, Dad," Peter said, regaining some of his energy, "Ken wasn't in his right mind. He kept calling the girl Laura."

John looked at Peter, who was sitting in the passenger seat with his eyes closed, remembering the events of the night. John decided that he wouldn't tell the police about Ken and that he would let Peter handle the problem his own way.

John couldn't believe how busy it was at the hospital emergency room. It was packed with patients. After he had walked in with Peter, they were immediately sent over to a triage area, where a nurse examined Peter's condition. The nurse got a wheelchair and rolled Peter into one of the examining rooms, where another nurse quickly came to take some blood. Meanwhile, an IV bag was brought in to deliver fluids to Peter's body. "He's lost a lot of blood," the nurse said. "We'll be giving him some whole blood once we determine his blood type." Then the nurse turned away from John and said under her breath, "If we have any, that is."

The blood test came back in less than five minutes, and a nurse brought a bag of whole blood. "It's a good thing he's type B," the nurse said, hanging the blood bag on the IV pole next to the bed. "We have plenty of type B but almost none of any of the other types."

Peter had been lying on the examining table for about half an hour before the doctor came in to examine his injuries. "There doesn't appear to be any major damage," the doctor said as he cleaned the wounds. It took over twenty stitches to close the one in Peter's arm and another twenty-five stitches to close the one in his leg.

Peter and John were in the hospital for over six hours as the health-care providers pumped blood and antibiotics into the patient. The cops who had questioned Peter indicated that they were having trouble with gangs in that area. One of them had even said there had been several killings in that area and many other areas within their jurisdiction. He also indicated that the police were almost helpless to do anything about it as they were shorthanded as a result of the disease. He indicated that the overall police department had experienced more than a 40 percent decrease in manpower in the last two months and that things would only get worse.

As Peter listened to the cops tell their story about what was happening in the community, he wondered how many crimes, like the ones Ken and the guys had committed that night, were going on uncontested. Were citizens that vulnerable?

Peter and John got home at about four o'clock in the morning. Beth was asleep on the floor next to the couch, where her mother was also sleeping. John told Peter to go to bed. He then walked over and picked up the little girl and carried her to bed. Then John climbed into bed himself, exhausted after a very strange day.

CHAPTER 17

The next day, Peter was resting comfortably on the couch in the basement family room, partially doped up with some painkillers. He was half asleep on the couch but still had one eye on the afternoon movie playing on the TV. Beth was upstairs watching some kids' show but was primarily there to help her mother if she needed something. Paula was still on the living room couch, still very weak from the effects of the disease.

Peter wasn't too interested in the movie, so he decided to see what else was on. As he reached for the remote, he heard the front door open. He could hear footsteps as the unknown trespasser walked down the hallway. He didn't know who it could be. Everyone was home but his father, who wouldn't be home from work until about six o'clock. Then Peter heard the soft footsteps of his sister running toward this individual, and heard her call out, "Daddy!" It was only one o'clock. What was his father doing home so soon? Peter got up from the couch, but his efforts were cut short as he saw his father coming down to the family room with his precious princess on his back.

"Dad," Peter called out, puzzled by his arrival, "why are you home so early?"

"This disease has caused three doctors' offices on my route to close and four offices on Mark's route to close. There isn't much of a need for two couriers. So Mark and I are going to be splitting the courier responsibilities. I'm going to do the morning pickups, and Mark will do the afternoon pickups. This way we both still have some sort of a job."

"Does this mean you won't be making as much money?" Peter asked.

"We'll get by," John said, seeing that Peter was getting a little concerned.

"Daddy," Beth asked, still hanging onto his back, "are we going to be poor?"

"No, princess," John said after he'd flipped her over his shoulders and deposited her onto the overstuffed chair next to the couch.

"Dad," Peter said. He was about to ask another question, but before he could ask it, John turned toward him and gave him a look that told him not to ask any more questions.

"Honey," John said to Beth, "can you go up and watch your mom for a while? I want to talk to your brother for a minute."

"You're in trouble now," Beth said in an energetic tone as she ran for the steps.

"What's up, Dad?" Peter asked, concerned about the way his father had sent his sister out of the room.

"I didn't want to say anything in front of your sister," John began. "I don't want her to start worrying about something she doesn't even understand. I found out today that a large number of employees at the hospital are having their hours cut back or being laid off. The hospital has lost some key people in certain areas, and there isn't enough staff to run those specialized areas. Some of the employees are being moved around to cover the basic functions, but I'm afraid that this is only the beginning of something worse."

"But you still have a job, right?" Peter asked, questioning his father's appraisal of the hospital's situation.

"Oh yeah," John said, trying to reassure Peter. "I'll have that job for a while."

"But," Peter said, expecting that his father was hiding other bad news.

"Well, as a part-time employee," John started, pausing for a second to see if he could figure out another way to present the facts, "I am no longer eligible for health insurance. There is no way we can take you or your mother to a doctor's office, that is, if we could even find one that is still open."

"Don't worry about me," Peter said, trying to reassure his father. "I know basic first aid, and as long as I keep this clean, it should heal with no problems. I'm just a little worried about Mom. I can't go out and find a blood donor, and I don't even want to talk to Ken."

"Don't worry about your mom," John said in a sad tone. "I think she'll be okay for a while. Right now the big problem is the cost of things like food and gas. Gas is over five dollars a gallon, and they say it could reach six to eight dollars a gallon by the end of the year. So we will need to be very careful with our money."

"I'll do what I can," Peter said. "Maybe I can get a part-time job if you think it'll help."

"No," John said, looking at Peter's leg, "That needs to heal first. Afterward, we'll see."

"But, Dad," Peter said in protest, "I can get a job over at Kroger's or one of the other grocery stores."

"No," John replied in a stern tone, "not now, anyway. Plus, school should be starting up soon." John was heading for the steps, when he turned, saying to Peter, "All we have to do is keep track of how much we are spending each week and fine-tune it so that we spend as little as possible."

"In other words," Peter said jokingly, "no more ice cream, right?" Ice cream was Peter's favorite dessert, especially in a banana split with all the fixings.

"We'll see," John said with a chuckle. "We may still be able to afford ice cream from time to time. Get some rest," he ordered, and turned and headed back upstairs.

Peter sat on the couch thinking about what it would be like not to have the money that his father had made in the past. John was no millionaire, but his paychecks weren't half bad. Plus, they had his mother's income. All he could do now was rest and try not to think about all the bad things that were happening.

Several days had passed with Peter limping around the house, trying to find something to do. He had been given crutches to help him get around, but he didn't like using them, so he just limped around most of the time. Normally, he would spend hours playing his Game Boy, but lately, he seemed to have lost all interest in the game. Instead, his mind kept going back to the problems of the night when he'd been stabbed, and thoughts of his dad, who was at work but could be laid off at any time. He also had thoughts of his mother, who was still resting on the living room couch.

She was very weak but seemed to have the energy occasionally to sit up and watch a little TV. However, this afternoon she was resting quietly, which left Peter with basically nothing to do. Finally, he went to the back door, from where he could see Beth sitting on the porch drawing another picture using charcoal, instead of pen and ink. But he couldn't see what she was drawing. "Beth!" he called out after opening the door. "I'm going to take a walk down to the corner store. You want anything?" he asked. Peter loved his sister, and occasionally he liked to bring her something as a surprise, but today he felt like only offering to get her something.

"No thanks," Beth said without looking up from the picture she was drawing.

"Okay," Peter said and headed out the door. He walked the two blocks to the end of the street, where the small store was located. It wasn't anything special, but it was close to the house. The store offered a variety of everyday essentials, but most of the time the place was much more expensive than other places. Peter went in and bought a soda and some chips to nibble on. As he was pushing the door to go out, it seemed that someone else was pulling the door to come in. As Peter stepped out into the sunlight, he saw who had been opening the door from the outside.

"Hi, Peter," Ken said, trying to be friendly. "I haven't heard from you all week. I hope everything is all right."

Peter didn't respond. He just looked past Ken and walked around him.

"Everything will be all right," Ken said, trying to get Peter to talk to him. "Trust me."

Peter stopped in his tracks and turned to face Ken. "Trust you?" Peter asked in a loud, sarcastic tone. "I wouldn't trust you to take out the trash."

"Hey, man!" Ken hollered back, following Peter back up the hill toward his house. "I'm sorry about cutting you with the knife. I don't know what got into me. It was as if I was outside my body watching the whole thing."

Peter stopped again and turned to look at Ken. "And you mean you didn't intend to rape that girl?" he growled, anger in his voice.

"I didn't know what I was doing," Ken said, a little ashamed. "But it was so easy to do. There were no cops around, and even when our voices started getting loud, no one came. You could have raped her too," Ken said to see if he could get Peter on his side.

"I may have had the opportunity," Peter replied in a stern tone, "but I had enough decency to know that it's wrong to rape a girl."

"But it's easy," Ken said, still trying to get Peter to understand how little law enforcement there was on the streets. "You know how easy it is?" Ken asked.

"No!" Peter said in a loud, angry voice. "And I don't want to know." Then he turned to continue his trip to the house.

Ken ran after him and stopped in front of him. "It's so easy that we've done it two other times. We even went inside one house and raped this girl who was sitting at home watching her little brother. Boy, did that kid get a little education that night," Ken said with a tone of pride.

This simply infuriated Peter. "I don't want to hear it!" he yelled, pushing past Ken and continuing up the hill.

"You have no idea of what it's like out here on the streets!" Ken hollered back. "You can do almost anything!"

Peter just waved him off and continued home. As he reached the top of the hill, his leg was starting to throb, so he walked a little slower. However, his plan of a slow return home was changed when he saw an ambulance sitting in the driveway. Peter limped as quickly as he could the rest of the way to the house, only to find Beth sitting on the steps crying.

"What's wrong?" Peter asked as he knelt down next to his sister. He feared the worst and was right to do so.

"Mommy's dead," Beth said in between sobs. "She died," she repeated in a loud defeated tone as she started beating her brother with her fists. She was younger, but she wasn't weak. The blows she was landing were painful, especially the one that hit his wounded arm. Finally, exhausted, she fell into her brother's arms and cried.

Peter just held Beth in his arms, and the two cried together. Paula had lasted quite awhile after the first blood transfusion. They all had hoped that she would survive long enough for them to get another donor or until a cure was found. Peter felt that he had failed his mother by not finding another donor. He felt that he had murdered her, as if he had stuck a knife into her heart. And now he felt as if the same knife had stabbed him in the heart. Overwhelmed with guilt and sorrow, Peter just wept.

It was about ten minutes later when John came flying down the street. He had received the call while he was out on his rounds. John was still driving the courier car, which he had never driven home before. He pulled up onto the grass as his driveway was cluttered with an ambulance, the medical examiner's vehicle, a paramedic's van, and several cop cars. He jumped out of the car and ran up to the porch. He saw the kids on the porch crying profusely. He quickly went past them and headed into the house, where Paula was still lying on the couch. John dropped to his knees beside the couch and lifted her soft hand. "Oh Paula," he cried out, and then broke down weeping as he buried his head into her chest. He wrapped both arms around her and tried to hold as much of her as possible.

After about ten minutes, the coroner came over and told John he had to take Paula now. John slowly released his grip from the lifeless body of his wife and gave her one last goodbye kiss. As he stood up, two soft hands, accompanied by a soft voice, came over to meet him and directed him toward the kitchen. "Come on, John," said the soft voice, "let's go into the kitchen and have a cup of coffee."

John cleared his eyes of the remaining tears and looked toward the voice. "Thank you for coming," John said to Marsha. "How did you know so fast?" he asked, surprised to see Hailee's mother standing in his kitchen.

"Hailee was with Beth when they noticed that Paula looked different. Beth didn't know for sure if she was breathing or not, and Hailee called me," she said, directing John to take a seat on one of the kitchen chairs. "I told her to call 911 and said that I would be right over. So we've been here for quite some time."

Marsha poured John a cup of coffee, and the two sat quietly, listening to the individuals in the living room as they prepared to transport Paula to the morgue. Beth and Peter watched in silence as the paramedics rolled her out of the house. The thought of someone stealing their mother triggered Beth's emotions. She ran to the gurney and tried to pull Paula back into the house. A female police officer pulled Beth out of the way, then the paramedics rolled the two children's mother to the back of the ambulance and put her inside.

Beth ran into the house to her father and cried in his arms. He didn't know what to do. He just held his little princess and told her everything would be all right, even if in his own mind he didn't know whether he would be all right. Finally, Marsha came over, picked up Beth, and carried her over to the rocking chair that Paula used to sit in when she cross-stitched. Beth curled up into a ball and continued to sob softly. John just sat at the table, staring out the kitchen window, not looking for anything in particular. He was dazed, thinking about the paramedics pushing the gurney with the lifeless body that was his wife. He'd watched her being wheeled out of the house and out of his life. John couldn't get the vision of that gurney out of his mind—the sheet protruding up with the impressions of her body. He thought of the paramedics pulling a sheet up over her face. Had they really taken his wife out the door off the living room, or was she still on the couch, this whole thing being a big mistake? The more he thought about the whole scene, the more it appeared to be a dream. However, dreams don't last forever. He was interrupted.

"Dad," Peter said in a soft tone, standing at the kitchen door, "I'm sorry I failed her."

This caught John completely by surprise. "What do you mean, you failed her?" he asked, confused about what Peter was talking about. He hadn't yet returned to reality from his dreamland visions when Peter had first addressed him.

"I wasn't able to get another donor for her. She died because I failed," Peter said in a tone of despair as yet more tears fell from his eyes. He could feel the pain of failure burning a hole in his chest.

John, now understanding what Peter was saying, jumped to his feet and ran over to him. "It's not your fault," he said, putting his arms around his son. "Even if you had gotten another pint of blood, there is no way to know if it would have worked," John continued, not knowing what else to say. "It was God's turn to make the decisions," he continued, hoping a different twist might do the trick better, "and he decided it was time for her to go. It's not your fault. It's just one of those things that God has control over and we don't." John didn't know what else to say to convince his son it wasn't his fault.

Peter continued to break down over losing his mother. Deep down he knew it wasn't his fault that she'd gotten the Sanguis virus, but he had had the ability to help keep her alive and had failed her. These feelings were tearing Peter apart. He didn't know what to do. "Look at me," John demanded. Peter looked up into his eyes. "It wasn't your fault." He thought nothing he could say at this time would convince his son, so he hugged him close. They both cried again.

After about fifteen minutes, they settled on the couch in the living room. Beth sat up in Marsha's arms and called out to her father. "Daddy," she said in a soft trembling voice, "is that what's going to happen to me?"

John looked at his little girl and was struck with the fear of what reality could impose on them. He was struggling with that fear and wished to comfort her after their sudden loss. He ran over to her and picked her up. "Of course not," John said, hoping that his answer would have some truth to it. Only time would tell. "You're too young to catch the Sanguis virus," he said in a soft, reassuring voice. Although in the back of his mind he had the thought that maybe she would catch the virus and die from it.

"But, Daddy," Beth said, beginning to cry again, "I'm going to get older, and I might catch the disease and die like Mommy did."

"That's a long way off," John said, hoping there would be some truth to this statement, "and by then, they will have found a cure. You'll be fine."

John carried Beth over to the couch. He put one arm around Peter and gave him a big hug while Beth sat on his lap, cuddling up against John's stomach. He sat there, thinking about his two kids and what they had been through, and said a soft prayer that God would protect them in the days to come. He didn't know what was in store for them, but he feared that the worst was yet to come. Sometimes life puts us in situations where there are no words that can help ease the pain we are feeling. We just have to learn to deal with the situations and deal with the tough times, and with God's help, we will overcome them.

The next day Peter woke up late to find that his father had gone out on errands related to the funeral arrangements. Beth was still asleep; he didn't want to wake her up. A note Peter found on the table indicated that Marsha would be over later to look in on them. So for now, Peter was all alone, which was not a comforting situation, being in the house where his mother had died because he wasn't able to provide the blood she needed to stay alive. Peter felt that if he didn't do something, he would go crazy. He decided to contact Ken over the internet. That way, if Ken got too bossy, he could just sign off.

"Are you there?" Peter typed on the screen when he saw Ken's username, indicating he was currently active on the instant messaging system.

It was several minutes later, but Ken finally responded with, "I'm here." He wasn't sure why he had logged into the system. He wanted to talk to Peter but wasn't sure he would talk to him. He had logged into the system almost every day, waiting to see if Peter would log in. When he saw Peter's log-in, he wasn't sure how to respond. He didn't know if Peter was still mad at him.

"My mom died last night," Peter typed. Usually, Peter could type quite fast, but today he felt he was lucky if he could type more than one word a minute.

There was a long pause before Ken responded, "Sorry." He felt that her death was his fault. If he hadn't been so obsessed with that one girl that night, they might have been able to find Paula a donor.

There didn't seem to be anything else to say. Each of the boys just sat there, waiting for the other to respond, but neither made a move. What do you say after telling your friend that your mother died? It wasn't as if Peter could talk about the weather or how life was going with his friends. So what was he to say?

Ken finally ended the stalemate by asking, "Is there anything I can do?"

Peter just sat there, wondering what someone *could* do. Ken couldn't bring his mother back, and there wasn't a whole lot he could do to make Peter feel better. "No," he replied.

Again the stalemate between the two continued, each wanting to continue the conversation but not knowing what to say.

"How is your sister taking it?" Ken asked.

"Not good," Peter replied, another short response.

Ken figured that since he had asked about Peter's sister, he might as well ask about his father. "How's your dad doing?"

Since the conversation was drifting away from him, Peter responded with more information. "He's doing all right considering," he typed in reply, "but with everything going wrong, he's pretty stressed out."

"What's going wrong?" Ken typed back, becoming more curious about how things were going over there. After all, since his father had died, Ken didn't have anyone to call family. Peter was his best friend. So to Ken, Peter and his family were the closest thing Ken had to family.

"My dad got his hours cut, and he's afraid we may have financial problems."

"I might be able to help get you some food if you need it," Ken typed back. "I found several vacant houses. I'm staying in one of them. This house is behind a small store, and I found a way in to get food."

248

"You're stealing now?" Peter asked once he'd read Ken's previous message.

"I'm not stealing a lot," he replied, "just enough to survive."

"Aren't you afraid you'll get caught?" Peter asked.

"All I'm looking to do now is to keep from starving to death. Plus, the cops have almost no control," Ken sent back. Before Peter could reply, Ken sent a second line: "I could probably steal city hall right out from under the cops' noses if I could figure out what to do with it."

"LOL," Peter responded.

"If I can be of any assistance, let me know," Ken replied.

"Okay," Peter replied. There was a short period where neither seemed to have anything to say. Peter looked out the window, wondering what to do, when the computer beeped, bringing his attention back to the screen. The message indicated that Ken had signed off.

Peter had been feeling a little better since having talked to someone, even if it was over the internet. Now he was feeling alone again. He again looked out the window and was wondering what to do. He didn't want to leave Beth alone in the house since she was still asleep. He got up and walked into the living room just in time to see Marsha pull up into the driveway.

"Come on in," Peter said as she walked up to the door with a basket of food.

"Hello, Peter," Marsha said as he held the door open. "I thought I would bring you some sandwiches for lunch." She walked into the kitchen, where she placed the basket on the counter. "There is some of my homemade potato salad and some cookies in here," she said, removing the various dishes. "I didn't know what kind of sandwiches you liked, so I made several different types." As she finished unpacking the basket, she looked up at Peter and could see the defeated expression on his face. "It'll be okay," she said in a soft, loving tone. "I know how you tried to help your mom stay alive. I'm sorry she passed away."

Peter looked up at her in surprise, wondering how she knew what they'd been doing to keep his mom alive. "How did you know?" he asked in a puzzled tone.

"Well, your mom became sick with the disease almost three weeks ago, and I haven't heard of anyone lasting more than a week to ten days without an infusion of fresh blood. Plus," she said with a small smile, "I saw the bruise from the puncture wound on her arm. When I thought about it, I realized you were trying to give your mom a transfusion. And since she lasted longer than was expected, I knew you'd been successful at least once."

Peter was astonished that she knew what they'd been up to. "Why didn't you call the police?" he asked, concerned that she might call them now.

"Because I knew you were just trying to help your mother," she said, walking over to Peter and putting her hands on his shoulders. "And I didn't think you meant any of the kids any harm, so I decided to keep quiet about it."

"Thank you," Peter said, a little relieved that she would not blow the whistle on him. But now he started to reexperience the feelings he'd had earlier. He limped over to the back door and looked out the window.

"How's your leg?" Marsha asked, noticing he was limping. She had heard about the stabbing attack from Hailee, who had heard the story from Beth. Kids loved to tell stories.

"It's okay, I guess," he replied.

"How's it look?" she asked, concerned about how well it might be healing, especially since puncture wounds can be a problem to heal.

"Okay" was all Peter replied.

"Come over here and sit down. Let me take a look at it," Marsha said, turning one of the kitchen chairs around so he could sit down.

Peter sat down and pulled the hem of his khaki shorts up high enough to reveal the gauze that was protecting his injury.

Marsha removed the gauze, revealing a six-inch wound sewn shut with twenty-five stitches. Once the wound was revealed, she lightly pushed on the red sections of skin. The skin appeared not only red but also puffy. "It looks like it's getting infected," Marsha observed. "Did the doctor at the emergency room give you a prescription for an antibiotic?"

"They gave me some pills for pain, but I don't think they gave me anything else," Peter replied, trying to remember that night. His memory of the hospital was blurry. "My dad would know," he continued, "but I'm not sure when he'll be home."

"Okay," Marsha said, "do you know where the alcohol is located?"

"In that cabinet," Peter replied, pointing to the corner cabinet where they kept all their medical supplies.

Marsha cleaned the wound as best she could with the limited supplies that were in the cabinet, then applied a clean dressing. "I'm going to see if I can get some antibiotics from work tomorrow," she told him. "In the meantime, you need to keep this as clean as possible."

"Thank you," Peter replied in a low disheartened tone.

Marsha, seeing that Peter was still feeling depressed over losing his mother, knew that he needed someone to talk to. She was sure that she wasn't going to be of much help as he needed to talk to someone closer to him. "Why don't you go over to Carla's house?" Marsha said. "It will give you someone to talk to." Marsha knew a lot about Peter and Carla from comments from Beth and Hailee. She knew how much those two meant to each other, and she felt it would be good for Peter if he could get together with Carla to talk.

"Beth is still asleep. I don't want to leave her here by herself," Peter said with a tone of concern.

"I'll stay until she wakes up," Marsha said, trying to let Peter know he didn't have to take on that responsibility. "Then she can come over and play with Hailee. That will help her also. Now go on and get out of here," she said with a smile on her face.

"Thank you," Peter said. Before Marsha could say goodbye, Peter was out the door.

Peter felt better as he walked over to Carla's house. It would be good to talk to someone about what he was feeling. Even though it was only a short walk over to Carla's, his leg was bothering him some, so he walked slower than normal. He surveyed the streets, which seemed deserted. The kids who normally would be playing outside seemed to be missing. There was an eerie silence in the air, almost as if he were standing in the middle of a graveyard. Peter looked around as if searching for a set of eyes that might be watching him walk down the street. It was unsettling, especially when he thought of all the things Ken had said about what it was like on the streets. Might someone jump out of the shadows and kill him with no consequences? This terrified Peter.

Peter approached Carla's house and walked up the sidewalk to the porch. He could hear the TV in the living room as the front door was open about ten inches. He also noticed that the porch light was still on. This seemed unusual since everyone was watching how much electricity they were using. The cost of electricity had doubled since the disease had killed off many workers. The ability to generate electricity had been compromised because of the manpower shortage.

Peter walked up and knocked on the door. He expected Carla to be stretched out on the couch, watching some show on TV. However, no one seemed to respond to his knock, so he knocked harder the second time. The doorbell hadn't worked for some time, so he was restricted to knocking. Still no response. "Carla," he called out, leaning close to the opening of the door. Still no answer. He was getting worried. He walked to the end of the porch to look down the driveway to see if the car was still there. As he peered around the corner of the house, he saw that the blue Chevy Blazer was still parked at the top end of the driveway. Her mother usually parked up there and then went into the house by way of the back door.

"Carla!" he yelled once more through the front door, assuming everyone must be somewhere upstairs. But still, all he got back was silence. He stood there, not knowing what to do. He looked around the neighborhood to see if Carla and her family might be over at a neighbor's house, but no one was to be found anywhere. Concerned that something was wrong, he decided to go into the house and look around.

"Hello," he said, slowly opening the door and stepping into the front entrance area. There was a small closet to the left, and the doorway to the living room was to the right. From there he could see there was a soap opera on the television. He continued his slow advance into the living room when he saw someone sleeping on the couch. As he walked up to the couch, he couldn't tell from the jeans the person was wearing if it was Carla or her mother. "Hello," he said, loud enough that whoever was sleeping should have awakened. However, there was no response from the sleeping soul. He walked up to the couch and slowly lifted the light blanket off the shoulders of the individual, revealing a female body facing the back of the couch. Carla and her mother could almost be identical twins, they looked so much alike. They both had the same eye color and hair color. Most of the time they even had the same hairstyle, so whoever it was sleeping on the couch was not identifiable from the way she was positioned. Peter didn't want to wake the person, but he wanted to talk to Carla. Still, he had no idea if this was Carla or her mother.

"Hello?" he said, reaching down and lightly shaking the individual. The person didn't respond. He shook the individual a little harder in an attempt to wake her up. However, he still received no response. Now he reached down and pulled the hair back from the person's face. He could see some age lines, confirming that this person was Carla's mother. However, when he pulled the hair back from her face, he noticed that the skin was cold. He reached out with both hands and rolled her over, finally realizing that Carla's mother had died in her sleep. He got a cold shiver up his back as he realized he had just found a dead body. When his mother had died, he didn't get to see her body. The only dead body he had ever seen was his grandmother's at her wake, where she was made to look nice and normal. But here he had just found a dead body that was not made up for a show. It caused him to shudder.

He backed out of the living room and into the entranceway, wondering where Carla was. *Had she discovered her mother and left the house?* he wondered. But as he thought about it, he recalled that the body was covered as if for sleeping, so he was probably the first one to have found her dead. So, then, where was Carla? He walked into the kitchen to see if there were any signs of her in there. However, the kitchen was nice and clean as it usually was. Carla's mother always stressed that they clean up their messes when they were finished eating. So there was no way to determine if Carla had eaten breakfast or not.

Peter went up to her bedroom. He had been in her bedroom many times in the past, not for anything unmentionable, just to watch TV or play on her computer. As he reached the door to her room, he noticed it was partway opened. Concerned that she might still be asleep, he knocked lightly on the door. However, there was no response from inside. "Carla," he called out, slowly opening the door. He didn't want to catch Carla in an indecent situation. However, there was still no response from inside. He opened the door the rest of the way and walked into the room. Her bed was neatly made, which meant that she must have gotten up and made her bed already. Most teenage kids are sloppy, but Carla liked to be organized and relatively neat.

Peter was now wondering if Carla was even in the house. There didn't seem to be a response from anyone anywhere, so he decided to come back later. As he turned to go back down the steps, he thought he heard a noise from the bathroom. "She's in the shower," Peter said to no one but himself. "That's why she didn't hear me." Peter walked over to the bathroom door and listened at the door to see if he could hear anything. In the background, he could hear the sound of a small radio. "Carla!" he called out again, knocking on the door. No answer. *Could she have left the radio on when she finished her shower?* Peter wondered. He knew that she liked to listen to music in the shower as they had discussed what radio stations played the best music. But to leave the radio on was not like her.

"Carla!" Peter called out, much louder this time, as he tried the bathroom door. The door wasn't locked, so he slowly opened it. As he peeked into the bathroom, he could see the reflection of the bathtub in the vanity mirror. He could see what looked to be Carla's dark hair at the end of the bathtub. "Carla," he called out again, assuming she was asleep in the tub. He didn't want to startle her as she realized that she was in the tub while a boy had walked in on her in the bathroom. He continued to slowly open the door as he waited for some response from inside. Once the door opened the rest of the way, he had a full view of the bathtub. In the tub was a fourteen-year-old girl with dark hair who appeared to be asleep. Peter feared the worst.

Peter walked over to the tub and reached down to shake Carla to see if she was asleep. However, her body was as cold as the bathwater she was submerged in. She had become so weak that she couldn't get out of the tub and died where she was lying. Peter didn't know what to do. He didn't want to leave her in the cold water with nothing to cover her, so he reached down and lifted her out of the bathtub. The cold water hit his shirt and made him shiver. He carried her to her bedroom, where he laid her on the bed.

In front of him was this very pretty girl he had known so well. Now she was lying in front of him with no clothes on. He had always dreamed that someday he would get to see her this way, but this wasn't how he had pictured it. Her hands and feet were all wrinkled from being in the water for so long. Her skin was partly tanned except where her bathing suit prevented the sun from changing the skin tone. Peter didn't like the idea of her lying there all wet, so he went to the bathroom and brought in a towel to dry her off. He slowly rubbed the towel over her entire body. The thought of touching a naked girl's body made him shiver. He didn't know why; it was just something he had never experienced before. He continued, drying off her chest, paying close attention to the feeling he had when he touched her breast. The feeling was mesmerizing. He dried off her arms and then started on her legs. He paused at her thighs, wondering if he should continue up her legs. For some reason, he felt that he was betraying her. He could have done almost anything he wanted to, but he couldn't get past the idea of who it was in front of him. He started to understand why Ken had gotten so carried away when he molested that girl they had raped. Here lay a girl's body fully exposed, available for whatever he wanted to do. But in this case, he just couldn't because it was someone he cared for. But it made him wonder. If this girl was someone he didn't know, could he do some of the gross things that Ken had done to that girl? Peter just didn't know and was afraid to find out. Could he sink to the depths that Ken had sunk given the right circumstances? All he could do was pray his conscience would guide him down the right path.

Peter decided this was more than he could stand. He took the towel and used it to cover Carla's body. He bent over and gave her one last kiss goodbye before going downstairs. Once downstairs, he stood at the front door and looked out at the deserted neighborhood. What should he do now? There was no one to talk to. His father wasn't home, and he had no friends who were still around other than Ken. He took one last look around the house and started to go out the door, when he stopped. He walked into the kitchen and picked up the phone to call 911. When the operator answered, Peter, reporting that he had found two people who had apparently died from the disease, requested that someone come by and take care of them. The 911 operator took some information from Peter and told him that someone would be there as soon as they got free. Peter didn't want to wait, so he walked out the front door and headed home.

CHAPTER 18

The funeral arrangements for Paula were hard to set up as the funeral homes, the ones still open, were busy night and day processing the dead. Wakes were scheduled almost around the clock to accommodate the numbers of deceased people being processed. With the increase in deaths, funerals were getting to be very expensive as the undertakers could ask for almost any price. Many insurance companies that handled life insurance were on the verge of going bankrupt because of the number of claims being filed. If one's file did get processed, it could take up to three or four months, which was substantially longer than normal. However, the funeral went off without a hitch. John was glad it was over, although he still missed Paula, as did the two kids.

John was sitting at home watching the news while Peter and Beth sat at the kitchen table playing a game. School was supposed to start up on Monday, but it had been canceled due to a lack of teachers. There was no indication as to when school would start up again, if ever. John sat, listening to the newscasters as they discussed the number of deaths from the disease. They indicated that there had been over eighty-six thousand deaths in the local area alone, and nationally the number was estimated to be over eight million. These numbers reflected the number of deaths from the disease, mostly adults. However, the number of deaths from other causes was also on the rise. In this case, a lot of children had died. These younger victims had been killed by gangs or had died while doing dangerous things while part of a gang. The newscaster started to read off the names of certain communities that viewers should avoid because gangs of children had overrun these areas. The number of homeless kids was impossible to estimate, but they were definitely present. The number of fire, burglary, murder, and rape calls coming into the police department was more than the authorities could handle.

John could remember last week when, just three houses south of his home, some gang had set a vacant house on fire just to watch the neighbors as they tried to keep the fire from spreading to their own houses. John and Peter were both there, trying to help the neighbors save their homes. Those people were lucky as the fire eventually burned itself out, but it had taken hours to do so. They had called the fire department, but the firefighters never did show up. The news also indicated that some gangs had started a fire in a house in Andover that had oxygen acetylene tanks inside, and the tanks blew up, killing three of the boys. The fire spread to ten other houses before it finally burned out. A few firemen were helping to control the fire, but firemen were few and far between. One school in Norwood had been set on fire, and when the firemen arrived, gang members, armed with rifles stolen from a sporting goods shop, fired upon them. The National Guard was called in to provide cover, and eventually the whole gang was killed and the fire put out. However, the school had been totaled.

The news also discussed the economy, which in a word was bad. You would think that the unemployment rate would be almost zero as everyone was trying to hire people to keep their businesses running. However, the loss of buyers for products manufactured by the larger companies dropped off, so these companies went out of business. As a result, unemployment had risen. There were almost no jobs to be found, including government jobs, which in other times always seemed to be plentiful. John sat in his chair and thought about how long his job would be there, or at least what little job he had left. The number of doctors' offices still open was getting smaller every day. Soon the hospital wouldn't need a courier if there weren't any doctors' offices from which to pick up blood specimens.

Peter and Beth were playing a game of gin rummy, but Peter wasn't paying any attention to it. He was watching his father's reaction to the news stories that were being presented. He could see that the topic of unemployment was bothering his father, but there was nothing Peter could do to help. Peter lost the hand and decided that he didn't want to play another round. Instead, he walked over to his father and knelt down by his recliner.

"Dad," Peter said, "I can try to get a job to help earn money."

John looked down at his son and could feel a tear forming in his eye. The thought that his son would have to go to work to help support his family made him feel ashamed and proud simultaneously—ashamed that he couldn't earn enough money to keep the house going, and proud that his son would help carry the burden he was feeling.

"That's all right," John said to Peter with a slight stutter as he tried to swallow his feelings. "You'll be starting school soon. I don't want you to miss out on a good education."

"What school?" Peter replied in disappointment. "I'll be surprised if the school ever starts up again."

"Well, I don't want you to have to go to work," John said, pausing as he thought about his response, "at least not yet."

Before he could finish his thoughts on the subject, there was a knock on the door. John got up and opened the door, to see Marsha standing outside with tears in her eyes. Her face was red, indicating that she had been crying tears for a while. "What's wrong?" he asked with a tone of concern as he opened the door and let her into the house. So many people had died from the disease that he was afraid someone close to her had died.

"I got fired," she replied, starting to cry.

Taken completely by surprise, John had to stop for a second to reevaluate the thoughts in his head. "Is there anything I can do?" he asked. He tried to come closer to her, thinking that maybe if he held her, she might feel better. However, she didn't want any comforting from him. She pushed him away and walked down the hallway to be alone.

It was a good minute before she started to compose herself and explain what happened. "I was alone in the hallway near the pharmacy. There was no one around. So I went into the pharmacy and opened the drug cabinet. I don't have access rights to the cabinet, but I know how to open it without a key. I pushed on the cabinet door just enough to let the latch push in, and then I used a card to hold the latch in place while I opened the door. Anyway," she said, taking a deep breath in an attempt to recover from her period of sobbing, "I took out a bottle of antibiotics, and before I could close the door, the head nurse came in. She caught me with the drugs and"—Marsha began to cry again—"she told me I was fired and to leave the hospital immediately." Marsha continued crying for several minutes.

"You'll get another job," John said, trying to raise her spirits but knowing he wasn't having much success.

"Oh yeah, who's going to hire a nurse who was caught stealing drugs from a hospital? No one," she snapped back in a loud, aggressive tone. "They'll all think I'm some kind of drug addict or, worse, a drug pusher." She buried her head into her hands and sobbed again, this time with renewed energy.

John didn't know what to do. He didn't know why she was taking the drugs. "Who were the drugs for?" he asked, trying to understand her motivation.

Marsha looked up with eyes that would have killed a weaker man. "For your son," she said in an accusatory tone, pointing a finger right in his face. Had she been any closer, her finger would have poked him in the eye.

"I'm sorry," John said, not knowing what else to say since he had no idea why she would be stealing drugs for Peter. She hadn't ever informed him of any medical concerns associated with him. "Why were you trying to get antibiotics for Peter?" he questioned.

"His leg is infected. He needs an antibiotic to clear up the infection," she answered.

She had been trying to do something nice for John and his son, and she'd gotten in trouble for it. It probably wasn't fair, but still, it wasn't John's fault. John said nothing else. He went over to the kitchen counter and made Marsha a cup of tea, hoping this would help her feel better.

"Is there is anything I can do to help?" John asked as Marsha drank her cup of tea.

"There's nothing you can do," she replied. In a disgusted tone, she asked, "Don't you think you've done enough?"

John didn't know what else to say. She'd been trying to help his son and had lost her job. Not only had she not gotten the drugs for Peter, but also now she had no way to make a living. John just then remembered some antibiotics left over from last summer when he'd cut his foot open. He didn't want to tell Marsha he had some upstairs in the master bathroom, so he decided just to be quiet and let her drink her tea.

Marsha put down her teacup, apparently feeling a little better; at least she had stopped crying. She had been a good friend to John and his family. He wondered if this was the end of that friendship or if it was just a bump they had to get over.

Marsha got up to walk out of the house, but John stepped forward. He gently put his hands on her shoulders and looked deep into her eyes. "I'm so sorry that you got fired," he said in a soft, sincere voice, "but if there is anything I can do to help, please give me a call."

Marsha left without saying another word.

Peter, having witnessed the confrontation between Marsha and his father, went out into the backyard to escape the scene inside. He was depressed about his father's situation, mourning his mother's passing, concerned about Beth's safety, upset at the loss of his girlfriend, and all in all just downright confused. He didn't know whom to talk to. He decided that the only one who knew him well enough to talk with him was Ken. Peter slipped into the house from the front door and proceeded up to his room, where he got online to see if Ken was around. Funny how everything in business was falling apart, but the internet systems seemed to run like clockwork.

It took over a week before Peter got a response from Ken. He told Ken he was depressed and wanted someone to talk to and was wondering if he was available. Ken agreed to stop by and see him later that night.

It was about nine o'clock when Peter heard a knock on the front door. "I'll get it," he said, expecting it to be Ken.

The two boys sat on the front porch steps, listening to the crickets chirping in the shadows. Neither wanted to start the conversation. Peter didn't know where to start with all the problems he was facing, and Ken didn't know where to start because he didn't know what Peter wanted to talk about. They sat there for almost twenty minutes waiting and, in Ken's case, hoping the other would say something.

"Carla's dead," Peter blurted out with no warning that he was even going to speak.

Ken quickly looked over at Peter, surprised by the news. He knew how he felt because of his loss of Laura. "I'm sorry," Ken said, not knowing what else to say. It wasn't as if they were starting a nice casual conversation, but to blurt that out with no warning? What could he do but say "I'm sorry"?

The silence returned as neither could figure out what to say. "She died ten days ago," Peter said, finally deciding he had better say something. "Her mother died the same night. I called the police, and they said they would take care of them."

"I'm sorry to hear that," Ken said sincerely. "Is there anything I can do?"

"No," Peter replied, still in a depressed mood.

"Did you go to the funeral?" Ken asked. There had been so many victims of the disease that sometimes the bodies went straight from the morgue to a casket and into the ground. They weren't even embalming the bodies as they normally would. As time went by, it was getting harder for the authorities to locate next of kin to come and claim the bodies. This was the case with Carla and her mom. Without someone to claim responsibility for the deceased, the authorities buried people with whatever information they could obtain.

"No," Peter replied. "I never heard anything about when it was supposed to be, and the cops weren't sure either." The authorities just didn't have the manpower to handle all the problems on the streets, let alone keep up with the paperwork on all the deceased. After Peter finished this statement, the two boys fell back into the realm of silence.

This time it was Ken's turn to start the conversation. "Did you know that Cory is dead too?"

This time it was Peter who looked over at Ken, surprised by the news. "What happened?" Peter asked, knowing that Cory was type B and shouldn't have died from the disease.

"We were chasing these two girls," Ken started, pausing a second as he tried to think of another way to tell his story. He was going to say they were chasing the girls to rape them as they had done several times in the past, but Ken felt this would upset Peter. "We were going to have some fun with them," Ken continued, although deep down he knew it didn't sound much better. "As we chased them around the corner of some warehouse, we ran into a gang who had guns. They didn't even tell us to get lost; they just started shooting. Cory got hit in the chest and, as far as I could tell, died instantly. Justin ran away. I haven't seen him since. I dove behind some garbage cans, but one bullet grazed the inside of my arm." Ken pulled up his shirt and displayed a three-inch Band-Aid he had applied to the injury. "From there I started crawling down the street. When I got to the end of the building, I looked back to see if they were going to chase me. From where I was, I saw them strip the clothes off the girls. That's when I decided to get the hell out of there, and I've never been back. I don't even know if anyone has picked up Cory's body, and I'm not going back to find out."

Peter, knowing why Ken had paused at the beginning of his story, had been concerned about his actions since that night he'd seen them rape that girl. "Have you bothered many girls?" Peter asked, emphasizing the word *bothered*.

Ken looked up at Peter, knowing what he was asking. "You mean have I raped a lot of girls?" he asked with a touch of anger in his voice as he responded to Peter's insinuations. Ken, pausing a moment for the anger to subside, lowered his head. "We've raped six girls since that first night." He paused for another second, ashamed of the number he had quoted and about the fact that there was a number at all. As he thought about it, he felt that the number should have been zero. Ken looked back up at Peter. "Listen," he said in a soft voice, "I haven't even looked for another girl since I saw that gang attacking those girls. I felt terrible when I realized that if we had caught them, we would have been doing the same thing that the gang was doing, and that was enough for me. You won't see me doing that again."

Peter was glad to hear that Ken would not chase girls for the twisted pleasure of raping them. However, he still wasn't ready to trust him either. "What else have you seen out on the streets?"

"Well," Ken said, a little reluctant to describe some of the sights he had seen over the last two weeks, "two nights ago, I was checking to see if this one house was empty. I wanted to go in and see what kind of food might be in there. Anyway, as I was watching the house, I saw three boys and two girls come up and break the front window. They weren't even being quiet about it. Then one of the girls climbed through the window and opened the front door. Since they were in the house, I figured I had better go to another location. I found some food in another house about a block away. When I was coming back, the boys were throwing what looked like water balloons at the house. The only problem was that the balloons must have been filled with gasoline or something, because they exploded into flames. The boys must have started a fire in the house and were using the balloons to burn the outside of the house. I hid behind some bushes and watched the whole thing. I didn't want them to see me, or the cops to see me, but the cops never showed up. I left after about an hour. The house was pretty much burnt to the ground with the kids sitting on the curb watching."

"I've heard of other gangs setting fires," Peter offered. "You know the Olsons' house down the street?" Peter paused a second to let Ken reply.

"Yeah, I noticed the house isn't there anymore," Ken responded.

"A gang burnt it down about a week ago," Peter continued. "My dad and I went over to help the neighbors keep the fire from burning down their houses."

"There's been a lot of torching going on," Ken said, envisioning some of the burning sights he had seen over the last couple of weeks, "but that's a small problem when you look at the number of girls who are being attacked."

What do you mean?" Peter asked with a touch of concern in his voice.

"About a week ago, I was down in the Avondale area, and I saw a gang of about ten boys torturing a middle-aged woman. They made her do all sorts of disgusting things. When they were done, they tied her between two trees, naked, with her arms and legs pulled apart. Then they smeared something all over her that seemed to attract bees. I think it was sugar or honey or something. Anyway, the bees kept coming in. The boys stood and watched for a while. From time to time they would throw stuff at her to make her jump, and then some of the bees would sting her. After a while, the woman passed out, and the boys got tired and left. When it was safe, I worked my way over to where she was tied up and cut her loose. Then I dragged her into the bushes to hide her. Then I got the hell out of there."

"I've heard several stories about gangs on the streets," Peter said, "but nothing as bad as that."

"It's really bad in some sections of town," Ken said in a serious tone. "You're lucky it's not bad around here. But I have seen several gangs in this area, so if I were you, I wouldn't let Beth go outside at any time. These gangs may be watching and looking for opportunities. There are also certain parts of town that I wouldn't even drive through because the gangs are so bad."

"What do you mean?" Peter asked, his curiosity piqued.

"I was on my way home along Route 42, but back away from the streets, traveling in the shadows, when I saw a gang of about seven kids come running across the street. I couldn't tell at first what they were doing, but apparently they were laying boards with nails in them across the street. They had painted them black, making them hard to see. Anyway, I saw this car come down the street and run over the boards, blowing all four tires. A young couple got out of the car and was attacked by the gang. The gang apparently had guns. They shot the guy and then dragged the woman into the woods. I don't know what happened to her; I just got the hell out of there."

"So what have you been doing these last couple of weeks?" Peter asked, wondering how Ken had seen all this and survived.

"Well," Ken said, "I found an abandoned house over on Marshall Road to stay in. I found an abandoned car, and I'm hiding it in a garage over on Pine Street. I know where to get things like food and clothes. I can break into almost any store and get something to eat. The cops are nowhere to be found in most cases. As long as I avoid the gangs, I do all right."

"You mean to tell me there are no cops around anymore?" Peter asked, questioning Ken's description of the way things were.

"Oh, they're around," Ken said in a sarcastic tone, "but they only patrol the safer parts of town. They won't go into some of the bad areas. Even the army won't go into some areas unless they go in force. So if you need something, you go to an area where the cops don't go and just watch out for the gangs. Being by myself, I can hide pretty easily. The gangs generally make so much noise that I can hear them coming and can get out of their way.

"The house I'm staying at right now still has power and a computer. I get online from time to time to see what information there is on gangs. There are a lot of websites now identifying bad sections around the country. That's what I was doing when I saw your message, checking out different areas to relocate to, as several gangs are now getting too close to the house on Marshall. I only get on the internet during the daytime. It's too easy to see the lights from the monitor at night, and I don't want anyone to know I'm there, especially after last Friday."

"What happened last Friday?" Peter asked, his curiosity rising again.

"I was sitting up in the front bedroom of that house at about eleven o'clock at night when I saw a gang come down the street. I made sure they couldn't see me, but I listened in on what they were saying. The leader was giving instructions on attacking another gang. I couldn't believe all the weapons these guys had. Apparently, they attacked several soldiers and stole their weapons. They had M-16 machine guns, grenades, and even a rocket launcher. It scared the hell out of me. So I've been looking around for another house to stay in."

"Why don't you stay in the house where you have the car parked?" Peter asked, wondering why Ken hadn't just done that initially.

"Well," Ken replied with a slight chuckle, "most of the main part of the house is missing. The house was burned to the ground, but the garage is still standing. That's why I put the car in the garage. No one is going to be too interested in that place because there isn't a house worth looking into."

"Good thinking," Peter replied, surprised at Ken's ingenuity. "Is there anything I can do to help?" he asked, trying to rekindle his friendship with Ken.

"Just keep an eye open for an abandoned house where I can hole up," Ken replied.

Peter sat there for a second as an idea formed in his mind. "Why don't you just stay here?" he asked, not really thinking about the possible consequences of this arrangement. At the beginning of the summer, he would have loved to have Ken stay over, or at least more than he had before all the trouble started. However, with the changes that Ken had gone through, Peter was concerned about how he was going to fit into a family environment. Not that there was much of a family environment left after his mother had died and now that his father was about to lose what little job he had left.

"Are you sure you wouldn't mind?" Ken asked, hoping that Peter would forgive him for his past transgressions. "I could help you get things like food and clothes," he continued, trying to rationalize the idea.

"Well," Peter started as he assessed the situation. Here was a young kid out on his own in a world that was falling apart. Ken's knowledge of the problems Peter's family might encounter could be very useful. Also knowing how to get food and clothes when there was no money would be of great help. However, Ken's actions toward young girls scared Peter. With no consequences to restrict his actions, would Ken return to his newish old ways and begin to rape girls again? If so, how safe would Beth be around him? But on the other hand, Ken knew what to watch out for with gangs and their actions toward young girls. This could help Peter keep his sister safe.

As Peter took the time to run all these ideas through his mind, Ken started to get the feeling that Peter didn't want to provide an answer for fear of hurting his feelings. So Ken provided his friend with another avenue. "I appreciate the offer," Ken started, "but I will be all right on my own. But," he continued, hoping to make Peter feel he still needed him as a friend, "if you see a place where I can stay, let me know. And if I can be of any help, let me know."

Peter continued to weigh the risks of trusting Ken with his sister against the advantages that Ken could provide to keep Peter's family safe and help get them needed supplies. "Well," Peter finally said, "we'd have to check with my dad. He would have the last say. However, a couple of rules," Peter continued in a serious tone. "You keep your hands off my sister—and any other girl for that matter."

"What if I meet a nice girl?" Ken said with a smile. "Can I kiss her good night? I don't want her to think I'm shy or something."

"You know what I mean," Peter replied with a smile, knowing Ken understood his meaning.

"I would never hurt your sister," Ken continued in a serious tone, "or any other girl for that matter. Beth is the sister I never had."

"Okay," Peter said as he stood up. "Then let's go inside. It's getting late."

"Hey, Peter," Ken said as he got to his feet, "how would you like to go do some shopping?" A big smile formed on Ken's face.

"What do you mean?" Peter asked, not sure what Ken's facial expression meant.

"Do you need some food?" Ken asked. "I know where to get some."

Peter looked at the front door of the house and tried to remember what was left in the refrigerator and the cabinets. He knew there wasn't much. They could use some food, especially if Ken was going to be staying with them. "I suppose we could do with some food," Peter replied, "but we don't have a lot of money."

The smile on Ken's face stretched to its limit as he smiled back at Peter. "I didn't ask if you had money, just if you need food."

"You mean, steal it?" Peter asked, wondering if Ken had had a change of heart and wanted to go back to a life of trouble.

Ken stood there, looking at Peter. "Of course I mean to steal it. If you don't have the money, then you are going to have a hard time buying food. On the other hand, I know where the government has their food storage, from where they distribute food to the poor and needy. It sounds like you fit the needy category. Want to go?" Ken asked.

Peter stood there thinking about it. *Maybe he's right,* Peter thought, confused as to what was the right thing to do. Stealing was wrong, but starving wasn't much of an alternative. *If the government distributes the food to the needy anyway, we might as well help the government by helping ourselves.* "Okay," Peter replied, deciding he would rather steal some food than starve.

"Great," Ken said in an excited tone, "let's go." Ken led the way with Peter close behind. As the two boys headed down the street, they stayed close to the shadows. After about two blocks, they changed direction and maneuvered through some back fields. It took them about thirty minutes to come up on the back of a brick house with all the windows busted out.

"What happened to the windows?" Peter asked quietly, trying not to attract the attention of anyone who might be watching.

"Most of the abandoned houses all have busted windows. That's one sign that I look for when hunting for a place to stay or when looking for food. If the house has busted windows, I sneak in at night and hang out until daylight. Then I search through the house to see what I can find. Then I sneak out again after dark. This way, no one sees me going into the house. And I don't use a flashlight that might be spotted by someone on the street, especially a gang. I can only imagine what would happen if a gang came by and saw the light from a flashlight inside some abandoned house.

"That sounds like a good plan," Peter said, quite impressed with Ken's survival techniques.

"Learned that the hard way, unfortunately," Ken continued with a small chuckle.

"What do you mean?" Peter asked, concerned about his statement.

"The first couple of nights I was on the streets, I went into an empty house using a flashlight. This gang came busting into the house, screaming that I was in their territory and that I was dead. They scared the hell out of me, screaming the way they did. I jumped out the window onto the front porch roof and climbed down a tree to get the hell out of there. Unfortunately, I left my bag of supplies and my flashlight behind. That's when I decided on a different strategy for searching for houses. So far, it seems to work.

"Hold it," Ken said quietly, stopping by the corner of the house. He was watching something around the front of the house. However, from where Peter was standing, he couldn't see it.

"What's up?" Peter asked, his curiosity causing him to become impatient.

"Shh," Ken replied. Ken watched for several more seconds before slipping back behind the corner of the house. "It's a small gang who hang around this neighborhood. They don't seem to be too bad, at least not as bad as others I've seen. They just appear to be going down the road. We'll give them a couple of minutes to get out of sight."

They had been waiting for about ten minutes when Ken got up and checked the surrounding area. "Okay," Ken said, after checking again to see if the gang was gone. He led Peter along a row of bushes to the next house that had been burnt to the ground. Ken continued along the edge of the destruction to the back door of the garage, where he reached down and lifted a small rock. Under the rock was a set of keys. Ken quickly and quietly unlocked the door. When the two were inside, Ken closed the door and relocked it. "Be careful," Ken said in the dark, "the car is right in front of us. Feel your way around to the passenger side while I go and open the garage door. But don't get in yet," Ken cautioned.

"Why?" Peter asked, thinking it would be safer to close the car door while in the garage, where it would be harder to hear.

"If there is anyone around when I open the garage door, we may need to make a run for it. And if you're in the car, it will take you too long to get out. I don't want to have any delays." Ken went over and pulled on the rope to release the garage door from the drive assembly used to open the door. Ken paused and placed his ear against the door to see if he could hear anything suspicious. When all seemed safe, he lifted the door to open it. Ken didn't want to use the garage door opener as it made too much noise, not that he could have anyway; there wasn't any electricity since the fire. Also, if something should happen outside the garage, he wanted to hear it before the door was open all the way.

With the door opened, Ken took one last look around. "All clear," he said as he turned and walked to the driver's door. "Get in, but don't slam the door." The two opened their car doors and jumped into the car. After carefully closing his door, Ken reached for a small red light he had in the cup holder, shining it on the keys he had in his hand. It was difficult to tell one key from another in the dark, so Ken used a small light on the key chain to find the right key. Ken inserted the key into the ignition and then stuck his head out the window for one more listen for any threatening sounds. All seemed quiet. Ken started the car and pulled out of the garage.

The boys headed over to some warehouses on Malhouser Road. "There is one warehouse," Ken started, heading down one of the major roads, "that has food for distribution to the poor. I found a brochure in one of the houses asking for donations. Anyway, I went there late one night and watched the place for several days. I noticed a car sitting by the side entrance area and assumed it was a night security guard. I never saw anyone come or go from that warehouse all night. Now people were coming and going during the day, but I counted how many went into the place and how many left the place. The numbers indicated that no one was left inside, but that car was still sitting there. The next night was the same way. On the third night, there were two cars there, and I saw this security guard walking around the outside of the building several times during the night. Anyway, I snuck in one night and marked the tires of that one car that always seems to be there, and to this day, it has never moved. So when two cars are sitting there, I don't go near the place. When there is only one car, then I know it's safe to go in. They only have a security guard a couple of nights a week."

"Boy, you surely checked the place out," Peter said, amazed at Ken's survival abilities.

"Well, I've learned to survive," Ken replied, feeling a little strange having someone admire him for his abilities. "Anyway, I don't take a lot of food for fear that they might think something is wrong. So I only take enough to last about a week. And then I go back again."

Ken drove for about two more miles and then drove to the back side of an office building. Some lights were on in the office building, indicating that it was occupied. "The cleaning people haven't left yet," Ken said, relieved to see several other cars in the parking lot. "I try to get here when they're here," he continued. "I'm afraid that the cops are watching this building. We are in an area that doesn't have a gang problem, so the cops aren't afraid to come by. So to prevent attracting attention with only one car in an empty parking lot, I come when the cleaning crew is here."

Ken parked the car at the far end of the row, away from the building and close to some bushes beside the parking lot. He started to open the door. "See," he said, pointing upward as he opened his door about two inches, "I've disconnected the dome light so no one can see us getting in or out of the car. Also, when you go to close the door, close it gently. It doesn't even need to catch. Just make it appear to be closed."

Ken and Peter quietly left the car, staying down and ducking into the bushes along the far edge of the parking lot. Ken led the way over to a chain-link fence. "Over here," he said in a whisper. Ken headed down the fence to one of the fence poles. "Looks like the fence is intact," he said, pointing to a section chain link, "doesn't it?"

"Yeah," Peter said, wondering why he would ask such an obvious question.

Ken reached up and untied a piece of rope from the top of the fence pole and another rope at the bottom. He then pulled a section of the fence out far enough for the two of them to enter the property of the warehouse. "I cut the fence and put this pole in to keep it tight. From a distance, the fence looks intact." Ken quickly retied the ropes to hold the fence in place.

"Come on," he said, leading the way past the dumpster behind the warehouse. When they reached the back of the building, Ken stopped and crouched down in a shadow. "The only way into this building without tripping the alarms is a hatch up on the roof, and the only way to get to the roof is to climb up that fire escape over there," Ken said, pointing to a dark corner of the building.

"How the hell are we going to get up to the fire escape?" Peter asked, seeing that the bottom rung of the ladder was about ten feet in the air.

Ken just chuckled. He reached behind a pallet of bricks sitting by the wall of the warehouse and pulled out a makeshift grappling hook. "Now watch this." He got up and walked over to the fire escape. He tossed the grappling hook up and caught the bottom rung of the ladder. Then he pulled the retractable ladder down to about a foot from the ground. "Are you afraid of ladders?" he asked as he waved for his friend to go up the ladder.

"No," Peter said. Then he climbed to the roof. It was quite a climb to the top of the building, a lot farther than it looked from the ground. Peter was concerned that someone might see them.

Ken was right behind him. As he reached the roof, the fire escape returned to its retracted position.

"See," Ken said, "we can stay up here as long as we want. No one can even tell we're up here. Come on." Ken took the lead across the roof of the large warehouse.

Peter followed, amazed at the size of the roof. He'd been on the roof at his house but never on a roof like this. The size alone made him feel very small.

Ken approached a square box located about a hundred feet from where they had climbed onto the roof. He stopped and bent down beside the box. He lifted a large lock hanging on the clasp, keeping the cover in a secured position. "Looks locked," Ken said. He lifted the lock up so Peter could examine it.

"Yeah," Peter replied, wondering how they would get in. "Do you have a key?"

"Oh yeah," Ken replied in a sarcastic tone, "as if the owners are going to give me a key so that I can break in whenever I want." After a second, Ken said, "Of course not." He stood up and walked to the other side of the lid. He pulled two pins out of the backs of the hinges on the lid and lifted the lid from the opposite direction. "Not bad, huh?" Ken announced, proud of his accomplishment in outwitting the building's security. "Come on, let's go."

Ken climbed into the hole in the roof and dropped into the darkness inside. "Where are you?" Peter called after Ken.

"Just lower yourself down," Ken's voice replied from the darkness. "It's only about seven feet to the floor."

Only seven feet, Peter thought to himself. *That's like falling into infinity when you can't see where you will land.* Peter lowered himself down until his arms were stretched out and he was dangling in the air.

"Let go," Ken said, reaching up to grab Peter by the waist. "I can reach you. Just drop."

Peter let go and fell the few feet to the floor. "Man, that's scary," he said as he stood up and realized how short of a drop it really was.

"Yeah," Ken said. "The first time I did this, I lowered the rope down to see how far down the floor was. Then I did just what you did: I lowered myself down and let go. I've done this quite a few times so it doesn't bother me anymore. Come on," he said, walking into the darkness.

"Hey, where are you going?" Peter called into the darkness. But before Ken could answer, the small attic utility room was illuminated with a dim light.

"Come on," Ken said, "let's go do some shopping." Ken opened the utility room door and headed down a long metal stairway to the warehouse floor. The floor was covered with pallets of packaged foods. All the food on the pallets were nonperishable items. Ken walked past a long line of pallets and took a turn to the right. As he reached the far wall, he paused at a large section of shelves with lots and lots of food, some of it in cans, some of it in jars, and yet more of it in boxes. Ken walked over and picked up a box about the size of a Xerox box. "Come on," he said, handing the box to Peter. "Let's go shopping."

"What is all this?" Peter asked as he surveyed some fifty feet of shelving full of food.

"Well, from what I can tell," Ken replied, "this is all the excess stuff that has fallen out of damaged boxes. They throw it all here and later distribute it to local food shelters. As long as you don't take a lot from one spot, they'll never know we were here."

Ken grabbed a second box and started filling it with various cans and boxes from the shelves. Peter followed his lead. As they were about finished filling the boxes, Peter turned to Ken and looked up at the steps going to the utility room. "How in the hell are we going to get back up to that hole in the roof with these boxes?" he asked, afraid he would have to climb back up through the hole and onto the roof. The thought of climbing down that fire escape carrying a box of food didn't sound like something he wanted to try, either.

"We don't," Ken said with a small chuckle. "I found another way out. Come on." Ken turned and walked toward the steps that went to the utility room. Passing those, he went through another door below the steps. Ken opened the door and turned on the light. "Wait in here," he instructed. "I've got to go turn off the lights."

Peter walked into what he assumed was the disposal room. To one side was a large compactor, apparently for cardboard, and on the other side was a metal door that Peter thought might lead to an incinerator. After about two minutes, Ken returned to join Peter.

"How do you get out of here?" Peter questioned, concerned about what Ken had in mind.

"Watch this," Ken said. He walked over to the door to the compactor and lifted the handle. Looking inside, he saw that the area was empty as if someone had run the compactor. "Come on," he called. He climbed into the compartment, out of Peter's sight.

Peter walked up to the open door and found Ken climbing out of an access door at the top of the compactor. Ken lifted his box of food onto the top of the compactor. "Give me your box," Ken said, taking Peter's box and putting it on the top also.

"Why do you go in through the roof if this is such an easy way out?" Peter asked. He followed Ken's lead and climbed into the compactor.

"Because," Ken said, climbing back into the compactor, "the door to the compactor latches on the inside. I can open it from inside to get out, but I can't open it from this side to get in. Wait a second. I have to turn out the lights."

Peter watched Ken climb back through the compactor door, then suddenly everything went dark again. A small red light in the distance indicated that Ken was using the small light on the key chain to find the door. Ken climbed back through and swung the door closed. There was a familiar clang as the latch snapped into the closed position. To make sure it was shut, Ken pushed on the door. It didn't move.

"See," Ken said, shining the small red light on the door, "it's secured. No one will ever know we were inside." As the two climbed out onto the top of the compactor, Ken looked around to make sure no one was in the area. Of all the times Ken had traversed this route, he had yet to find someone in the area. "Okay," Ken said. They huddled behind the same pallet where they'd started. "Wait here while I go close up the roof access."

"Oh yeah," Peter replied, realizing that the hatch on the roof had been left open.

Ken quickly went over to the fire escape and pulled the ladder down again. He climbed up onto the roof and disappeared. Peter sat there watching the dark surroundings, wondering if they were being watched. It had been only three or four minutes when Peter saw Ken climbing off the roof onto the fire escape. As he reached the retractable section, he stepped onto the top rung and rode the ladder down to its extended position. He then climbed down and stepped off the ladder, allowing it to return to its retracted position.

"Okay," Ken said, picking up his box, "let's go home with the groceries." After one more quick look around, the two scurried across the small parking lot to the back of the property. Ken untied the fence section, allowing him and Peter to slip out of the secured area, and then retied the section, making it appear unbroken. Then the two headed over to the car.

Ken paused at the edge of the bushes. "We need to make sure there isn't anyone coming out of the building," he said, checking the area from behind the bushes. "Looks clear," he said, and headed for the car. The two boys quietly opened the car doors and placed the boxes on the back seat, quietly closing the doors once they'd done so. With one more look around to make sure everything was clear, Ken started the car and pulled out.

"How's that?" Ken asked as they were driving down the road.

"I was scared to death the entire time," Peter replied, relieved to be safe again. "How did you figure all that out?"

"Well," Ken started, heading down the road toward Peter's house, "it wasn't easy. The first couple of times I climbed back out onto the roof, but then they came and cleaned out that utility room, and the crate I was using was no longer there. So I had to find another way out. I looked at all the doors and windows and could see the alarm sensors, so I knew I couldn't go that way. I even tried looking in the incinerator to see if I could climb up the chimney. Then I noticed the compactor. They didn't need an alarm on it because it latches closed from the inside. I was just lucky that the access door on the outside didn't have a latch; otherwise, I would have been stuck in there."

"What about the cleaning crew at the office building?" Peter continued questioning. "Have they ever caught you coming back?"

"Once," Ken replied. "I was scared that day. The supervisor of the cleaning crew was coming out and saw me by the car. I just put the box of food in the car, having already opened the front door. This was before I had disconnected the interior lights. Anyway, I told the guy I stopped by to see if they had any openings for helpers. I told him my dad was out of work and that he was willing to do almost anything for a job. The guy bought my story and gave me a card for my dad to call. Talk about being lucky. After that, I found another car. I didn't want that guy to see the same car in the parking lot."

"Man, you're lucky," Peter declared, amazed by Ken's stories.

"I must be," Ken said. Ken drove home to Peter's house, where they took the groceries inside. Ken stayed that night and many nights after that.

CHAPTER 19

The winter months were upon John and his family earlier than they had hoped. Winters in Cincinnati were generally on the mild side with temperatures in the low teens and not a lot of snow. However, history had shown temperatures as low as negative twenty-five degrees and snow of up to twenty-four inches from one snowfall. Everyone hoped this would be a mild winter with warm days and not a lot of snow.

The temperatures in mid-December weren't that cold, but the amount of snow was more than expected. Travel on city roads was extremely dangerous since the city didn't have money to pay for snow removal. With many roads becoming impassable, transportation had ground to a halt. Stores, those that were still open, had little supplies to offer, and variety was greatly limited. If your favorite cereal was Raisin Bran, all you would find is Cheerios. Many companies that had multiple products produced at multiple sites consolidated those sites, trying to keep at least one of the major plants running.

Ken and Peter also had fallen upon hard times. The first time they'd tried to steal food after a snowfall almost got them in a lot of trouble with the cops. During one of their trips, it started snowing while the boys were inside. When they climbed out, they quickly secured the hatch on the roof and went home. The opened hatch allowed snow to fall in, leaving a puddle of water in the utility room once it had melted. The next time they went on a shopping trip, Ken opened the hatch, only to find a light was on. This was the first time they had ever seen a light on. They decided to get out of there instead of going shopping. When they reached the bottom of the fire escape, four security guards came running out from the side of the building. Ken dashed for the fence line with Peter on his heels. Ken quickly untied the fence, and they escaped to freedom. That was the end of their opportunity to get free food.

Peter and Ken tried to get some work doing odd jobs. They did some repair work on some houses, mostly roof work after a bad storm in late January. They helped an older woman who had lost her husband, who'd fallen victim to a small mob in the community. The boys didn't make a lot at first, but every little bit helped.

The government had hired several teams to go door-to-door to see what houses still had survivors living in them. If no one replied to their knocking, they were instructed to gain access to the house whatever way they could without being too destructive and to search for anyone now deceased. Ken and Peter thought this was a cool job, or at least until they found their first dead body. They were checking houses over on Chestnut Hill Road when Ken knocked on the door and no one answered. He tried the front doorknob, which was unlocked. Ken walked into the living room, only to find two dead adults who had been dead for a while. The stench of decaying bodies inside a weather-sealed house had made him almost barf from the smell. The coroner came by and indicated that they had been dead for over two months.

The position of some bodies Ken and Peter had found indicated that they weren't the first to arrive on the scene. Peter walked into one house and found three girls tied spread-eagle on different beds. Each girl was left naked and apparently had been tortured. The coroner identified burn marks on the girls' bodies, along with bruises. And finally, whoever the culprits were had cut the girls' wrists and left them to bleed to death. There was so much blood all over the place that Peter almost got sick from the sight, never mind the smell.

All in all, out of the three hundred homes that the two boys checked out between mid-November and early February, they had discovered forty-two bodies. By late February they had investigated most homes within their area, and they'd had enough of stumbling onto dead bodies.

John was now the only courier for the hospital. Tom had died in early November in a car accident. The rumor was that he had the disease, which caused the accident. Mark also caught the disease around Thanksgiving and died, leaving John with the entire route. However, the number of doctors' offices still open was now down to only four for both routes. By Christmas, the number of offices that were still open dropped to three. The hospital changed its policy; now those individuals who needed blood work had to go to the hospital. This was devastating to John. What a way to start the New Year. He had some savings and was able to make ends meet, but times were getting very hard. He didn't use the normal furnace to heat the house as the cost of gas was so high that it would have been cheaper to use electricity. Instead, John put the fireplace into service. They started with a pile of wood they received from his uncle's farm, but that was less than two cords. By mid-January, they were burning whatever they could find. Peter and Ken were going out in search of wood to burn for heat. Since they had done the house-to-house search, they knew what houses were empty of residents but not empty of wood furniture. The two would go from one house to another, taking wooden furniture and breaking it up for firewood. It worked well. John didn't like the boys stealing furniture from homes that didn't belong to them, but he knew this was the only way they would keep the house, and therefore their bodies, from freezing.

The news broadcasts during the winter months told basically the same sad story. The number of deaths from the disease was still rising with no hope of finding a cure. In the local area, some sixty thousand had died, and more than forty-five million had died across the United States. The news had no idea of how many had died around the world but estimated the number to be close to a billion people. The population of the world was dropping fast. There were a lot of deaths associated directly with the disease, but there were also many others that were an indirect result of the disease. Gang fights were the number one killer of young people. Most fights were over territory that the gangs had claimed in search of supplies to survive. Many kids died also during the winter months from exposure or malnutrition. Yet another large number of kids, having been strung out on various drugs, died from overdosing. This was one commodity that was plentiful for all who wanted it. Robbery was also a big problem. Not only was there stealing from empty stores and houses, but also some of the desperate kids had started robbing people on the streets, including the cops. Occasionally, a cop would shoot some of these kids with no warning.

Actually, it had become common practice to shoot first and ask questions later. The number one crime against young girls was rape. Gangs were raping many of the young girls on the street, but there had even been cases where the cops or people in the military were raping girls. Their belief was that they could get away with it because there was no one to stop them. Some girls came forward and informed the authorities, but this was a small number compared to what the authorities estimated was going on. Even when the perpetrators were convicted of the charges, regardless of the crime, the authorities were so shorthanded that the punishment was a verbal reprimand, and the perps were back out on the streets.

By early March, things started to look up. Not only did it appear that spring weather might arrive early this year, but also John had found a job at a food warehouse. He gathered food for orders from various stores and assembled it to be loaded onto trucks. Sometimes, a box of cheese would fall off a pallet, and John would hide it somewhere in the warehouse. After he had stashed a quantity of supplies, he would have Ken and Peter go into the warehouse through a door that someone had forgotten to lock and pick up the supplies.

It was now early April, just two weeks before Beth's birthday. John came home from work and checked the mailbox for mail. Mail was delivered only twice a week. "Beth, honey," he called out again as he shuffled through the letters and flyers, "are you home?" At first, he didn't hear a response as he finished looking at the mail. As he stood there contemplating what to do next, he heard a soft cry from upstairs.

"Daddy," he heard again. This caused a shiver of fear to move through his soul. It wasn't a happy cry, like the way his daughter called him when she wanted him to see something special she had done. This cry was more like that of a defeated animal hit by a car and now dying.

John turned and ran up the stairs, taking them two at a time. He turned down the hallway and ran into his daughter's room. There on the bed, his precious daughter was lying curled up in a ball. "What's the matter?" he asked as he ran to her side.

"I don't know," Beth replied in a weak voice. "I just have these terrible cramps in my side, and I feel very sick to my stomach."

John looked her over, not knowing what to look for, and touched her forehead to see if she had a fever. His brief examination indicated that he didn't have the slightest idea of what to look for or what to do. He quickly grabbed the phone and dialed Marsha's number.

"Hello," came a response from the phone.

"Hello, Marsha?" John asked, even though he could tell by the voice that she was indeed the person on the other end.

"What's wrong?" Marsha asked, wondering why John's voice sounded strange.

"Can you come over?" John asked with an increased level of fear in his voice. "Beth is having cramps and feeling sick to her stomach. I don't know what to do." Since Marsha had been fired, John had been spreading the word around that she was a nurse for hire. The hospitals were so understaffed with nurses, and so many people were coming down with the BARD disease, that Marsha was pretty busy. John didn't know if she was going to be free to come over and see Beth.

"I'll be right over." It didn't take her long to travel to John's house, and she didn't even knock on the door when she arrived. She walked in and went straight upstairs to Beth's room.

"Okay," Marsha said as she walked into Beth's bedroom. "Beth," she continued as she knelt down by her bed, "tell me where it hurts."

"Right here," Beth said, pointing to her lower right abdomen.

"Okay," Marsha said, "let's check this out. John, can you leave us alone?" she asked, looking at John with a small smile of reassurance.

"Can't I stay?" John asked. "I'm worried about her."

"I know," Marsha replied, standing up and walking John to the door. "But I need her to be relaxed, and you're not going to help being all concerned. Plus," she said with a smile, "we girls don't like to have our dads around when we talk girl talk."

John was too worried about Beth's condition to pay any attention to what Marsha was saying. He just stayed in the hallway, pacing back and forth like a first-time expectant father. He continued his tracking back and forth for about twenty minutes, wondering what the heck those two could be doing this entire time. Several times he almost broke down and knocked on the door to see what was going on, but he decided that might make Beth feel more uncomfortable.

Finally, after half an hour, the door to Beth's room opened and Marsha escorted Beth, now dressed in a bathrobe, past her worried father and into the bathroom. Now the waiting vigil began. John could hear the water in the tub running. *Must be for Beth.* Another fifteen minutes passed, then Marsha came out of the bathroom by herself. "What's going on?" John asked, still concerned about Beth's health. "Is she all right?"

"She's fine," Marsha replied as she smiled back at John. "She's just growing up." John just stared back, waiting for an explanation of Beth's condition. "She's becoming a woman," Marsha continued, hoping for some sign that he understood where she was heading. She could see that John had no idea of what she was hinting at. *I guess guys are that way,* she thought. *Time for the direct approach.* "She's having her first period," she said with a big smile on her face.

"So what do we do to help her feel better?" John asked, still not understanding that this was not something one could take an aspirin for and feel better. It had to run its course.

"Don't worry about it," Marsha replied, trying hard not to laugh out loud. "I've told her what to do, so she'll be all right. If you have any problems, just give me a call. I'll try to get some Midol tomorrow after work that she can take for the cramps." Marsha began preparing to leave.

John still didn't understand what was going on, but because he trusted Marsha, he agreed to let her handle the situation. After she'd left, he went outside to work in the yard so he had something to keep his mind busy.

Beth rested most of the next day. She would occasionally doze off for several hours, and then the cramps would return, waking her up. Then she'd take some aspirins and go back to resting on the couch. Ken and Peter spent time on the computer, reviewing possible jobs they might get. The school systems never reopened, and they had time on their hands. Also, they both knew they needed the money.

John came home from the warehouse on time. The traffic was much lighter because the number of drivers had dropped drastically since the BARD outbreak. "How's Beth?" John asked as he walked into the kitchen and saw the boys raiding the refrigerator.

"She was watching TV," Ken replied first, since Peter had just taken a big bite out of an apple.

"She was complaining about cramps," Peter chimed in after swallowing the big bite, "but she took some aspirin and went upstairs to take a nap."

"I'm going to go upstairs and check on her," John said. He quietly walked up the stairs and bypassed the one step he knew would answer to his weight with a loud squeak. He opened Beth's door and peeked in to see her lying quietly on the bed. Satisfied that she was all right for now, he closed her door and started back down the steps.

Later that night, John was sitting in the living room reading the paper, looking for a possible job for Peter or Ken. Peter and Ken were busy looking for job openings on the internet. Because of the cold winter, Peter had moved the computer from his colder room downstairs to the warmer living room. Beth had had more cramps and had gone upstairs to take another hot bath. After about twenty minutes, a sudden fearful scream came from over by the stairs. Everyone jumped up and ran, with Peter in the lead. When they arrived at the bottom of the steps, they found that Beth had fallen down the stairs. John pushed past the boys to see what had happened to his little princess. Seeing her on the floor, he scooped her up and carried her to the couch. "Beth!" John called out to the barely conscious girl with a touch of fear in his voice. "Are you all right?"

"My back and foot hurts," she replied as she reached for her right ankle.

"Can you move your foot?" John asked, concerned that she may have broken her ankle.

"Yes," she replied, slowly moving her ankle.

"I think you just sprained it," he said, trying to reassure her even though he had no idea if he was right. "Did you trip coming down the steps?" John asked, wondering how this graceful little girl could have tripped.

"No," Beth replied in a weak voice. "I just don't feel very good. I feel a little dizzy."

"Do you still feel sick to your stomach?" John asked as he tried to get a better picture of the situation.

"No, not really," Beth replied, looking a little dazed.

"Do you feel tired?" John asked, not wanting to know the answer to this question.

"A little," she replied. She lay back and closed her eyes.

"Well, you lie here on the couch and get some rest," John said, placing a pillow under her head. He got up and walked into the front room, waving to the boys to follow him.

"I don't know what's wrong with her," John said to Peter in a soft voice so as not to have Beth overhear. "I don't know if she's just sick or if she has that damned blood disease."

"She's not old enough to catch the disease," Peter replied, hoping his father's interpretation was wrong.

"I'm going to call Marsha," John said, heading over to the phone. "Marsha," John said when he heard her answer the phone, "I think Beth is dying."

There wasn't a sound from the other end of the line. "Please," John pleaded, fearful she didn't have the time, "she just fell down the steps, and she says that she is very weak and dizzy. I'm afraid that she's come down with the BARD disease and is going to die."

Silence remained at the other end of the phone, but soon John heard Marsha reply, "I'll be right over."

Returning to the Davison house and going into the living room, Marsha knelt down next to Beth to get a close look at her. "Beth," she said in a soft voice, "I understand you fell down the steps." Beth wasn't quick to respond, but she did affirmatively shake her head. "Can you tell me what happened?" Marsha asked.

"I just got really dizzy," Beth replied in a weak voice, "and fell down the stairs."

"Do you have any aches or pains?" Marsha asked, noticing several abrasions on the side of Beth's face where she must have hit the steps.

"No," she replied, "not really."

"Beth, I want you to squeeze my hand as hard as you can," Marsha said, putting her fingers into Beth's left hand. Marsha saw the small fingers curl around her three fingers; however, they exerted almost no pressure. "Okay," she replied. "Now I want you to raise your left leg six inches and hold it up as long as you can." This time Marsha did nothing but watch as Beth strained to lift her leg only about three inches and, a second later, plop it back down on the couch. "Okay," Marsha said, "I'm going to make you some warm tea. It'll make you feel better."

"Thank you," came Beth's soft response.

Marsha got up and walked into the kitchen, where she heated some water. Then she tiptoed into the front room, followed by John and the boys. "Okay," Marsha said quietly so as not to be overheard by Beth. "She is very weak, which could be the result of the fall. However, I kind of doubt it. She said she was feeling dizzy before she fell, and that's what bothers me. I hate to say it, John, but there's a good chance she has the disease."

"I thought that you couldn't get the disease unless you reached the age of puberty," Peter shot out quickly, not wanting to believe Marsha's assessment of his sister's condition. "That's like thirteen or fourteen, isn't it?"

"That's true," Marsha replied, seeing the fear in Peter's eyes. "But some kids reach puberty sooner than others. You know the cramps she's been having?" she asked, looking at both John and Peter, who shook their heads in response. "She's having her first period."

John knew that was what Marsha had been trying to tell him yesterday. But he hadn't wanted to believe it because that would mean his little girl was growing up and could fall prey to the disease.

Marsha didn't know what else to say. After all, what can you say when you just told a father and a brother that the youngest member of their family may now have the disease and there isn't a thing they can do to keep her from dying from it? "If I can be of any help," Marsha ventured as she turned and headed for the kitchen to finish brewing Beth's cup of tea, "let me know."

John just stood there, not knowing what to do next. He slowly walked to the corner of the living room and stood there, watching his little angel resting on the couch. *Or is she lying there waiting to die?* he wondered. He felt as if someone had pulled his heart out and crushed it in a vise. His world had fallen apart when Paula died, and now he might have to relive the entire scenario all over again just because his little girl was growing old enough to die. He wanted to go over to her and hug her so hard that she would merge with him. All he could do was just stand there and watch his pride and joy from across the room.

"Ken," Peter said, nodding his head, indicating that he wanted Ken to follow him. "We have to go out and see if we can find a blood donor for Beth," Peter said when they were in the backyard.

"Do you think there are any kids left in this area we can draw blood from?" Ken asked, concerned about the number of people left.

"I don't know," Peter said with a tone of uncertainty, "but we have to try." It had been a long time since they went roaming the streets, and there was no way of knowing if there were many kids still around. It was too cold to go out in the winter months. When they went looking for odd jobs to earn money, they usually returned home before it got dark. Now they would have to try again to find a blood donor. Otherwise, there was no telling how long Beth would live.

"You're right," Ken said, agreeing with Peter. Ken stood there remembering the past excursions they had been on. Remembering the failures, the close calls, and the one successful mission, Ken tried to tell him that it was possible to find another donor. But deep down, he felt this would be an exercise in futility.

"Okay," Peter said, "let's go get ready. I have all the stuff from before down in the basement."

"Do you know what Beth's blood type is?" Ken asked.

"I believe it's type AB," Peter answered.

The thought of trying to find type AB blood made Ken nervous. The news had announced that so many had died from the disease that there couldn't be many left. Now to have to find someone with this rare blood type just made the journey seem nearly impossible. As Ken ran through his memories of some of their past trips, he remembered finding a boy with type AB blood, so maybe they had a chance.

"If we do find someone," Ken said, still running through the expeditions from the past, "we will have to carry the kid back all by ourselves. We don't have anyone to help us this time."

"You're right," Peter agreed, remembering how they had transported the one donor using the stretcher and four pole-bearers.

Peter wouldn't be able to call his father for a ride back because cell phones were virtually extinct. Since the start of the plague, the use of cell phones had become more and more expensive, until it got to the point where only the rich could afford them. Most of the workers who'd had jobs in cellular communications had gone back to supporting the old landline systems.

"We'll just have to do the best we can," Peter concluded, looking up at the house as if peering through the walls at his sister lying on the couch. "We have to for my sister's sake."

The boys got their supplies together and were ready to head out the door at about nine o'clock. It was dark, but not so dark that they couldn't see. A small moon helped them to see where they were going. "Where do you want to go?" Peter asked, not sure which way to head.

"We could go over to the Lake View Apartments," Ken answered. "If my memory serves me correctly, we found a type AB donor there when we were out looking for donors for your mom. Maybe we'll get lucky again."

"Lead on," Peter replied, hoping Ken's memory was accurate.

The route to the apartment complex was harder to travel because so many yards now looked like overgrown fields because the homeowners were now gone. So, instead of cutting across nicely cut lawns, the boys were forging through fields of tall grass. Most of the lights around the apartment complex were out because someone had shot them. However, the lights over the entranceways were still functional, providing some light around the apartments. Ken and Peter could hear voices, which was encouraging as it indicated there were people around. However, many of the voices belonged to adults. That meant either they were very lucky not to have contracted the disease or they all had type B blood. Ken and Peter needed to find a kid who had type AB blood.

On the steps of the first apartment building, Ken and Peter saw several kids with their parents playing out on the front stoop, which made the kids a nontarget. The two boys stayed in the shadows so they wouldn't be spotted.

They advanced cautiously as they entered a bad section of town. This section was known to be overrun with gangs. Ken told Peter that he'd been through this section of town before, adding that if they were going to find a kid without any parents around, this was the part of town to look in. Ken had heard stories of kids running free. And the cops and military rarely entered this area because the gangs here were large. When the military sent in several squads to manage the gang problem, they couldn't find anyone because everyone went and hid. But when they sent in one or two men, those men usually got jumped. This area previously had been known for robberies, but now the robberies had stopped as there wasn't much left to steal. The cops and military had succeeded in limiting these gangs' ability to move out of this confined area.

As Ken and Peter walked down a small alley, they could hear cries from a young voice. They couldn't tell what the voice was saying, but it sounded as if it were yelling "Stop!" They approached the sound slowly and cautiously for fear that this could be a trap. Some gangs used such tactics as this to attract their victims.

"Quiet," Ken said as he and Peter approached the back corner of a small abandoned store. They each slowly peeked around the corner, trying to see who was crying, but being ever so careful not to reveal their presence. What they saw was almost too horrifying to imagine. A young girl of about eleven years old was lying on a crate with most of her clothes torn off. A soldier was standing there with her shoulder pinned and with his pants down around his knees. The two boys stood there, stunned, as this soldier proceeded to rape the young girl and at the same time slap her across the face because she wouldn't stop crying.

Peter pulled Ken back around the corner so they wouldn't be seen. "We have to help her," he requested with a tone of concern.

"Okay," Ken said as he looked around the area. "You stay over there,"— Ken pointed at a dumpster about twenty feet away—"and get ready to throw some rocks. If he pulls out a gun, I don't want you to do anything but run around the corner of that building and get the hell out of here." Ken pointed to the corner of a neighboring store, where the dumpster was sitting.

"What are you going to do?" Peter asked.

"Pray I can distract him long enough for the girl to get away without getting shot," Ken answered with a tone of confidence. But deep down he was scared to death as he felt he was out of practice, not to mention being out in the bad part of town.

Peter took up position behind the dumpster, holding two good-size rocks. Ken stood at the corner, also holding two large rocks. Ken stepped out from behind the corner and let fly his first projectile at the soldier. At the same time, he yelled, "Hey, stupid!"

The rock caught the guy in the back and made him jump. He turned around just in time to see the second projectile coming in. However, this time he dodged the rock. It soared behind him and crashed into a metal trash can. "I'll get you!" he yelled, trying to reach down and pull his revolver from its holster. However, it was hard to get the gun out since it was snapped securely in place, and the holster itself was lying on the ground at his feet with the waistband of his pants lying over it. The soldier continued to struggle to remove his firearm.

"You're an asshole!" Ken yelled again. He heaved another large rock at the soldier, this time catching him in the arm he was using to get the gun out. This infuriated the soldier to such a degree that he actually tripped on his pants as he was trying to pull his holster up, while at the same time trying to run. This caused Ken to start laughing, which infuriated the soldier more. As Ken watched for another second, he saw the girl get up off the crate. Standing there with only a torn shirt to cover her body, she reached down, picked up a bottle, and used it to hit the soldier on the head, causing him to crash onto the ground crying out in pain.

"Come on!" Ken cried out to the girl, who looked up to see Ken waving at her to get away from the soldier. She immediately ran past the soldier and over to where Ken was standing. "Let's get out of here," he said once she had caught up with him. The two of them took off, heading toward the dumpster where Peter was waiting, armed with his rocks. Once they joined up with Peter, Ken said, "Let's go!" The three took off around the corner and disappeared into the shadows.

After taking about three more turns around different buildings, the three stopped. The girl, realizing she was basically naked, covered herself with her arms. Ken and Peter looked at her and then looked at each other. Ken removed the dark-colored Harley-Davidson shirt he was wearing— he'd chosen a dark color so that it would be hard for others to see him— and said to the girl, "Here, put this on for now." The girl quickly took the shirt and turned her back to Peter and Ken as she slid the large shirt over her head. She turned back around to let the boys see how the large shirt fit. It made a nice dress for her small body. She looked both boys in the eyes and thanked them as she began to cry.

Ken and Peter looked at each other; they were thinking the same thing. "My name is Peter," Peter said to the girl. "I have a sister who is dying from the disease and needs a blood transfusion. Do you know what your blood type is?"

"No," the girl replied, not understanding much about what Peter was talking about other than the point about his sister dying.

"Can we test your blood to see what type you are?" Peter asked in a kind voice. "It won't hurt. We just stick your finger and get a drop of blood."

The girl still didn't understand, but she agreed to let them test her blood. Ken took out the alcohol wipes and wiped off the end of her finger, which was pretty dirty from living on the streets. Then Ken held her finger as Peter took the lancet and stuck her. She jumped as the point penetrated her finger and a small drop of blood came through. Peter quickly put the blood on a slide. Hopeful, Peter tested her blood. Peter looked up at Ken. "She's type O," he said, obviously disappointed.

"I'm not the right type, am I?" the girl asked, reacting to the boys' disappointment. She didn't understand what the boys were talking about, but she did grasp that they were disappointed.

"No," Peter said, "but thank you for letting us test you."

"You're welcome," she replied in a shy voice.

The girl stood there and thanked the boys for having helped her, feeling a little disappointed that she couldn't be of some help to them. Without another word, the girl turned and headed down another alley. "Good luck," Peter said in a soft tone, barely audible to Ken, who was standing next to him. Peter knew that she, too, would die soon from the disease if the city itself didn't get her first.

"Let's go," Peter said once he had finished packing the testing supplies. The two boys continued their search for a blood donor for Beth.

"This looks like a good place to cut through to the other side of the street," Ken said, pointing to what was left of a large sporting goods store that had been destroyed by gangs. They entered the store slowly in case someone was inside. However, the building appeared to be empty. They stopped at the back of the store to get a more expansive view of the interior and check out the area in front before going out onto the street. Just as they were about to step out onto the sidewalk, they heard something crash to the floor behind them. The two quickly crouched down to hide from whatever or whoever was in the store.

Curiosity can sometimes be a strong urge that is difficult to ignore. Ken motioned to Peter to go one way around the store, motioning that he would go around the other way. As they approached a counter over by the wall farthest away from their starting point, they came across a young boy of about nine or ten years of age. He was crouched down behind the counter, wearing only his underwear. Ken shined the red flashlight at the boy, who appeared to be only skin and bones. His shoulder blades stuck out of his back. Ken also noticed several bad bruises on his back. When the boy looked up, Ken almost dropped the flashlight. His face had been badly beaten. He had one black eye and several bad cuts on his cheeks. His lips were blistered and swollen. Ken motioned that he and Peter should leave the boy alone and go try to find another donor. This boy had had enough bad things happen to him; they didn't want to add to his suffering.

Ken and Peter continued to search for a donor for Beth. As they were about to step out of the store, they saw the silhouette of a girl running into the doorway of one of the stores across the street. She stopped just inside the doorway and sat down, puffing as if she had just run a marathon. To get a closer look at this new prospect, Ken and Peter moved slowly along some abandoned cars parked along the road. They were about twenty feet away, looking through the side windows of an old Chevy pickup truck. "How old do you think she is?" Ken asked, wondering if they should try to test her.

"She looks like she's a little older than Beth," Peter replied, trying to determine her age. The glimmering light of the quarter moon was casting a dim light onto the girl's face. Her face was all broken out with acne, and the shirt she had on was small, revealing that she was much more developed than someone who hadn't reached puberty yet.

"Think she might be a good candidate?" Ken asked as he started to plan on how to put her to sleep.

"No," Peter replied in disappointment. "If she is older than Beth, either she is type B and immune to the disease, or she could be the right blood type but just not showing signs of the disease yet."

"Let's go over to that housing complex," Ken suggested, pointing to a housing complex north of the parking lot. The boys crossed the parking lot and headed over to several houses that appeared to be empty. "Let's go in there," Ken said, pointing to an open door at the back of a brick house. "Then we can get a look out the front windows to see if anything is going on."

As the two boys entered the house, they heard a strange sound coming from the living room. The sound seemed familiar, but neither boy could determine what it was. They went to check it out. As they walked carefully through the dining room, past the kitchen table, they could hear the sound more clearly. "It seems to be coming from over there," Ken whispered, pointing to the couch. The two continued their advance until they were standing next to the couch. On the couch was a small boy who had some nasal problems, snoring away.

"Let's check him out," Ken whispered ever so softly so as not to wake the boy.

"Okay," Peter said, "but I would still put him out."

Ken pulled the white washcloth from the bag, where it had been stored, and applied some chloroform. Instead of holding the rag against the face of a fighting victim, Ken kind of just laid the cloth near the boy's nose and let him breathe in the vapors. However, since he wasn't fighting back, there was no good way to tell if the boy was under or not. "That should be long enough," Ken whispered, removing the cloth and returning it to its Ziploc bag.

Ken and Peter performed their respective tasks as they tried to determine if this boy would be a good donor. "No luck," Peter replied in a disappointed tone. "He's type A."

The two packed up their supplies and left the boy sleeping where he was. They continued to the front windows to see what, if anything, was going on in the neighborhood. "Look at this place," Peter said, amazed at the way the neighborhood looked. There was trash everywhere. Several cars had been vandalized. The house across the street had been burned to the ground. The area was a mess. There didn't appear to be anyone on the streets, which was good news and bad news at the same time. The good news was that there apparently weren't any gangs in the area, and the bad news was that there might not be any donors around either.

"Well," Ken said, a little disappointed, "I guess it doesn't matter which way we go."

"Well, let's go that way," Peter said, hoping that his selection would prove to be a wise one.

The two boys slipped out the front door and headed down the street. They remained within the shadows to limit their chances of being spotted. A couple of houses had lights on, indicating that someone was home, but all the streetlights were out.

Several houses down from where they had checked out the street were two boys sitting on lounge chairs looking at some magazine by the light of the back porch. The older boy looked to be about ten years old, and his apparent brother appeared to be about eight or nine.

"What do you think?" Ken whispered as he gauged the situation.

"They look about the right age," Peter said, "but we've never tried to take two at the same time." He was feeling a little nervous about trying to put two to sleep at the same time since he would have to be the one to put one of them out. Ken always had been the one who put the kids to sleep; Peter's job was to determine the kid's blood type.

"I know," Ken said, looking back at Peter. "That means you have to put one of them to sleep at the same time. Do you think you can do that?" he asked, hoping for an affirmative answer. If Peter couldn't do this, they would have to pass up this opportunity and move on to see if they could find someone else who was all alone. One of these two boys could be the donor they needed to help Beth.

"Yeah," Peter replied reluctantly, trying to sound as if he were comfortable with the situation.

"Okay," Ken said as he surveyed the area. "We'll cross over to that side of the swimming pool and come up on the far side. Then, when I give the signal, you take the younger boy and I'll take the older one. Okay?"

Peter looked over at the pool, where the boys were sitting, and agreed that this would be a good plan. The pool was only about twenty feet from the spot where the boys were sitting, and they had their backs to it.

Ken pulled out a knife, took the cloth they had been using, and cut a slice along the edge of the material. Then with a sudden pull, he ripped the cloth into two pieces. Ken and Peter quickly ducked out of sight because, what with the noise created by ripping the material being a lot louder than Ken had thought it would be, the two boys sitting on the lounge chairs looked up from the magazine they were reading. However, because the noise didn't appear to them to be anything of concern, they returned to looking at the magazine.

"That was close," Peter whispered, a little shaken up from the sudden need to duck out of sight.

"Sorry," Ken replied with a little giggle. "I've never done that before. I've seen my dad do it, and it never sounded very loud to me."

Ken gave one piece of cloth to Peter and then pulled out the chloroform bottle. "Okay," Ken said, about to give last-minute instructions. "When we get behind the pool, I'll pour the chloroform on the rags, and when I give the signal, we go put them to sleep."

"All right," Peter replied—but a disturbing thought came into his head. "Now we're going to have two sleeping kids. How are we going to carry two kids back here to be tested?"

Ken looked at Peter. He hadn't thought about that. He took a moment to think about how to address this problem. "I know," he said as an idea came to him. "We'll put them both to sleep and then carry the older boy behind the pool to test his blood. If he's the lucky one, then we will take him home, and his brother can just sleep. If the older one isn't compatible, then we can put him back and test his brother."

"That sounds good to me," Peter said, still not sure he could do this.

"Let's go," Ken whispered. He started to make his way through the edge of the woods and to a place where they could approach the pool without being seen. Once they were in position, Peter removed the backpack, leaving it behind the pool. He didn't want to have it become an additional problem if he were to have trouble putting his candidate to sleep.

Ken looked around to make sure the coast was clear. He pulled out the chloroform bottle and poured some of the liquid on his torn piece of cloth. Then he motioned to Peter to hold up his piece as he applied some to his piece of cloth. With both rags ready to put their respective potential donors to sleep, Peter and Ken made their way around the pool to where the two other boys were sitting.

The two boys were quietly talking about something they'd found in the magazine and had no clue of the approaching boys. Ken, confident, moved slowly, step by step, toward the two boys. Beside him and a little behind him, Peter slowly followed Ken. However, Peter's stomach was doing cartwheels as the fear rose within him. He had never tried this before. What would happen if the little boy struggled and he couldn't put him to sleep? What would happen if the boy screamed? Everyone in the neighborhood would come running to save the boys and to kill Peter and Ken. Peter's nerves had him shaking so bad that he was afraid his knocking knees would give his and Ken's position away. He'd never even realized what Ken had to go through every time they went to put a kid to sleep.

Step by step, they got closer. They were now within two feet of the boys. Ken motioned to Peter that this was it. Peter was afraid that he might freeze up when it was time to attack. That would be disastrous as the younger boy would probably try to fight off Ken and might scream. Peter had to do his part or else die right there on the spot. Suddenly, Ken made his move. It was Peter's turn to make his move. He didn't know how, but he felt himself moving forward. He wrapped his arm around the little boy's shoulders and placed the rag over the boy's face. Ken got his arm around the shoulders of his victim and had both arms pinned so he couldn't resist. Peter wasn't as lucky as he had only one arm. The boy's right arm was still free, and he was using it to try to pull the hand in which Peter was holding the chloroformed rag away from his face. Peter almost let go when the little boy buried his fingernails into his right arm. Peter wanted to scream out and hurt the kid back, but he was too busy concentrating on keeping the cloth over the boy's face. After what seemed like an eternity, the little boy finally went limp in his arms. He carefully lowered the boy into a lying position on the lounge chair and looked over at Ken. Peter wiped the blood from the small wound the younger boy had made with his fingernails.

"Good job," Ken said confidently as a big smile formed across his face. He knew this was probably the hardest thing Peter had ever done.

"Thanks," Peter replied, exhausted from the ordeal. Not that it required a lot of physical strength, but the emotional effort had been exhausting.

"Okay," Ken said, reaching beneath the arms of the older boy, "grab his feet and let's get behind the pool." The two quickly carried the older boy behind the pool, where they commenced the routine of testing his blood. Ken looked on with anticipation as Peter applied the antigen to the blood samples, hoping this boy would be a match for Beth. However, the test revealed that the older boy was type O.

"Well," Peter said in a disappointed tone, "I guess we might as well take him back and try his brother, but I would venture to say that he's going to be type O too."

Ken and Peter carried the older boy back to the lounge chair and laid him down as if he had fallen asleep. Then they lifted the younger boy and carried him behind the pool to repeat the routine. Again Ken sat in anticipation of the results, hopeful this would be the last one they would have to do this night. However, Peter's understanding of the genetics was right as this boy was also type O. Disappointed, the two carried the younger boy back to the lounge chair and positioned him as if he, too, had fallen asleep.

Still nursing their disappointment, Ken and Peter returned to the woods, where they could talk without being overheard. "This is getting very frustrating," Ken said, somewhat agitated.

"I know," Peter replied, also upset, not because they hadn't found a donor yet, but because if they didn't find one, then his sister would die. "We need to keep looking," he said with hope in his voice. "We'll find someone." *We have to,* he thought, deciding to keep this statement to himself.

"I wish I were as optimistic as you are," Ken said. There was a pause between the two boys as if a truce were being implemented. "All right," Ken continued, "let's start heading home. Maybe we will find someone on the way back."

"Okay," Peter agreed, a little disappointed. But the later it got, the less chance they had of finding anyone outside. Peter turned and followed Ken through the woods and back to the house where they had made their initial observation of the street.

They were as cautious upon entering the house this time as they had been before. When they stepped through the door, a voice from the darkness called out, "Who's there?" It caught them totally off guard. Ken almost jumped backward, right into Peter.

Surprised by the voice, Ken wasn't sure what to do next. Had the boy they'd put to sleep earlier already awakened, or was there someone else in the house who'd been hiding earlier? A quick glance at the couch revealed that the boy they had tested earlier was still asleep; he had rolled over and wasn't snoring. After several seconds of silence, Ken replied to the question in a soft voice, saying, "No one special. We're just looking for a place to stay for the night."

From the shadows in the far corner of a badly trashed living room came a soft voice. "Do you have any food?" It sounded like a young boy. The voice sounded very weak.

"I'm sorry," Ken replied, sympathetic to the requester, "I don't have any right now. But," he continued, in hopes of not losing the attention of the owner of the voice, "I can get some."

From the corner of the room came a young boy about ten years old. He was nothing but skin and bones. He looked as if he had been freed from a German concentration camp during World War II. His eyes had sunk deep into his skull, and his lips appeared to be chapped. His face had signs of bruising, indicating that he'd had some bad times in the past. Ken felt sorry for the boy and wished he had some food to offer him.

"No food in the kitchen?" Ken asked, hoping that the boy hadn't thought of that.

"No," the boy replied in a disappointed tone. "I've checked out the entire kitchen."

"Would you like to go with us to go get some food?" Ken asked, feeling sympathetic toward the boy.

The boy just looked out the window at the empty street and stepped back. "No," he replied, fear rising in his voice. It was obvious that he was terrified of the world outside this house. He had been treated badly by some of the gangs in the area and was more fearful of them than he was of starving.

"Well," Ken said, looking at Peter for reassurance, "maybe we can bring some back."

The eyes in the boy's head seemed to pop out at the possibility that they might come back with food.

Peter reached out and jabbed Ken in the arm. "Should we test him?" Peter asked in a very soft whisper so that the boy wouldn't hear him.

"He's not going to have enough blood to give," Ken said in a slightly sarcastic tone. In a way he was right; this boy's skin was sucked in around his bones.

"We don't have a lot of choices at this point in time," Peter argued in a more forceful tone, worried that if he were to fail, it could cost him his sister. "A little good blood has got to be worth more than no blood at all."

"Okay," Ken said, knowing that Peter was right about the time they had to find a donor. But this boy didn't look as if he had a whole lot to give. "Before we get some food, can we test your blood?"

The boy just stood there, confused by the question. He had never heard of a test related to blood.

Ken could see the fear in his eyes. "It'll be okay," he said in a friendly tone, trying to win the boy's confidence. "It won't even hurt."

Reluctant, the boy agreed to the blood test. As the boys performed the testing ritual, they explained to the boy what they were doing and why, hoping that if he understood what they were doing, he wouldn't be so afraid of what would happen. Peter applied the antigens to the blood samples as the boy watched in amazement and as Ken watched in anticipation. However, Ken and Peter were both disappointed when the blood test revealed that the boy was type B. He was going to be one lucky kid in that he would not die from the disease. Now, whether he would survive life on the streets could not be known by anyone, but the signs were leaning toward a sad conclusion.

"Thank you," Peter said to the boy, trying to hold back his disappointment.

"Now," Ken said, "you hide in the corner where you were before, and I'll come back later with some food for you. Okay?" The boy nodded his head, indicating he understood. "My name is Ken," he continued. "What's yours?"

"My name is Lucas," the boy replied in a more optimistic tone.

"When I come back, I'll call out your name. And I'll also say my name so you know it's safe to come out, all right?"

The boy shook his head and disappeared into the shadows. Ken and Peter made their way out of the house, disappointed that they hadn't found a donor for Beth and, although a little less so, disappointed that they had had no food to give the boy. Chances were that they wouldn't be able to return with any that night as it would be much too late for them to return once they got home. Plus, they still didn't have a donor for Beth.

Ken and Peter decided to head back home using a different route than the one they'd started on, hoping to find someone who could be a donor. The night was dark as the moon had ducked behind some clouds, and it was getting late. Their hopes were dwindling fast. They had to make a stop to allow a military patrol to go by. The men didn't seem to be doing much to find anyone as they were talking and laughing so loud that they could be heard a block away. Ken and Peter just hid in an empty house and watched them roll by. When the men were out of sight and out of hearing range, the boys continued their search.

They had traveled about two blocks when they heard a gang approaching from down the street. Again, the boys found refuge in another abandoned house. They watched the approaching gang from an upstairs bedroom window. They never realized how close they were to being in the middle of a gang war. As the gang coming down the street reached the house where Ken and Peter were hiding, another gang came storming out of the house from across the street. The two boys would have been in real trouble had they gone into the other house. They watched for several seconds as the two gangs started fighting. However, this was no fistfight; the gang members had all sorts of harsh weapons. One boy came out of the house waving a machete, and another one came out firing a shotgun. His aim wasn't bad either as one boy fell to the ground. The gang in the street was also armed but had their weapons hidden. They too pulled out knives and guns and used them.

"Let's get the hell out of here," Ken said as he watched the boy with the machete swing and cut off a boy's arm. The boy stood there in shock at the sight of his missing arm. He didn't have long to stare as the boy came back with the machete and caught his victim squarely on the side of his head. He died instantly.

Peter needed no persuasion to depart this ghastly exhibition. Ken led the way down the steps and out the back door as the sounds of screaming and guns being fired could be heard out front. They ran as fast as they could while still trying to stay low so they wouldn't be spotted. After running about two blocks, they ducked behind some bushes to rest, when off in the direction of the gang fight, rifle shots. Ken surmised that the military had returned and, judging from the number of shots he'd heard, put an end to the fight by killing everyone there.

After a short break as they watched the street, Ken and Peter decided it was safe to continue on home. They stayed up close to the houses to stay in the shadows. Although there weren't any lights around, the moon cast a bright glow over the area when it peeked out from behind the clouds. The trip back to the house took a lot longer than expected as the boys tried to remain out of sight. As they reached the edge of the bad area, where all the homeless kids seemed to hang out, they paused as a shadowy figure in front of them ducked behind some bushes.

"Hold it," Ken said in a soft whisper, kneeling down by the corner of another abandoned house. "Look over there," he said, pointing to someone who appeared to be hiding. He and Peter waited for about five minutes, but nothing happened. The shadowy figure either had evaded whomever was chasing him or her or simply didn't want to be out in the open, which was understandable for this neighborhood. As Peter and Ken waited, the moon again popped out from behind a cloud, casting rays of light upon the area. The light filtered down through a tree to cast some light on the individual hiding in front of the house.

"It looks like a girl," Ken whispered to Peter, observing the way the moonlight bounced off the long strands of blonde hair.

"Yeah," Peter concurred, knowing what Ken was thinking: *Here was a possible donor, all alone, and there appears to be no one around.*

"Let's go," Ken said, pulling out the cloth and chloroform. Ken and Peter weren't fifty feet from the girl, making it easy to sneak up on her. Ken slowly approached her and had no trouble putting her to sleep. Once she was asleep, Peter joined Ken within seconds. They picked up the girl and carried her behind the house from which they first had spotted her. They laid her down and were able to tell that she was about ten or eleven years old, which made her the right age. She had nothing on but a long T-shirt and panties, making it easy to see she was a little thin but not as malnourished as some of the other kids they had seen.

"Now," Ken said, kneeling down next to the girl, "let's test her."

Peter quickly pulled out the testing supplies as Ken got the girl's finger ready to be punctured. With the drops of blood on the slide, Peter applied the antigens to the drops. The results were disappointing; she was type B. Here was another possible survivor.

"Should we take her back over to the bush," Peter asked, putting away the testing supplies, "or just leave her here?"

Ken looked over at the bushes where they'd found her hiding and noticed there wasn't a lot of cover. "I think she'll be safer if we leave her inside this house," Ken replied, pointing to the house they were hiding behind. "She'll also be warmer inside than outside, behind a bush."

"That sounds like a good idea," Peter replied. "We might even be able to find a blanket to cover her up with."

Peter and Ken picked up the girl and carried her through the back door of the abandoned house. They walked carefully through the house to where they thought the living room would be. It was hard to find their footing in the dark, especially for Ken, who was walking backward while holding the girl from beneath her shoulders. As they reached the living room, the moon came out again, projecting enough light through the living room windows to see a sofa over in the corner. The two boys laid the girl carefully on the couch and quickly looked around for something to cover her up with. However, the moon disappeared again, leaving them in total darkness.

"She'll be all right," Ken whispered. "Let's just head on home."

"Okay," Peter replied. The two slowly made their way to the back door. They slipped out the door and stopped at the corner of the house to check that the area was clear. Suddenly, they heard a loud bang inside the house.

"What the hell was that?" Ken asked, looking up at the windows of the dining room. "Could the girl have awakened already?" he asked, thinking she might have awakened and was trying to walk around in the dark. She would have been disorientated from having awakened in a dark room of some house she wasn't familiar with. But it was too soon for her to wake up.

From where they were standing, Peter and Ken could see flashlights moving inside the house. "Someone else is in there," Peter exclaimed, surprised.

"No kidding," Ken said in a sarcastic tone, louder than he should have seeing they were supposed to be hiding.

Suddenly they could hear someone kicking the front door of the house open. Ken and Peter quickly moved to the front corner of the house and peeked around it. There were seven or eight older boys running out of the house, carrying something large.

"It's the girl," Ken said, surprised at what he was seeing.

However, the volume of his voice was louder than it should have been as one of the boys in the gang overheard him. "Thanks," the boy yelled back with a tone of laugher. "We've been trying to catch her all night. Here," he yelled back. He pulled the girl's panties off and threw them in the direction where Ken and Peter were standing. The other boys tore her shirt off. They carried the sleeping girl off as if they had won a prize.

"We just gave her to them," Peter said in a frustrated tone.

"There's nothing we can do now," Ken said in a defeated tone. "We might as well go home." The boys walked home, defeated in their mission to find a donor and disgusted at what life had evolved into, from a world of good and bad to a world of bad and downright awful.

The boys walked into Peter's house shortly after two o'clock in the morning. They were tired and beaten down. Both of them just wanted to go to bed and sleep away the bad experiences of the night. However, John was in the living room, having waited for them to return, and he wanted to talk.

"Peter!" John called out in a tone of panic that made the hairs on the back of Peter's neck stand up. "It's Beth."

Peter and Ken bolted into the living room to see John kneeling next to the couch where Beth had been lying. John had one of his hands on her head as he ran his fingers through the shiny strands of hair on her head. He had tears in his eyes when he looked up at Peter.

"She's dying," John said, almost choking on the words. The thought of his one and only daughter dying in front of him was tearing him apart. Here in front of him, the life was slowly leaving the little girl's body, and he was helpless to do anything to stop it. It was that feeling of helplessness when he would rather die in her place just so she'd have a chance at life.

"Peter," came a small, weak whisper from the little girl's lips.

"Peter!" John said, jumping up when he heard the voice of his little girl. "She just called you," he said, jumping up out of the way so Peter could get down next to Beth and hear her voice. *She hasn't gone yet,* John thought. *She is still with us.* John's emotions were running in every which direction. The feelings he felt at the thought that she was still alive filled his heart with hope, even though he knew the situation was hopeless. But the feeling that she was still here, even if only for a few more minutes, made him feel glad, especially since she now would see Peter before she left them.

"I'm here," Peter said in a soft voice as he tried to hold back the tears. However, overwhelmed with emotion, he couldn't help but cry. "I'm sorry we couldn't find a blood donor for you," Peter said between the sobs that were now making it nearly impossible for him to speak. "We just couldn't find anyone."

Beth had been lying there too weak to move, but her brother's overwhelming emotions generated a spark of energy within her. She raised her arm and put it on her brother's shoulder. "It's okay," she said in a soft whisper. "Mom's calling me."

Peter paused and looked at his sister's face. Her eyes were closed, but they were darting around behind her eyelids as if she were looking for something. Then the movement of her eyes stopped, a small smile formed on her face, and in an almost inaudible voice she said, "Hi, Mom." Seconds later her face went blank as if the soul that had just recently occupied this little body had left to go to a place much better than the one she'd left behind. Her arm also became limp. Peter slowly lowered it and laid it across her chest. Tears ran down Peter's face, partly at the sadness of losing his sister, partly because of the happiness he felt upon knowing that his sister was experiencing being with her mother again, whom she loved dearly.

John came over and put his hand on Peter's shoulder. Peter, looking up, could see the sorrow in his father's face, along with the bloodshot eyes and the red cheeks from wiping the tears away. Peter stood up and fell into his father's arms. The two just stood there and cried.

Peter looked up and noticed that Ken was standing at the opposite end of the couch, looking down at Beth. He, too, had tears in his eyes as he felt he had let another person die from the disease. He just stood there, not really crying, but not relieving the tension of the moment. He was trying to absorb all his emotions and shove them deep into his unconscious to avoid the pain. Peter could see he was slowly tearing himself apart when he noticed Ken's hands slowly molding into fists. "Ken," Peter called out, trying to direct his attention away from Beth, but Ken never took his eyes off the little body lying on the couch.

Peter stepped out of his father's embrace and walked over to Ken. "Ken," he cried out as he touched his shoulder. Ken still didn't move. "Ken," Peter called out, this time in a voice too loud to be ignored.

"What?" Ken replied as he looked up at Peter.

The look in his eyes indicated to Peter that feelings of anger were growing within his friend's mind. Peter remembered what had happened the last time Ken lost control, when he lost his father and his girlfriend. He had gone crazy and raped a girl and stabbed Peter with a knife. The thoughts of that night made Peter's arm and leg hurt. "It's all right," Peter said, placing a hand on Ken's shoulder to get him to calm down. "She's with our mom."

Ken's reaction caught Peter by surprise. Ken flung his arm up to knock Peter's hand off his shoulder. "Leave me alone!" Ken cried out at the top of his lungs, catching Peter and John both completely off guard, so much so that they each jumped about two feet. It was such a sudden reaction that Ken almost scared the two of them to death. And he was so loud he might have brought Beth back from the dead, if such a thing were possible.

"Calm down," Peter said as fear rose in his soul, not only for his own safety but also for Ken's. Ken was very good at surviving amid the chaos they were living in, but he'd been able to survive because he used his head. It was obvious now that he wasn't thinking; he was reacting.

"Leave me alone!" he cried out again, swinging his arms wildly.

John just stood there in amazement. He had never seen anyone react the way Ken did. "Ken!" he hollered in an attempt to get Ken to know that there were others in the area. However, it didn't appear to do any good.

Ken started to push past Peter en route to the front door, but Peter decided to stand his ground. "Where do you think you're going at this time of night?" Peter asked, afraid that Ken was going crazy. He didn't know what Ken would do, but having seen his worst, he didn't want to see it again.

"Get out of my way," Ken commanded in a low, threatening tone that gave Peter the chills.

Peter didn't want him to go out at such a late hour, so he stood in front of him, blocking his way to the front door. However, Ken had other ideas. Ken walked up to Peter and, with a mighty push, lifted Peter into the air and sent him sailing into the kitchen. Peter slid across the floor and crashed into the trash can. His arm hit the stack of pans on the counter. Ken then turned and headed for the front door, not even stopping to say good night. Peter didn't know what to do as he slowly got to his feet. The front door slammed shut, indicating that Ken had departed for places unknown.

"Come on," John said to Peter, extending a hand to help his son to his feet. "Let's go take care of Beth."

Because of the chaos happening all around the world and in their local community, having Beth buried by an undertaker was almost impossible. Almost all the undertakers had a blood type other than type B. Instead of going to see an undertaker, the next day Peter and John made a small wooden casket in the garage and lined the inside with sheet metal to keep out most of the crawling bugs that would be in the ground. John got Beth dressed in her prettiest dress and laid her in the casket on some soft pillows and blankets. Peter put in several of Beth's more treasured drawings so they would always be with her. Finally, John invited Marsha and Hailee to come over and say goodbye to Beth. The four of them said their last farewell as John closed the cover to the wooden box. It was hard for John to do so without crying, but he was trying to be strong. John and Peter then carried the small box into the backyard, where John had dug a grave for Beth's final resting place.

John said a few words, ending with a prayer. Then he and Peter filled the grave while Marsha and Hailee stood by. After they had finished, the four went inside and sat down in the living room. John was in his chair, and Peter was sitting on the floor next to the couch. Marsha just sat down on one of the dining room chairs with Hailee on her lap. It seemed no one wanted to sit down on the couch where Beth had died the night before. It seemed strange how, at most funerals, everyone attended some sort of Mass before going to the burial site. Afterward, all the friends and family would return to someone's house, where everyone would grab a bite to eat and talk about losing their family member or friend. In the Davisons' situation, there was no formal Mass, no formal burial, and no get-together afterward to talk about the recently deceased. It was just a solemn procedure of putting their loved one into her final resting place, then each could reminisce about their loss in their own time and in their own way.

CHAPTER 20

As we go through life, there are periods when time seems to move extremely fast, and other times when it seems to stand still. At the beginning of the epidemic, time seemed to fly by. As time went on, the lives of the survivors slowly improved, becoming less harsh. The social environment was improving. Small stores were starting to open up; the number of gangs was decreasing; even school had started up again. It had taken almost thirteen years to reach this point, but life was slowly returning to normal.

John looked at those sitting around the table. Across the table from him was Marsha, whom he had married. Marsha and Hailee had lived very close to one of the gang zones. In great fear for their safety, John had arranged for them to stay with him. Marsha had helped with the meals, laundry, and housecleaning in an attempt to say thank you to John, but then after several months of cohabitating, he'd asked her to marry him.

After the two of them had married, they pooled their financial resources and opened what turned out to be a very successful small mom-and-pop store where they sold just about anything their customers needed, from socks to car batteries.

Sitting to John's left was Diane, Peter's wife, whom Peter had met at the hospital.

About a year after Beth died, Ken was driving home with food for the family. A gang jumped the car, shooting him and stealing the food. He was found by an army squad and was rushed to the hospital. Peter and John also rushed to the hospital, where they met Ken's nurse, named Diane

Masters. Even though Peter was not a member of Ken's family, Diane allowed him to see Ken.

"Hey, friend," Ken whispered with a little chuckle. "It looks like they got me."

"Hi, friend," Peter replied, not sure of what to do next.

"Looks like dinner will be a little late tonight," Ken said, trying to give a little chuckle.

"That's all right," Peter said, trying to follow Ken's lead with some humor, "my dad's not that good a cook anyway, so you may have saved us from an upset stomach."

Ken put forth a small smile. "I'm going to miss you, my friend," he uttered in an almost inaudible tone as he reached up and grabbed Peter's hand.

"I'm going to miss you too," Peter said, wondering if Ken was giving up on life. How do you say goodbye to someone you know is dying? How do you know what words to say, knowing that they may be the last words your friend will ever hear?

"It looks like I'll be able to see my dad soon," Ken muttered, looking deep into Peter's eyes and remembering Beth's comment about her mother. The sensation of living seemed to drain slowly from his body, as did the pain from his injuries.

"It's okay," Peter replied in a soft tone. As Peter continued to gaze into Ken's eyes, he could see the spark of life slowly dim as his friend's eyes became dark and motionless. "Go meet your father," Peter whispered, knowing his friend hadn't heard his last comment.

Diane put her hand on his shoulder. "Are you all right?" she had asked Peter, who appeared to be in some sort of trance.

Peter looked at her and smiled. "I'm all right," he said in a soft, calm tone. "He was my best friend."

Diane stayed with Peter for several hours as he described his relationship with his friend and all the things that had happened to Ken and him. Diane started to like Peter, which soon developed into a friendship. After three years, he asked her to marry him. Now, she and their five-year-old daughter, Crystal, were sitting across the table from him.

"What are you doing?" Diane asked Crystal as she kept stacking blocks and knocking them down.

"I'm knocking down buildings like Daddy does," she replied as she knocked the stack of blocks down. Peter had a job working for the government, going around and restoring buildings that were in need and tearing down other buildings and houses that had been demolished.

Next to Peter sat Hailee, who was now a pretty young woman. She had seen John as a father figure ever since her father died. She became somewhat of a replacement for Beth, but John was careful never to compare Beth to her. Hailee was Hailee and was now a part of his life. Beth was Beth and was a part of his memory. Hailee was following in her mom's footsteps, working at one of the hospitals as a nurse's aide. She had plans to eventually go to college. She had married Mike Shea, a doctor at the hospital, who was now sitting across the table from her. He was holding their ten-month-old little girl, Violet, on his lap, trying to keep her from taking all the utensils off the table.

John looked at his family and wondered about the strange events of the past that had brought these individuals together. A tear came to his eye. The past had so much sadness, and now the future seemed so bright. Everyone at the table had a story to tell concerning lost loved ones. But now these individuals sitting around the table were smiling at one another and talking about things that had happened recently and their expectations for the future. The horrors of the disease had been replaced with hope and love, both of which were easily visible to John in the faces of those around the table.

"Okay," John said, trying to get everyone to settle down a bit. "Let's say a prayer thanking God for all the blessings we enjoy." John bowed his head and was followed by the others. "Dear heavenly Father," he started, trying to find the words to express his feelings, "we are so grateful to be here today as a family as we look forward to the future that lies before us. We, who have survived this holocaust that thou have sent forth into our lives, ask that thou help us to remember the ones whom we have left behind. Also, help us to cherish their memories until we see them again. Let us strive to be more like thee and, to rebuild this world following the plans that thou would want us to follow, plans of family and friends and of a simpler life that doesn't overwhelm the soul with worries and sorrows of the high-tech, high-speed world we have left behind. And those who have survived this ordeal, may we remember thee and strive to follow the examples that thou have revealed to us. May we always help one another by providing kindness and mercy to all in need. In Jesus's name, we pray. Amen."

John looked up at the family around the table. Not a word was spoken as all faces were turned toward John. Many had tears forming in their eyes as smiles formed across their faces, acknowledging that his prayer had touched them all. They were in full agreement to make this a better world.

Suddenly an announcement on the TV caught John's attention:

"We interrupt the *Today Show*'s presentation of the 2016 Macy's Thanksgiving Day parade for a brief announcement from the president of the United States."

"Go turn it up," John requested. They all sat around the table, waiting for the president to come out and make an announcement. The president who'd been in office during the outbreak had caught the disease and died, along with more than half the individuals holding public offices. The government of the United States was in shambles for several months until they filled vacant key positions with individuals who had type B blood. They had trouble trying to put this request through as a law because the Supreme Court had ruled this action as unconstitutional. However, after much debate, it was allowed to go into effect until a cure was found.

"The president will be reading a short announcement," the speaker told the audience, "and then she will answer some questions." The speaker looked to the right and noticed that the side door was open. "Ladies and gentlemen," the announcer said, "the president of the United States."

President Sheryl C. Monroe came out onto the platform. "Good afternoon," she said once she had stepped up to the podium. She paused as she looked around.

"It is with a sad heart that I have to announce that Joseph Armstrong of Debut, Minnesota, passed away today at one twenty-seven this afternoon. It is believed that he was the last individual in the United States who did not have type B blood and the last to die from the disease. Joseph was born six months after the outbreak. We don't know if any others around the world are still alive with a blood type other than type B, but scientists have indicated that they have not been able to find a cure. If there are other survivors, they too will not live long. I would like the nation to remember those who have lost their lives to this global disaster and to say a prayer on their behalf. Thank you," she concluded, looking back up from her notes. "Now I will take a few questions."

Many hands went up as the president singled out one reporter. "Tom Davis of the *Herald News*. Can you tell us how we, as a country, are recovering from this disaster?"

"The human race has gone through a rough time, but times are getting better. The good news is that the world we live in is returning to a new norm. The schools are back in session, the economy is continuing to improve, and people are getting back to work. As you can imagine, we still have a lot of work to do. Many of our basic infrastructures are running, but we have reliability issues as we have to train a whole new workforce. But as I said, times are getting better."

"Errol Rodriguez of the *New York Times*," the next reporter announced. "Can you tell us about how many deaths are attributed to the epidemic?" he asked.

"Well," the president said, looking down at her notes, having known that someone would ask this question, "there is no way to obtain an accurate count, as many have been buried without notifying authorities. According to my scientific advisor, the world had more than seven billion people before this crisis came upon us. Now it is estimated that there are only six hundred million people left. Now, I know that sounds like a big number, but this is the estimate for the entire planet. To put it another way," she continued, "if you were to write your name down and the names of nine friends and relatives, you would be the only one who has survived. Many, many years ago," she continued, "God, upset with the way humankind was behaving, sent forth a flood to wipe out most of humankind, save for a handful of faithful followers whom he allowed to be spared. After the Flood, God said that he would present a sign to indicate that he would never destroy the earth again with a flood. He never promised that other events would not plague humankind. Maybe this plague was God's way of telling humankind that he was not pleased with the way we had been living here on earth. Maybe he was upset by our lack of care for others; our greed for money and lust for power, especially at the cost of others; our loss of morality; and the increase in pornography, illicit sexual behavior, drug use, alcoholism, and the many other activities humankind has ventured to partake in. Maybe this plague is God's way of cleaning up some of the filth in the world and allowing humanity to step back and review what we have so as to take a different step forward, to follow God's guidance and create a world that will allow us to live happy lives."

The president's statement seemed to catch all the reporters off guard, as none of them jumped in to ask the next question. Even those in John's house seemed paralyzed by her thoughts of God's wrath upon humankind and her hopes for the future. "Peter," John said after several seconds of silence, "let's not listen to the news of the past. Why don't you turn off the TV, and let's have some dinner and try to do as she said: to live happy lives in a way that would please our heavenly Father."

Peter turned off the TV, and the family sat down and enjoyed the meal and each other's company.